THE LAST THING TO DIE

DI FENCHURCH
BOOK NINE

ED JAMES

OTHER BOOKS BY ED JAMES

DI ROB MARSHALL SCOTT BORDERS MYSTERIES

Ed's first new police procedural series in six years, focusing on DI Rob Marshall, a criminal profiler turned detective. London-based, an old case brings him back home to the Scottish Borders and the dark past he fled as a teenager.

1. THE TURNING OF OUR BONES (Feb. 2023)

Also available is FALSE START, a prequel novella starring DS Rakesh Siyal, is available for **free** to subscribers of Ed's newsletter or on Amazon. Sign up at https://geni.us/EJF9FS

SCOTT CULLEN MYSTERIES

Eight novels featuring a detective eager to climb the career ladder, covering Edinburgh and its surrounding counties, and further across Scotland.

1. GHOST IN THE MACHINE
2. DEVIL IN THE DETAIL
3. FIRE IN THE BLOOD
4. STAB IN THE DARK
5. COPS & ROBBERS
6. LIARS & THIEVES
7. COWBOYS & INDIANS
8. HEROES & VILLAINS

CULLEN & BAIN SERIES

Six novellas spinning off from the main Cullen series covering the events of the global pandemic in 2020.

1. CITY OF THE DEAD
2. WORLD'S END
3. HELL'S KITCHEN
4. GORE GLEN
5. DEAD IN THE WATER
6. THE LAST DROP

CRAIG HUNTER SERIES

A spin-off series from the Cullen series, with Hunter first featuring in the fifth book, starring an ex-squaddie cop struggling with PTSD, investigating crimes in Scotland and further afield.

1. MISSING
2. HUNTED
3. THE BLACK ISLE

DS VICKY DODDS SERIES

Gritty crime novels set in Dundee and Tayside, featuring a DS juggling being a cop and a single mother.

1. BLOOD & GUTS
2. TOOTH & CLAW
3. FLESH & BLOOD
4. SKIN & BONE
5. GUILT TRIP

DI SIMON FENCHURCH SERIES

Set in East London, will Fenchurch ever find what happened to his daughter, missing for the last ten years?

1. THE HOPE THAT KILLS
2. WORTH KILLING FOR
3. WHAT DOESN'T KILL YOU
4. IN FOR THE KILL
5. KILL WITH KINDNESS
6. KILL THE MESSENGER
7. DEAD MAN'S SHOES
8. A HILL TO DIE ON
9. THE LAST THING TO DIE

Other Books

Other crime novels, with Lost Cause set in Scotland and Senseless set in southern England, and the other three set in Seattle, Washington.

- LOST CAUSE
- SENSELESS
- TELL ME LIES
- GONE IN SECONDS
- BEFORE SHE WAKES

PROLOGUE

He had to stop to catch his breath. Doubled over, his heart still galloping away. He grabbed his bicep through the thin fabric. His arm was throbbing, like someone was digging an ice pick into his bicep. While an elephant squatted on his chest.

He couldn't breathe.

He couldn't breathe.

There. A long suck of cold air and he was back in the land of the breathing.

Even let himself laugh at the thought.

The night was cool, the sun still down below the tower blocks in the East End. He stood on a dark patch of the walkway on the South Bank, between cones of overhead lights.

The Thames was at low tide, swishing away below. The Millennium Bridge wasn't far away – it flashed with lights, shooting across from this bank to the North like lasers in a *Star Wars* movie. Over the other bank, St Paul's glowed in the early morning sky. Cranes slept, all lit up with red dots.

The other bridges each had a different light show that

seemed to run all night. Otherwise the early morning was quiet, just some kids shouting in the distance and that heavy background noise you always had in London.

He stretched out his arm, feeling much better. Must've brushed that wall. It was all numb now, like it was somebody else's limb.

Footsteps behind. Heavy. Multiple feet.

Shit.

Too quiet here – he needed to get over the bridge and find someone to help in the busier part of the city. He had to move again.

He tried to push off but his knee locked. His bloody knee. He stretched it out until it clicked.

There.

The thick pop, then a buzz of pain up his thigh, up his hip. He stretched it, swivelled it. It felt good. Strong. Ready now.

The footsteps were closing on him.

He pushed off, running along the wide walkway. He cut up the slab path leading to the steps, the Tate art gallery looming over his head as he bolted up the steps. His knee felt fine, stable, but that ache was back in his arm again. Tight, sharp. Repeated, like someone drumming on it with mallets. He couldn't stop – they were closing on him.

Smart enough not to shout, not to draw attention to themselves. He couldn't see them, but he could hear them. They were definitely there.

At the top of the steps, he swung around the tight turn and headed north now, feet pounding over the Millennium Bridge, heading towards the glowing skyline, the metal resonating with each step. He was bouncing. Floating. The whole bridge was empty, nobody in his sight line. He was running straight towards St Paul's, like he could just fly off and land on the roof.

He chanced a look behind and they were following him.

Two men. Big, though, and slow. Slower than him. Even with his aching knee. The throbbing was so bad now. He hadn't noticed. Not as bad as the ache in his arm.

He crossed over the midpoint and started descending towards the other side of the river.

A couple walked hand in hand, heading away from him.

He swerved past them, but turned to face them. 'Can you help me?'

Got a confused look back.

'I need help.'

They shook their heads. He guessed they were tourists – Japanese, Korean, maybe Chinese – he didn't know which, he wasn't an expert. Didn't matter where they were from, what mattered was they didn't understand a word he was saying.

Over their shoulders, he saw *them* approaching, felt each step through his shoes, up his legs.

'Don't worry about it.' He turned back and raced away again, pushing himself harder and faster. The pain in his arm was getting worse now. He needed to get over the bridge, climb the path to the road at the far side, then flag down a car.

Flashes of traffic between the buildings at the end – there were people driving. Someone would stop. Someone would help him.

He tried to power on, but he was too tired. Adrenalin only went so far. He hadn't eaten for two days, he reckoned. He needed more energy and he had nothing left.

A gang of lads spread across the bridge, walking towards him, singing that Oasis song, arms wide, heads back. Blocking his path.

Last thing he needed.

He tried to get through, but one stopped him, grabbed his arms. A big guy, heavy. Bearded. Shaved head. Face full of rage, but softened when he looked in his eyes. The guy was drunk, stinking of booze. They all were. Heading somewhere – *anywhere* – after a club, to keep the night going. His face twisted into a frown. 'Hey, it's *you!*'

Shit.

He'd been recognised.

'Boys! Look who we've got here!' The big guy wouldn't move to the side, wouldn't let him pass.

'Come on, mate, I need to—'

'You know who this guy is?' The big guy grabbed his wrist. Tight. 'He's the—'

'Mate, I'm being chased. Can you help me?'

The big guy was swaying a bit. He ran his hand over the stubble on his head. 'Sure, man. What's—'

'Just stop them. I need to get away. I'll buy you all dinner as a thank you.'

'Cheers.' The big guy stared at him, a daft grin filling his face.

'Thanks.' He tried to ignore the stinging pain in his arm, but he needed to get away. This was his chance. 'Thank you.' He passed them and bombed away towards the street. Just climb up there, nothing too hard.

The footsteps behind were heading away. The group of lads was chasing them off.

He stopped on the step and turned back to look. The lads were running over the bridge. One tripped up and went down, taking another with him. Daft bastards.

Well, it worked. He wasn't being chased anymore.

He took a deep breath, but it stuck in his throat. Like he was thirsty and couldn't get enough water. His fingers were tingling. His breathing was hard, way harder than it should be. He had to grab the handhold at the side, like he was an old man. He had to hold on to it.

Just get up to the road.

He managed a step, then slid down on one knee, sucking in breath. Gasping. He couldn't catch his breath, couldn't hold on to the rail. Pain burnt down his left arm and up the side of his neck.

He tumbled over, rolling onto his back.

Lay there. Staring up at the sky.

'Can't... catch my breath...'

Felt like the elephant on his chest was lying down now.

'Mum... No!'

CHAPTER ONE

T he reception area was like something from a Netflix show set in a clinically clean future. Very early, but the place was lit up like New Year's Eve.

Everything was white. The floor, the walls, the ceiling, all of the furniture, though that wasn't much. A white sofa, a white coffee table and some white chairs. The reception desk itself was white.

The only colour in the room was the receptionist's deep red hair, coiled together and resting on one shoulder. She looked at him through the Perspex shield, but didn't smile. 'Dr Deacon will be with you in a moment.' She pointed behind him. 'Please, take a seat.'

'Thanks.' DCI Simon Fenchurch gave her a smile, though his face mask hid virtually all of the gesture, leaving just some warmth around his eyes and maybe the stretching of his ears. Nope, he got nothing back from her, and she just went back to her white computer. He limped through the reception area and managed to make it to the seat. Collapsed into it like his old man.

The room smelled of freshly brewed coffee, but she wasn't offering any.

No out-of-date magazines on the low table, thanks to covid. Besides, everyone there was staring into their smartphones. The businessman diagonally opposite was twitching like he was in the middle of a nightmare. He blinked awake and stared at Fenchurch. 'Morning.' The kind of polite you only got in Middle England, not in Shoreditch.

'Morning.' Fenchurch adjusted his facemask and sat back. He'd spent umpteen years wearing masks at crime scenes most weeks of his adult life, but having to put one on in his civilian life was still taking some getting used to. Not that he wanted covid again. Twice was quite enough. Still had that cough on cold mornings.

A door in the corner opened. 'Mr Fenchurch...' Dr Edwin Deacon didn't even make eye contact, just looked in his general direction, then sloped off back through the door, scratching his arse through his trousers.

Fenchurch got up and his knee buckled. He gripped the chair arms and went back down.

Christ.

The only good thing was he couldn't feel any pain. He felt shame, though, especially from the look he was getting from the businessman opposite. He stretched out his leg and the knee popped. Had to swallow down his grunt. Still, it was enough – he managed to get up and walk over to the door without it being an obvious hobble.

Deacon was sitting behind his desk, checking his computer screen. Not a medical page, more a stocks and shares tracker. A frown clenched his lined face. Long and square, like he'd been carved from granite, but not enough chiselling had been done. 'How are you?' He looked over at Fenchurch and snorted. 'That knee still giving you bother?'

'Bother I could live with.' Fenchurch eased into the seat and rubbed at the knee. Numb. Everything felt numb. 'It's just like it's not there. And it barely works. If it was a phone or a car, I'd have replaced it years ago.'

Deacon smiled at that. 'Yes, well. Thanks for coming in.'

'You want to have a look at it?'

'Not really. I can tell enough from your walking gait, Mr Fenchurch.' A smile flashed across his thin lips. 'Good news. Your date is looking like early December.'

It just collapsed out of his mouth, dropping onto Fenchurch's lap. Hitting him in the bollocks. 'That's.... That's *six months* away.'

'That's actually a good outcome in this day and age. Without my pull, it would be eighteen months.'

It'd been six years since that smackhead scumbag had taken him out on a stairwell and he'd been seeing this clown for over two years now... 'You know how badly it's impacting me?'

'I do know. You tell me every six weeks, Inspector.'

'I don't think I can stress this enough. I've got a young son and I can't run after him in the park. Can't play football with him.'

'I'm truly sorry, but you of all people should know we've had to put off surgery because of the small matter of a global pandemic. It might have faded into the background of every-one's lives but it's still affecting things now.'

Fenchurch tried to stretch out but his knee was silently throbbing. No pain, but waves of ... *something* pulsing up and down his leg. 'Christ.'

'Listen, the existence of these sub-variants might play to your advantage. With covid on the rise again, the hospitals are cancelling so many procedures. It's possible we might be able to fit you in early.'

'There's a standby waiting list?'

'Indeed. You'd need to be available at a morning's notice.'

'I've been fasting until noon every day on the off-chance.'

'Excellent. Excellent.'

'I'm a DCI, so I can go off at a moment's notice. Standing agreement with the boss. I'm serious. Ten minutes, and I'm in the Royal London, stripped and waiting for the needle.'

Deacon sniffed. 'Well, it won't be that short a notice.'

'Well, you call me and I'm there. How likely is it to get the go ahead on the standby list?'

'Hmm... I'd say about five to ten percent.'

'But...' Fenchurch swallowed, but his mouth was dry. 'I've been on the list for two years.'

'No. You've been seeing me for two years, but it was only in November last year when you decided to take my advice seriously and I added you to the waiting list.'

Fenchurch stared down at his shoes. The toe of the left one needed to be polished. 'Can't believe it's taking this long, that's all.'

'You have the option of going private.'

'Isn't *this* private?'

'Well, yes, I am. But I mean for the actual surgery.'

'I don't have the money for that.'

'I thought you were investigating selling your other flat?'

'I was. I did. But... I'm guiltily renting it out to a friend, so it's a complex situation.'

'Can't your friend guiltily buy the place?'

'My friend isn't in steady employment.'

'I see. In that case, it's just you, me and the NHS waiting list.' Deacon smiled. 'How has your knee been?'

'I'd say agony, but I can't feel anything below my nipples just now.'

'Well, that's a good sign. For now, it's all about pain

management. Is the medication helping you to function adequately?'

'Adequate is a bit of a stretch.'

'Indeed. But you're still functioning?'

'It's mostly fine. At my level, it's a desk job. At home... Like I say, being able to kick a ball about with my boy would be nice.' Fenchurch felt himself frowning. The one place he had sensation.

'We can increase the dosage if you'd like?'

'I'm on a strong dose as it is. I started off on one or two a day, but now I'm taking eight and the strength keeps creeping up.'

'The problem with medicine is it's not an exact science.' Deacon laughed. 'It's entirely usual for us to have to taper up the dosage until we reach the optimal level. Until you're under the scalpel, we have to keep you functional and pain-free. Aside from your mobility issues, the fact you're not in constant pain is a strong sign. You're taking a mild and controlled therapeutic dose under the care of a professional. You're only taking the bare minimum to remain functional in your activities. You're an educated man, you should know you're in safe hands.'

'I left school after my O-levels.'

Deacon laughed. 'But you've got a PhD from the University of Life, right?'

Fenchurch returned the smile. 'Something like that. But these are opioids I'm on.'

'And they're very low level. Once the surgery's over, you'll be fine. Besides, if this level of pain relief isn't enough, we can start you on a course of fentanyl, which is significantly stronger. And you're nowhere near there... Yet.'

'You think I might get there?'

'No, but I'm reassuring you that you've got a long way to go until you reach the pain-management ceiling.'

'Feels like I'll smash my head off it soon.'

Deacon grinned wide. 'How are you doing on that dose?'

'I'm fine.' Fenchurch felt his fingers twitch like he wasn't in control of the motion. 'I could do with another prescription. Almost out.'

'Of course.' Deacon grabbed his pad and scribbled on it, then tore it off. 'Here you go. That should tide you over until next we meet.' He slid it over the desktop but didn't let go, even when Fenchurch tried to take it. 'We're still awaiting the fee for last month's consultation and prescription.'

'I don't just need a new knee.' Fenchurch sighed. 'These consultations are costing me an arm and a leg.'

CHAPTER TWO

Fenchurch joined the end of the queue and took his empty tub out of his pocket. He flipped the cap off with his thumb. Then on again. Then off.

The pharmacy wasn't as swish as Deacon's surgery. Not by a long shot – probably the only shop within a mile that hadn't stripped back the walls to bare brick, shoved the word "craft" in front of whatever it was they were selling and quadrupled the prices. One of those pharmacies that specialised in the weirdest stuff – perfumes, picture framing, printing camera film, a whole section of knock-off Lego – to supplement their core income. The place hadn't been touched since the Eighties, judging by the dust covering most of the stock. Some of the aftershaves were so ancient even Fenchurch's old man wouldn't think about splashing them on.

A woman sprayed perfume on her wrist and sniffed it, recoiling. Seconds later, the smell reached Fenchurch and he had the same reaction – that stuff should be used to kill weeds, not provide allure.

He was still popping the bottle lid, so he stopped and put it away. He checked his written prescription – hard to decipher the handwriting. Made him think that doctors used a secret code only pharmacists understood.

Eight pills a day. Some days, after a long shift, it felt like he was rattling when he walked up the stairs to the flat.

He put the paper back in his pocket.

His knee was throbbing. The bugger of this injury was his ankle and hip were compensating and carrying the load. A load they wouldn't naturally bear. The whole thing was taking a toll – his back ached worse than his knee, going from a low hum to a growl.

In twenty minutes, he'd either need to have another pill or be horizontal.

What a way to live...

He looked up and the queue had moved forward.

Three to go.

His phone rang.

He checked the display.

Younis calling...

His heart rate surged, throbbing in his neck.

What it was when the person you'd worked years to put away was back out on the street...

He could kill the call, but Younis would just ring back.

He could block him, but he'd just visit in person.

Sod it.

He hit answer and put his phone to his ear. 'Morning, Dimitri.'

'Alright, Fenchy, my love?' He giggled. 'See you still haven't blocked me, my sweet prince. I feel so honoured!'

'What do you want?'

'Oh, nothing much. Just my daily check-in. See how my favourite copper is.'

'I'm still alive. Just about.'

'Oh, I know. That queue is bloody slow.'

Shit.

He was watching.

Fenchurch fought the urge to swing and scope out anyone around. Instead, he used the chintzy mirrors dotted around the place to spy on his spy. No obvious contenders. Maybe they were outside, watching him from a distance. He stepped forward in the queue, acting all calm. 'It's a bugger, that's for sure.'

'Fenchy, always remember that I know where you are at all times.'

'Well, that's good news. You'll see me coming when I finally arrest you and send you back to prison.'

'Ain't going to happen, sweet cheeks.' Younis cackled. 'Now, the reason for the call is I was wondering about you and me going for a nice sweaty sauna together.'

Fenchurch let out a weary sigh. This again. 'Afraid I'm more of a steam room kind of guy.'

'Oh yeah?'

'Yeah. Prefer a moist heat.'

'If this was a text exchange, I'd be using those eyes emoji.' Younis cackled. 'But it sounds like a date, my sexy soldier. I've got one fitted out in my office.'

'I'm not going into a sauna or a steam room with you.'

'Oh, you will. You know you will. Love you, bye.'

The phone clicked.

Younis was gone.

Fenchurch felt his shoulders slump, but he couldn't let his guard down. He needed to act calm.

Younis had him under constant surveillance.

Or he was just lucky and wanted him to think he was.

Best to operate on the basis he was always being followed, always being watched.

That knowledge would've saved Jon Nelson's career a couple of years back.

Christ.

Fenchurch stepped forward in the queue and watched the old guy charge out of the chemist. He looked like the businessman he'd seen in Deacon's surgery – was *he* stalking him? He'd managed to get here before Fenchurch, but this place was only two doors down and he looked like he could walk like he was under ninety unlike Fenchurch.

His phone blasted out again.

He answered it. 'Fenchurch.'

'Simon, it's Jason.'

Detective Superintendent Jason Bell.

Meet the new boss, same as the old boss.

'Hi, Stringer. What's up?'

Like Fenchurch wanted to know.

'Simon.' That little pause that showed the joke name was needling him. 'I'm calling to say I've assigned you to a high-profile death investigation.'

Fenchurch felt himself frown. 'Not a murder?'

'Well. That's the thing. We're not sure. Could be a murder, but if not it's certainly the kind of death I need someone I can trust running it. And you're my number one guy.'

'Okay, I'll take that as a compliment rather than you blowing smoke up my arse to get me to agree to this.'

'Millennium Bridge, soon as you can make it.'

'Sure thing. See you there.' Fenchurch ended the call and pocketed the phone.

Another new case. Great.

The woman in front seemed to be getting half of the store put in a family-sized McDonald's paper bag.

Time was, Fenchurch would've left the queue without getting his drugs. But without them, he'd soon feel the dam burst and the reservoir of pain would flood him. He'd tested the limits a couple of times and the only conclusion was he'd be off work without his prescription. Wouldn't be able to climb the stairs down to the shops or walk more than twenty feet.

No, as much as he needed a prosthetic knee, he needed this prescription more.

Like Deacon said, his drug use was legitimate, and he was following Deacon's orders.

People got into trouble with this stuff when they messed about with dosage.

This was his lifeline...

Fenchurch waited in the queue, popping the empty drug container in his pocket.

He was going to be fine.

CHAPTER THREE

Fenchurch stood just off the Millennium Bridge and slid his crime scene trousers up to his waist. The elastic snapped on and he pulled the jacket down.

'Simon.' A man walked past him, tall but stooping. Fenchurch took a few seconds to recognise him – but nothing came up. Just fog.

'Morning. You here for business or pleasure?'

He let out the long sigh that usually precluded a longer story of woe. 'Business.' Instead of elaborating, he marched off up the path towards the street.

Fenchurch continued on, none the wiser. Way too many people in his life.

Two sets of steps led down to the walkway along the river-bank, either side of what looked like the longest escalator in the world.

Back the way, a brick office building led all the way to the road, where St Paul's Cathedral stood like a sentry, already glowing white in the morning sun. The other side was a brown marble carbuncle that must've been raised from Hell sometime in the Eighties. The glass thing between it and the road looked like it'd been built upside down.

He had to bend over to tighten the overshoe covering his brogues. Got a throb of pain from his knee – the morning's drugs hadn't kicked in enough to dull the rest of it back to normal service. The pills gave a blanket of euphoria – a blanket he hugged tight around his shoulders.

He must've looked a sight, putting his jacket and mask on first before his trousers. Had to do it that way, didn't he?

The metal foot passenger bridge spanned the river from the grim outer reaches of the Square Mile that comprised the City – anonymous buildings that had something to do with the financial sector or servicing it – down to the tourist attractions south of the river: the Tate Modern and Shakespeare's Globe Theatre. He'd only visited one of them and he should correct that, though whether his son would enjoy *A Midsummer Night's Dream* was anyone's guess. Still, some of the tragedies would no doubt resonate with his own life.

Get over yourself, you old goat!

Fenchurch was now dressed and ready to enter yet another crime scene.

Deep breath.

He took the last few steps slowly, the calming numbness tingling up and down both legs, and stopped outside the tent erected at the entrance and smiled at the crime scene manager. Took her clipboard and signed himself in.

As he handed it back, a round figure stepped out of the tent, more a fat cloud than a human being. 'I know what you mean, Tom.' Bell laughed, but no mistaking the furious eyes glowering through the goggles at Fenchurch. 'There you are,' his harsh Birmingham accent rasped out. At least Fenchurch couldn't see his lips move. 'And what time do you call this?'

'Traffic was bad, sir.'

'I needed you here.'

'And here I am.' Fenchurch got a spasm of pain in his back, as if to remind him. He barged past Bell and peered inside the tent.

Several people in there, all working away. Forensics and pathology, as well as cops.

Fenchurch looked back at Bell. 'Surprised our chums from the City of London aren't here.'

'Right behind you.'

Fenchurch swung around and there they were, just outside the locus. Suited and booted, but like they were off to the trading floor rather than into a crime scene.

DI Steve Clarke's spray tan looked a bit more natural for once and his hair was whiter than Fenchurch's. 'Morning, Si.' His barrow boy accent would be at home selling socks on the street.

Fenchurch didn't recognise Clarke's colleague, but smiled at him all the same. He pulled his goggles up and mask down, breathing in the heavy London air again. The harsh tang of someone smoking nearby. 'How did you know it was me?'

'Can spot that old man limp from a mile away.' Clarke chuckled. 'How you doing?'

Fenchurch flashed his eyebrows at Clarke. 'Win some, lose some.' He thumbed at Bell. 'You know my new boss?'

'Don't think I do, no.' Clarke folded his arms. 'What happened to the last one? Did you burst him?'

'Kind of.' Bell stood up tall, though he was the shortest of the four by some distance. 'Julian's now the Commander of Specialist Crime.'

Clarke snorted. 'Climbing the greasy pole, eh? Commander to Commissioner is, what, four remaining moves, right?'

Bell winced. 'Doesn't have to be. Some people jump a few in one go.'

'From what I've seen of Julian, I'm sure he thinks he's capable of the top job.'

Bell laughed. 'Everyone thinks that at his level. It's all about not messing up. Or getting caught messing up. Or having people who can carry the can for it when you do.' He shifted his gaze between them. 'What brings you here, gentlemen?'

Clarke and his mate were keeping a distance from them. Other side of the pile of crime scene suits. Clarke put his hands in his pockets. 'Well, our bosses are being a bit forceful about territory.' He waved his hand up and down the steps. 'This here is City land.' He pointed at the bridge. 'That's technically on the river, so it's Met land.' He folded his arms again. 'Trouble is, this body's on the cusp of both. So we could arguably have a claim on this case.'

'That would've been better to know before we got our forensics and pathology here, as well as over forty officers.'

'It would've been, yeah.'

Bell stepped forward, right up to the inner locus. 'Thing is, Inspector, you've turned up late to the feast because you knew we'd take this. Because all you lot are good for is spreadsheets and financial scams. This is real policing.'

'Real policing.' Clarke laughed. 'You've no idea, do you?'

'Inspector, I'm a superintendent. Show me some respect.'

Clarke nodded. 'Quite surprised to see a super out of uniform and at a crime scene.' His grin widened. 'But I'm here on the orders of my *chief* super to make sure we take this case.'

'Who is your—'

'Guys!' Fenchurch stepped in front of Bell, still inside the inner locus, hands raised. 'Can you stop arguing like kids? Both forces have had an understanding since before our great-grandfathers were born, but you're standing around arguing like this is the good old days where you'd drag a body to the other side of a street so the other lot would take it. It's 2022, for crying out loud; policing has evolved.'

Clarke was nodding along with it. 'So?'

'So this is a Met case.' Fenchurch gestured to the steps behind them. 'If we have to venture north of here, we'll contact you.'

'Show us how it's done, right?'

'No. Just the courtesy of two police forces working together to catch a criminal.'

Clarke looked at his mate, got a nod, then smiled. 'That sounds good to us.'

Maybe that was the chief super he was with. Trouble with the City cops was they were thick as thieves, almost literally. Hunkering down in their little part of London where nobody lived – not really – so the murders and rapes and assaults were few and far between. Focusing on whatever financial crimes were being committed by the great and good, or in their name at least.

Fenchurch taking this case would be a relief to them – they were probably more interested in who'd been killed. Like some top banker.

Bell blasted a smile at them. 'We'll be in touch, lads.'

'Sure.' Clarke stepped away, then walked up the steps towards street level. His phone was out by the time they hit the cordon, which was still blocking angry commuters and tourists from using the bridge.

'Well, that's not exactly what I expected to happen.' Bell snapped his goggles back into place. 'You know we need to solve this now, right?'

'I'll do my very best, sir.' Fenchurch nodded. 'What did you—'

'I mean it. We could've handed this off to them. A suspicious death isn't the same as a murder.'

'I'm not working for the Met just to fob crimes off on to that shower. This isn't a contest, sir. I know you've been out of active policing for a few years while you focused on strategic matters. You might want to get into a pissing contest with them over who takes it, but this is our skillset. There are protocols. It's on our patch. And—'

'You don't get it, do you?'

'Get what?' Fenchurch pointed back into the tent. 'That body in there might be another line on a spreadsheet to you or to them, but he has a family and loved ones who need answers, if not justice for what's happened to him.'

'Well.' Bell tugged his mask and goggles over his face and stepped back into the tent.

Fenchurch hadn't seen Bell that pissed off with anyone for a while. Not one to fight his own corner, just retreat into silence and grass to his boss. In an hour, there'd be a telephone call between the chief supers of the two forces to argue the toss.

Arseholes.

Fenchurch snapped on his goggles, secured his mask and stepped inside the tent.

And saw why Bell was acting that way.

A young man lay on his back, staring up at the tent's roof. Designer jeans, long-sleeve T-shirt with a SUGARMAN logo on the front. Brown skin laced with tattoos up both arms. Instantly recognisable even with his head shaved to rasping stubble, rather than his trademark ginger afro.

Bell was squatting down, his giant belly stretching the crime scene suit almost to bursting. 'You recognise him?'

'Curtis Archer.' Fenchurch felt a sickness in his stomach. 'Superstar footballer. The Cockney Mbappe.'

'Seem to know a lot about him.'

'Season ticket holder at the London Stadium, sir.'

'Tell me about him, then.'

Fenchurch peered at the corpse and just saw tragedy. Huge hope for the club, both financial and sporting, now wiped away. 'What's there to say? Scored on his debut for West Ham at sixteen. Scored on his England debut at seventeen. One goal shy of the Golden Boot winner at the 2018 World Cup in Russia when he was nineteen. Heading to the top of the game. Summer 2020 was going to be a big one for him, secure a massive transfer to one of the big boys.' He looked at Bell, saw he'd lost him, but continued regardless. 'Man City and Chelsea were supposed to be in for him. Real Madrid, Paris Saint-Germain and Barcelona too.'

'But the pandemic ruined it?'

'Nope. Early March, last home match before the lockdown, he got scythed down outside the box. Snapped both ligaments in his knee, tore his hamstring. Hasn't been seen inside the London Stadium in over two years now.' Fenchurch sucked in a deep breath. 'That's my bit done. What happened to him?'

'This isn't a murder case, Simon, not yet.' Bell pointed outside. 'Initial reports suggest he might've been chased, hence us treating it as suspicious.'

'Wise.' Fenchurch's brain was pinging with a billion different possibilities. From the trivial, like a rival club doing it – Millwall up to their old tricks again, as his old man would say – to any number of personal reasons he couldn't grasp. 'With the right advice and backing, a kid like Curtis is loaded from the age of sixteen, independently wealthy by twenty.'

'Unbelievable.'

'I'm not judging whether that's right or wrong, sir, just stating facts.'

'No, I get it. People will say all that money for kicking a ball, but it's the lifeblood of the country, isn't it?' Bell grinned at Fenchurch. 'I'm a Charlton fan, for my sins.'

'I didn't know that.'

'There you have it. Now, where there's money, there are any number of people looking to exploit those with talent. Agents, managers, family, friends, lovers.'

But that was all going to have to come out in the wash. Right now, they needed to get as much information from the corpse as possible.

'Om pom tiddly om pom.' Dr William Pratt was working away at the body. Lifting and checking. His bushy eyebrows filled his goggles with a frown. He glanced up at Fenchurch. 'Aha, there you are.' He levered himself up to standing. 'Way too young to die.'

Fenchurch nodded. 'Just turned twenty-two.'

Pratt frowned at him like Fenchurch had just developed an ability to ascertain the age of someone from a glance. 'Oh?'

Fenchurch pointed at himself. 'West Ham fan.' Then at Curtis Archer. 'West Ham player.'

'Well, for once I'm glad you're at my crime scene.' Pratt bellowed out a laugh, muffled by the mask. 'Anything else I should be aware of?'

'That's my football sticker knowledge exhausted, William. He was a great player. Headed to the top, either with a much bigger club or by dragging West Ham up with him.'

'I understand now why you're the right party to lead this, Simon.'

'Party?'

'You know what I mean.' Pratt smiled at Bell, like he'd only just noticed him. 'As we discussed, I shall perform a full post-mortem, which I will arrange for later this morning.' He tilted his head to the side. 'I appreciate that for you, requesting I shift it up the pecking order seems like a trivial matter, but my office contends with processing the bodies of several MITs. This will have a knock-on effect for other crimes in the city.'

'Thanks for doing it, William.' Bell clapped his arm. 'I get it. I wish we had the resources to prioritise everything, but the tragedy is we just don't. And this is the one the media will be shouting about as soon as they get wind of what's happened here. You mark my words...'

'Oh, I get it. Seen it before, several times.'

Fenchurch caught Pratt's attention. 'So, what's happened to him?'

'Well, he's dead.'

'I know that. What killed him?'

'There are no marks on the body. No signs of external trauma or track marks in traditional places. No signs of any blows or cuts or what have you. So my assumption is it's a medical emergency. Could be a heart attack, stroke, aneurysm, overdose, poisoning, obstructed airway, sepsis, kidney failure... the list is endless. If there's no anatomical cause once I open him up then, given his age, blood toxicology will be a big tell.'

Bell pricked up at that. 'And you're—'

'I'm fast-tracking blood toxicology, yes. Already taken the bloods and they're on the way to the lab in Lewisham. She's got some whizz-bang new kit that'll have it done in a jiffy.'

'Okay.' Bell looked at Fenchurch. 'Let's leave him to work in peace.'

CHAPTER FOUR

'It just never ends, Simon.' Bell kicked off his bootees and tossed them into the discard pile. 'Never. Bloody. Ends. I'll have to get back to base and arrange press releases for nine different cases, plus this one on top of that. I'm going to have to bring in the senior media officer and she *hates* me. With a burning passion.'

Fenchurch wondered why...

'I've got a media debrief pencilled in for noon.' Bell looked back at the tent, then checked his watch. 'That's going to be cutting it really fine to have anything meaningful to add, if you ask me. All the while, the Acting Commissioner's going to be calling me up every fifteen minutes or, rather, getting one of her lackeys to call me up every fifteen minutes. Dude!' He thrust out his hands in the air. 'If there's any news, *I'll* be calling *you*. They don't get it, Simon, they really don't.'

Out of his crime scene suit, Bell was a sight to behold. Everything bulged. His trousers were like sausages on the barbecue, ready to burst open. His belly hung over them – his shirt must've been extra-long to cover that stomach.

Fenchurch looked him in the eye instead. 'Sir, as SIO shouldn't I be leading the media activities?'

'No, Simon. It's on me. This is a priority case. When a celebrity dies, it goes up to the Commissioner's office. It shouldn't be that way, really it shouldn't, but if we didn't handle it in that way, the other cases would be swamped. The Lord doesn't care how many Instagram followers you have or what your income is, when he rings the dinner bell, you take your seat at the table. It isn't illegal to run from someone – our investigation is to rule out foul play.'

'I get it.'

'And *she* wants to make a good impression until the permanent replacement is announced. And obviously, she wants it to be her.' Bell sighed. 'Anyway. I need to go and handle all of that.' He clamped his hand – a bunch of bananas made from sausages – on Fenchurch's shoulder and squeezed. 'Get to the bottom of what happened here, Simon, will you?'

'That's my intention, sir.'

'This is nothing but a tragic *medical* death, not a murder. Now, hurry up and say so, because I can't afford anything more than that, resource-wise.' Bell dragged his hand down his face. 'And get this bridge open soon, yeah?'

Fenchurch smiled at him. 'On it.'

'Oh, I've secured DI Carling and his team from the South MIT. Keep an eye on him.'

'What's that supposed to mean?'

'Oh, just that he's going far, Simon. Might bring him into your team sooner or later.' Bell waddled off towards the cathedral. He had to stop halfway to suck in a deep breath under cover of checking his phone. Pulling up the Travis Food app on his phone, planning his second breakfast. There might be a slight incline, but nothing to get out of puff about. How the hell he was still a cop absolutely baffled Fenchurch.

THE LAST THING TO DIE

Completely unfit, physically and professionally. Still, he talked a good game – he must have a really low par on the golf course of office politics – and he seemed to constantly land on his feet.

Nice to be asked about having a knee that needed to be replaced...

Fenchurch shook off his trousers without any pain, miraculously, and dumped it all in the discard pile, surveying the outer locus.

People standing around, cops taking statements from eyewitnesses. A lot of faces he recognised, people who worked for him and those on the South London MIT he didn't. Still early, but the day was warming up.

Like this case. He looked back at the tent. Pratt was right – twenty-two was no age to die. How the hell could someone go from being watched by over a billion viewers on the TV to lying on a bridge, dead?

How?

It just didn't compute.

'Si.' A toothy grin walked over. Brown hair slicked back like a mobster. Black suit, lime shirt, no tie. Not an ounce of fat on the guy – and he could've done with it, his face was that gaunt. Not skinny, though – stacked, like he could do twenty reps of Fenchurch without breaking a sweat. DI Tom Carling, his right hand proffered towards Fenchurch. 'Hey, big guy.'

A foot shorter than Fenchurch, give or take. Fenchurch had no idea who called him Tom Thumb first, but it had stuck. Just not to his face. *Never* to his face.

Fenchurch shook the hand. 'Tom. What are you doing here?'

'It's my patch.' Carling motioned towards the bridge. 'Anything from Sutton up to the river.'

'This is north of the river.'

'Not quite. That's City territory. Anything from this bank south is ours.'

If Fenchurch ever had another argument about jurisdictional pissing contests... 'Well, this comes from the top. I'm the SIO, reporting to Superintendent Bell.'

'That fat wanker.'

'Inspector, please don't voice your thoughts like that.'

'Sorry, it's a joke. Jason's a good mate of mine. Would say it to his face and he'd call me something relating to my height.' Carling grinned wide. 'But South London's my patch, so I'm a just a bit miffed that you've been allocated, that's all.'

'It's okay, Tom. You'll have it back once I'm done with it.' Fenchurch smiled at him. 'Promise I won't break it.' The joke didn't land. 'Listen, let's just stick our heads together in a way that doesn't fracture any bones and get this off our plates. You'd step up for most cases, but this is far from normal.'

'Right.' But Carling didn't seem too sure about that. Thin lips twitching, his grey eyes narrowed. 'It's Curtis Archer, isn't it?'

'Afraid so.'

Carling shook his head. 'Bell said you've got this because of that teacher case a few years back?'

Fenchurch exhaled. A painful case in way too many ways. 'That was all over the papers. TV. Social media. You name it. Big controversy at the time and that was before we found her body. But I handled it. Even got a conviction.'

'I've never had that kind of thing.'

'You're lucky, Tom. You can watch and learn from my mistakes.' Fenchurch grinned at him. 'Bell mentioned you've been seconded to my team.'

'He gave me no choice in the matter. First detective on the scene.' Carling stepped back to let the gurney past, two white-suited pathology staff carrying the body towards the steps. All zipped up, nothing on display. Next stop, Lewisham.

Carling watched them struggle up the steps with it, yawning. 'Been here since six. Got a good look at the crime scene.'

'Oh, well, that saves me a job. Care to bring me up to speed?'

Carling frowned. 'Weird thing is, Archer had nothing on him. No phone, no wallet, no keys. This drunk lad called it in.' He looked around, then stuck out his chin. 'Him over there.'

Fenchurch turned around. The guy was built like a bear, but his face had a softness to it. And he looked like his hangover kicked in a few hours ago. 'Shouldn't he be off somewhere giving his statement?'

'That's the thing.' Carling pointed up at the walls either side of the steps up. Two pairs of cameras, one directly above them, the other halfway up. 'Caught him going through the victim's pockets.'

'Then I need a word with him.' Fenchurch walked over, his knee rattling and clicking like it was filled with broken glass. He didn't say anything, just listened to the guy talking.

Scottish, but his accent was hard to place. Dressed for the nightclub, smart trousers and a white shirt, though the red and yellow stains showed he'd probably been kicked out of somewhere. He stared right at Fenchurch. 'I didn't rob him. Swear.'

'I want to believe you. How about you tell me what happened?'

'We'd been at Waikiki.'

'That's a nightclub, right?'

'Left at lights up. No coats, so we just headed out, going back to Deezer's place.'

'One of your mates?'

'Lives in Brixton.'

'Fair old walk there from here.'

'Travis were price gouging on fares for some reason. When you don't need a ride, they're cheap as chips. When you really need them, time for a second mortgage just to get to Southwark. Pricks.' He yawned into his fist. 'Sorry. That kid ran past us. Almost knocked me over. I grabbed him, stopped him going. And I recognised him, but he tried to shrug us off. Said someone was after him.'

'You see anyone?'

He shook his head. 'We ran over the bridge, but there was nobody. A couple from Korea were walking over, seemed a bit confused to see us.'

'How do you know they were from Korea?'

'Deezer speaks Korean. Big into K-Pop, spent a year in Seoul before uni.' He laughed. 'But there was nobody else there. Got a couple of the boys to run along the walkway in both directions, while I came back here and...' He swallowed, let out a slow breath. 'Curtis was lying there. Dead.'

Fenchurch looked at Carling and raised his eyebrow. He got a nod in return – that all checked out with the CCTV. He focused on the bear man again. 'You know his name?'

'Been to West Ham a few times, aye.'

'Heard a story you might've been rummaging through his pockets. I don't want to—'

'Aye, I was.'

Well, that was unusual. 'You *were* going through his pockets?'

'Sure.'

'What did you find?'

'Nothing. I was looking for ID to confirm it actually was him, you know? And the state of him... You can put in medical information on your phone nowadays. Maybe he had a condition, that information could've saved his life.'

'He was still alive?'

'I don't think so. But you can bring people back to life, right?'

'Not really. Did you find his phone?'

'No. Was going to call 999 on my way back, but the paramedics were here already. Swear I didn't take anything.'

'Can anyone back this up?'

'My pals weren't with me.' He frowned. 'There were two cops...'

Carling nodded. 'Two uniformed officers were nearby, sir. They responded immediately. And two paramedics were attending a nearby accident.' He narrowed his eyes. Fenchurch had forgotten how much of a habit that was, like he only had one trick to use while intimidating people. 'Trouble is, they didn't see anything. And the CCTV is inconclusive.'

The big guy turned out his pockets – he had nothing on him. 'I haven't taken anything!'

Carling frowned. 'Where's your own phone, sir?'

He looked at him like he'd lost his mind. 'Eh?'

'You're on a night out. Where's your phone, your wallet, your keys?'

He eased his sleeve up to his elbow. 'Just need my watch. Pay for drinks, order Travis cars, can even unlock my front door with it.'

Carling was shaking his head.

Fenchurch smiled at the cop next to him. 'Get him home and arrange for a statement to be taken this afternoon.'

'Will do, sir.' The big lump grabbed the Scottish bear by the arm. 'Come on, Jamie, let's get you home.' He led him away, two giants in need of a punchline.

Carling watched them go. 'That doesn't stack up for me.'

'You think that guy might be a suspect?'

He nodded. 'Curtis told him he was being chased and CCTV backs that up.'

'You've found his assailants?'

'No, but we've got Curtis running across the bridge. He spoke to Jamie and his mates, who ran off. Minutes later, big Jamie ran back and found Curtis dead or dying.' Carling nibbled at his cheek. 'I still think he took the stuff from Archer's pockets.'

'How, though?'

'Look around you, Simon.' Carling pointed over the sides of the bridge. The walkways headed in both directions. 'Easy to lob his plunder down there. Get someone to grab it. Be on eBay already or at some shop in Mile End.'

'That's some drop, though. Have you got anything on CCTV to back it up?'

'Camera cuts off. That Jamie lad slipped off the bottom.'

Fenchurch thought it through. It'd make a prosaic explanation, that's for sure. Drunk guys mug a celebrity as he died. 'Okay, keep on it. Get to the bottom of what happened.' He waited for a nod. 'How are you getting on with next of kin? Friends, family, all of that?'

'Got my team working that side of the case. Archer's got a mum and a dad. Both alive, as far as we know. And he's got no siblings.'

'Wife or girlfriend?'

'Hard to separate truth from tabloid rumour, you know?' Carling stuffed his hands into his pockets. 'But whatever. We'll find them, if they exist.'

Fenchurch wasn't sure about that. 'Thing is, an England international out without an entourage seems a bit strange to me. People with that sort of profile are never on foot or alone. Usually got some mates from school or a manager or whatever who follows them everywhere. And pretty much always in the back of a blacked-out four-by-four.'

'Kid can't wipe his arse without someone asking if he

wants two-ply or to use the bidet.' Carling laughed. 'See your point, mind. Someone should've been with him.'

'Get me names, Tom. And find out why he was alone.'

A female detective walked over, one hand in her pocket. She smiled at Fenchurch. 'DS Susan Inglis.' Scottish, but not stab-your-throat Glasgow. Softer.

'DCI Simon Fenchurch.'

She seemed defensive as she held out a written note at arm's reach. 'Tom, I've got an address for Curtis's mother.'

Fenchurch took the note from her. 'Tom, you stay here and manage the crime scene. Get all of those kids vetted, their parents spoken to. All that jazz. Our biggest priority is knowing where Curtis Archer was last night.' He smiled as he started walking off. 'And get the bridge open.'

CHAPTER FIVE

Fenchurch trundled his car through a sprawling brick estate. Three-storey blocks of flats opposite semi-detached homes. Been a while since he'd been in this neck of Canning Town but it wasn't anywhere near as bad as he remembered. Not that he'd want to live there – his own experience in Limehouse put him off living near where he worked. His professional career had made staying anywhere in London feel like an ordeal. His fantasy of moving out to Essex or Kent would be the first thing he'd get on to once his new knee was bedded in. Run a station in Chelmsford or Tunbridge Wells. Lovely.

A woman was leaning against her car, checking her phone. She looked up as he passed and gave her customary scowl. Acting DI Kay Reed. Red hair cut practically short, her fringe tucked in behind her ear, almost matching the colour of her blouse.

Fenchurch pulled in at the next available space and got out. 'Sorry, Kay, traffic's been crap.'

'It's London, guv, it's always crap.' She sighed. 'How's your knee?'

'It's still there.' Fenchurch looked down at it. 'Though I do have to check.'

'Weren't you at the doctor's first thing? Or did you just want to get out of doing the briefing?'

'Yeah. Feels like a decade ago.' He smiled at her. 'Where's this address?'

'Follow me.' She set off along a back lane towards a terraced block overlooking a park. Even had goalposts up on the grass, but the pitch ran diagonally across it – presumably to minimise balls smashing through windows. 'Heard Tom Carling is working this case too.'

'That's right.'

She glanced over. 'Keep an eye on him.'

'On Tom?'

'You call him Tom Thumb and make him the butt of your jokes, but he's...' She sighed. 'Never mind.'

'Come on, Kay, what's he done?'

'He's... He's very handsy.'

Fenchurch stopped dead. 'Are you kidding me?'

'Nope. My mate Emma reported him for touching her up in the evidence locker at Sutton three years ago.'

Fenchurch felt like slugs were living in his guts. 'What?'

'They investigated, but didn't conclude anything.'

'Shit. You think there's something in it?'

'That's the problem, guv. Because there was no conclusion, it means he'll keep on doing it.'

'But you think he's done it?'

'The guy's notorious. Never get into a cab with him. Or be last in the pub with him.'

'Shit, how come I didn't know?'

'Because of what's between your legs, guv.'

Fenchurch felt even more sickened than from the drugs. 'This parallel world happening right in front of my eyes. Jesus.'

'He tried it on with me, once. Years ago. I was pissed. Stupid of me, but when you're with cops, you think it's okay. I could barely walk. I got away and found three female officers who separated us. One of them rode with me in the cab home.'

'Jesus, Kay. I'd no idea.'

'It's different for women. You put up with the comments, the looks and leers, and the odd boob or bum grab. The world's becoming more enlightened, but seems like the consequences for those who tell are far worse than for those who are doing it.'

Fenchurch felt his mouth go dry.

'You and I know how little that's changed.'

Fenchurch stopped himself. 'I've got a daughter on the job, Kay, I know how—'

'Guv.' Reed was shaking her head. 'Why do most men have to have daughters to see how bad this shit is?'

He didn't have a defence against that.

'I should be a full-fledged DI by now but, as a woman, I have to work twice as hard with half the recognition.'

'Kay, I offered you a promotion and you—'

'My fucking mother was dying, Simon! I didn't have the brain space!' She stomped away from him.

'Kay!'

'Leave it, I'll fight my own battles.' She stopped outside a house and pressed the buzzer.

Fenchurch followed her over. She was right – he saw it as a problem to be solved, whereas all she wanted was some sympathy. Some equal treatment. And now he'd have to keep a very close eye on Tom Carling.

Carling was a mate, or Fenchurch thought he was. Going to

be hard to look past that. But if even ten percent of it was true, he needed to drum him off the force. For good.

Fenchurch joined her on the front step. 'I promise to keep an eye on him.'

She nodded. 'Thank you. That's all I ask.'

The door opened and a middle-aged black woman looked out, arms folded, looking them up and down. 'Jehovah's Witnesses aren't allowed in this borough.'

'Police.' Reed held up her warrant card. 'DI Kay Reed. DCI Simon Fenchurch. Looking for Candace Archer.'

'That's me.' Her arms got even more tightly folded, stretching the skin. 'What's this about?'

'It's best we do this inside.'

'Fine.' Candace turned heel and charged inside.

Her house was immaculate. White floor tiles that shone in the morning light. Cream walls filled with pictures of her and her son, from a young age through to him as a grinning teenager. She didn't appear to get any older, but her smile waned over time, seemed that little bit more forced, and the bags under her eyes grew.

An odour of rich cooking hung over the place, heavy on the coconut and coriander.

The living room had a blue leather suite, the glass coffee table matching it down to the Pantone colour code. A dining area sat behind it, in the exact same colour. A television was on, playing some cookery show. The garden was filled with a conservatory, itself rammed with expensive rattan furniture and so many candles.

Candace walked over to an ironing board in the middle of the oatmeal carpet and muted the TV. Her iron hissing – the clothes basket was half-full, the rest up on hangers along the curtain pole. She picked up a pair of jeans and ran the iron across a leg with the precision of someone who'd done that for a long time, week in, week out. Her gaze was locked on the television as she hung them up and grabbed a T-shirt from the pile. 'Well?'

'It's better if you sit.'

'My hip's so bad these days, it's better if I stand.'

Fenchurch hadn't noticed her limping. Maybe some people hid it better than he did, or were just on stronger drugs. 'I'm afraid to say that, in the early hours of the morning, a man collapsed on the Millennium Bridge and, despite efforts to revive him, he died there. I'm very sorry to have to tell you we believe your son is dead.'

Candace reached for a hanger and slid the T-shirt on to it. SUGARMAN, so presumably her son's. She hung it up. Then let out a sigh. 'It's definitely him?'

'We believe so.'

'And you're here to ask me to identify the body, aren't you?'

'That's not—'

'Half of London could identify my boy.' She slammed the iron down on the board. It rattled and hissed. 'I need to see him.' She looked at Fenchurch, eyes twitching, tears on her cheeks. 'I need to see my boy.'

CHAPTER SIX

Reed grimaced, but didn't look around at Fenchurch. Both thinking the same thing. Poor woman. Both of them being parents, this was their worst fear.

Candace Archer stood on her own, head bowed, arms dangling at her side. The image on the screen zoomed in on her son's body – her only son's body – on the slab, covered from the chest down. Cold, dead. She sucked in a deep breath, then looked over at Dr Pratt, standing in the doorway, and gave him a tight nod. 'That's my boy. That's Curtis.'

His nod was solemn. His exit was swift.

The screen flicked off.

Fenchurch gave her an understanding look, or as close to it as he could manage. 'Take all the time you want.'

'I wish I had.' Candace rubbed at her cheek. 'But there's never enough time.' She muttered a silent prayer to herself, touching her St Christopher and crossing herself. She smiled at Fenchurch, then picked up her handbag and left the room, walking right past Fenchurch.

'Mrs Archer.'

She stopped, dipped her head, then turned around to look at him with a frosty glare. 'It's *Ms* Archer. I took my ex-husband's name for my son's benefit, but we divorced a long time ago.'

'Would it be possible to have a word?'

'I'm sorry. I need to get back home. I've got a mound of washing. And I got two houses to clean this afternoon.'

Reed walked over, tilting her head at her. 'You don't have to work on a day like this.'

Fenchurch was just surprised she had to work at all. 'She's right. You should take some time out to focus on what's happened.'

Candace was rocking, her whole body fizzing with energy. Maybe her son meant she didn't have to work, financially, but she still had some physical urge to. 'I'm in shock, I think.' She stared hard at Reed. 'Have you got children?'

Reed nodded. 'Two.'

'And you?'

Fenchurch gave his own nod. 'Two, as well. Boy and a girl.'

'How old?'

'Al's five. Chloe's... She's twenty-five.'

Candace seemed to recoil at the age gap. But she didn't seek answers – a different mother, an adopted son, or a daughter who'd been abducted and raised by another couple... She stood up tall. 'Okay. Well. Both of you will know how I feel.'

'I do.' Fenchurch held her gaze. He wasn't letting go. But she was – eyes shut, jaw clenched. 'Ms Archer, I'm in charge of investigating what happened to your son.'

'He died. That's all I need to know.'

'He told some men he was being chased.'

Her eyes burst open wide. 'Chased?'

Fenchurch grimaced. 'I'm going to find out if that's true. I want to know who by. I want to know if that's why he died.'

'Well. I don't care.'

Reed was scowling. 'You don't *care*?'

'I don't care. My boy's with the Lord. His race is run.' Candace brushed her eyes, smearing her makeup across her cheeks. 'I need to put his affairs in order.'

'Ms Archer, I'm a season ticket holder at the London Stadium. I watched your son play for West Ham. Every home game until the pandemic.'

She swallowed. They might worship at different altars, but she maybe saw that Curtis Archer had left an impact on both of their lives.

'My son's a huge fan.'

'You mean until the injury.'

'No, he barely saw him. But now, Al watches his videos on YouTube. That hat-trick away to Newcastle, I could recite the commentary off by heart. My son wants to do what your son did. He wants to be the Hammers number nine.'

'I wish him well.' She shook her head. 'But what Curt did? What he achieved? It's virtually impossible. My boy was lucky. I told him that all the time. Stupid boy thought he deserved it. He didn't see what it cost to get where he had. Didn't see how he lost his childhood.' She looked around the room, then at both of them through eyes thick with tears. 'Where can we get some privacy?'

CHAPTER SEVEN

Reed led her into a family room. Tastefully decorated with comfortable sofas opposite each other. Four boxes of tissues sat on the coffee table.

Reed sat down next to Fenchurch, tore off a tissue and handed it over to Candace. 'Here you go.'

She sat there, hands clasped around her bag. 'I don't need it.'

'Everyone does, Candace. Everyone does.'

She reached over to take it, lips pursed. Then dabbed at her eyes. 'To make it as a footballer, you need skill, of course, but you need to give up so much of your life. Curt never had a girlfriend at school. Never had friends. Barely had school. He wanted to be a footballer. That was it. But I saw other boys with that laser focus on the same goal Curt had. And you know what set him apart? His faith. My boy had God's will. He said his prayers every night. It was all that was in them. And the Lord blessed him with so much. He had it all. He was good on the pitch. Fast, skilful. But that's only part of the battle. My boy had the kindness of a saint. Me and my sister and her family.

44

He took us all to the World Cup. He put us up in the best hotel in Moscow. He was such a generous boy. He gave me money to buy my house from Tower Hamlets council. Where I raised him.'

'You're from Canning Town?'

'Born and bred. You?'

'Limehouse.'

A smile flickered across her lips.

Fenchurch leaned forward. 'Can I ask you about his father?'

She was shaking her head. 'His father is a difficult man.'

'What's his name?'

'Oliver. Ollie.' She crossed herself again. 'Last I heard, he was in Monaco.' Her eyes fizzed with rage. 'Monaco! And I'm in Canning Town! Raising *his* son!'

Fenchurch left her some space. He had a sudden throbbing in his knee. He needed to stretch out but there was no room. The room felt too hot, too dry. He needed to get out of there. He tried to swallow it all down, to focus on her. On her son's life. On his death.

'When I met Olly, he was nothing.' She was shaking her head. 'And now he thinks he's something. A player. A big deal.' She sighed, long and deep, years of stress and resentment escaping. 'Met at school. My first love. Last love, really.'

Something still flickered in there. The opposite of the resentment and bitterness, something like affection and tenderness.

Fenchurch couldn't get a read on how old she was. Those eyes had seen a lot, but her skin was smooth and not a trace of grey in her hair. If someone told him she was thirty-five, he'd believe them. He figured forty, maybe. Eighteen when Curtis was born.

'Ollie tried to stand by me when I... When I got into trou-ble. His words. Married me just after Curt was born. But it

ED JAMES

didn't work. I had a screaming baby and he... He was Ollie. We split up when Curt was a year old. Ollie divorced me. He... He went to university, didn't he? Southwark. Thought he was something. Never paid me a bloody penny for his son. I raised Curt myself. Me. My mum and my dad didn't help. His parents never bothered, did they? Just me and my boy.'

'That must've been tough.'

She swallowed hard. 'I've sacrificed so much for him. Took him to training and matches on my own. Didn't have a car, so I took him there on the bloody bus. Waited in the rain for him. But he loved it and they told me he could make it. At seven, they knew he was a special talent. The Lord had blessed me with a special boy. He had the pace of a runner and the balance of a ballet dancer. They said it was just a case of keeping him going in the right direction. Keep him on the straight and narrow. Which the Lord helped me with. And he did. Of course, his boys' club fed into West Ham.'

The clock on the side table ticked. Five to ten.

Candace snarled. 'That's when his dad became interested. His boy signed up to West Ham's academy. It was like *he'd* made that happen. All of a sudden, he's round at our flat with football boots and strips and words of encouragement. Building up my boy to being Pelé or Maradona.' She looked at Fenchurch. 'What happened to Curt?'

'We're investigating it now.' Fenchurch waved back through to the identification room, now empty and being sterilised by a cleaner. 'Dr Pratt will be conducting a post-mortem this morning, so we'll know full details then. I'll have a Family Liaison Officer assigned to you so you're not left alone.'

'Thank you.' She was focusing on the room's door, like her son could just walk in, then a sharp jerk of the head and she was staring right at Fenchurch. 'Be honest with me. Do you think someone's killed him?'

46

'We'll know more when the pathologist has completed his examination. Do you have a reason to believe it is anything other than a medical cause?'

'I don't know.' Candace lurched forward, head in her hands. Now she had a use for the tissue, rasping as she blew her nose. 'Curtis was a great kid.' Her voice was muffled. 'He was very popular, you know? Everyone loved him. At church, at school, on the street. Everywhere. At the club.' She balled up the tissue and tossed it onto the table, then stared hard at Fenchurch with those almond eyes. 'Did he die because he was famous?'

'We don't know. DI Reed and I work for a Major Investigation Team covering East London. We need to understand why someone would target your son. There are obvious potential reasons which we are investigating already. Such as his fame, like you say. It could just be he was in the wrong place at the wrong time. But it'd be incredibly helpful if we piece together as much of his life as we can. It can close off doors that might be wasting time.'

Candace tore off another tissue and blew her nose in a loud honk. 'Curt was a quiet boy. Kept himself to himself. Part of the problem.' She slammed the balled-up tissue down on the table. 'At school, I told him to keep his head down and he did. But... He didn't lift it back up. Just did the work, in case the football didn't happen. He could've gone to university like his father. But he didn't have a lot of friends. Never seemed to trust people. I don't know if that's because of what happened between me and his father, but...'

'No friends?'

'Not that I know of.' Another tissue, but she just held it.

Fenchurch rested his hands on his lap. 'What was your relationship like?'

'I'm there every day. At his flat. I clean his place. Cook

meals so he has something proper to eat. If it was up to him, he'd be eating deep-fried chicken or pizza. Most of his job is being fit, so I made sure he ate a high-protein, high-energy diet. The club's dietician gave me recipes. I love to cook. He loved to eat. I trained him to like that food. Said my touch made it taste much better than at the club.' She was smiling, wistfully. Then she clamped her eyes shut.

Candace was present in her son's life. A lot of parents weren't, but she was someone who had that daily connection. And she seemed supportive of him and his career.

'Candace, mapping out his last twenty-four hours are going to be crucial in determining what happened to him. When was the last time you saw him?'

'Not since his birthday.'

'When was that?'

'Two days ago.' She sighed. 'He seemed distracted, but I couldn't get out of him why. He was supposed to go to Dubai for this corporate thing, but... He didn't, did he? He told me he didn't want to fly. I was going to see him today after work, but... Obviously... I've...' She took another tissue and turned away from them.

Fenchurch sat back and let her tend to her tears. Forty-eight hours was a long time to fill. 'Why didn't he go to Dubai?'

'I don't know.'

'Okay.' Fenchurch smiled at her. 'Does your son have any management?'

'He's got an agent, if that's what you mean.'

'You got a name for him?'

'Mark Primrose.'

God.

Fenchurch knew him from the TV. He looked at Reed and she nodded – didn't even have to ask the question. He focused on Candace. 'How did your son get on with him?'

'Well. I was in all of the meetings with Mr Primrose. He looked after us since Curt was fifteen.'

'Isn't that illegal?'

'It was just advice at that stage. But his advice paid off, so Curt signed up with him when he could at sixteen.'

'What about an entourage?'

'An entourage? My son wasn't a rapper.'

No, but young players liked to hang out with people they knew. 'Any friends who hung around with him?'

'No. Aren't you listening to me? My boy kept himself to himself. He didn't have friends growing up. He was very cagey.'

'A lot of footballers have—'

'—very expensive cars. I know. I've seen the car park at the training ground. But my boy wasn't one of them. Trouble was, he couldn't take the Tube to work, could he? So he had a driver. A big black Range Rover, picked him up and dropped him off. I think the club paid for it.'

'He didn't drive himself?'

'No.'

'Okay. Did he have a security detail?'

'All I ever saw was that driver. Maybe he was security too. I don't know. Not that he went out much. That injury broke my son. He was never the same after.'

Reed tilted her head to the side. 'Off the pitch as well as on?'

'Both, yes. Both. Obviously not on the pitch – he hasn't been able to train since. Hasn't even been to the training ground since it happened. He's tried to keep up his fitness at home. Got a gym. But... His knee operation wasn't a success.'

'Oh?'

'He went to this place in Switzerland his *father* knew about. And it didn't work. Didn't repair the damage fully. He had a second operation in the States. He had to go to a place in

49

Denver. They were angry about what'd happened to him. Said his knee had been butchered.'

Reed leaned forward. 'Could I get the name of both clinics?'

'I'll have to look them up.'

'There's no immediate rush.'

'Okay.' Candace stared into space.

Maybe they were pushing her too far, too soon. But she seemed to know pretty much everything about her son. Or enough to be able to give a good first impression to prod and poke away at.

'Fenchurch.' Candace's glare drilled into him. 'Curt's been very distant from me. Evasive. Almost dishonest. I figured he was just growing up, hoped it meant he was spending time with his girlfriend.'

'His girlfriend?'

'I never met her.' Candace swallowed. 'He said he was in love with her, but how could he not introduce her to his own mother?' She winced. 'I was looking forward to being a grandmother, but that's not going to happen now.'

'He didn't mention her name?'

Candace shook her head.

Fenchurch was in danger of losing her here. His knee was throbbing like a bastard and he needed to get out of there. He leaned forward, his toes feeling numb in his shoes. 'Candace, we didn't find any keys on him.'

She frowned. 'What about his phone?'

'Erm, no.'

'And his watch?'

Fenchurch tried to think back to seeing him on the bridge. His arms had been tattooed but empty. He covered it with a cough. 'I'll need to check into that.'

'It was a gold smartwatch. He was very proud of it. Cost him enough money.'

'You said you go into his home every day?'

She nodded. 'Curt has an apartment in Wapping.'

'You've got a key?'

'Not quite.' Candace reached into her bag and got out a black fob. That will get you into the building and into his apartment. 'Please take good care of this.'

'Okay. I will return it in due course.' Fenchurch got up. He needed to take his next dose. 'DI Reed will stay with you for the next while until a Family Liaison Officer's been allocated.'

'Thank you. Do you think my boy was murdered?'

'We'll find out.'

CHAPTER EIGHT

Fenchurch stopped on the concourse and shivered. It might be June, but that wind was still bloody cold. He felt it deep in his bones, like he'd never be warm again. He reached into his pocket for the fresh bottle of pills and put two out on his hand. Little white bastards, ridged in the middle to let someone split them. Maybe he should do that. Maybe he should just go cold turkey.

His knee sent a spasm of pain riding up his thigh, as though it was demanding another hit of pain relief.

He popped one in his mouth and swallowed it down with ice-cold water. The shiver was like he was being electrocuted.

Jesus Christ, get a hold of yourself!

Fenchurch put the other one away and pocketed the tub, then got out his phone. He started tapping out a message to Reed:

Thanks for staying with her. She'll probably stand to inherit. Coax it out of her. And get in touch with the father and the clinics. Thanks.

He sent it and felt like a loser. Getting out of there because he wanted to get the forensics started. Not because he couldn't stand to be in the same room as a grieving mother. He'd done that so many times in his career. This time felt worse than anything else, though, and he couldn't figure out why.

He pocketed his phone and walked over to the car park as fast as he could move.

The rubbery tang of a cigar hit him.

Dr Pratt was in the smoking shelter, standing next to a cleaner who was watching a video on his phone, volume up full. Pratt was sucking on a cigar, while giving the guy some serious side-eye.

Fenchurch smiled at him. 'You're surely at risk of setting fire to that beard.'

Pratt bellowed out a laugh. Something Fenchurch had never seen in the pathologist.

Fenchurch clutched the key to Curtis Archer's flat. 'Catch you later.'

'Not so fast.' Pratt left the shelter and walked over to Fenchurch, shrouding him in a fug of smoke. Not the worst smell in the world, less the harsh bitterness of cigarettes and more the memory of his maternal grandfather's own cigars making the room smell of that at family get-togethers over the years. 'Not official yet, but young Curtis died of a heart attack.'

Fenchurch felt his whole body collapse. 'You're sure of that?'

'That is my working theory, yes.'

'He was a twenty-two-year-old professional footballer!'

'Don't get angry with me.'

Fenchurch raised his hands. 'Sorry, it just doesn't fit.'

'The exertion from his early morning run taxed his depressed respiratory function. Cardiac arrest secondary to severe respiratory distress aggravated by severe opioid use.

And the blood toxicology came back very early, showing high levels of opioids in his system.'

'So he was using heroin?'

'Opioids rather than opiates.'

'What's the difference?'

'Not much, chemically. Opiates are derived from natural products, namely poppy sap. Heroin, codeine, morphine. Opioids are created in the laboratory, though some are partially derived from natural sources.'

He tried to shift so he was downwind of the cigar smoke. It might be nostalgic, but he didn't want that in his lungs. 'You know what he was taking?'

'Well, I'd say we're looking at oxycodone...'

Jesus Christ.

The exact same drug he was on.

It hit Fenchurch like a punch in the stomach. 'You think that killed him?'

'Well, it certainly taxed his system, yes.'

What the hell was it doing to Fenchurch's own body?

'How much was he on?'

'I don't know yet. In fact, I'm unlikely to unless you are able to find a prescription. I can merely say what killed him. How it got into his system is your realm.'

'But you must have an idea about the dosage?'

Pratt took a puff on his cigar. 'Well, I'd say he was taking about six to eight eighty milligram tablets a day.'

And guess who else was taking that...

'If it was indeed a prescribed dosage, Simon. You don't start there, though. Most physicians start at a much lower level. But to have that level in his blood, he would have been opioid-tolerant and that shows a long-standing addiction.'

'Addiction?'

'Sorry, I'm being crass. Young Curtis had a serious injury

and, from what I can tell, failed surgery. That needs serious medication to manage the pain. I will be following up once his physician has been identified to see what precisely they were treating him for.'

'It's not just his knee injury?'

'Not necessarily. Oxycodone is a broad-spectrum painkiller. It's commonly prescribed for bone cancer, for example, although there's no evidence of that here. Could be any number of uses, including recreational. It's a weird one, Simon, unless of course he has been buying pharmaceuticals on the street...'

'That's unlikely. He's a household name. Famous. Anyone would recognise him.'

Pratt took a suck on his cigar. 'Well, it's not uncommon for rich kids to not so much use what's sold on the street, but acquire it through other means. Lot of theft goes on, sure I don't need to tell you.'

'With you now.' Fenchurch stared at the cigar smouldering in Pratt's fingers.

Curtis Archer's heart had given out.

A twenty-two-year-old. One of the fastest footballers Fenchurch had ever seen, like that goal where he zipped past six Crystal Palace players or when he outstripped that Liverpool right-back like he was an old man or that run in the World Cup last sixteen where he won that free kick.

Dying of a heart attack. Because of what was in his system. Because of what it'd done to his system.

Fenchurch knew he needed to get off that. He couldn't let Al grow up without a father.

He stepped in close. 'William, I need to ask you some confidential advice, both as a friend and as a doctor.'

Pratt took a puff of his cigar and exhaled it slowly. 'Go on?'

'Nobody else can know.'

'Of course. You have my word.'

'I'm on a similar dose of oxycodone.'

'For your knee?'

'Eight eighty milligram pills a day.' Fenchurch sucked in the second-hand cigar smoke. 'I want to stop.'

'Have you got an operation date?'

'No. Well, still six months away.'

'Curious.'

'William, I'm on a really strong dose and I don't want to die of a heart attack.'

'Thing is, it's hard to step down from heavy-duty oxycodone to nothing. If you're serious, you need to do it gradually.'

'How gradually?'

'I'm not a specialist, but I've some expertise. It's called tapering. You space out the pills farther and farther apart, until you're down to half the dose.' Pratt clapped Fenchurch on the arm. 'Then you make sure you see a bona fide addiction specialist.'

Addiction.

Jesus Christ.

Curtis Archer was an addict.

Was Fenchurch?

No. No way.

Fenchurch was under a doctor's care, with a legitimate injury.

Pratt pursed his lips. 'I know one who I'd personally recommend after my son's ... issues.'

CHAPTER NINE

Fenchurch zipped into a space marked "Car Club only" and stuck his "On Official Police Business" sign on his dashboard. Hopefully they'd cancel each other out. Besides, anyone using that club should be at work or driving the car out to the country.

He got out into the warming air, blown by the Thames flowing just beyond the big park. Wapping. Last time he'd been here, that'd been waste ground, some vestigial remnant of this area's docking history. And he knew a fair chunk of the history after that. Growing up nearby, him and his mates had cycled here to play and this area had always felt strange even then. Stuck between the big docks, but not getting the same gentrification treatment as Canary Wharf. The big print works ensured all the pubs were workers' boozers that continued the same hours as sailors' drinking dens – open at five on the dot and any Tuesday morning felt like Friday night by half past eight.

Not a great place to have a paper round. Nobody lived here, so Fenchurch had to go long stretches on his dad's old boneshaker between deliveries. Always locking it to a lamppost, then running up and down the tenement stairs.

Now, though, it felt like everyone who was anyone lived here. The ancient bond buildings were luxury flats – this one had a pizza restaurant in the ground floor, with prices that meant a slice would be more than Fenchurch paid for a whole pie, as his old mates in the States would say.

A grimy van pulled up on the pavement outside, almost hitting him.

Fenchurch was about to kick off, felt that blood rising in his ears, when he spotted who was behind the wheel.

Mick Clooney hopped out onto the street, his limbs thin like the frames of a racing bike. 'Morning, Si.' He smiled wide, running a hand over his bald head. Seemed to have another ten piercings stitched into his eyebrows, not that there was much room left. 'Been ages since I've seen you. Come here, you big bastard.' He wrapped Fenchurch in a hug, like he was wrestling a bony snake, then broke off and gave Fenchurch the up and down. 'You got the key?'

'I've got the secret too.' Fenchurch handed over the fob and stepped back. 'Been a while, Mick.'

'Missed doing the doing, you know?'

'Oh, I know that feeling almost too well.' Fenchurch felt a twinge in his back, probably from riding a desk too long. Good to be out on the street, where he could do the most damage. He checked into the van, where a big lump of a man was tapping something into his phone. 'Where's Tammy?'

'In the Maldives on her honeymoon, so they needed someone who knows the ropes.' Clooney gave a theatrical bow. 'And here I am.' He laughed. 'You don't need to look so pleased.'

Fenchurch gave a grin. That was all it deserved. 'Didn't know she was getting married.'

'She's a secretive one. Took one of the girls in the team four months to find out. Doesn't wear a ring.'

Fenchurch shook his head. 'Need me to suit up here?'

'Are you expecting a body in there?'

'Mick, I'm *always* expecting a body.'

Clooney laughed. 'Do it then.' He handed Fenchurch a pair. 'Hope that's big enough.'

'Cheeky sod.' Fenchurch started suiting up, trying to puzzle it all through.

His painkillers matching Curtis's. His tolerance for opioids...

Made him swallow down thick mucus.

Jesus Christ. Who wanted to have any tolerance for opioids?

Clooney frowned at him. 'You okay there?'

'Why wouldn't I be?' Fenchurch just had to put his goggles and mask on.

'Well, you're not listening to a word I say. Usually you reply to everything I say. Some snark. Some grumpiness. Chasing me up on progress at the crime scene. Either Tammy's got you well-marshalled or... Why are you being so quiet?'

'Sorry, just thinking about Curtis Archer.'

'Right, right.' Clooney walked over to the door and tapped the fob against a reader. The door pinged and he opened it. 'Like being on *Star Trek*.' He stepped inside. 'I mean, it's quite something that a kid that young could afford a place like this.'

Fenchurch followed him up the carpeted stairs, the walls dotted with black and white shots from Wapping's past.

'You ever see the lad play?'

'A few times, yeah. More than a few.' Fenchurch let out a deep breath. 'I was at the match when he got crunched by that big Palace lump. Could hear the snap from the stand. Opposite side of the pitch, Mick.'

'Jesus.'

'Usually when it's a fake injury, you see them rolling around, slapping the turf. A real one, arms flailing in pain. With Curtis, he just lay there. Out of it. Either he knew it was bad or his body did and just shut down. Seeing him getting stretchered off like that, my old man thought he was dead. Just glad my boy wasn't with us or it would've traumatised him.'

'That was over two years ago, right?'

'Think so.'

'You've got some memory.' Clooney stopped at the top. 'Struggling to see how we get in here?'

Fenchurch checked along the corridor. All white, with some purple lighting. One tiny window at the end that barely let any light in. Only two apartments on this floor, one marked 'CA'.

Clooney tapped the fob against the door lock. The door clicked. 'Aha.' He went in first.

Fenchurch followed him into a massive living space. It was immaculate, though. Just like his mother's flat. Scented with a fresh citrus smell. Double-height unit, taking up two rows of the small windows, but it still felt dark, even in the height of summer. These buildings were designed to store and preserve, which meant keeping the light out. This living room was bigger than Fenchurch's flat with Abi. Bigger than both of them put together.

The walls lined with a rainbow of framed football shirts: Ronaldo's famous number seven shirt from a pre-season friendly against Real Madrid; Salah's Liverpool red; De Bruyne in the sky blue of Manchester City; Maguire in both the blue of Leicester and the white of Man Utd away; Lascelles in Newcastle's disgusting orange-and-tangerine stripes from one away season. Most were grass stained, the Lascelles one torn on the sleeves, which showed how much Curtis Archer revelled in the physical side of the game.

A blue sofa in three sections filled a corner, not so much L-shaped as a U. The latest game consoles sat on a unit opposite, but no sign of a television.

'No telly.' Fenchurch looked over at Clooney. 'Has someone nicked it?'

Clooney was back out in the doorway. 'In here.' He turned to face Fenchurch. 'What was that?'

'You're going deaf. I said there's no TV.'

'Blind as a bat, you.' Clooney walked over, picked up a remote and pointed it at a long box, maybe sixty inches wide. A sound bar, maybe.

Silently, a hatch slid back and a TV rose out of the top, unfolding into a huge screen, like having your own personal cinema.

'What the hell?' Fenchurch crouched down and ran his hand under the gap beneath the screen. Nothing. 'Where did that come from?'

Clooney was grinning. 'The screen rolls into a tube.'

'Are you kidding me?'

'Nope. Very experimental tech. Can't just walk into John Lewis and pick one up, mind. Costs the best part of a hundred grand.'

'Wow.'

'Tip of the iceberg, mate. This one's three years old. Should see some of the later models. Knock your socks off.'

'Mine are already knocked off, so I'll take your word for it.'

'Shows how much cash is in football, though. I mean, I hate football, but even I've heard of him.'

'That's fame for you.' Fenchurch walked over to the window and looked out at the park below, lining the Thames. Cracking view over Rotherhithe, though why anyone would want one was maybe beside the point. 'Kid's still got a presence from his celebrity endorsements, shampoo ads, even some *Fortnite* skins... But how long that lasts, who knows?'

'Will he ever play again?'

'He's dead, Mick.'

Clooney winced. 'You know what I mean. Did people think he'd play again?'

'A lot of serious football fans wrote him off. My son didn't. Still holds him up as a god. Hard to let that go.'

'What about you, Si?'

'Well, if you want my honest appraisal?'

'Always.'

'I think Curtis had become a liability to the club. All the fans knew he wasn't coming back at the level he was at before, but the club acted like they thought he was and didn't invest. Before the injury, they'd supposedly agreed a deal with Chelsea or Man City for over a hundred million. Then... Well, they'd be lucky to get his contract paid by the insurers.'

'Tough world.'

'Sure. But Curtis Archer would've been financially okay. Even at his age, with the money he'd made, he'd still be loaded for a long time. And with the right people, he could've built a media career.' Fenchurch turned away from the window.

Money was always a motive.

The club had a contract to pay him for a set period. When he'd signed his new deal, there were rumours it was for six or seven years. And that was just over two years ago, right before the injury. A hundred-and-fifty grand a week. A lot of cash going out all the time, meaning a big incentive to stop paying him off. Yeah, they'd probably be insured for a chunk of that, but maybe not.

Fenchurch walked over to the doorway Clooney was standing in.

A kitchen that hadn't been used, or at least had been cleaned so well it looked like it. A designer coffee machine was the only thing on the counter, not even a kettle. Maybe it had one of those daft taps that would scald you with boiling water. Even more than the living room, it was like Curtis's mum's place, just on a much grander scale. Same colours or lack of. Just blue as a highlight or accent or whatever the term was.

Fenchurch realised he'd been too quick to get out of there with Candace. As soon as she gave him the fob, he was gone. Footballers' parents had a reputation for being controlling or pushy. And usually they earned from their sons, either directly or indirectly. Definitely needed another chat with her, no matter what Reed got out of her.

He tried another door and it led into a hallway. Blue carpet, bare walls. Four doors. The first two led to smaller bedrooms with en-suites. Double beds in each. Tasteful artwork, black-and-white photos of East London given a wash with blue to match the rest of the place. Someone had commissioned that.

At the end was a tiny window looking into a thin sliver of garden at the back. Another two rooms. On the left, a small room filled with memorabilia of a career that had barely started.

The far wall was filled with West Ham shirts from the smallest kid up to the adult, all grass-stained and worn, mounted in blue frames. Archer on all of them, but his famous 9 bookended the display, with his breakthrough 23 filling the middle.

England shirts filled another wall, a wider range of numbers, 21, 18, 14 then all the 9s he'd made his own.

Seventeen green England caps rested on the heads of eyeless mannequins. Kind of creepy, really.

England v Scotland.

England v Germany.

England v San Marino.

FIFA World Cup 2018.

There were another forty-odd heads waiting to be filled and a whole other wall just waiting for the shirts from the rest of a career that wouldn't happen.

Fenchurch shook his head. 'Kid kept everything.'

But he was alone in there.

No sign of Clooney.

Clattering came from the living room, the tell-tale sign that some of his team had arrived.

Clooney himself was in the master bedroom. The window looked north over the rooftops of Wapping towards the less gentrified parts of East London. 'Well.'

Fenchurch had never seen a bigger bed. Could fit a whole football team in it. And subs. And coaches. Black sheets, with the duvet tucked under the mattress. 'Well what?'

'This place is like a hotel. Clean as one, too.'

'His mother comes in to clean every day.'

'If she's been here, she's removed any sign of her son.'

'What do you mean?'

'Si, there's *nothing* here. Clothes in the wardrobe, sure. But that's it. No books, no magazines, no tablet or laptop, no food, no mess. We thrive on mess, Si. But aside from that, what your lot have been saying to mine, I'd expect to find some pots for his drugs. Even slips of medication. All I've got is a Samsung phone charger. There's not even a toothbrush in there.'

'You think someone's cleared their tracks?'

'Two possibilities. One, he never lived here. Two, someone's cleared it out.'

Fenchurch took a peek into the en-suite. A recessed bath in the middle. White tiles, blue counter top. Sure enough, it was empty. Not even a bottle of designer bath foam.

'Look, Si, we'll finish cataloguing it all, obviously, not that there's much. But I'll get some dusting done in here, see if anything's fallen through the cracks.'

'Appreciate it, Mick.'

'It's going to be days, though. We're backed up.'

Fenchurch felt bits of him tighten and clench. 'This is the highest priority. Orders from the top.'

'Still, all the favours you owe me, I doubt I can do it in the timescale you want.'

Same as it ever was...

CHAPTER TEN

Fenchurch found Candace where he'd left her, back in the family room. Staring into space, onto her second box of tissues.

No sign of Reed, though.

Fenchurch stepped back out and spotted her on a call about something else, scowling at the handset. He killed his and waved an apology at her.

She turned away from him, shaking her head.

Charming...

Fenchurch joined Candace in the family room. 'Hi.'

It was all he had to say. All he could think of. Didn't want to open up her feelings too much.

Candace looked up, eyes narrow. Reddened by tears. 'She's chasing up a family officer. But I don't want one.'

Fenchurch took the seat opposite her, the air puffing out of the cushions as he sat. 'I hear that a lot from people. Everyone's different. Believe me, it's good to have a conduit into the investigation. Questions you won't have now, you—'

'Save it.' Candace pointed out to the corridor. 'I heard it all from your colleague.'

'Okay...' Fenchurch smiled at her. 'Ms Archer, when I—'

'Candace. It's Candace.'

'Okay, when—'

'Have you been to Curt's home?'

Fenchurch nodded. 'I've got a few more questions.'

'What kind of thing?'

'Well, your son was obviously very affluent.'

'What's that supposed to mean?'

'This isn't the right time. Sorry, I should come back later.'

'No, what do you mean?'

'Your son's apartment is worth a lot.'

Those almond eyes narrowed further. 'You think I killed him?'

'No, I didn't say—'

'But you think I clearly stand to benefit should anything happen to him. Right?'

'There's a lot of money for someone to gain now.'

'Listen to me.' Candace leaned forward, clasping her hands. 'All I wanted in life was for my boy to be okay. Since I found out I was pregnant at sixteen, every second of my life has been focused on making sure he had everything. That he was okay.' A tear rolled down her cheeks. 'Curt's dead. That's not okay.'

'I'm sorry.'

'Don't give me that. You think I killed him, don't you? Let's hear it. Don't hide behind platitudes. Don't pussyfoot around me.'

'There's nothing to hear.'

'Come on. Why would I kill him?'

'Well, you would inherit his estate.'

She shrugged. 'He hasn't got a will. Kept telling him to sort one out, even if all the money went to the Battersea Dogs Home. Something, anything. But he wouldn't listen.'

'Okay, but still. You must see how it looks?'

'You think I'd arrange for my son's death?'

'I've dealt with that scenario before. More than once. And I don't have any evidence of anything here, okay? I just want to know what the truth is.'

Candace swallowed something down. Bile, tears or just saliva, Fenchurch couldn't tell. 'The truth is Curtis gave me a third of everything he made.'

'A third?'

'He took the rest. *And* he bought my house. Believe me, aside from the obvious, I've much more interest in my boy being alive than dead.'

'I get that. I'm sorry, but I do need to ask these questions.'

'The truth is, I invested all of the money I took from him. There's a small fortune in his name. I was going to give it all back to him when his career was over.' She shook her head. 'I know my boy. I know he won't save enough, whereas I live a simple life and don't need much. I just want my boy to be okay.' She reached for the tissue. 'Now I have all this money but no son.'

Reed stepped back into the room, but Fenchurch gave her a warning shake and she backed off.

'Candace, at your son's flat, we... Well, we haven't found anything. It's spotless.'

She nodded. 'Cleanliness is next to godliness.'

'That's not what I meant. There's nothing there. It was like a hotel. Nothing to personalise it. Just some clothes and one room with his footballing memorabilia.'

'I cleaned it every day, like I said.'

'Even so, I'd expect a toothbrush or some medication.'

'What kind of medication?'

Crap. 'Prescription. For his injury.'

'Why would you think he was on anything?'

Fenchurch scratched at his chin. 'It came up in the blood toxicology, I'm afraid.'

'What does that mean?'

'We test the blood for common things. Alcohol, drugs, you name it.'

'*Drugs?* You think my son's a junkie?'

'Candace, your son was on strong painkillers. Oxycodone. It's an opioid.'

'Shame on you! You think that, just because I am poor, that I should be slovenly. And that my son's a drug addict!'

'I don't mean anything by it.'

'Sure you don't.' She stood up, clamping her hands on her hips. 'Listen to me, okay? My son was a great athlete, an amazing son, and a decent person. And you sit there and you... you... you accuse him of being on *drugs?*'

'Look, it's a fact. Your son had drugs in his blood. It looks like he'd been taking them for a long time. I'm sorry to have to ask, but you didn't know about those drugs?'

'I swear. And I know all about opioids. I've watched that show with Michael Keaton. If I'd known he was taking *that*, I would've stopped him.'

'They were probably prescribed by a doctor.'

'I'd still have...' Candace collapsed back onto the sofa, pinching the bridge of her nose. 'Oh my God. My poor baby.'

'You don't know the name of his doctor?'

'No. The club handled all of that. They wouldn't speak to me directly.'

Bingo. 'Why was that?'

'Everything went through his agent. He didn't want Curtis or me to speak to them directly. Gave him all the power in the relationship.' Candace waved behind Fenchurch. 'I gave your colleague his number.'

'Thank you.' Fenchurch took a deep breath. 'Look, I'm sorry for the hard questions. I do need to ask them. And thank you for answering them.'

She smiled at him. 'I'm not angry with you. It's reassuring, actually. I just want to know that no stone will be left unturned in finding out what happened to my boy.'

'How did you get on with Mr Primrose?'

'We had a professional relationship.'

'Sounds like a whole story.'

'Well. Mr Primrose is a master of the dark arts, as they say. Sure, he got my boy good deals, but I don't trust him.'

'Is this your way of saying you think he might be the source of the oxycodone your son was on?'

'That's right.'

CHAPTER ELEVEN

J on Nelson sat back in the seat, pushing as low as he could go. Keeping an eye on the rear-view, watching the man approaching the front door.

Shifty, eyes scanning in every direction. Athletic build, but sharply dressed. He rattled the red door's knocker and stepped back, arms folded. Got his phone out and checked it. Tried the knocker again.

Nelson noted his appearance. Definitely a Barbour jacket. But 501s too judging by the red tab. Strange combination. No idea about the shoes, but that was immaterial. The hat, though... One of those stupid flat caps hipsters wore these days. At this distance, looking at him through a wing mirror, Nelson couldn't tell if the guy had any hair under there or if he was bald.

And nope – he definitely didn't know him.

He wasn't his target.

So who the hell was he?

This case was worse than anything he'd done as a cop.

Well, worse was stretching things. Hardly the brutality of a murder case or the toxicity of a long-term drugs operation.

It was... boring.

Working for Waheed and his stupid mate as a private eye wasn't the best career move, but he wasn't even a beggar, let alone a chooser. It was work, work with good-enough pay, but it didn't fill the gaping hole in his heart where a career used to be.

His phone rang. 'Call from Marie Deacon.'

Nelson kept his focus on the twat in the hat, who had his own phone to his ear, talking to someone on his own call. He got the deep sigh out of the way and tapped his AirPod to answer. 'Hey, it's Jon. Are you okay?'

She was out of breath. 'Jon, my husband's just booked a Travis.'

Nelson jerked up. 'He's on the move?'

'Right now.'

'I'm just around the corner from his office.' And his home, but he didn't mention that. He twisted the key in the ignition and the car roared into life. 'Do you know where he's going?'

'No. I tried following your instructions, but I could only hack the Travis app. It doesn't tell me where he's going, just that he's going.'

'Okay, call me if you get another notification.' Nelson hared past the house, but there was no sign of the man in the hat now. He took the corner on the wrong side of the road and swung right, cutting in front of a bus.

The surgery was gleaming white like a dentist's smile. A Prius sat outside the front. Lights on, idling. No plume of exhaust, so just using the battery.

Nelson parked opposite and waited.

The guy in the hat crossed right in front of him, dashing

across the road and heading into the old-school pharmacy next to the surgery.

Where was Deacon? Keeping a Travis car waiting wasn't going to get him a five-star rating, not without a hefty tip.

It hit Nelson – this could just be a ruse. Call a cab to see if he was being tracked by his ex-wife.

No.

That was a twist too much. It implied suspicion and they had nothing to suspect that Deacon knew anything was going on.

No.

This was legit.

He was heading somewhere. Hopefully to meet his lover. Nelson had his camera, all charged and ready to use the tele-photo to spot them at it. Just needed to know which hotel they were meeting in.

The surgery door opened with a swoosh and Edwin Deacon strolled out, swinging his briefcase and whistling. A man without a care in the world, not a man facing a toxic divorce. He dipped his head and got in the back of the Travis. Seconds later, it pulled out into traffic.

Game on.

CHAPTER TWELVE

Nelson kept it slow as he followed, held to a two-car distance, but his focus stayed on the Prius. Knew all of the details of it, save another one cut between them and he lost his target. No, he knew which one Dr Edwin Deacon was in.

This far south of the river and Nelson felt like he might turn into a pumpkin. Peckham, and not the bit that'd been hauled upmarket and filled with expensive shops, bars and cafés, with the nicer houses sold off to a generation of up-and-coming London professionals.

No, this was the worst sink estate in the area. Sixties housing that looked like it hadn't been touched since it was erected, just left to fester, without a care given to the poor bastards who lived there.

Deacon's Travis car pulled in on the right.

Bingo.

No spaces nearby. Typical.

Nelson followed on and got one on the left. He knew this car and could angle all of the mirrors to see anyone.

Deacon was outside an old Victorian school smothered in scaffolding – the gentrification machine was hitting another target, as his old boss might've said. Wooden barriers surrounded the site, advertising the development of yet more executive apartments. One thing London had a lot of was executives, or people who wanted to call themselves that.

Deacon got out and looked around. A man completely out of place. He wasn't on his own patch, wasn't swinging his briefcase around now. He crossed the road, heading towards a block of flats.

Not here for the property developers, then.

The site was at least twelve identical buildings, with maybe two hundred flats in each one. Great place to get lost.

And Nelson had no idea why Deacon would be here. He sifted through his notes, but couldn't figure it out. Must be a house call.

Deacon ducked his shoulders and walked up the thin path to the nearest door.

Well, that was a good sign. At least Nelson wouldn't have to get out and go hunting in the wild to see which address Deacon went to. This parking space was hopefully good enough to keep an eye on him – he got out his camera and powered it on, trailing Deacon up the path until he slipped inside the door.

Six floors, though the ground floor had a few blank units. Probably communal washing areas and post rooms for parcels. The staircase was visible from here and Deacon appeared through the window, skipping up like a man heading to a brothel.

Perfect place for one – no cops would be watching out here.

Just a former one.

Yeah, this was starting to match Deacon's MO. A man who got himself into some sticky situations and seemed to thrive on

danger. The risk was the ultimate turn-on. Danger the ultimate aphrodisiac.

Deacon stopped on the top floor and knocked on a door.

It opened and a silver-haired woman stepped out. Tall and
slender, but hard to tell her age from down here. Could be mid-
forties. Could be sixties.

Not what Nelson had expected – an eastern European girl
or a local one, maybe. But girl being the operative word –
young. Deacon liked them that way. Dangerously so.

Or so his wife believed. All part of the rush to risk.

Maybe she was the madam and the girls were inside, or in
another flat. A lot of ways you could organise a scheme like
that.

Deacon raced off down the stairs, hands in pockets, and
he burst out into the morning air again, then up to the
street.

The Travis had driven off, but a giant Range Rover pulled in
where it'd been, driven by a skinhead. A passenger, but Nelson
couldn't make him out from here.

The passenger got out and shouted, 'Deacon!'

Shit.

Fuck.

Shit.

Younis.

Tall, like a praying mantis towering over Deacon. Dark hair
spiked up, with a blond streak in the middle.

Younis.

A man with his fingers in so many pies they needed a
hundred bakeries.

Younis.

The man who'd fucked Nelson's career. His job in exchange
for his freedom.

Younis.

Ten metres away, completely oblivious to Nelson's presence.

Nelson reached into his glovebox for the bundle of clothes he'd stashed there. Felt way too heavy.

Deacon crossed the road and headed towards Younis.

Nelson got out and crossed the road a few cars up. He kept himself to the wooden barriers lining the work site, taking it slowly, each step closing in on his target. An angle grinder shrieked out.

Nelson was five metres away now. He reached into the bundle and grabbed the handle.

Younis swung around just in time to see Nelson pull out the zip gun and train it at his face. 'What the fuck?'

Nelson held the gun, aiming it right at Younis.

Deacon and the skinhead driver were watching. It was all they could do.

Witness a murder.

But Nelson couldn't pull the trigger.

All those times he'd thought about it, fantasised about it. Here he was, and he only found out he wasn't a killer at the worst time.

'Fuck!' Younis grabbed the gun and wrestled it away from his face.

Nelson lost his footing and fell back against the barrier, cracking his head against the wood.

Younis was on top of him now, pointing the gun at his face. 'What the fuck are you trying to do, Nelly?'

Nelson twisted around and shook Younis off, toppling him onto the pavement with a thud.

The gun went flying, then landed and rolled along the slabs.

Nelson shut his eyes and waited for the explosion, for the zip gun to fire.

Nothing.

He opened them again.

A boot was resting on the bundle. Gloved hands reached down to pick it up.

Someone else had Younis pressed up against the wall.

'Jon?' PC Chloe Fenchurch stood there in full uniform, inspecting the gun. 'What the hell are you doing?'

'Chloe? I—'

'He fucking attacked me!' Younis was trying to shake off his cop. 'Pointed that thing at me!'

No sign of Deacon, the skinhead or the Range Rover.

Chloe grabbed Nelson and led him away. 'My partner thought it was two lovers doing the nasty on my beat at this time, but no. It's you. What the fuck's going on?'

Younis was close to squealing now. 'That's a fucking gun!'

Chloe looked into the rags. 'Oh shit!'

Nelson swallowed hard. He had to play it cool here. Really, really cool. 'It looks like a zip gun to me.'

'What's one of them?'

'A one-shot improvised firearm. Firing pin on a spring. Point the tube at the target, bang. Wrapped in clothing so it doesn't burn your hand and doesn't look like a gun. Deadly at short range, useless at longer range... As risky to the assailant as the target.'

'You tried to kill him?'

Nelson scowled at her. 'Me? That's his!'

'What?' Younis had his eyebrows raised. 'That's nothing to do with me!'

Chloe shook her head. 'Great. Since you both wrestled for it, your prints and DNA are going to be all over it.' She pulled out a large evidence bag. 'Right, whoever this belongs to, it's mine now. I'll write this up.' She leaned in close. 'Go home, Jon.'

He nodded, but caught a sour look from Younis.

Yep – he should've killed him when he had the chance.

CHAPTER THIRTEEN

'Poor woman.' Reed was staring out of the window. 'Can't imagine what that must feel like. Losing your kid like that.'

Fenchurch tightened his grip on the wheel. Didn't say anything. Just trundled along the car park that was Whitechapel Road. The speedo barely moved, just the occasional tick. Still, at least the traffic did move every minute. 'Bloody roadworks.'

'Shit.' She looked over at him. 'I didn't mean that.'

'Didn't mean what?'

'About losing a kid. It was insensitive.'

Fenchurch looked right at her, into her eyes, and smiled. 'Got both of mine in my life, Kay.'

'I know, but—'

'This Primrose is in Aldgate Tower, right?'

She frowned briefly, then nodded. 'Second floor.'

'Been in that building a lot over the years, even though it feels like it only went up last week.'

'Ten years, isn't it?'

'It's where that Travis shower are based too.'

The traffic on the left turn lane somehow ploughed through, so Fenchurch pulled out and joined them, cutting along Commercial Road – completely the wrong direction, but he was one turn away from being on the right path.

There – he swept in front of a bus and shot back along Alie Street.

Bollocks.

Six cars idled at the end, waiting to turn right.

Two spaces on the left, though, so he took the first front-on.

'Come on, let's walk up.' Fenchurch got out onto the street. The air was thick with petrol and diesel fumes, but the usual London dryness had given way to a humidity where even the lampposts were sweating.

Her door slammed and he plipped the locks, then set off along the street. 'All change along here, isn't it?'

The old concrete post-war buildings were mostly levelled now, turned into a corridor of glass and chrome towers – not the tallest in London but more than enough to totally change the landscape. Despite Brexit, so much of the City's functions were spreading out into the lower-case city, surrounding land that used to feel a million miles away but was now a continuum of the financial sector from the City to Canary Wharf. Land was cheaper here and it was under a different police force.

'You getting anywhere with the club?'

'Doctor's up in Edinburgh for some reason they won't disclose.'

'What about the manager?'

'Busy with training.'

'Well, keep on them, yeah? Surely there's someone in the medical staff who can talk to us.'

'I spoke to the family doctor in Canning Town. He hasn't given him a thing since he was thirteen.'

'So it's got to be through the club?'

'That or private.' Reed was jogging to catch up with him. 'I feel like such a bitch, guv. I didn't think.'

'Kay, it's fine.' Fenchurch stopped outside Aldgate Tower, barely ten years old but feeling ancient in amongst all the new building work. He smiled at her. 'If I apologised for every time I put my foot in it, well, I'd still be apologising when I pop my clogs in fifty years' time.'

'But I didn't—'

'Kay. It's fine.' Fenchurch gave her one last smile, then went inside.

A security guard sat back, elbows resting on the arms of his chair, scanning their every movement. Saying nothing.

The board behind him listed the businesses. Travis now had the top four floors, and the rest of the names were firms Fenchurch didn't recognise. Probably all accountancy and law firms. Probably some money laundering fronts.

Not his problem until it became his problem.

Bingo – Primrose+Mercer were on the second floor, just like Candace said.

Reed was already at the lift, foot wedged inside, ready to take them up.

Fenchurch stepped in. 'Time was, I'd take the stairs to the top floor here. But this bloody knee.'

The door shut and the lift rumbled up. 'Still giving you bother?'

'Never stops, Kay. Never stops.'

The door opened again. A wide atrium filled with pot plants as big as security guards. Doors led to four different quadrants. Primrose+Mercer's green and purple logo sat above a glass door.

Reed stepped out first and stormed over to it.

Fenchurch took his time following her. His knee wasn't so much playing up as just really bloody sore. This tapering wasn't going very well. He stopped by the water fountain to swallow down another pill, then joined Reed in their reception area.

The straight-backed receptionist spoke into her headset, staring through them like they weren't even there.

Reed was standing up, arms folded. 'You okay there?' Her voice was low.

'Just thirsty.'

The receptionist frowned, then focused on Reed. 'Did you say you were with the Met or City of London police?'

'Met.'

'Okay, Mark. They're with the Met. Sure thing.' She stood up and waved towards a corner office. 'Mr Primrose will see you now.'

'Thank you.' Reed walked over to the door. The sign above read 'The Daddy'. 'Well.' She opened the door and stepped in.

Fenchurch followed and felt like he'd entered the lion's den.

Unlike the spartan reception area, this office was an absolute state. Papers on every surface. Shelves bursting with books. A bigger collection of football shirts than Curtis Archer, but stacked up against the wall. A Spurs scarf was the only thing hanging there.

Mark Primrose stood behind a desk, headset on, arms folded. Six-foot. Silver hair, but his salt-and-pepper stubble was more salt-and-crushed-chillies, betraying the red hair he would've had in his youth. Big bruiser, from the old East End. Gruff and arrogant. Face like a bulldog, one that had been trained to bite people's throats. 'Well, you can tell Harry that my client won't do it for less than ten grand.' He nodded at

Reed, then gave Fenchurch the old up and down. 'An hour. Do you think I'm a bloody idiot?' He laughed. No computer on the desk, just a sleeping iPad in amongst all of the British daily newspapers and a couple of the big Spanish and German ones, though Fenchurch couldn't fathom why he'd flung the *London Post* across the room. 'Yeah, you let me know what Harry says. Cheers, buster.' He smashed his chunky thumb into the receiver and rested his headset on his shoulders. This was a man who talked a lot on the phone and who needed the convenience of a hands-free call. No mobile for him, just an old-school landline. 'Cops, yeah?' Deep voice, betraying a long history of smoking. Essex accent, but more Colchester than Southend.

'DI Reed, DCI Fenchurch.'

'Ooh.' Primrose shifted his gaze between them. 'I do feel honoured to have such high-ranking officers in my humble office. Please, have a seat.'

Despite his knee, Fenchurch stayed standing. 'Mr Primrose, we're here to—'

'Shelly!' Primrose was looking between them. 'Three espressos, when you've got a minute.'

Reed smiled at him. 'I don't drink coffee.'

'I ain't asking you, princess. They're all for me.' Primrose cracked his knuckles. 'Now. Who did it and how much do I have to pay to keep it out of the papers?' That laugh again. With the right people, it'd be infectious.

Which spoke volumes about him.

'Anyway.' Primrose's eyes shifted between them. 'Listen, I'm being serious here. Who's done what to who?'

'Curtis Archer.'

Primrose sighed. 'He's a good kid. Great player. Being a top footballer is about two things.' He raised his thumb. 'One, being good at football. Obviously. But a shit ton of kids are.' He raised his index finger. 'More important, though, is determination. You need an iron will to make it in this game. That's what separates the top ones from the rest. You play fives against someone who played for Cheltenham or Coventry, you'll know all about it. They'll run rings around you. Not much difference between those lads and someone like Curtis. Sure, he might be that little bit faster, but the real difference was that kid put in the hours on the training pitch. Wasn't an aspect of his game he took for granted. Always trying to improve. And—' His phone rang and he checked the display. 'Oh, crap. Sorry, I've got to take this.' He put his headset back on and hit the button. 'Harry! How's your bollocks?'

Reed was looking like she was going to shove the phone somewhere uncomfortable.

'I told him ten grand an hour because he mugged me off last week about young Jack. Yeah. Him.' Primrose made eye contact with Fenchurch, nodding his head quickly, signifying that he was in control. 'Eight for the whole thing would work for me, just don't tell him I told you, yeah? Make him sweat, that's my plan anyway.'

Fenchurch took a look out of the corner windows. Across Leman Street, they were building a narrow tower that looked like New York's iconic flatiron, fitting a tower into a very narrow angle. No doubt it'd carry the same name and have a flatiron steak restaurant on the top floor.

'Alright, Harry, let me know how it goes. Love to the girls.' Primrose thumped the button. 'Bloody never rains but it pours, eh?'

Fenchurch turned to face him again. 'Nice view you've got.'

'Had better. We were up on the third-top floor but Travis wanted it, so we... came to an arrangement. Hence it being a bit of a pigsty down here.' Primrose laughed. 'Anyhow, what's Curtis done?'

He had no idea, did he?

Football agents were supposed to be the most well-connected men in the business, and he just didn't know.

Fenchurch could prise some information from him before he hit that bombshell. These guys traded in rumours and gossip, about how what you shared got you more than that back. 'You've worked with him for a while, yeah?'

'Since he was sixteen.'

'Not that long, then.'

'Well. He was one of my first clients. Used to work for... Let's say an Italian geezer and leave it at that.' Primrose bellowed with laughter. 'Anyhow, Curtis is a great kid. Wonderful footballer and he's smart too. Listens to what I have to say. Plays along with it.'

'I sense a but?'

'Biggest issue with Curtis is he's too loyal to the club. He could play for anyone, but he was a fan as a boy. All he wanted was to play for West Ham. Kept trying to lure him away from that shower.'

Fenchurch waved at the scarf on the wall. 'You're a Spurs fan, yeah?'

'I mean, yeah, but if you let that sort of bollocks affect your business dealings, you're in the shitter.'

'I get it. But you're saying Curtis can't separate his emotions from the business side?'

'I reckon I've fleeced Spurs more times than any other club, but I still support them. And bless his socks, but Curtis was worth a lot more than West Ham.'

Fenchurch smiled at him. 'I sense another but here?'

'His mother was enabling that kind of thing. She's got a reputation at the club for being pushy. I mean, I love Candace, but she was always in there, every day, demanding this, that, the other thing. Had to sit her down and make her promise to let me do all the talking. She listened and I used that to my advantage. To all of our advantages. I got an extra ten grand a week for the kid just so his bloody mother didn't turn up there.'

Fenchurch laughed, hoping it didn't sound fake.

'Trouble is, Curtis would speak to his manager about business stuff behind my back.'

'You weren't happy about that?'

'Eh? No, that happens all the time. The clubs all try to influence their players. They see themselves as farmers and the players as cattle. I mean, I influence my clients to suit my own agenda. How the game works. Everyone knows that, but what the clubs and the players should understand is that I hold the power in the key relationship.'

The door opened and the receptionist teetered in on eight-inch heels, carrying a tray with three tiny espresso cups. She laid it on top of the stack of newspapers and sashayed off.

'Thanks, Shell.' Primrose reached for a cup and slurped at it. Must have been close to eighty degrees and he didn't even wince. 'Not enough salt in this. Bloody hell.' He finished his coffee and slammed the cup down on the table. 'Thing with Curtis is, well. He doesn't know it, but I do – his career's finito. Kaput. Over. Certainly at the top level. But!' He reached for a second espresso and put it on the table in front of him. 'I'm all about the money, yeah? Even with Archer out of the game, I could still make Primrose a ton of money with endorsements. Getting him a line of clothing. Hell, I've got a couple of offers for him to hawk private healthcare. *Strictly, I'm A Celebrity, Big Brother*. You name it.' He slugged the second coffee. 'Now, I've given you a little bit of inside gen on the kid, how about you tell me why you're here? What's he done?'

There it was.

The cheeky cockney geezer who spoke out of turn, who was a bit loose-lipped, who over-shared...

Hiding underneath was a steely-eyed businessman.

Charm was a weapon to be deployed. Candour was a weapon.

Well, Fenchurch had ammo of his own. He fixed Primrose with his own glare. 'He's dead.'

'Shit.' Primrose collapsed back onto his office chair and rolled backwards. 'Shit.' He stared through the window and ran a hand down his face. 'What happened?'

'Heart attack.'

'*Heart attack?* Is this a wind-up?' Primrose craned his neck around to look at Fenchurch, like he expected a film crew to burst in. His phone rang and he checked the display. 'Sod him...' He let out a deep sigh. 'Is this on the level?'

Fenchurch nodded.

'Curtis had a heart attack. How?' Primrose was shaking his head. 'How? The kid just turned twenty-bloody-two!'

'His blood was full of opioids, Mr Primrose. It depleted his immune system.'

'Woah, woah.' Primrose was holding up his hands. 'You think I gave him them?'

'Now why do you think someone gave him them?'

'Eh?'

'They could've been prescribed.' Fenchurch shrugged. 'After an operation like he had, I presume he'd been on some strong painkilling medication. But you seem to think there's something shifty going on here. Why?'

Primrose's gaze shot between them. He licked his lips. He was jittery, like he was on something stronger than the empty coffee cups lining his desk. 'Anything to do with that operation is entirely down to the club. Okay?'

'Okay.' Reed folded her arms. 'Trouble is, I can't get hold of anyone at the club who'll speak to me about medical matters.'

'I'll put in a call and sort you out.' Primrose picked up his third coffee then put it down again. 'Shit. I can't believe this. Why are you pair investigating him? You think this is a murder?'

Reed shrugged. 'We're working this case because of the public profile of your client. So we are being discreet. But there are several unanswered questions here that are making us feel a bit off about the whole thing.'

'Such as?'

'Well, the fact nobody will talk to me about his medical history.'

'I've said I'll sort that out for you, darling.'

She winced. 'Sure, but why don't you tell me what happened with the operations?'

'Operations?'

Reed nodded. 'Plural.'

'You heard about the second, then...' Primrose stood up again, but took off his headset and rested it on the desk. 'Well, the first one was a complete disaster. Curtis was in a lot of pain after. Didn't heal properly. When you do your ligaments like that, it's a complete nightmare. Botched. No other word for it. They botched it. Tried to do it on the cheap, didn't they? So I got the club to send him to America and the Yank doctor reckoned he'd sorted it. Thing is, by that point, Curtis was never going to be the player he would've been. The first op put paid to him being the best in the world.'

'But he still had a career?'

'When he came back, maybe.' Primrose stared into space. 'Lucky for him I'd got him a new deal six months before. Got Curtis a lot of cash, really. It'd set him up for life. Term was until 2027, but they were due him all of that, come rain or shine.'

'What did the club get out of it?'

'The Hammers inserted a release clause in his contract. Meant anyone who wanted him would have to pay up nine figures. Manchester City and Chelsea were super keen. Mate of mine in Madrid reckoned he could get Real or Atleti to pony up too. Would've been a good payday for Curtis. Any club willing to pay the hundred mill they were after, he was walking away to get his cash and the club got their fee. Everyone's happy. Cushty.' He sighed. 'And then he got injured and that's all she wrote.'

'So that injury means they're liable for his wages?'

'Well... I guess it's an insurance job for them.'

Reed frowned. 'You guess?'

'I hear a few things about this new lot that took over.' Primrose tapped his nose. 'Like they believe insurance is too expensive, so they insure themselves by sticking the money aside.'

'So they're paying his salary?'

'Until 2027.' Primrose tapped his nose again. 'I mean, he would've come back and played. Probably not half the player he was. Got loaned out, maybe. Sold. It was mostly a case of Curtis seeing out that deal, then I reckoned I could get him over to the MLS.' He looked at Reed. 'That's Major League Soccer. In America and Canada.'

'I know what it is. Saw the Tampa Bay Rowdies play a few years back.'

'Well, well.' Primrose laughed. 'Even with his injuries, someone like Curtis would be a superstar over there. Or I reckon I could've got someone in Turkey interested. Pay a lot over there and nobody really knows why.'

Fenchurch glanced at Reed, letting her know he was taking over. 'How had he seemed recently?'

'Listen, the truth is, I haven't heard from Curtis in a bloody long time.' Primrose picked up his third coffee and drank it this time, eyes shut. 'Seemed a bit frantic on the phone last week.'

'Any idea why?'

'Wouldn't say.'

'Wouldn't or didn't?'

'I asked, he said he'd tell me face-to-face. Supposed to meet for dinner last night. Didn't show.'

'Okay. Where was this?'

'Noir. Place up in Shoreditch.'

Fenchurch nodded. 'I know it. Craft beer place, used to be a strip club.'

'Did it?' Primrose clattered his cup down onto the desk. 'Anyway, I waited. I hate eating alone, so I tried calling but he didn't pick up. I left after half an hour.'

'What time was this?'

'Be about eight, I think.'

'You know anyone who might've spoken to him recently?'

'Struggling to think. I mean, I try to keep my clients apart, you know? Don't want them talking shop about me. Sharing secrets. Bad enough with their mates at the clubs.'

'So you don't know any close friends?'

'Sorry, no.'

'The reason we're investigating this is it's possible he was being chased.'

'Good luck to them. Nobody's catching that kid in a sprint. But I want to help. Whatever happened to Curtis, I want to know. For myself, for Candace and for his fans.'

'We believe he'd been taking oxycodone.' Reed left a pause. 'But we can't find any prescriptions.'

'Woah, woah.' Primrose raised his hands. 'I ain't involved in whatever you think I am.'

'What might that be?'

'Well... I don't know. You think he was getting illegal back-street oxy?'

'Know anything about that?'

'Nothing to do with me. But, come on. Curtis would never buy drugs off the street, would he? It'd ruin his reputation. We talked about that a lot and he understood it. His playing career might be in the toilet, but all those celebrity endorsements and corporate gigs would dry up if he was a naughty boy.'

'He ever been a naughty boy before?'

Primrose laughed. 'No, but my clients come from very diverse backgrounds, shall we say.'

Fenchurch would drill into those backgrounds. If there was anything, he'd find it. Anything.

'Now, you're asking me if I know anything about him taking drugs? Nope. I'm a football agent, not an apothecary, so you'd have to check with the club. I told you, the only time I intervened medically was about the second op. But if you want my suggestion, I think what you're looking for is a doctor who'd prescribe those drugs and be very discreet about it.'

Fenchurch left him some space. He didn't disagree with the idea, but wanted to know if Primrose had anything further.

He was drumming his fingers on the desk. 'And if you're looking for a Dr Feelgood, there was one player who was friendly with Curtis. An ex-client of mine. Suffered a big injury, so knows a thing or two about needing medication. Heard a rumour or two that he can sort you out.'

CHAPTER FOURTEEN

Big clubs like West Ham or Chelsea would have a custom-built training complex out in the green belt somewhere. The media would refer to it by name, as if they were in the know about what went on there. All the secrets the club held there. Transfers, player injuries, managerial squabbles. All the gossip.

Shadwell United, on the other hand, had a small corner of Hackney Marshes earmarked for their permanent use. Four pitches fenced off from the ones used on a Sunday by amateurs, kept in slightly better nick by semi-pro ground staff. A big changing complex looked like a school built during the New Labour era.

The first team huddled in the centre circle of the nearest pitch, basking in the heat. Panting. Sweating. Listening to the manager as he laid out a plan.

They weren't their target, though.

Reed was charging up a different touchline like an angry dad at his kid's football.

The under-seventeens were playing a rough-looking game

of seven-a-side. A bibbed defender lunged into a tackle on a striker, not dissimilar to the one that tore Curtis Archer's knee apart.

'Good tackle!' Their coach clapped his hands together. 'Come on, lads. More intensity! I want to see you *bleeding* out there.' Had the build of a rugby player. Big and with that presence, like he commanded more space than he occupied. He turned around to them and scowled. Or it just looked like that. His nose had been broken in three places and looked like a sausage someone had dropped into a barbecue but had struggled to retrieve using their tongs. His dark hair was short and spiked up like it was 1986 and he'd just watched *Top Gun*. Looked early forties even though Fenchurch knew he was only twenty-nine. 'Can I help you?'

'DI Reed.' She held up her warrant card. 'This is DCI Fenchurch.'

Nervous eyes swept between them. 'Which of my lads are you looking for?'

'Terry Monaghan.'

His smile revealed missing front teeth. Six, both top and bottom. Presumably kicked out and not eased back in straight away. 'That'll be me, darling. How can I help you?'

She smiled at him. 'Thought you were still playing?'

'Oh yeah, I am.' He leaned forward to rub his thigh. 'Trouble is, I can't train anymore because of my dodgy knee. Every time I play, it balloons up like a watermelon.'

'An injury?'

'Bad one, yeah. First day of the 2016/17 season. Never the same after it. Man Utd were after me, supposed to sign me early doors in the transfer window, but they kept arguing over the fee. Kept getting pushed back towards deadline day. If I'd signed a week earlier, well. Who knows? But after that little incident, I had to settle for playing for Charlton, Portsmouth and now bloody Shadwell. But at least they're putting me through my coaching badges. After I hang up my boots, I'll be kept on as coach full-time. Maybe even become a manager. Who knows, might manage Man U one day?' He stopped smiling, hiding that gap in his teeth. 'So why are the Old Bill here? You finally going to charge Jack Stead with injuring me?'

Reed fixed him with a hard stare. 'Curtis Archer is dead.'

Monaghan shut his eyes and snarled, 'Ah, shit.' He screwed up his face and burst into tears. Mouth hanging open, jaw juddering. Wailing. 'Oh my God.' He turned away from the pitch, arms wrapped around himself. 'Curto....' He took a deep breath then rubbed at his eyes, clearing his cheeks.

The kids were standing, hands on hips, mouths open, staring at him.

'Don't stop playing, you little sods! Go on!' Monaghan glared at them until they kicked off again. 'Sorry, that was... unexpected. We played together at the Hammers, right? Me and Curto. He was young and breaking through, whereas I'd done that a few years earlier and was a cruciate away from being cast out by the club.' He focused on the pitch, like they were discussing a shortage of water bottles or practice cones. 'What happened?'

'Heart attack.'

Monaghan was off again, lips quivering.

'You were close, then?'

'Oh, still are, yeah. Loved that geezer like a brother, you know? Mentored him since he was fifteen. Could see his talent. Cockney Mbappe they called him, but he was going to be even better than the real thing, until that injury. Broke the poor sod's soul in two.'

'When was the last time you saw him?'

'Meet up for a coffee every week. Curto didn't drink, but he loved a latte. Supposed to meet him for a beer last night. Coffee for him, obviously. Sat there, waiting. Got late, still not answering calls or texts.'

Similar story as with Primrose. 'So you left?'

'Eh? No, he showed up when I was paying the bill.'

'You *saw* him?'

'Yeah.'

'Last night?'

Monaghan looked at Fenchurch then back at Reed. 'You not listening to me?' He shook his head. 'He looked in a bad way. Like he was whacked up on something.'

'You know what?'

'Well. They had him on some strong pills for his recovery, I can tell you that. Supposed to be just to ease it, like with mine, but it's been two years now. And you want my opinion? The club were cheap on the op. Should've sent him to the US first, but nope. Manager and Curto's mother didn't want him over there, so it was done over here. Place in Birmingham.'

'I thought it was Switzerland?'

'Whoever told you that lied. Same place that butchered *my* knee. Made a right meal of it too. Two years later and it was still dogging him. Said he's in constant pain. Had to get it done again in the States, didn't he? That worked but... Still sore. It's why he's addicted to those drugs.'

Reed exchanged a look with Fenchurch. 'Addicted?'

'Pops them like sweeties. And he was muttering about someone trying to kill him.'

Shit.

'It's a delusion.' Monaghan brushed more tears from his eyes. 'Kid was broken. Never get back to the top of the game. And those drugs do funny things to your brain. And Curto didn't have many people in his life. He couldn't talk to his mother about this. So it was just me.'

Fenchurch nodded along with it. 'We think he was possibly chased by someone when he died.'

'Man. Shit. Seriously...' And he was off again, crying into his elbow. This time, his players didn't seem to notice.

'You know what he was taking?'

Monaghan shook his head. 'I was on codeine, but I think he was on something different.'

'Well...' Reed was frowning. 'We found a lot of oxycodone in his bloodstream.'

'Oxy? Christ.'

'Probably what caused his heart attack.'

'Ah, shit. Hillbilly heroin, eh?'

Fenchurch looked away from them both. Watching the kids shouting at each other over a goal. Monaghan didn't seem to notice.

Hard to listen to that. But also, he could see how it was a slippery slope to taking them.

Monaghan squatted down and picked at a blade of grass. 'Look, I kept telling him to stop. Get off those pills. I mean, I'm clean myself. Never take anything stronger than a cup of tea these days. Aside from booze. I kicked the painkillers, but he didn't seem to be able to. Not even sure he was physically in pain anymore.'

Fenchurch looked at Monaghan. 'Trouble is, we don't know who he was getting it from.'

'You mean, what doctor?'

'We haven't found a prescription or a bottle anywhere. Don't have anything, really. Just got it in his bloodstream.'

'You think he got it from a dealer?'

'No idea. You had a prescription for your codeine, right?'

'I did. And it ran out. I was still in a lot of pain during the recovery.'

'So you got some.'

Monaghan snarled. 'Right.'

'From who?'

'I know people.'

'Drug dealers?'

Monaghan laughed. 'Primrose told you this, yeah?'

'I'm not able—'

'Yeah, yeah.' Monaghan tapped his nose. 'Primrose has spread lies about me dealing to people before. Absolute bullshit. I've told him if he does it again, I'll see him in court. And he's done it again, hasn't he?'

Reed stood her ground. Stayed silent.

'Don't believe a word Mark Primrose says. After what I went through with my injury, he told me I'd be okay. Then he sacked me. He'd taken fifteen percent of my bigger deals, but I was no longer likely to make him anything in the future.' Monaghan looked down that wonky nose at Reed. 'Primrose gives all the big talk when he needs to, but he only cares when the money is rolling in from his stallions. After all, they shoot horses when they fall.' He sniffed, then rubbed at his eyes. 'I do all that side of things myself now. I talk to the club myself, agree what's happening, then get a lawyer to check it over. Saves having some sexual deviant coke fiend taking fifteen percent, eh?'

'What do you mean by—'

'Just joking. He's not into kinky stuff and, as far as I'm aware, the strongest thing he touches are those coffees of his. Surprised his heart's still beating, I tell you. Primrose is a total bullshit artist. Plays everyone off against each other. Acts the big man, but he's just an arsehole, you know?'

Fenchurch knew. Only too well. Had to deal with too many small men who thought they were titans. 'Did he arrange for your codeine?'

'I'm not going to say.'

'Do you deal controlled substances to other players?'

'Of course I don't. Who do you think I am?' Monaghan waved a hand over at the pitch. Somehow the lads had continued their game again without it descending into a fourteen-man brawl. 'I want to help those lads fulfil their potential. Nobody's as good as Curto. Nobody's even as good as I was. But I want to help them be the best *they* can. And not just on the pitch. Off it too. I want to listen to them, to guide them. I'm not going to screw any of that up just for a few extra quid.'

Fenchurch didn't know whether to believe him or not, but it made sense. Still, he knew better than most that someone dealing drugs could make it sound like they were doing it for the most noble of reasons. 'We're serious about him being chased. It's why we want to know who was giving him the drugs.'

'There's something you're not telling me here.'

'Of course. It's a police investigation and you're not a police officer or a relative of the deceased.'

'So you *do* think it was me?'

'I'll ask you this straight, okay? Did Curtis ever ask you for help sourcing drugs?'

'No. And like I bloody told you, I'm very anti-drugs these days.'

'But back then?'

'Club doctor told me to kick the codeine, and he took me off it quick smart.' Monaghan looked over at the pitch, his head rising and falling to trace the arc of a hoofed clearance. 'But the truth is... I still needed it from time to time, you know?' His focus went to his boots. 'One of the guys at the club got me sorted out. Just a few months' worth, cost me a pretty penny, but it tided me over until it stopped hurting so badly. Saw an addiction specialist my cousin went to. End of.'

'Who was the teammate?'

'I can't tell you...'

'Come on. It's crucial here. If Curtis was being chased, they might as well have killed him.'

Monaghan let out a deep sigh. 'Fine. The lad I got my drugs from back in the day, he's the academy boss at West Ham.'

CHAPTER FIFTEEN

West Ham, as opposed to the other United along the road in Shadwell, were a Premier League club and had all the riches that entailed, which came with a few barrows full of pressure. They had to compete with Chelsea, Arsenal, Liverpool, Newcastle United, Leicester, Tottenham and both Manchester clubs. And if they slacked off, they'd get relegated down to the level of Shadwell. But the money meant a near-as-damn-it-top-class training complex out in Romford, where Fenchurch swore he could see the Dagenham and Redbridge stadium as he crossed the car park, but it could've been a supermarket.

The first-team players were all leaving now. Faces Fenchurch saw on the TV during the week and on the pitch at the weekend. Wee Ben McBride got into a Tesla X and swept across the tarmac like he was on the pitch, the jinky Scottish winger harkening back to an earlier age of speedy players from north of the border.

The first-choice defensive pairing of Carlos Alberto and Dean Morgan were beside their matching Lamborghinis, chatting to youngsters, signing their autograph books, posing for selfies with schoolkids.

Four TV crews were filming it all. Only one journalist was talking to camera, the rest were scribbling in their pads.

Reed caught up with Fenchurch. 'What's going on?'

'First week of pre-season training, Kay. Winter World Cup in Qatar, so this season starts early. Still lots of chat about us replacing Archer with two lads from France and Spain, so the press want to know how that's going and also see who's on their way out.'

'God, they're as bad as the lot who we deal with.'

'Eh, not *that* bad.'

Reed's phone blasted out. 'Well, well. It's the club doctor. I'll leave you to it.'

'Thanks, Kay.' Fenchurch squeezed between a Uruguayan holding midfielder and his almost-sensible Ford Mustang, then entered the training complex.

The reception was like a plush golf hotel, all marble floors and sweet flower smells. The desk was manned by a security guard who looked like he'd seen things. Narrow eyes, darting everywhere, watching everything. Ex-services, that's for sure, just which service and what had he seen? He raised his finger. 'Just a second.'

That Eustace lad who'd broken through the previous season was chatting to a lanky guy with hair like an open fire.

Fenchurch got out his phone and called Carling.

Bounced.

Second time.

The guard drilled his gaze on Fenchurch. 'Can I help you, sir?'

'Police.' Fenchurch rested his warrant card on the desk, all casually. 'Here to speak to the academy manager.'

'Ah, well, I'm afraid he's at a conference in Qatar.'

Bugger.

Fenchurch let out a sigh. 'Any idea when Jack's back?'

'Jack?' The guard frowned. 'Jack's not the manager, son. He's the director.'

Fenchurch almost rolled his eyes. 'Well, is he here?'

'Oh, sure. Come on through.' He led over to a security door and swiped a card against the reader. His limp was even worse than Fenchurch's. 'Second door on the right. Can't miss it, but if you do, I'll be back here smashing reporters' skulls together.' No smile.

Fenchurch set off down the corridor, the terracotta tiles leading through to a huge swimming pool. Must be the women's team in there, some of them relaxing by the side, others going hard at it in the pool, others splashing around in the shallow end.

Sure enough, the second door on the right was marked:

Academy Director
Jack Walsh

Fenchurch rattled on the opaque glass.

'Busy just now.'

'Police, sir.'

A sigh. Chair legs scraped back. Footsteps. The door opened and Jack Walsh peered out, looking at Fenchurch and laughing. Fred Perry polo shirt, pink. 'You can fuck right off.' He slammed the door.

Charming.

Fenchurch hauled it open and stepped in. 'In case you didn't hear, I'm a police officer.'

'Yeah, I know.' Walsh was sitting behind his desk, feet up. Polo shirt tucked into navy jeans tucked into cowboy boots. 'And, like I told you, you can fuck right off.'

'Sir, we need to—'

'You cost me my job at Shadwell.'

Fenchurch laughed. 'But you're academy director at a top—'

'I should be the bloody manager here, but no. I'm not. All because of you, DI Frenchman.'

'DCI Fenchurch.'

'Yeah, I bloody know your name.'

'Well, what happened to you is nothing to do with *my* actions, more to do with who you were sleeping with in those hotel rooms.'

Walsh just shook his head, fizzing away like he was going to explode. 'What are you here for, Frenchman?'

Fenchurch looked around the room. A green Barbour hung on a rack with a flat cap stuck on the top. Then at Walsh. 'Curtis Archer.'

'In case you've not noticed, this is the academy. We teach the young lads coming through. Curto's a first team player now. I mean, the poor sod's crocked and our manager's on a scouting mission trying to sign a Bulgarian lad who might replace him long-term, but he ain't my concern anymore.'

'Curtis was found dead this morning.'

'Shit.' Walsh leaned back in the chair and stared up at the ceiling. 'Are you shitting me?'

'Yes, sir, the Metropolitan Police are just a bunch of cheeky wind-up merchants.'

Walsh reached over for an open can of WakeyWakey energy drink and took a bracing sip. 'How did he die?'

'Heart attack.' Fenchurch didn't want to get into the rest of it just then. Walsh was in shock and he needed to exploit it now. He'd seen him clamming up a lot before. 'Did you know Archer well?'

'When I joined the club five years ago, Curto was on the

cusp of breaking through to the first team. I mean, he was only *technically* one of my charges. Kid was already a first-teamer and he was just incredible.' Walsh was staring into space, like he was watching mental footage of Curtis Archer playing. 'Just no holding the kid back. Like Rooney or Michael Owen when they broke through, way back when. Played against both of them and they had nothing on Curto. Kid was a phenomenon and had all the tricks. I mean, he was the kind of player who probably wouldn't be playing at that level into his thirties, so you just had to harness it while it happened. And I was trying to be a mentor to him, helping him cope with breaking into the first team at that age and with the fame that came with it. And the pressure. Mother was something else, mind. Talk about pushy. In here all the time, asking why he's not starting every game. He was sixteen! I mean, sure, he was soon the first name on the team sheet but it wasn't because of her.'

'What about his father?'

'He wasn't on the scene while I looked after him.' Walsh rocked back in his chair again. 'How could he die of a heart attack? He was twenty-one!'

'Just turned twenty-two, I believe.'

'Right, right.'

'We think his system was depleted because of the medication he'd been taking.'

'Painkillers, right?'

'Right. You know anything about them?'

'Not my bag. I manage the academy. Dealing with dickhead parents, mainly. Getting shouted at by the first team manager. Ian's a good lad, but he can be a bit vociferous. Don't even speak to my lads much. Got a big team to train them.'

'But you know a thing or two about oxycodone, right?'

'Well, yeah.'

Fenchurch froze. He was just admitting to it?

'My bleeding back.' Walsh rubbed at his spine. 'Injury from my playing days. Not from the pitch.' He gave a grin. 'Jumped off a makeshift diving board in Corfu. Pool was a bit too shallow, landed on the bottom, popped a disc. Didn't get renewed here the following summer. That's why I tumbled down the leagues.'

Fenchurch frowned. 'Thought you played for Charlton?'

'Where I ended up, yeah. Never made the first team here, but I was a West Ham boy. Why I got this job, in truth. They want to make sure we take care of the lads who don't make it so much as the ones who do.'

'When did you start taking the oxycodone?'

'Club doctor gave me a script.'

'Curtis ever speak to you about oxy?'

'Nope.'

'Sure?'

'Sure. Never spoke to him since he left my care, four years ago. That mother of his made sure he didn't speak to any of us lot directly.'

'Here's the thing, Jack. We found a lot of oxycodone in Curtis's system, but we don't know where he's got it from.'

'Why's that important?'

The first person to ask that.

Fenchurch knew there were a hundred reasons, but this was the one that didn't stack up.

Why was a professional footballer using a controlled substance? Possibly without a prescription. The controlled substance that might've killed him. That felt more like a murder case, where Fenchurch would be on home turf.

'We believe it's central to ascertaining why Mr Archer died.'

'You think he was murdered?'

'No, but we've got a big gap in time covering his last few

days. He seems to have been in some distress.'

'Shit. Right. Look, I don't know anything about that. I can ask around.'

He was being way too helpful, especially to the man he blamed for ruining his beautiful managerial career.

'You ever share your drugs with anyone?'

'You think I'm his dealer?'

'Are you?'

'No!'

'You've never supplied painkillers to a teammate?'

'Now listen here—'

'You have done. Admit it.'

'Listen, I know sharing medication is a crime, so I'm not talking about that.'

Fenchurch didn't nod. Kept his poker face up.

'Look, I'm not saying this on the record, but I might've given an old mate some way back when. He was a young kid, just been through an op. Unlikely to get renewed. Came to me, and he was in deep pain. Doc at the time tried to get him off the oxy. He just needed a little drop. I had a bottle that I never used. Back was going through a decent spell, as it happened, so I gave him it.'

'I can guess who that player was.'

'Terry bloody Monaghan.'

Fenchurch didn't know whether to believe him or not.

Scratch that. Jack Walsh was a liar. A cheat. A sex fiend.

'It's quite hurtful that he'd suggest I was dealing.'

'Where did you get the oxy from?'

'My doctor! I was at Shadwell at this point. Doctor Riches gave me a script. Bosh.' Walsh sat there, twiddling with his thumbs. 'But I ain't done nothing. So, if you want to arrest me, be my guest.'

Fenchurch really wanted to. But he needed more.

CHAPTER SIXTEEN

Fenchurch only had to follow the raised voices to find Reed along the corridor.

'Just get him on the phone!'

'It's not as simple as that.' A male voice, young.

'Please. Call him!'

'I can't.'

'Why not?'

A long pause. 'Because he told me not to.'

Fenchurch found them in a room at the end. A big place like a public library, and not a grand Victorian one. Black rubber floor tiles. Pine shelving units. The pong of spicy Pot Noodles and cheesy Doritos. A bank of computers along one wall, nobody working at them, but the perpendicular wall had a long bench table crammed with young geeks working at laptops. Most had those daft in-ear headphones all the kids wore these days, a couple those over-sized dad headphones that were popular for a bit, all bopping their heads to different beats as they worked.

Right in the middle was Reed, hands on hips, talking to a

cherub from a Raphael painting, but one that had grown up and wore a West Ham tracksuit.

She shook her head. 'Just. Call. Him.'

'Fine.' The cherub got out a phone as big as his head and tapped the screen, then held it out to Reed.

Fenchurch joined them, tilting his head.

Reed waved a hand at him. 'Chandler here is the head of data analytics.'

'Welcome to the data room.' Chandler stared at his phone, frowning. 'This is only a stopgap while they—'

His phone crackled into life. 'Hello?' Scottish accent. Sounded like Scottish rain in the background too.

'Tom, it's Chandler. I've got the police here asking to see Curtis Archer's medical records.'

'Aye?' Didn't seem like a surprise. Maybe he knew about the death already.

'This is DI Kay Reed.' She grabbed the phone off Chandler. 'We need access to his records as part of an investigation into—'

'Well, it's going to have to wait, love. I'm—' Huff. '—doing a hike of the Southern Upland Way in the Scottish Borders.' Deep breath. 'Should really be at the club now, but it's a charity thing, delayed from covid, and it would've been bad form to pull out of it. My old boy died of MND, so the club understand how important this is to me.'

'All we need is approval for the medical records you've got on Curtis Archer.'

'Listen, I heard the boy died. I want to help, really I do, but I'm in the arse end of nowhere and there's nothing I can do about this just now. You're lucky I've even got reception here.'

'You just need to let our pathologist gain access.'

'*Chandler.*'

The lad sparked into life, nudging his head closer to the phone. 'What's up?'

'Are you—' Huff. '—playing silly buggers here?'

'Well, it's—'

'When the police come asking for records, you give them. Okay?'

'But you told me to—'

'I told you if it was... Never mind. Just let them have it. Okay?'

'On it.'

'Take them into the data room and open your firehose wide enough to share Curtis's medical records with them. Now, I've really got to go. Got a tough incline ahead of us. I'll be back in the smoke on Wednesday if you need me. Ciao!'

The line clicked dead.

Chandler stared at his phone. 'Okay. Sorry about that.'

'What does he mean by firehose?'

'It's a joke. Twitter has a data feed of everything on there they call the firehose. I made a reference to it once, saying we could get money from—'

'I see.' She patted his arm. 'How about you go and get us those records?'

'Sure thing.'

'Boy!' Heavy footsteps cannoned over from the door. A fight wearing a business suit stormed towards Chandler. Red-faced, with the stubble of someone on a three-day bender. 'Here, boy!' He beckoned him towards him.

No mistaking Ian Stanton or his thundering Geordie accent.

Fenchurch had seen him on the sidelines every fortnight since he'd joined West Ham from Newcastle, after he got them promoted back to the Premier League. A handy centre back at both clubs in his playing days and one of those men who seemed to dominate every room he was in. Including this one.

Stanton got in Chandler's face. 'Boy, can you get me that report on the Bulgarian lad?'

Chandler stared down at his feet. 'Printed?'

Stanton chuckled. 'Obviously.' He didn't seem fazed by the two cops standing around. 'Quick as you like.'

'Okay, sir.' Chandler scuttled off across the room.

'Good boy.' Stanton folded his arms and watched him go. He smiled at Fenchurch. 'Time was, the manager would have a secretary to do all this stuff. Nowadays, we've got so much more staff but I've got to bust heads myself.'

Fenchurch returned the smile. 'Heard you were away on a scouting mission?'

'Flew back this morning on the owner's private jet.' Stanton was frowning. 'Do I know you from somewhere?'

'Hopefully just the stands. DCI Simon Fenchurch.' He held up the warrant card. 'We're investigating the death of Curtis Archer.'

Stanton rolled his eyes. 'Don't let me stop you.'

'You did hear the fact that he's—'

'Aye, man, the lad's dead. What can I do about it? Kid was some player, like, but he's been crocked for over two years. Took me all that time to line up the money to replace him, and now the Bulgarian lad's people are asking for more bloody money.' Stanton shook his head. The death seemed to be more of a nuisance than a tragedy.

'When was the last time you spoke to him?'

Stanton blew air up his face. 'Well, you'd need to get the boy over there to confirm it, but I don't think Curtis has been into the training ground in over a year.'

'Not since the operation in America?'

Stanton gave him some side-eye. 'You're not supposed to know about that.'

That was a bit fishy.

The whole thing was.

Seemed like the club just didn't care about the kid. Maybe the metaphor of stallions and horses stretched to the club – they just saw them as disposable objects. Not real, live human beings.

Or dead ones.

Chandler returned carrying something.

Reed walked over to him, but Fenchurch couldn't tell if it was Archer's medical records or his scouting report.

Stanton took Fenchurch to the side. Smiling. Eyes burrowing into him. Christ, this guy had enough charisma to light up Wembley Stadium. 'Listen, I have to project this image of being a right hard bastard, okay? I care for all the lads, especially Curtis. He scored so many goals in that promotion season, feels like one of my family. You lot, you're not just normal cops are you? You think he was murdered, don't you?'

'We're investigating along those lines.'

'Well.' Stanton smoothed down his lank hair. 'Wouldn't surprise me. Kid had a darkness to him. I could use that, mind, point him to the opponents and he'd destroy them.'

'What do you mean by darkness?'

'You know.' His eyes bulged. 'I don't mean the colour of his skin!'

'I didn't think that.' Fenchurch had him clocked as a racist now. 'What did you mean?'

'Most of the lads are singled-minded in their lives with, you know, a steely determination. Football is all they know, all they want to know. All they've got. Curtis... It felt like he'd lived a life, but he was so young.'

'So you mean parental stuff?'

'Not that. More school stuff. Kids he grew up with. I don't know. Maybe just me imagining things to make me sound all poetic, like.'

Fenchurch smiled at that, but it was something to investigate. 'Anyone who'd stand to benefit from his death?'

'Too many, probably.'

'Like the club?'

'Excuse me?'

'I understand Curtis Archer was on a long-term contract, but most of that time he'd suffered a serious injury. Hundred-odd grand a week going out the door. Gather you didn't have him insured?'

Stanton glared at him. 'That's none of my business.'

'None of *yours*?'

'Yeah, you'd need to speak to the owner about that.'

'He about?'

'How am I supposed to know that? Only time I hear from him is through that bloody director of football he's put in place between us. Like he doesn't think I can do all parts of the job. Just wants me focusing on coaching the lads, not building a squad or that.' Stanton shook his head. 'But I'll tell you this for nothing, I did have a rapport with Curtis. Lad called me up a few months ago, so I went around to that pad of his down in Wapping. Sat with him and had a long chat. Kid makes a great coffee, I'll tell you that for nothing. But he was in a bad way.'

'What about?'

'I mean, I asked how he was getting on and he said fine. Doing some running on it.'

'So why did he call you?'

Stanton clicked his tongue a few times, thinking through which lie to use to cover it all over. He let out a sigh. 'One of the first things I did when I started here was to speak to the players' parents about their financial planning. I wanted to stress how important it was for me and my team when our careers were over. I'm doing okay as a manager as I get a good salary, and my boys are okay as coaches. Lot of lads gamble it all away. Lot of them just piss it away, or fritter it away on shite. I'll tell you this for nothing, if you've just wasted all your money as a player and you don't work, it's a short retirement from the game. You'll be on the building sites or driving a cab. I'm trying to make sure they focus on that side.'

'Very kind of you.'

'All part of the job.'

'So what was Curtis asking you about?'

'Way he told me it, he'd listened to my advice. Got himself stressed about it. Someone at the club had put his *mother* on to an accountant.'

Everyone seemed to have it in for Candace Archer. Poor woman. All she'd done was try the hardest for her son.

'Same bloke a lot of us use to manage our affairs.' Stanton held up a hand, smiling. 'Not those kinds of affairs, before you start.' The smile faded. 'But Curtis... He called me up, said he was worried his money was running out.'

This was new.

'But he was earning a lot of money every week.'

'So? Anyone can still spend any amount. Well, almost any amount. Curtis seemed to be distressed about it. Asked me how he could get it all back. I didn't know the first thing about that stuff, but I gave him a pep talk. You know how it is, told him to focus on his fitness and get back to the training ground. Soon enough, he'd be banging them in again. Get a big move, a lot more cash. You know how it is.'

'Why did Curtis want to speak to you instead of his agent?'

'Because I suspect his agent made the recommendation to his mother. Mark's my agent too.' Stanton let out a deep breath. 'Si's a good guy.'

'Si?'

'Simon Fisher. Si-Fi Investments or something. He's legit, apparently. Regulated by the Financial what-do-you-call-it Authority, so what do I know?'

'But Curtis thought he'd stolen his money?'

'Not quite. Si doesn't just do tax returns and all that shite. He manages my investments and takes charge of my bank accounts, all that jazz.'

He'd know what state Curtis's finances were in.

And if he had been siphoning money off, well – Fenchurch knew a few people who could spot that.

If there was money going out the door for the drugs that killed Curtis Archer, Simon Fisher might know where to.

Fenchurch smiled at him. 'Thank you, sir.'

Stanton clapped his arm. 'Just find out who did this to him. If it was himself, if Curtis killed himself... Do me a favour and keep it from Candace, would you? Poor woman must be going to hell over this.'

CHAPTER SEVENTEEN

'Haven't had one of these in ages, guv.' Reed was covering her mouth while she ate. 'Like going back in time.'

'Back to the future, more like.' Fenchurch tried swallowing down the burrito but his mouth was on fire. Bloody hell, even his eyes were watering. He took a bit of a breather then got it down. 'Too much hot sauce.'

'You didn't leave much in the bottle.' Reed opened the glovebox. 'And who keeps hot sauce in their car?'

'Me, that's who.' Fenchurch hovered over taking another bite. 'What's your take on this?'

'My take?'

'On this whole case. Murder or accident?'

'Well, we don't have enough to say it was a murder, but it seems like a lot of people stand to benefit from his death.'

'Like who?'

'That's a big question, guv. Do *you* think he was murdered?'

'It's a tricky one, isn't it? He wasn't stabbed or shot, was he? But it's pretty suspicious to me how we can't find any trace of him getting access to the medication that caused his death.'

The same pills Fenchurch himself was on.

But he had to reassure himself that he was on regular blood and urine tests, and everything was working fine. His heart felt okay. He wasn't straining it, but he was still getting exercise at the gym.

Why it had taken such a toll on Curtis was a mystery.

'What ideas have you got, guv?'

'The club stand to gain the most, I think. They're on the hook for five years' salary. Sounds like he wasn't insured, so that's over five million quid a year out the door to a player who isn't playing.'

'Five million?'

'It's probably closer to seven or eight.'

'Christ.'

'Yeah, and they've lost a massive payday on him. Over a hundred million quid. And they'll have to spend thirty-odd million on this Bulgarian striker to replace him. Even then, he might not settle.'

'Jesus, guv, the money...'

'I know, Kay. I know.'

Her lips were twitching. 'Seems a bit coincidental that the manager's scouting a replacement just as he dies, doesn't it?'

'Not so sure. Someone like Stanton's up against it. Battling against an owner who might not want to spend. Probably just finally beat him down and wanted to strike while the iron's hot.'

'Sounds a lot like you, guv.'

'Lot to admire in a man like that.' Fenchurch sighed. 'What do you think of the mother as a suspect?'

'She's not done this.'

'Are you sure?'

'Come on, guv. Her own son?'

'I know you spent a lot of time with her, Kay, but she's the one who stands to gain the most.'

'She was going to give all her money back to him.'

'We've just got her word on that.'

'It was in a separate account, put in his name. She's the sole beneficiary of his will too.'

'Still...'

'Come on, guv, you don't really think he was murdered, do you?'

'Not yet. But it's all just so suspicious. Why someone's cleaned out his flat before we went around there. Who was chasing him. I just don't get it at all. None of it.' Fenchurch put the last of his burrito into his mouth, spicy juice sliding down his chin. He chewed in silence, mulling it all over.

Maybe Reed was right and he was too suspicious, but there was definitely something up about the whole thing.

'You think he's been poisoned?'

Fenchurch looked over at her. 'You mean someone's slipped the drugs into his system?'

'That kind of thing.'

'Kay, his stomach had a couple of partly digested pills. High dose. The opioid levels in his blood tell the tale – this guy was always walking around with opioids on board. When the level started to taper off he'd feel the crash and need to take more. A normal person starting at those levels would simply stop breathing as soon as it hit their bloodstream. With Curtis, he'd had them in his system a long time.'

'But over a long period of time, you could make it look like he'd been taking the medication.'

'Well. That's...' A bit of chilli was stuck between his teeth. 'Candace cooked for him, every meal she said. Easy to slip the drug in.'

'Exactly. Explains why we can't find a prescription.'

'Her own son, though?' Fenchurch shook his head. 'I mean, I've considered something along those lines, but that's... wow.' He bunched up his foil and tossed it back into the bag. 'Come on, then. Let's see what this accountant's got to say for himself.'

CHAPTER EIGHTEEN

Fenchurch crossed the road. That noise in the rear speakers he'd been ignoring was now full volume up front. Surround-sound withdrawal. He needed another pill and soon. He clenched his teeth and tried to ignore it all.

Si-Fi Financial Services didn't look like the most legit business on Hoxton Square and that was saying something. The giant glass window showed the reflection of the busy street and Fenchurch had to squint to see through the glass, where the accountants were hard at doing absolutely bugger all. A crowd had gathered. Mostly hipsters – young men sporting heavy beards and flannel shirts rather than clean shaves and navy suits.

'Who'd trust this lot to manage their finances?' Reed stepped up to the door and was blocked off by a massive man, more a wardrobe than a human being. She stepped aside and let him thump down the steps, his jewellery jangling. She was shaking her head at him as he went. 'My daughter's obsessed with him.'

'Who is he?'

'A rapper. Kanyif Iqbal.'

Fenchurch laughed. 'Glaswegian?'

She was frowning. 'Why do you ask?'

'That sounds like "can you fuck, pal".'

Reed's eyebrows shot up. 'Well. Anyway, his music is absolute dog shit.'

'Should hear the stuff Chloe listens to. When did music die, Kay?' Fenchurch followed her inside.

No reception area, just a lot of desks around a central area. In the middle was a table football setup, two men either side, roared on by the crowd. A whistle went and one of the men pumped his fists in the air, then vaulted up onto the table and held his arms aloft like he'd won the World Cup in grass football. Table-less football. Football. He pointed at his opponent, then at his groin. 'Suck it, bitch!'

The loser shook his head. 'Well played, Si.' He walked away, still shaking his head.

The crowd started to disperse, heading back to their desks, the laughter fading to background chatter.

The champion hopped down off the table, still laughing. He wore beige cargo shorts and a bright-red T-shirt with the sun image from Primal Scream's *Screamadelica* album. The clothes hung off him – the guy was skin and bone.

And someone who acted like that must be pretty senior in an organisation, so Fenchurch made his way to him. 'Looking for Simon Fisher.'

'You've found him, mate.' He looked at Fenchurch through thick lens, bloodshot eyes blown up, but he barely registered Reed's presence. 'If you're looking for financial advice you should speak to Tina, who heads up the—'

'Police.' Fenchurch had his warrant card out. 'This is DI Reed. I'm DCI Simon Fenchurch.'

'Oh. Another Simon. Well, I'm not so simple. Suspect

you're the same.' Fisher tilted his head back and bellowed with laughter at his own joke.

Fenchurch thumbed at the table. 'Take it you won?'

'Oh, yeah. Yeah, man.' Fisher was nodding enthusiastically. 'I'm in training. World championships in Germany next year. Played in this year's finals in France, but I only got to the last sixteen. I want to win next time.'

'That's a big leap.'

'Yeah, but you've got to have hashtag life goals.' Fisher folded his arms across his chest. 'What brings the police here?'

'Relax, we're not investigating your firm. It's about a client of yours.'

'Which one?'

'Curtis Archer.'

Fisher checked his nails. 'What's he done?'

'He died.'

'Right.'

No reaction other than indifference.

'You don't seem upset.'

A shrug. 'They come and go, I can't do anything about it.'

But still suspicious.

'There's something you could maybe help us with.' Fenchurch's turn to lean in close. 'We found oxycodone in Curtis's bloodstream, but no prescription. No doctor we know of has prescribed it.'

Fisher's eyes were like saucers. He seemed to get off on being on the inside track. 'So why are you here?'

'Just wonder if there was a Dr Feelgood on the books? Someone he paid a—'

'Dr Feelgood. Cracking band. Canvey Island. Where I grew up.'

Fenchurch nodded. 'That's right. Bit before your time.'

'Bit before yours too.'

'Very true.'

'I'm into all sorts of music.' Fisher swung around. 'Kegsy, stick on *Milk and Alcohol* by Dr Feelgood.' Then back to Fenchurch. 'Anyway. Kid like that, though, who knows if he's been buying drugs off the street.'

Shuffling drums burst out of speakers Fenchurch couldn't see. Clanging guitars followed. Way too loud, so he stepped even closer to Fisher. 'What's that supposed to mean?'

'Well.' Fisher was dancing along with the music, mostly in the shoulders. 'Curtis is from the wrong side of the tracks. Canning Town is a bad place. He was edgy, pretending he was more street than he was. Probably comes from insecurity. Growing up in a place like that, without an old man. It does a lot to you.' He put his fingers in his mouth and blew a loud whistle like a shepherd. 'Mr Hodges!'

A man stood up and raced over. Like a walking pencil, tall and thin, and all stretched out. His hair tapered off to a point, held in place by gel. 'What's up, boss?'

'Cops here need to go through the books for young Curtis, who died today.' Loud and unsubtle.

'Okay.' Hodges beckoned them over to his desk with his fingers.

Reed walked over, perching on the edge of the desk.

Fenchurch focused on Fisher again. 'You see Mr Archer often?'

'Last week, as it happens.'

'In here?'

'Spoke to him on the phone. Seemed agitated.'

'You know why?'

'I told him his investments are in the toilet.'

'In what way?'

'They're sitting on top of soiled toilet paper, ready to flush.'

'How badly?'

'Bad. Like, really bad.'

'He blame you?'

Fisher shook his head. 'We just do his books.'

'I thought you're an investment firm.'

'We are. But we only do his accounts. Well, we do his mother's investments. Both of those accounts are in his name.'

Which backed up her story. Still, if she was the beneficiary in his will, it just made her look innocent. A layer of innocence.

'But Curtis's own investments are held elsewhere?'

'Right, right. And I'd warned him when he started shoving money over there, but he wouldn't listen, would he? Stuck all of his wonga over there.'

'All of it?'

'Eggs, baskets...'

'Over where?'

Fisher sighed. 'BRO Capital.'

'As in Bro?'

'No. Well, maybe. But it's B-R-O.' Fisher scratched at his neck. 'They're not a great firm. Bad rep. New too, so no track record. Certainly not to warrant the amount he was throwing at them. I told him that, but he still wouldn't listen. Thought I was pitching for his portfolio. Man, I was just looking out for him.' He stepped closer and cast his gaze between Fenchurch and Reed. 'Between us three and the table here, the City of London Police are investigating them. A DI Clarke was in here asking stuff about them.'

Fenchurch nodded. 'I know Steve.'

'I suggest you pick up with him, then.'

'What am I picking up with him about?'

'Just the word on the grapevine. That's all.'

'Must be a pretty specific word if you're advising clients against them.'

'I can't say any more. The rest is a matter you need to take up with DI Clarke.'

Fenchurch was fizzing – something concrete to go on, finally.

Reed was beckoning him over, so he followed her.

'What's up?'

Hodges cracked his knuckles. 'I've got every receipt for every transaction he's ever made from a pharmacy or a private doctor's surgery.' The screen of his computer filled with scans in a six-by-three grid. 'These are the last receipts for paid prescriptions from multiple pharmacies.'

Fenchurch squinted to read them. Sure enough – 80 mg oxycodone, eight to be taken daily. 'Any idea where they were dispensed?'

'A few, yeah.' Reed sighed. 'Seems like he didn't use the same pharmacy twice. Or not within this timeframe. But nothing on the system about who prescribed them.'

Fenchurch looked at Reed. 'Do you mind following them up?'

Reed gave him that look. She minded, but she'd do it anyway.

CHAPTER NINETEEN

Nelson sat in the kitchen, pressing his fingers against the crumbs on his plate and putting them to his lips. Could still taste the Chantilly butter and the strong mustard, but maybe that was from his fingers. He wanted another sandwich. Still had half the packet of roast beef. And the tomatoes wouldn't be as crisp tomorrow. The lettuce would wilt like a Prime Minister.

Anything to avoid thinking about what he'd almost done.

Stupid prick.

And Chloe had the gun. In police custody.

Nelson just hoped his word was good enough for her sergeant. That it was much more likely to be an East End ganglord's weapon than an ex-copper's.

Despite that ex-copper having a bear-sized grudge against the ganglord.

Stupid, stupid prick.

What was he thinking?

The front door clunked.

He got up and padded through on his bare feet.

Lisa was at the door, dropping her bag on the floor and hanging up her coat. Time was, she'd just be DS Bridge to him, but now she was his fiancée. 'Well, there you are.'

'What are you doing home?'

'Jesus, Jon.' Lisa rolled her eyes at him as she kicked off her shoes. 'I was coming home for a quick lunchtime shag as it's my peak ovulation time, but you obviously forgot so I'll head back to work.'

Nelson put his hand to his forehead. 'Crap. I'm sorry. It's been a busy morning.'

'I've heard.'

'What?'

'I heard a story about Chloe Fenchurch arresting you?'

Shit.

'Arresting? Nobody was arrested. Do you want a cup of tea?'

'Jon, I want the truth. Susan spoke to Chloe. Said Younis had a gun?'

'I'm putting the kettle on.' Nelson padded back through and stuck the kettle on. His mug was still warm from the last one, so he got another out for her. Then two teabags out of the little storage pot they'd bought in Italy.

The kettle hissed and rattled.

'You've not been answering your phone.'

'Battery was low so I was charging it.'

'Likely story.' Lisa leaned against the fridge, arms folded. 'Well?'

'I saw Younis.' Nelson swallowed hard. 'There no arrest. Not me, not Younis. We were caught fighting over a weapon.'

'A weapon? Jesus, Jon. Was he trying to kill you?'

'He said it was mine, I said it was his. Chloe seized the

weapon and sent us both on our merry ways, without charge or arrest.'

'Okay. That's what you'd tell Fenchurch or Waheed. What's the truth, Jon?'

'I... I saw red. Everything I've been through over the last two and a bit years... My testimony falling apart, meaning they let him go. Getting kicked off the force.'

'Well, I'm glad you're actually recognising that, rather than burying your feelings like you always do.'

'I'm sorry. I can't be easy to live with.'

'Jon, you're fine as long as you tell me the truth.'

Nelson swallowed it all down. The rage, the fear, the guilt, the shame. He poured boiling water into her mug, then into his. 'It wasn't his gun.'

'What?'

'I tried to shoot him with a zip gun.'

'A zip gun? Jesus, Jon! What the fuck?' She grabbed his arms and shook him. 'I'm trying to have a baby with you and you're *shooting* people?'

'I didn't.'

'Oh, well done.' She clapped. 'Good work. You got through a morning without murdering someone.'

Nelson flicked her teabag into the compost and tipped in some oat milk. He grabbed a spoon and mashed his teabag against the side of the mug. 'I had this weird thing where... I saw what I was doing. I had a gun in my hand. I could've killed him...'

She was staring at her feet.

This was it. Their relationship was over. Four years, now it came down to this.

What had he been thinking?

Killing Younis.

Why did he think he could get away with it?

The sheer arrogance.

She looked up at him. 'You'll have to think of another way.'

'What?'

'Killing Younis would be the wrong thing to do on so many levels. You need to put him back inside. He needs to face the justice he's escaped.'

'Are you serious?'

Her gaze drilled into him. 'Deadly.'

'I thought you'd be angry.'

'I'm livid. But I've been a cop for long enough to appreciate the nuances in things. I've been in a relationship with you for long enough that I can see how badly this has affected you. I love you, Jon, so I want you to not fuck this up. Don't kill him. You might be a dad again – do you really want me to raise our kid on my own because you're in jail or you've been killed?'

'No. Of course not.'

'If you do anything like that again, it's over. Am I clear?'

Tears stung his eyes. 'Crystal clear.'

'Look, I get it. There are people I've wanted to kill. Seriously. But actually doing it is fucking stupid, Jon. And you're not stupid.'

'I've been stupid.'

'Are your prints on that gun?'

'Sure, but the gun has his prints on it too.'

'And Chloe Fenchurch has it?'

'She does.'

Lisa sighed. 'Knowing Chloe, she's honest. You've just got to stick to your story. It's not yours.'

'Right.'

'Did you make it yourself?'

Nelson shook his head. 'Got it from an old firearms officer.'

'Do you have any others?'

'No.'

'Well. Don't even speak to him again.'

'Her. Jenny Southall.'

'Will it be traced back to her?'

'I doubt it. She's extremely clean.'

Lisa picked up her cup of tea and sipped it. 'Jon, I get that this is personal for you. Younis represents what happened to your brother. You felt good about yourself because you'd helped take him off the street. Then he got out of jail, you felt like it was all because of you.'

'It *was* all because of me.'

'No, it wasn't. It was a legal technicality. Some unlucky bullshit. Most cops do stuff that's in a grey area, but you just happened to get caught. That's it. That's all that happened.'

'It doesn't feel like it.'

'No. But you're clearly not enjoying working for Waheed.'

'This morning, he had me watching our client's home. Wouldn't tell me why. Then she called me and I had to chase around East London following her husband. That's when I saw Younis. Last time he was inside, he still ran everything from in there. I just don't see how he'll ever be off the streets, how he won't be inflicting misery on people.'

'Jon, it's breaking my heart seeing you obsessed with him. It's not healthy. You need to move on. Maybe join another police force. Maybe the NCA. Start your own private business, maybe...'

'I could...'

'Jon. I can help you, but I want you to make sure you don't damage yourself here. Be smart, not emotional. I'll speak to Chloe about burying the evidence, but that's—'

'Don't do that.'

'Jon, it's okay.'

'I don't want you to get caught.'

She smiled. 'I'm a better detective than you.'

'But you're aren't going to be lucky forever.'

'No, but Chloe owes me. I've helped her a lot in the past.'

'But her dad...'

'Are you telling me Simon Fenchurch has never bent the law?'

'No, but he doesn't get caught. Just fails upwards.'

'Exactly, Jon. You haven't got his luck. Stop trailing Younis...'

'Okay.'

'Thank you.' She walked over and kissed his cheek. 'We haven't got time now, but let's see how we both feel tonight.'

'Are you sure?'

'Jon, this has been a fuck of a lot to take in. Okay?'

'Can I get you a sandwich?'

'Jon. It's fine.'

He leaned over and kissed her on the lips. 'Thank you for listening without judgment.'

'It's what a relationship is. Or should be.' She wrapped her arms around him and he held her. 'Jon, I'm not working the case against him and his organisation, but I know people who are. Younis is so far removed from the frontline now that getting to him is going to be difficult or impossible.' She broke off and looked up at him. 'But his hands are bloody, Jon. There's a smoking gun somewhere; just make sure you're not holding it.'

CHAPTER TWENTY

The last thing Fenchurch told Carling was to get the bridge open.

It was still shut.

He raced down the lane as fast as his knee would allow him. Getting close to the time where he needed to think about another pill. Which meant adding another hour to the time.

He could handle it. He was in control.

He could handle it...

He was bigger than the average guy, plus he'd been putting a bit of extra strain on the joint.

Sod it.

Just take one a bit early because it was sore.

He popped a pill and swallowed it down with some water.

Oh okay.

Yeah.

There it was.

Signal up, noise down.

That silence just washed over him as the pain receded, like waves on the beach.

He walked up to the locus and snatched the clipboard out of the uniform's hand, getting a shocked look from her. He handed it back. 'Sorry, I'm not annoyed with you.' He entered the outer locus and scanned around.

Carling was lurking near the crime scene tent. Why it was still there, Fenchurch didn't—

His phone was ringing.

He fished it out and spilled his tub of oxycodone onto the concrete. Stupid sod. His knee creaked as he bent over to pick it up. Daft old bastard. He stood up with a crunch and answered the call. 'What's up, Kay?'

'You okay, guv?'

'Surviving. Just about.' Bloody Carling was heading back into the tent. 'What's up?'

'I'm still waiting on a call back from Steve Clarke, guv.'

'Need me to—'

'No, I've got it. Wanted to let you know that I've just finished at the first pharmacy and it's a bust. Their records are all filed at head office. Have to put in a request to get the scans. It'll be a day or two. Might need a warrant, depending on how arsey they get.'

'I thought technology was supposed to make things quick?'

'Depends, guv. It's great if you want to delay and obfuscate things.'

'Think that's what they're doing?'

'Nah, it's a big chain, guv. Just bureaucracy. I'll call you after the next one.'

'Thanks, Kay. I know it's donkey work, but it's very important donkey work.'

'Which is why you've got your best DI on it. I get it.' She laughed. 'Catch you later.'

Fenchurch hung up and set off towards the tent.

'Sir.' DI Uzma Ashkani was standing over at the side, arms

folded, eyebrow raised. Dark hair scraped back in a ponytail, her eyes like lumps of coal. She looked exhausted – they called it the terrible twos for a reason, though Fenchurch knew the threes were worse. 'Was just about to call you. We're kind of needing guidance here.'

Fenchurch nodded along with it. 'Just been digging into the kid's background.'

'Yeah, yeah, swanning around football clubs and so on.' She shook her hair. 'You need to give me and Pinkie some guidance, not just Kay.'

'Pinkie?'

'Tom.'

'Why do you call him Pinkie?'

'Same reason you call him Tom Thumb or we call you "the twat". It's his nickname.'

Well, it made a change from people accusing Carling of being sexually inappropriate.

'Okay, so what do you need guidance on?'

She shrugged. 'Just that this is looking *weird*. The fact the flat is cleaned out means someone is trying to cover their tracks. And no sign of the key he surely had on him.'

'So now you see why I wanted to explore it all for myself. Someone cleared out his flat and we're no closer to finding out who or why.'

'You think it's got something to do with the Oxycontin he'd been taking?'

'That's the brand. He'd been taking generic oxycodone.'

She nodded slowly. 'Chemically they're the same, just the additives that vary. Rare to get the branded stuff on the streets, though.'

'Is it?'

She nodded. 'I could speak to my old colleagues in street drugs about anyone who might've be selling oxy?'

'Sounds good to me.'

She pursed her lips again.

'You seem annoyed, Uzma.'

'Well, it's a needle in a haystack job. I know I put myself forward, but still...'

'Taking one for the team. DI Reed's hunting down prescriptions for me. I appreciate the hard work. Superintendent Bell appreciates it.'

'Thanks, sir.' She walked off looking a little bit taller.

'What's up with her?' DS Lisa Bridge was frowning at Uzma. Dressed in jeans and leather jacket, ready to go undercover.

'Nothing much.' Fenchurch smiled at her. 'What's going on in your world?'

'Just back from lunch.' She stared into space. There was a story there, but Fenchurch wasn't going to hear it from her. 'Uzma's asked me to focus on the apartment, so I'll head there soon.' She sighed. 'Thing is, he hadn't been there for a couple of days.'

'Really?'

'I ran his phone records. Been off for two days too.'

'Weird for a kid in this day and age.'

'You're telling me. No calls or messages, guv. It's all done in apps now, which are encrypted so even if we got the data, it'd all be gibberish.'

'Makes sense. We still haven't found the phone. Right?'

'Right. Thing is, he could have another phone or a tablet or laptop.'

'But?'

'It's unlikely. I did get his last-known location as Hammersmith.'

'Other side of the city. What's he doing there?'

'No idea. Been in Brentford and Kensington a bit too.'

Bridge got out her notebook and flicked through the pages. 'I've got some of my lads investigating Curtis's friends. I was going to catch up with them and see if they could shed any light on that mystery – maybe some of them live over there. Could be other footballers. Who knows.'

'Or a girlfriend or a boyfriend?'

She laughed. 'He's footballer, sir, none of them are gay.'

'Not publicly.' Fenchurch rolled his eyes. Despite the progress the world had made in the last thirty years, the fact that Justin Fashanu was hounded out of the top flight before he even came out. And there's been nobody since. And what happened to him was... even more tragic. Hell, even the police were a lot more advanced than that. 'What about privately?'

'Archer is seeing Casey Bosch. American actress. Was in that Netflix show about vampires in the Scottish Highlands. *Shot Through the Heart* or something?'

'Sounds like tripe.'

'It's not bad, actually. The book was shit, but the screenplay filled in a lot of the gaps.'

'Can you track her down? Might want to take some garlic with you.'

'On it.'

'Anywhere with the entourage?'

'Didn't have one.'

'That's unusual.'

'But he did have a security contract. Well, a personal management contract with an ex-footballer's wife. One of those WAGs with Coleen Rooney and Rebekah Vardy. Sacked her nine months ago and binned the security detail. Could set up some time with her, if you want?'

'Do it. Doesn't tally with the story from his mum about a driver, though.'

'Want me to dig into that as well?'

'Please. We need to know where he was while his phone was off. Build up a picture. Right now, we've got precious little to go on. He was supposed to meet his agent, but didn't. He met a friend, Terry Monaghan, but he seemed to be out of his head. That's the only movement we've got.'

'On it.' Bridge nodded and scooted away from the crime scene.

Carling walked out of the tent. Fenchurch didn't waste any time in grabbing him. 'Tom, how's it going here?'

'Getting there.'

'I expected you to get there a lot earlier. Been phoning you and you've been bouncing my calls.'

'Sorry, Si. It's been manic.'

'Why isn't the bridge open yet?'

'Clooney wanted to do a detailed scour of this place.'

'You're kidding me?'

'No. Because of this missing phone.'

'You won't find a phone on the bridge.' Fenchurch sighed. 'Wrap it up.'

'Will do. Just waiting on the team to finish searching the nearby bins. Will get you an update soon.'

'Can you get the tent down and that bridge open?'

'That's what I was doing in there – telling Mick to dismantle it.'

'Perfect.' Fenchurch watched him strip off the crime scene suit. 'What's your take on this, Tom?'

'Mine? I'd say he was being chased.'

'Definitely? Not just going out for a run?'

'Nobody would go running in ten-grand trainers, would they?'

'With the amount he earned? That's like half a morning's work.'

'Jesus. Seriously?'

'You're a man of the world, Tom. You should know.'

'The cricket world. Can't believe footballers earn that much.' Carling shook his head. 'Anyway, we finished speaking to the kids who helped him. They all agree with the first lad, Big Jamie. They said he was definitely being chased. Curtis was their hero, so they split up to distract his assailants. One of them reckons they spotted three guys.'

'Sure about that?'

'Sure. He was faster than the others, got across the bridge.'

'Find them. CCTV, the whole works.'

'On it already.' Carling held his gaze. 'Do you think I need orders to do my job?'

'Less of that, Tom.'

Carling looked away, then back again. 'If you don't mind a bit of feedback, sir, I think you're taking on too much direct work.'

'You too?'

'Well, Uzma and I talk.'

'Right, Pinkie.'

Carling shook his head. 'Great.'

'Tom, this is a high-priority case. That's what I do best. Bell puts up with me because I get results like nobody else. I may not be the best on spreadsheets, budgets, politics and organisational strategy, but I can solve big cases. Now, I appreciate your concern, but I need you to focus on doing your job. And I need you to attend the PM.'

Carling's mouth hung open. 'Seriously?'

'What part of me doesn't look serious, Inspector? Anyone who gives me a "Seriously", gets a game of rock, paper, scissors, rank. Hint: rank always wins.'

'Is this revenge?'

'Hardly.' Fenchurch grinned at him. 'If I was enacting revenge, you'd be counting paperclips.'

Carling looked like he was going to say something about it.

'Tom!' One of his team was charging towards them, DS Inglis leading – the same female officer who'd uncovered Candace's address. 'Got something.'

Fenchurch and Carling walked towards them.

Inglis held out a bag, which reeked of off bananas. 'Looks like someone took stuff off the victim, dumped it into a bag and tossed it into the bin. Wallet's in there.'

Carling winced. 'Shit, so Big Jamie did rob him?'

'Not sure.' She shook her head. 'We let him go a few minutes ago.' She nibbled at her lips. 'DS Bridge is doing a phone trace on that number. She's smart too – she's using the FindMy from Curtis's Apple Watch so it's much more accurate. The phone's on and it's moving.'

CHAPTER TWENTY-ONE

Fenchurch was in the passenger seat, grabbing the handle above the door as Carling took another turn too fast. Felt like he was at Brands Hatch or Silverstone rather than tracing the southern perimeter of the City. He had his phone out, on speaker. 'Lisa, can you give me an update?'

'I think whoever it is... They're heading here, sir.'

'You mean Wapping?'

'Correct. I'm at the flat now.'

The area around the Tower opened up to their right.

Carling floored it and overtook four cars, before slamming back in and stopping at the lights. 'Bloody hell.'

'It's okay, Tom. We'll get him.'

'Don't want to lose him, Si.' Carling flicked the indicator to the right. Didn't say anything. Just sighed.

'Sir?' Bridge's voice crackled out of the speaker. 'The signal's gone left up Leman Street.'

'Towards the *station*?'

'Maybe.'

'Sod this for a game of soldiers.' Carling hit the siren button and got a squeal as he blasted through the red light and cut up the Minories. The street was busy even at this hour, with a crowd gathered outside the pub. More lights at the end, which meant he slowed but didn't stop.

A slight gap in the traffic.

Carling shot through it, turning right to head along Aldgate High Street.

Nobody was pulling in. Typical.

'Where is it now, Lisa?'

'Whitechapel Road, I think.'

Straight ahead, then.

More lights a hundred metres away when it became Whitechapel High Street.

East London.

Home turf.

'Where the hell is he heading?' Carling swung around a bus and hit the brakes. Squealing loud. An Audi flashed the lights and honked its horn, oblivious to the siren. Carling pushed forward, getting it to reverse back. Then they were off again, as Whitechapel High Street became Whitechapel Road.

Fenchurch was scanning everywhere, but nothing stuck out. Two buses, a load of cars and a couple of ambulances from the nearby Royal London.

'Sir, I think it's gone into the hospital.'

'Thank you!' Carling roared along, then swerved in. 'Where exactly?'

'Car park on the right.'

Carling killed the siren and the lights, then took it slowly through the hospital complex. Sure enough, a car park sat on the right, almost filled. In fact, Fenchurch couldn't spot a single free space.

Only one vehicle was idling in the hot afternoon. An old BMW, with blacked-out windows. Parked headfirst, so there was no sign of a driver behind the wheel.

Carling eased his pool car into a blocking position – the only way the BMW was going out was through. 'Let's get it.'

Fenchurch was out first. His foot hit the tarmac and his knee locked. He went down. Only thing stopping his teeth hitting the floor was the palms of his hands biting against the tarmac.

'Jesus, Si!' Carling was frowning at him. 'You okay?'

Fenchurch waved at the car. 'Dead leg from the way you were driving.'

'I'm not that bad, am I?'

'No, but you're not that good.' Fenchurch pushed up to standing. Bloody hell, this knee was impossible. He adjusted the brace, tightening it that little bit until he felt the squeeze. He managed to put some weight on it, got it to click like a ratchet screwdriver. Managed to move across the tarmac.

Carling inched along the gap towards the door.

Fenchurch limped along behind him. Still no sign of a driver, just a song from that last Blur album playing.

Carling rapped on the glass.

Nothing.

'Here goes.' Carling tried the handle.

The door opened.

A man was reclining in the leather seat. Shaved head, combat trousers, black T-shirt. Left arm strapped up at the armpit, syringe hanging over a vein, biting on the end of the strapping. His eyes bulged. He let go of the strap and it pinged off. 'This isn't what you think.'

'Well, it looks like someone shooting up in a car park.'

The guy stuck the car in gear.

The syringe fell. The needle jabbed into his thigh.

The car stalled.

He lurched forward, shouting, and banged his head off the wheel.

The door bounced then battered off Carling's arse. He went down with a yelp.

Fenchurch hauled the door open and grabbed the driver's wrist. He tugged hard and pulled him right out of the car, then pinned him down to the tarmac. 'Okay, sunshine. How's about a name?'

'How about you fuck off?'

'That's a good way to get yourself smacked in the head by accident. You want me to rummage through your pockets for a wallet?'

Carling was on his feet again, dusting off his trouser knees. 'Si, don't you recognise him?'

Fenchurch shook his head. 'No?'

Carling pulled the needle out of his thigh. 'It's Jon Wardle.'

Fenchurch frowned at him. Christ, it was. The paramedic. Hadn't seen him in ages. That was who he saw that morning. 'You're a junkie?'

Wardle looked away. 'No.'

'Of course. What junkies do is admit they are. They don't deny it.' Fenchurch snapped on a glove and reached into the car to pick up the syringe. 'What's this? Too clear to be heroin.'

Wardle shook his head. 'It's water.'

'Water. Right. You're getting high on the placebo effect.'

Carling scowled at Wardle. 'Last time I saw you was this morning. You were first to attend Curtis's crime scene, weren't you?'

'Not me.'

'I saw you there, Jon. You took more than the lad's vital signs, didn't you?'

'No.'

'Come on, Jon. You've been a naughty boy.' Carling pointed at the syringe. 'What's this? Morphine? You steal it from the ambulance?'

'No.'

'Righty-o.' Carling laughed. 'How are you going to explain having Curtis's phone?'

'I don't have anyone's phone.'

Fenchurch limped around the car. Sure enough, a baby-blue iPhone sat on the passenger seat. He got out his own mobile and snapped a shot. 'I'm sure we'll find Curtis Archer's prints on this. Probably his contact details.' He tapped the screen with his gloved finger and woke it. Still on, but nothing showing who it belonged to. He held down the power and volume up buttons, then slid across the Medical ID option.

Curtis Archer

'Well, well, well.' He limped back around. 'Mr Wardle, why do you have Curtis Archer's phone in your car?'

'You just planted it there!'

'Son, you're in deep shit here. We've caught you injecting a class A in public. We've caught you with a phone stolen from a dead man. That's the lowest of the low.'

'Fuck off.'

'You stole it to support your drug habit, didn't you?'

Wardle's head went low. He kept his gaze on the syringe in Carling's hand. 'The morphine isn't enough. I can get some, sometimes. But... I need it more than I can get it.'

'So you stole from a dead body?'

'Not the first time. Not happy with myself. But they won't miss it.'

'Their families will!'

'I'm sorry.' Wardle was crying. Soon, a stream of tears

soaked his cheeks. 'I didn't mean to. It just... It started with a tenner in someone's pocket. Then a bracelet. Then a watch. Now... I'm stealing phones and... Curtis had a grand on him in cash. And some jewellery. Chain, rings. And that phone's worth a lot. Either just as a phone or as a memento of a dead footballer. Daft sod had taken the passcode off it. Who does that? I mean, maybe the physical changes to his face meant it didn't recognise him. Didn't bother to re-train it, just turned it off. Think of all the A-list celebs on the contact list... Must be worth ten grand. Maybe more. Don't you get it?'

'I do.'

Wardle dipped his head. 'Money is so tight just now. Fuel prices. Cost of living. It's ten quid for a tub of butter!'

'And you've got to feed your addiction. I understand. Well, you'll be looked after by Her Majesty for a good while, you daft sod.'

'What?'

Carling snapped a pair of cuffs on his wrist. 'I'm arresting you for the theft of a mobile phone.'

'But, come on! You know me!'

'Which makes this even harder.' Carling grabbed his wrists and finished the job. 'How do you want to play this?'

'You drive him around to the station. I'll find this supervisor. Break the bad news.'

'Come on, Jon.'

Fenchurch got a throb in his pocket.

Bridge calling...

'Lisa, we've got him. Thank you.'

Something crashed in the background. 'I need you at Curtis's flat. Now!'

'Why?'

But she was gone.

'Sorry, change of plan.' Fenchurch held out his hand. 'Need your keys.'

CHAPTER TWENTY-TWO

Fenchurch pulled in across from Curtis's flat and it didn't take him long to see why he'd been called out.

Candace Archer was kicking off. Arms wide, shouting. Holding a plant pot like she was going to throw it. Like the one she'd already thrown, splintered against the wall.

Fenchurch got out into the heat.

'You dare try to stop me from going inside?' Candace was in Bridge's face. 'That is my boy's *home!*'

Bridge was standing her ground, despite how close Candace was and how she was brandishing that plant pot. 'I totally get that. But we—'

'You need to let me in there!'

Fenchurch joined them on the pavement, but didn't step in. Bridge was good – she had this.

'We are performing a thorough forensic investigation of the property. It'll take time, Candace.'

'But I need to clean it. It's all filthy!'

'Nobody's been in there since yesterday.'

'You have! You all have!'

'My colleagues in forensics are in there just now, but they are wearing suits made from Tyvek, which stop any of their—'

'You don't understand.' Eyes shut, Candace shook her head. 'They will still be bringing *germs* in.'

'Candace, it's okay. We will make sure it's returned to you in the same state you'd leave it.'

'I very much doubt that.' She folded her arms, but still clutched the pot.

'It's a promise.'

'Well.' Candace glared at Reed then at Fenchurch. 'I'll be speaking to my lawyer about this.'

Bridge smiled at her. 'That's a very good idea. You know where to find us afterwards.'

Candace gave Fenchurch another look, like she expected him to jump in, then dropped the plant pot onto the pavement. Weirdly, it didn't smash. She huffed and strode off towards a tiny Fiat.

Bridge watched her go. 'Thanks for coming, sir.'

'You didn't need me.'

'Oh, I know.' She smiled at him. 'I didn't call you to help out with her, but I wanted you to hear the exchange.'

'Well, I didn't. What was it about?'

Bridge waved a hand around the building. 'This whole block has a concierge service. The guy's based in the entrance to the north and he's giving a statement to one of my lads.'

'About what?'

She looked hard at him. 'The CCTV covers the entrance to Curtis's flat. Candace was there last night.'

'Shit.'

'She spent lot of time there, too.'

Fenchurch sighed. 'So *she* did the deep clean?'

Bridge sighed. 'She turned up just after you hung up on me.'

'Sorry. We caught him, thanks to you. Jon Wardle.'

'The paramedic?'

'Him.'

'Shitting hell.'

'Anyway. What happened with Candace?'

Bridge pointed at the smashed plant pot. 'She came here and asked to be let in. So I asked her about the cleaning.' She held up her hands. 'Asked her nicely, in case you're worried.'

'I don't imagine you'd do anything else.'

Her lips pursed. She didn't believe him. 'Anyway. She insisted it was what she did every night. She said her boy's very messy. So many germs.'

'Sounds like OCD to me.'

'Well, obsessive cleaning, sure. I don't think anything could be clean enough for her. She let it slip that she hoovers seven times a day.'

Fenchurch laughed. 'When I lived alone, I didn't do it that much a year.'

'Jesus, sir!'

'I'm kidding. Once a week. Bear in mind I was hardly in that flat you and Jon live in now.'

'Right.' She was looking away, brow creased.

'Everything okay?'

'Oh, yeah. It's good. Just thinking... She started kicking off about not getting in. I mean, her compulsion might explain why she was here, but it also feels pretty convenient. Like she'd left something behind.'

'You're thinking it throws her into the mix as a suspect?'

'Only had a third, but she wanted more.'

'A third?'

'Of her son's money.'

'Oh.' Fenchurch stared up into the blue sky. A jet crawled across, leaving a contrail like a snail on a slab.

Could she have killed her son?

Really?

Why now? Why not wait until later, until he was richer?

'Okay.' He looked back at her. 'Listen, Candace told DI Reed about making investments in her son's name. We backed it up at their accountants. They had two investment accounts for his money.'

'That doesn't mean she didn't kill him.'

'I know, Lisa. Part of me can't believe she'd kill her own son, but a lot of me has been a cop for a very long time and has seen a lot of bad stuff. Maybe she's just a grieving mother with a cleaning fixation. But she's the one who stands to benefit most.' He sighed. 'Thing is, we don't have a lot of evidence, do we?'

'No. And we've got gaps in the CCTV.'

'So it might not all have been her?'

'Correct.' Bridge glanced at her phone. 'Bloody hell.' She put it away with a pout. 'The driver's wanting to speak to me.'

'The driver?'

'Curtis's driver. Nolan Roberts. The black Range Rover. You asked me to track him down. Spoke to the owner of the business Curtis was using, but we failed to find him. Then he turned up. DC Smith-Webster is speaking to him. Said he was here to take Curtis to the airport. He was flying to Dubai today.'

'Today? Shit. When was it booked?'

'A few days ago. Curtis told him to take the time off, then he was heading away on holiday.'

'He was supposed to be going three days ago.'

'Nope. Mick's team found the tickets. Definitely flying today.'

'But he told his mother it was three days ago.'

'Either he was wrong or she was. I mean, I'd say someone

THE LAST THING TO DIE

who was whacked up on those drugs maybe wasn't thinking straight.'

who was whacked up on those drugs maybe wasn't thinking straight.'

'Okay. When was the last time this Nolan guy saw Curtis?'

'Like I said, three days ago. Drove him to his mother's and back.'

'How does that tie up with his phone records?'

'It matches.'

'He didn't take him to Hammersmith?'

'Nope. He says he was "shit-faced in Dalston". Got names of mates who were with him at a hipster bar there.'

Fenchurch nodded. 'This is good stuff, Lisa. Thanks.'

His phone blasted out. Reed.

'Sorry, better take this.'

'Sure.'

He answered it. 'What's up, Kay?'

'Guv, I've got some news.'

CHAPTER TWENTY-THREE

Fenchurch stepped into his office, feeling like he'd swallowed molten tarmac. Sitting heavy on the bottom of his stomach, burning away.

Bell was standing in the window, staring out, jangling the change in his pocket. He swung around, forehead creased, lips twisted. 'Simon.'

'You got my voicemail then?'

Bell nodded. 'Indeed.' He perched on the edge of Fenchurch's desk. He looked like he was half-melted, dribbling onto the floor. 'Curtis Archer's been on smack?'

'No, sir.' Fenchurch hung his jacket up behind the door. 'He wasn't on heroin. He was prescribed a valid therapeutic pain reliever.'

'Well, there's very little difference between opiates and opioids. Just because it's prescribed doesn't stop him being a junkie.'

Fenchurch muttered, 'Like being prescribed a Big Mac.'

'What was that?'

'Sir, I've been seeing Deacon while I await my knee operation.'

'What?' Bell crossed his arms over his chest, like two sausages ready to burst. 'Simon. You should've told me. A long time ago.'

That old chestnut. Why didn't you tell me before? 'Sir, Dr Deacon wasn't connected to an open investigation before. There's no conflict of interest here. He knows I'm a cop. Everything's on the level. I'm seeing him for some pain management until my surgery. Have you any idea what my knee feels like?'

'Every time I have to take the stairs.' Bell laughed. 'It's not easy carrying this much weight.'

Didn't stop him eating two pizzas a day. 'But I'm totally in control of my situation.'

'You better be.' Bell stood up tall. 'Because I'm pulling you off that part of the investigation. Kay Reed can run it.'

Fenchurch nodded. 'She's already doing that, sir. I asked her to take charge of it. We'll hopefully get some leads.'

'Well, that's good of you. But I'm not impressed by this, Simon. It doesn't look good.'

All that focus on image... Constantly. Never about the substance, just on how badly it looked for him. 'Sir, Deacon's one of the few specialists in this side of the city, so it's just a coincidence that we both see him.' Fenchurch held up a finger. 'A bad one, admittedly. But it's all above board, I swear.'

Bell stared at him. The man was a walking spreadsheet, filled with calculations, constantly changing and redirecting. 'Anyway, while I was waiting—' He frowned. 'Where have you been, incidentally?'

'I was at Curtis's flat. His mother was kicking off there. I sorted that out but, after DI Reed called, I had a long chat with Mick Clooney about why we weren't finding any evidence of anyone even living there.'

'Okay, that's good. Thing is, I just got a call from the victim's mother's lawyer. Mr Unwin isn't impressed by DS Bridge's treatment of his client.'

Dalton Unwin... Just had to be him, didn't it?

But there it was again – the focus on image. Not on the fact there was a mystery that needed to be explained.

Fenchurch shrugged. 'Good. Unwin's a criminal defence lawyer.'

'What's that supposed to mean?'

'Candace Archer isn't out of the firing line here, sir.'

'You think she might've been involved in her own son's death?'

'Might not have killed him, but she could've poisoned him. She's the one who stands to benefit most from his death.'

Bell let out a long deep breath. 'I'm just asking you to be very careful with her.'

'We are being cautious, sir.'

'Glad to hear it.' Bell opened the door again. 'Is there anything else I should know about?'

'No, sir. Nothing.'

'Good.' Bell seemed like he wanted to get out of there but some page of the management textbook was keeping him there. 'Are you okay, Simon?'

'I'm fine, sir. My knee's an abomination but I'm okay. Once I've had my op, I'll be totally fine.'

'Good. But I'm your friend, Simon. You know my door's always open, yes?'

And you always speak in clichés. 'Thank you, sir.' Fenchurch tried to make the smile look authentic.

Bell seemed to buy it. 'I'll be at the Yard for the rest of the day, should you need me.'

'I hope I don't, sir.'

Bell laughed. 'Quite.' He tilted his head to the side. 'Are you

THE LAST THING TO DIE

honestly okay, Simon?' The way he was frowning, it felt genuine. Like he did actually care.

'I'm fine. Honestly.'

'Okay. Well. Godspeed.' Bell left the room, thumping along the corridor, listing to the left like a burst oil tanker.

'Thank *you*, sir.' Fenchurch walked over and shut the door. 'You're the *best*, sir. The *best.*' He sat on his desk and picked up the stress ball Chloe had got him. Thing had taken a lot of squeezing over the last year, that's for sure. A few cracks in the foam now.

Deacon was Curtis Archer's doctor. Not only were they on the same dose, but prescribed by the same man.

It still hadn't hit home.

Fenchurch knew he should get his physiology checked out independently. No way was he getting away without incurring any damage to his system.

He took out the pill bottle and rested it on the desk. He needed to get off these little bastards. As quickly as he could.

Those urges to keep taking them, though...

To stop spacing out the dose so he could taper off...

He needed to ignore the screaming pain in his knee and his head and just—

The door burst open and Carling stormed through, panting. 'Si. Bell said you were here.'

Fenchurch snatched up the drugs and pocketed them. 'What's up?'

'Not answering your phone?'

'Not when Bell's in the room.' Fenchurch reached into his pocket again. His phone wasn't there. Buggery. Where had he put it? He walked over and checked his jacket. Sure enough, there it was. He checked the display. '*Ten* calls?'

'You didn't answer the first, so I left a voicemail.'

'So you thought another nine would do it?'

'There was bad traffic on the way back from Lewisham.' Carling smiled. 'Okay. Bad news first, yeah?' He waited for Fenchurch's nod. 'After I lost all that time messing about processing our tea-leaf paramedic, Pratt had finished the PM before I got there.'

'I should've sent Uzma. Sorry.'

'Never mind. That paramedic, though. What a story. He'll be looking for a new job very soon.'

Fenchurch shook his head. 'He was too honest with us.'

'That'll stop as soon as he gets a lawyer in. I've got a couple of my best guys working it. Will keep you updated.'

'Good stuff.' Fenchurch sighed. 'Anyway. The PM?'

'Okay, right. Well, it was what Pratt expected. He reckons Curtis had an undiagnosed heart defect.'

'But he just signed a new contract with the club two years ago.'

'Turns out the club didn't do a medical when he signed it. Didn't show up when he signed for them initially five years ago.'

'So it's just come on?'

'Pratt thinks he could've contracted it from covid.'

'Covid? Really?'

'Affects everyone differently. People from... a ... eh, BAME background can get it worse.'

'Isn't that a myth?'

'Pratt thinks there's something in it, especially when it comes to Curtis. Anyway, there's evidence to support damage to the heart and lungs from it. And Pratt reckons the drugs he was on probably exacerbated it.'

'His lungs?'

'Both were damaged, so running like that put extra strain on his ticker. Just exploded.'

'Jesus.'

The good news was that Fenchurch didn't necessarily have the same heart defect. Hell, the daft shit he'd put himself through as an adult would've pushed it too hard. He'd know.

The other good thing was his gammy knee now stopped him moving at anything faster than a sprightly limp. His heart rate hadn't been above eighty in years. No danger of him straining himself, except when he had a hangover. And he hadn't touched a drop since he started on those pills.

'Pratt said he's been in touch with the club doctor. Dude's on some mad hiking holiday. Reckons he'll get to speak to him in detail about it later in the week.'

'Thanks, but I'm still waiting on some good news here?'

'Pratt says the club store data from every test, so he hopes to get to the bottom of whether they knew about this.'

'He hadn't been there in over year, though.'

'True.'

'Okay. Keep on top of them.'

'You think someone at the club could be involved in his death?'

'Don't you?'

Carling scratched behind his neck. 'I mean, sure. Everyone's a suspect in a case like this.' He shrugged. 'Bottom line. Undiagnosed heart ailment, lung damage, plus decreased respiratory function from the oxycodone, plus the strain from being chased equals dead. And Pratt won't conclude until he's done that deep dive with the club doctor.'

'Okay, thanks.' Fenchurch didn't know what to make of it. 'Issue is whether he was taking the drugs himself or someone was—'

A knock on the door.

Carling rolled his eyes. 'Someone was what?'

'Get that, would you? Could be Bell.'

157

'Sure.' Carling walked over and opened the door. 'Kay.' He folded his arms. 'We're kind of busy here.'

'You both need to hear this.' She barged past Carling and walked over to Fenchurch's desk. Had that look on her face. 'I've just been with Dr Deacon. Traced the last receipt I got from the accountant's bookkeeper to a prescription that came from him. He checked his computer system – turns out he *had* prescribed Curtis a strong dose of oxycodone to get him through the aftereffects of his operation. But that was eight months ago.'

Fenchurch frowned. 'Eight months?'

'Deacon said he came off it. Even gave him a prescription for methadone.'

Carling stuck his tongue in his cheek. 'Well, he very much wasn't off it.'

'I called Pratt about it on the way over.' Reed flicked through her notebook. 'If the idea was to kill him, methadone isn't the way... If Deacon killed—'

'Wait, wait, wait.' Fenchurch got to his feet with a jolt of pain lancing his knee. 'You think *Deacon* killed him?'

'We're trying to rule people in or out, guv. Pratt said if a doctor wanted to kill someone, they'd prescribe fentanyl. Much more likely to overdose on it. It's what killed Prince, for instance. Methadone is a substitute for oxycodone, but it's not as strong or as long- lasting. The idea is you take a drink of it at regular intervals instead of oxy, or heroin, so that you can gradually kick it without getting dope sick.'

Dope sick.

Shit, that's what Fenchurch was going through. Like that scene in *Trainspotting* where Renton saw a dead baby crawling across the ceiling.

What the hell was Fenchurch going to see?

Who was he going to see?

THE LAST THING TO DIE

Reed turned a page, snapping him out of his thoughts. 'Pratt reckons methadone clinics can "forget" to check if the patient is actually still taking opioids or opiates. They're supposed to have random pee tests. He says the methadone ends up being "as well as" rather than "instead of". Essentially legalised drug use.'

Carling was shaking his head, a sneer on his face. 'What's your take, Kay? Do you think Deacon's involved in this?'

'I'm not giving him a pass, put it that way. I've got people digging into his background.'

'Good idea.'

'Thing is.' Reed brushed her hair behind her ear. 'Deacon did save me a job.'

'Oh?'

'Gave me a contact with BRO Capital.'

Fenchurch frowned. 'Hasn't Clarke got back to you yet?'

'Still avoiding me.'

Fenchurch got out his phone and tapped out a text:

Steve, give me a call. It's extremely urgent. Cheers.

'Deacon's pissed off with them. Reckons they diddled him out of a load of cash.'

Fenchurch looked up at Reed. 'How did that come up?'

She tilted her head to the side. 'Turns out the O in BRO stands for Oliver Archer.'

'What? His old man?'

'Exactly.' Reed scanned the other. 'Neither of you knew?'

'No! I gave up on being psychic a few years ago.' Carling threw his hands up in the air. 'How does Curtis's dad connect with Deacon?'

'Well. Oliver Archer was seeing Deacon for an ankle injury he got from playing five-a-sides. Got a recommendation from the club doctor at West Ham. Referred his son there after the operation. Deacon said Oliver was very pushy about money, kept pimping some investments on him. And Deacon lost a ton of cash through it.'

'To BRO Capital?'

'Right. Way he described it, Oliver was trying to get a youth player to sign up to this investment scheme he's running. Deacon thinks Oscar had his son pushing those dodgy investments on people.'

'So we have more to add to Deacon being a suspect, then.' Fenchurch checked his phone. 'And we need to speak to his old man. Any idea when he's back from Monaco?'

Reed smiled. 'Turns out he's not in Monaco. Deacon was doing some consultancy work at the club to cover for the doctor's charity walk. Oliver Archer was there this morning.'

CHAPTER TWENTY-FOUR

Fenchurch sat behind the wheel, waiting. *Jingo* by Santana blasted out of the speakers, the fusion of hard rock and Latin rhythms that—

Reed snapped it off. 'That's absolute shit, guv.'

'Come on. You can't knock a bit of Santana.'

'It's even worse than Kanyif Iqbal.' Reed folded her arms. 'Has he responded to your text?'

'Who, Steve? Yes. Says he's on his way.'

'That's interesting. Just decided to come here without asking what it was about?'

'Just had to mention BRO Capital and, lo, he hath decided to getteth the fuck here.'

She laughed. 'Care to explain why you didn't go to see Dr Deacon?'

Fenchurch was fed up with lying. Lying was what addicts like Jon Wardle did. 'Because I've been seeing Deacon for my knee.'

'How long?'

'November.'

ED JAMES

'When those Scottish cops were down?'

'Doc reckoned I was supposed to get an op just before Christmas. I was travelling up to chilly Jockland in bloody midwinter for Operation Clusterfuck with Vicky. On the train, passing through Durham when he called to say it was postponed. Luckily, I could swap back at Newcastle rather than heading up to Edinburgh, then on to Dundee, but still...'

'Are you on some painkillers, then?'

Fenchurch nodded. 'Same dose as Curtis Archer.'

'Seriously?'

Another nod. 'Kay, I need to kick it. I know I do. I can and will kick it. But the drugs are what's keeping me working.'

'Does Abi know?'

'She does. Wants me off it too.'

'Things still tough between you two?'

'What's she telling you?'

Reed shrugged. 'Don't really speak much these days.'

'We're getting through it, Kay.'

'Guv, you want my advice—'

'Kay, with all due respect, I'm fine. It's under control.'

'Well, if you insist...'

'I do.' Fenchurch focused on the tower BRO were in, another of the new Leman Street buildings, one he'd barely even noticed, let alone been in. A ten-storey tower with a rounded corner that went up a couple of extra levels and formed a peak, like a Scottish castle. 'BRO' was stamped on the side in red letters. He got out his phone again and checked for missed calls and messages.

The back door opened. 'Alright, shaggers.' DI Steve Clarke collapsed onto the back seat. Beads of sweat on his forehead. 'How's it going?'

'Ah, the Scarlet Pimpernel...'

'Sorry I'm late. Got important stuff to do.'

'Like investigating BRO Capital?'

'Okay, so your text has me intrigued.' Clarke wiped at his forehead. 'What's going on?'

'Our victim, the one you shirked responsibility over, turns out he was—' Fenchurch frowned. 'He was involved in some kind of scam with them. Kay?'

She smiled at him, then round at Clarke. 'Selling NFTs.'

'Well, well. It's not illegal.'

'But?'

'We gather BRO were involved in some kind of scam involving them.' Clarke adjusted his jacket, like he was getting air in there. 'Where do I start?' He sighed. 'Either of you know what an NFT is?'

'Vaguely.' Fenchurch wished he could google it. 'Non-something somethings?'

'You, a DCI in the Met, must understand what they are.'

'Sure, but I want to know what a DI in the City Police knows about them.'

'Come on, Simon. You don't even know what it stands for.'

Reed was grinning like the class swot. 'Non-Fungible Token.'

'Okay, great.'

Fenchurch grinned. 'How about you explain like I'm five?'

'Hmm, that's more mature than I usually treat you.' Clarke smiled. 'Fungible means it can be replaced by an identical item. A pair of running shoes or a five-pound note are both fungible. You can get another running shoe or fiver and they're functionally identical. The Mona Lisa is non-fungible. Sure, you can make a copy of it, but it's not going to be identical. It's not on fabric that's hundreds of years old. The paint won't be exactly the same formulation. Wasn't painted by Da Vinci.'

'With you so far.'

'Now.' Clarke leaned between them. He stank of sweat and

cheap body wash. 'A fungible token is something that's easily copied. Most things on a computer are. Every copy is perfect, because it's all made of ones and zeroes, not atoms and so on. A *Non*-Fungible Token is a digital thing that's unique.'

'There's only one of them even though it's just ones and zeroes?'

'It's about the ownership. Si. You can prove you've got the master copy. The original gangsta. Think of a baseball card. You own that exact one, nobody else does. If it's a general card, you can swap it between you. But if they only printed one card, it's unique. You're the only one who owns it. Problem is it's hard to prove you do.'

'Other than the fact I've got it in my safe?'

'But that's possession, not ownership. If someone gets into that safe and nicks it, there's no way you can really prove it's yours. I mean, you can get an expert to verify it's unique and they could stand up in court and testify for you.'

'Okay. I'm with you.'

'Now, if you scanned that baseball card, you could send it to me, to Kay and to thousands of other people, but you'd still own the physical card. Right?'

'I get it. Digital files aren't unique.'

'Exactly. They're fungible. Say you sent a scan to me and to Kay. They'd be identical. We could swap them and there's no difference with your original scan.'

'Okay. I'm following you.'

'The thing that makes an NFT unique is it takes that scan's link and registers it on an open ledger called the blockchain.'

Fenchurch frowned. 'This is where I'm going to get lost.'

'It's not that complicated. The blockchain registers your unique ownership of your NFT. But it also tells *everyone else* that only you own it. Then if you sell it to me, the blockchain ledger gets updated to say I own it, but it's also got your previous ownership logged. And everyone knows I own it now.'

'Why's that special?'

'Well, if it's a real baseball card, the ownership would be logged on a ledger, but not everybody would subscribe to it and agree it's the master source of ownership. NFTs, they do.'

'Okay. With you.'

'An NFT is about creating digital scarcity. Giving something that can be easily copied a unique ownership. And it could be a photo of a painting or a video of a West Ham goal, though there aren't many of them at the moment.'

'Says the Millwall fan.'

'Hey.' Clarke grinned. 'That's harsh.'

'So who owns this blockchain ledger?'

'Nobody. It's decentralised.'

'How does that work?'

'Everyone submits changes and they're integrated and distributed by people who use very fast computers to do all this complex mathematics to mine, say, Bitcoins. Their reward for updating the ledger is to get some cryptocurrency back. And your changes are logged.'

'But who owns it? Microsoft? Amazon? Apple?'

'Nobody.' Clarke sighed. He was explaining it like Fenchurch was five, but it was clearly like dealing with a five-year-old who'd just learned the W-word – 'why?'. 'Okay. Remember when the internet took off, people would go out and register domain names like westham.com or westham.-co.uk and if you were West Ham, you'd have to buy that domain name from them for a fortune. And they did. Businesses paid through the nose. So think about the NFT as that name, then its value depends on how badly someone wants to own it.'

'With you so far.'

'But the difference with websites is there's a central register that says West Ham own westham.com, so anytime someone types that in, their browser does a lookup against that database and gets the code that takes them to the West Ham website's server, as opposed to little Brian's server, where little Brian is the guy who previously bought it. With domain names, an international standard emerged which slowed down the speculation. Aside from bad-faith actors, the only way you could register westham.com now would be if you ran a fan site or were from the village of Westham. It can't be malicious. With a blockchain, nobody owns it. Everyone can have access to the whole ledger of ownership, which is comparable to that domain lookup.'

'So anyone can look up my NFT code and see that I own it?'

'Precisely.'

'But nobody owns that register?'

'It means it's not open to exploitation or central control. Except that most of the transactions run through trading platforms. So there's a trader-bro purity and there's a reality. But either way, it's not as locked down as Web 2.0 stuff was.'

'Web 2.0?'

Clarke sighed. 'Web 1.0 was all about people putting websites up and you going in to read them. They still exist, stuff like google or the BBC Sport website. Web 2.0, as they called it, was all about user-generated content. YouTube, Facebook, Twitter. It's not about consuming stuff, it's about being part of it. Sharing and creating stuff on there. Interaction. But Web3 is all about a decentralised version of that. If you use Facebook, then the parent company called Meta says you own the account, but it's only useful on their platform. Posts, photos, videos. You can take it down but you can't easily put it elsewhere. A Web3 equivalent of Facebook would have looked like many different social networks accessing your own personal server for certain types of data, rather than one of them storing it centrally. So you share a photo or a text post where you want it to go. And if you don't like one platform, you can stop them ever having access to it.'

'This is all way over my head.'

'Simon, we're going to have to push salt and pepper shakers around a table for hours until you get it. I'm sure you'll get there eventually, but what's important just now is you understand the scam they were pulling.'

Reed was nodding. 'I know a lot about that.'

'Oh?'

'My husband, Dave, works for the FCA these days.' She looked at Fenchurch. 'Financial Conduct Authority. These things are unregulated. The whole thing is a badlands, worse than the Wild West. There are businesses selling cartoon photos that are supposed to be scarce and are provably so, but there are lots of ways hackers and chancers can swindle people.'

Fenchurch frowned. 'Such as?'

'What Steve was saying about ledgers and you showing ownership. That's by a key you have on your computer. A file that's unique to you. If someone obtains that key, that shows they own it, not you. Instead of transferring the NFT to them-selves, they transfer your key to them. They effectively become you.'

'That what you investigate, Steve?'

'Not so much. That's for the platforms to sort out.'

'So what do you do?'

'Well.' Clarke sighed. 'The blockchain is impossible to hack unless you own more than half of the tokens and even then, it'll be obvious you're doing it. Whatever your NFT is – paint-ings or tweets or baseball photos or West Ham goal gifs or whatever – they have no intrinsic value except what people will pay for them.'

'Same as in the real world.'

'The biggest scam we look at is artificially inflating the value of these things to millions of pounds. Then they lose their value over a few months, but they've made a ton of cash from the initial sale.'

'That's not really a scam, is it?'

'Depends on how you inflate it before you sell it. And people lose millions on it. Real money. Life savings. And businesses lose billions too. All because celebrities take money in exchange for pimping them out without knowing what they're pimping out. It's kids buying pictures of cartoon monkeys because their hero tells them to. And they lose a lot of cash doing it.'

'This is what Curtis was involved with?'

'Right.'

'I still don't get it.' Fenchurch sighed. 'Why?'

Clarke was shaking his head.

Reed leaned over and nudged Fenchurch's arm. 'Does Al still play *Fortnite*?'

'Can't get him off it.'

'Well, when you catch him buying skins for it so he can look like Spider-Man or Luke Skywalker, he—'

'He *pays* for that?'

'A few quid a time.'

'Bloody hell.' Fenchurch would need to have a look at that later.

'Anyway. Al's making payments online to a physical company, say videogame.com which is Video Game Inc., New York, NY. Imagine *Fortnite* hooks into the blockchain so only you can dress like a particular Spider-Man from a film, because

THE LAST THING TO DIE

you paid five million quid two years ago for the privilege. You can sell it to someone else, but then you can't use it.'

'I can see that.'

'But none of that's in place. All it is just now is stuff like cartoon apes or paintings or NBA shots. That's it. Doesn't do anything functional. Probably unlikely to because if you're the people who run *Fortnite*, you want to own all of that monetisation yourself and don't let someone else get in on it.'

'What's the problem with that?'

'If *Fortnite* suddenly lost popularity, like something better came out or it was tied to evil shit and the kids all hated that, then the character upgrades that you invested real money into would still be worth the same within the game in its own currency, but their external value would tank because there's no demand. So you paid a grand in real money for your character's unique look but you want out of the game economy and you can only get ten quid whereas last week a guy offered you twelve grand for it.'

Clarke was nodding. 'Yeah and if *Fortnite* closed down, that gear's worth nothing. You've lost the value. But if there's a new Spider-Man film coming out, your skin is suddenly worth four times what it was.'

Fenchurch felt like his head was turning inside out, even though he was starting to understand it. 'I think I'm with you. So, what problem is it trying to solve?'

'A combination of Californian hippies and libertarian criminals wanting privacy from the Man, man.' Reed smiled. 'The technology might be useful to someone, someday, but currently it's mostly just experimental at best, or a scam at worst.'

Fenchurch felt like he'd just got back to school after three months off. Everyone was so much further on than him. 'Okay.'

He waved at the BRO building up ahead. 'So what's their scam?'

'What isn't their scam?' Clarke laughed. 'NFTs. As I've explained to you, we're talking about secure transactions on a decentralised open ledger that nobody controls. They've got their own blockchain, and they mine about forty percent of the transactions on there.'

'Isn't that dodgy?'

'It's pretty common. It's open to everyone, but identities are hidden. So criminals used to use it until we got smart and could spot them taking money out by converting Bitcoin or Dogecoin into real money. But then the tech bros took over and it became an investment bubble. Used to be you could buy a pizza for three Bitcoin, then a Bitcoin was close to a hundred grand.'

'For something that doesn't exist?'

'Those pound coins in your pocket don't really exist. Money is a fiction we all subscribe to. We say that a pound coin is a pound coin because we all agree and we all accept them. It's just a digital version of that. Some people think the technology will change the world, but just now it's all a bubble. And one that's burst.'

'NFTs are burst?'

'Kind of, yeah. It's burst.'

'So it's all bullshit?'

'Well, who's to say? Thing is, if you buy a Spider-Man T-shirt in Ashworth's, that tee costs a quid for them to buy plus a quid for them to print. The difference in value is because of the importance you place on Spider-Man.'

'So my son wants to dress as Spidey while playing *Fortnite* and make sure nobody else can.'

'That's the idea, but the practice isn't there yet. Or

anywhere near. It'd be a specific Spider-Man suit, like from a film or an issue of the comic, or something, but yeah.'

Fenchurch waved at the BRO office. 'And this lot? Why were you investigating them?'

'They provide the backbone for some NFTs, but really the idea is to not mine for the gold yourself but to sell the shovels and the jeans for those that do. And yeah, they do mine cryptocurrencies, so the analogy doesn't work. They've got some data centres in the Highlands, right next to some hydro dams so the energy is dirt cheap and renewable. I mean, the idea is sound, but crypto prices crashed recently. Like ninety percent of the value gone in a few days. A lot of people lost their shirts and their whole wardrobes.'

'So they took a hit?'

'Not sure. But their clients? Big time.' Clarke clamped his hands on their shoulders. 'Now, how about we go inside and see what's what, yeah?'

CHAPTER TWENTY-FIVE

The BRO Capital office looked south across the Tower of London site, over the Thames to the Shard, like a glassy spike of a spaceship had crash-landed into industrial South London. The University of Southwark tower was its trusty companion. Fenchurch couldn't remember its name and it was bugging him. He'd... seen things up there.

What was it called?

He looked over to ask Reed, but the door opened and a blur of ginger energy waltzed in. Oliver Archer seemed to be so caffeinated that he experienced time at a faster clip than everyone else. Or maybe it was slower – Fenchurch couldn't decide. He was as tall and thin as his son's mother was short and curvy, and his skin was the colour of fresh paper, like he never went out during daylight. 'Well, well, well, it's the Old Bill.' Hardcore Cockney accent you only really heard in bits of Essex these days. He leaned against the back of a meeting room chair, but he seemed to hate being static, as though he needed to be continually moving. 'What can I do you for?'

'Thought you were in Monaco?'

'I was. Got a mate's yacht for a week. But they need me here. So here I am.'

'Making us all uncomfortable, Ollie.' Clarke gestured at the chair. First name terms. 'Have a seat, please.'

Archer stayed standing. Sharp suit, but rolled up to the elbows. Drainpipe trousers. 'Got a dodgy back, ain't I?' He rubbed at the base of his spine.

'Sure.' Clarke gestured behind him. 'Looking a bit threadbare through there, Ollie. Like you're shutting down this place.'

Archer scratched at his neck. 'Had to lay some people off, didn't we? Tough times.'

'So I heard. Last time we spoke, you said crypto was the future.'

'I did, didn't I?' Archer blew a slow breath up his face. 'It still is, but getting there's going to be a tough old slog, mark my words. And I'm deep in the shit now.'

'What's happened?'

'It's all crashed.'

'Sounds brutal.'

'I'll cope, just about.'

'But the rest of your company?'

'That's to be decided, I'm afraid.' Ollie looked at Reed, then at Fenchurch, like he was noticing them for the first time. 'So, what can I do you for?'

'Listen.' Clarke pointed at Fenchurch and Reed. 'My colleagues in the Met here have some bad news.'

'About me son?' Archer raised his eyebrows. 'Yeah.' He ran a hand through his spiky hair. 'Heard about it, yeah. His mother's mother called my mother who called me.' His Adam's apple bobbed up and down. 'Absolutely destroyed by it.'

Clarke sat there, nodding slowly. 'Not destroyed enough to not work.'

'Have to, Steve, otherwise I'm ruined. This'll clear me out if

I'm not very careful.' Archer shook his head. 'Don't think I don't care, either. Ever since my kid was young, I tried to make enough money for him. To pay for him, support him. Half my income went on him. Never made much until two years ago. Christ, he'd make more in a couple of weeks than me in all my career, the amount he was on.' He shook his head again. 'Can't believe he's gone. Imagine... Losing your son.'

Fenchurch'd had to, on more than one occasion. And losing his daughter. He knew the way the cogs whirred, the way the gears clicked into place on those thoughts. They didn't give you any peace. 'I'm sorry for your loss.'

'Thank you.' Archer was glancing behind him, into the chaos of the office, like he needed to get back through there to work.

Maybe things were that bad.

'Were you close?'

'As close as he'd allow, yeah.'

'You see each other often?'

A shrug, eyes still on the door. Like he'd left the oven on, or the front door unlocked. 'Once a week, if we were lucky. Course, I wasn't that lucky that often. Months would somehow go past and he hadn't got in touch. Broke my heart, but I'm made of stern stuff, ain't I?' Archer left it hanging. 'He came to me for financial advice, mind. His mother had him fixed up with this firm, but I know them. Know how little they'll grow your capital.'

Clarke perked up. 'So you gave him advice?'

Archer raised his hands. 'Oh no. Not my job, but he just wanted to run some things past me.' He finally took that seat, sitting carefully so he didn't crease his trousers, though ripping was more of a concern given how tight they were. 'My boy insisted on investing half of his money into cryptocurrencies.'

Clarke's puzzled expression made Fenchurch very worried. 'A half?'

'A third to his mum, half to this crypto investment, and he lived on a sixth. Thing is, he was on over a hundred grand a week, so that was still twenty k he was living off. Each week.'

'Has he lost much money?'

'Well, I'd need to have a look at his accounts.'

'He invested with you?'

Archer raised a finger. 'No, his investment manager did. We offer incredibly competitive management fees so we get a lot of business. I was impressed when they came in.'

'How much has he lost?'

'I'm assuming you've got a warrant?'

'Come on, Ollie. We go back a long way. I'm trying to find out what happened to your son here.'

Archer scratched at his chin now. Always something needed scratching. 'I suppose I owe it to his mother to help. Owe it to my lad.'

'What was he invested in? Bitcoin?'

'Nope. That's the one that'll be here for the long-term. That and Etherium. Both tanked but they've got legs. They'll stick at that level for a bit then slowly recover. Whether they'll get back to the previous level is anyone's guess. And I'm betting they will.' Archer grimaced. 'Trouble is, my boy was invested in all sorts of risky stuff that could go to a hundred grand a coin, or to nothing.' He stared at his shoes. 'And a lot has gone to nothing. Most of the coins he's invested in are gone. Like totally wiped out. All that money's lost. So he's got only one holding left. His whole future wrapped up in that. And it's touch and go.'

Fenchurch was struggling to follow. 'I thought this was all decentralised? Like you just needed a string of text on your computer?'

ED JAMES

'We manage it all for them. You've seen that story of the lad in Wales who accidentally chucked a hard drive with like a hundred Bitcoin on it. He's been trying to get approval to search his local tip looking for it. One of our services is managing all that for our investors. And not losing the hard drives the private keys are on.'

'And you did that for Curtis?'

'On behalf of... *Them*.' Archer folded his arms. 'I had the tech side covered.'

'And you needed someone with industry contacts so you could find other footballers to exploit.'

'Excuse me?'

Fenchurch smiled at him. 'Kids like your son. Young and impressionable.'

Archer looked right at Clarke. 'Steve, mate, what's this about?'

Clarke snorted. 'Ollie, we know Curtis was pushing your NFTs to his fans.'

'Well, I could deny it but there are so many videos out there of him doing it.' Archer let his arms fall to his sides. 'You got any kids?'

Fenchurch nodded. 'Girl and a boy.'

'They into football?'

'My daughter less so, but my son's five and a half. His iPad usage is a bit of an issue. He's always watching YouTube videos of Mbappe, Haaland, Salah... And your boy.' Fenchurch winced. 'I got him a West Ham shirt with "Fenchurch 9" on it, but he's grown out of it. For his birthday in November, he wants "Archer 9".'

'Even though he was out for two years?'

'Even though.'

'Nice to have a hero.' Archer was staring at his shoes again. He was definitely grieving in there, but struggled to show it.

176

Any sign of emotion was a sign of weakness in that land. 'Kids are obsessed by players now, rather than clubs. Know what I mean?'

Fenchurch nodded along with that. 'What took you to the club today?'

Archer looked up, frowning. 'The club?'

'You were at the West Ham training complex.'

Archer sighed. 'One of the young lads was getting really stressed about his money. His performances on the pitch will be affected by it.'

'How much had he lost?'

Archer sighed. 'Four million quid.'

'Shit.'

'Yeah. Lot of stress on his shoulders.'

'So why were you there?'

'He'd been trying to get hold of my boy, but only now do I see why he couldn't get hold of him. Wanted to... See what he could do. Needed to shore up his investments and... Well.'

'Did Curtis hook him up with these investments?'

Archer looked at Clarke, then Reed, then Fenchurch again. He swept a hand through his hair. 'Yeah.'

'So you were running the NFTs scheme with your son?'

'Me? Hardly. It was just that one kid. He was stressed about his money, needed something a bit more stable. A lot more. Us.'

'Just supposed to believe that, are we?'

'You should. My boy doesn't want anything to do with me. His mum poisoned him against me.'

'You did leave her when she was pregnant.'

'That what she told you?' Archer laughed. 'Hardly. Candace's old man and his brothers knocked seven bells out of me when they heard what happened. Warned me to keep away from her and the kid. I mean, they blame me but I wasn't the one who forgot to take the pill, was I? I would've loved to have been in his life. And Curtis blames me for what happened.'

'Are you sure this isn't your way of saying Curtis was selling NFTs for you to shore up your failing business?'

'Hardly.' Archer ran his tongue around his mouth. 'Oh, Curtis was pimping them out, but it wasn't for me. He was doing it for this firm based out of Seattle in America. Dodgy bastards, nothing like us.' He looked right at Fenchurch. 'There was someone locally he was working with.'

CHAPTER TWENTY-SIX

Fenchurch pressed the buzzer and waited. Old Kent Road in Elephant and Castle was one of those South London roads that just seemed to exist to let traffic through. Nothing of note on its own. No reason to visit, unless you had to.

'What do you make of that, guv?'

Fenchurch looked around at Reed. 'I don't know. Didn't seem upset that his boy was dead, but... Sounds like he had a rough time of it. Getting the shit kicked out of him by Candace's old man.'

'You actually believe that?'

'Hard to know what to believe, Kay. So many people lie to us. Every case. It's all people seem to do. Everyone is the star in their own film. Everyone needs a villain to blame and nobody takes on that role themselves.' Fenchurch pressed the buzzer again and stepped back until he could see inside the first-floor flat. No signs of life in there. If he was hiding from them, he was doing a great job. 'Wonder if we should try the training ground?'

ED JAMES

'It's probably shut now. Besides, uniform are having a trip up there.'

Fenchurch sighed. 'Well, this is a dead end. Let's head back to the station and regroup.'

'Sure.' Reed looked up and down the street. She stopped at the bottom of the steps. 'Son of a bitch.'

Terry Monaghan was marching up the street, carrying a bag of shopping. He stopped, mouth hanging open. Recognition flickered in his eyes. Two cops, outside his door. He dropped the bag and scarpered down a side lane.

Reed bolted off after him.

Fenchurch set off after her, his knee cracking and grinding. He passed down the narrow lane, barely wide enough for him let alone a car, then he came out into an L-shaped courtyard overlooked by more flats. No signs of an exit. No signs of where Reed or Monaghan had gone.

There was an underpass, a lane cut out beneath the flats, leading back to the main road. Back towards the car.

Fenchurch was useless on foot now. He needed to get back behind the wheel. Find Reed, maybe box Monaghan in somewhere. He jogged over towards the gap. His knee jabbed and he pulled up, grunting in pain. Panting. His head was spinning.

He needed to take the next pill. Kill all that agony.

He felt a burning in the pit of his stomach.

Acid, scratching his throat.

He doubled over and his lunch met the pavement.

He felt so weak, like a day-old kitten.

Couldn't stand up. The loose pebbles on the tarmac scratched his palms.

His heart was pounding in his chest. His smartwatch showed a heart rate of 160.

Too much for him. Way too much.

Shit.

180

All because he'd tried to run.

The oxy would've let him, but he was pushing himself too deeply into withdrawal.

He reached into his pocket for the pill bottle and stared at it.

He had to take another dose.

He just had to.

But he also knew he had to get off them.

He couldn't let what happened to Curtis happen to him.

He couldn't be a junkie cop.

Footsteps, walking towards him. 'Guv?'

Fenchurch pocketed the pill bottle and stood up tall. 'I'm here, Kay.'

'Jesus, guv, are you okay?'

'I'm fine. Just tripped in someone's sick.' Fenchurch shook his head. 'South London, Kay... Absolute animals around here.'

Reed scowled at him. Didn't believe a word of it. 'Well, I lost him.'

'Why was he running?'

'Must be something in this. Pimping out NFTs to young and impressionable kids. Maybe he's making a mint out of it. And maybe he had something to do with Curtis's death.'

CHAPTER TWENTY-SEVEN

Deacon was taking the piss with traffic, hitting at least forty in a twenty. And not an easy twenty. Lots of twists and bends this side of the river, in the old docks and wharves. Not like he was aware he was being tailed – Nelson didn't think so anyway – but that he had a precise rat run through housing that avoided the crippling traffic on the main roads.

And not that Nelson was physically tailing him within eyesight. The GPS tracker was still live, showing him cutting down More London Place at the back of Southwark, lining the Thames. A real dead-end street, though. That old battleship was along there. Schneider Consulting and another Big Five firm were based in bulbous modern offices down there.

Was he meeting someone? A management consultant for a consultation?

Nope.

Deacon stopped outside Southwark Crown Court, next door to the Schneider building. A giant brown blob of brick and concrete, with a long entrance hiding the denizens from the rain that wouldn't come for weeks. He got out and raced inside.

Weird.

Late for court?

Nelson could sit here, wait it out. But what was Deacon up to in there? Was it pertinent to the case?

Plus there was the fact that Younis had been keeping an eye on him. Even meeting him out in Peckham.

Why?

Why have a guardian devil like that?

It was all connected. Just, how?

Only one way to find out.

He drove down the narrow lane. Deacon's car was bumped up onto the pavement.

Nelson parked next to it and followed him inside the court. Not the first time he'd been there, not by a long shot.

Deacon was through security, staring into his phone, then putting it to his ear. That thousand-yard stare of someone listening to it ringing, then leaving a voicemail when really they needed to make the call.

Nelson walked up to the desk. 'What's on today, Chuck?'

The giant American security dude looked down at Nelson. Not many people could do that. 'Jon. Hey. Heard you're not a fed anymore?'

'Nope. News travels fast.'

'Don't it just. Well, take your pick, but it's all speeding fines this afternoon.'

Speeding?

So that's why Deacon was here. And he clearly hadn't learnt his lesson.

'Cheers, Chuck.' Nelson walked up to the security desk and dropped his possessions into the tray. Like being at the airport, but he had much less on him. No carry-on, no laptop or Kindle to get scanned. Keys, phone, wallet, too much change. He stepped up to the reader and waited for the next guy to go through.

Chuck walked over to the guy in front. 'Sir. Defendants go through the other queue.'

The guy turned around and it was like looking into a mirror – a black guy like Nelson, wearing a suit cut like his. Just a bit thinner and a few years younger. And a hell of a lot angrier. Simmering away, though, not exploding.

And Nelson knew him – Dalton Unwin. Criminal defence lawyer, world-class pain in the arse.

Unwin tilted his head to the side. 'Excuse me?'

'I said, defendants go—'

'Sir. I'm a lawyer.'

'Oh. Sorry, I just—'

'You assumed because of my skin colour that I could only be here because I'd committed a crime. Correct?'

'Come on, sir, that's—'

'I'm *outraged*. I'll be speaking to your supervisor.'

'Just because you're outraged doesn't mean you're right. I've been here for thirty years and I'm on a first name basis with all the lawyers that operate in this building. Check your assumptions before you accuse people of racism.'

Unwin looked him up and down, then walked through the reader, where he collected his briefcase and possessions with a sour look on his face.

Nelson gave a sympathetic raise of his eyebrows.

Chuck shrugged. 'Goddamn asshole.'

'Nobody believes a black cop. Or a black lawyer.' He walked through the scanner and didn't get the horrific beep that would lead to a body search. He filled his pockets again and looked around.

Deacon was talking to Unwin.

Nelson was in earshot, so he took his time looking through his wallet, listening. Counting his change, 10p by 10p.

'Why do I have to appear in person, Dalton? That's what I don't get.'

'Because, despite my advice, you refused to pay your speeding fine.'

'This is beyond the bloody pale. I should be able to drive how I like. I'm a doctor!'

'Edwin, you're not the kind of doctor who needs to make a house call to help an old lady out of the bath. Are you?'

'No, but it's the principle of the thing.'

'What, that you expect to be above the law?'

'No. But—'

'Your speeding fine was imposed by the court. You've got nine points on your license. Fifty in a thirty isn't a good look.'

'I'm still not going to pay it.'

'Well, it's been brought to court and they're going to send you to the cells for a day in lieu.'

'They can't—'

'They can. They'll let you out at five.'

'I've got to be somewhere!'

'Relax, Edwin. It's not today. But I'll get you off this. Just don't do it again. Come on.'

Nelson clocked a traffic warden outside, sniffing around Deacon's car. And his. Writing a ticket.

Shit.

He grabbed his stuff, then shot over to the front of the queue back through. 'Sorry, there's a parking ticket going on my car right now.' He squeezed through the doors then ran full tilt out of the court, back into the sunshine.

Nelson slowed when he saw the ticket being written for Deacon's car, not his. Yet. He raced over and got into his car. Started the engine, but took out his notebook and scribbled down a note about the speeding fine and Deacon refusing to pay. Trivial, but maybe there were other transgressions. Some that might be material to the divorce.

And Dalton Unwin. The human rights lawyer...

Nelson smiled at the ticket officer, who was motioning to wind down the window. 'What's up?'

'Gents, you can't park here.'

Gents?

Nelson looked behind him.

Younis was sitting on the back seat, reading the paper. 'Hello, sweet cheeks.' He smiled at the traffic warden. 'Sorry, mate, I've got a hiatus hernia so he's had to drive me here.'

'Well. Don't do it again or I'll give you a ticket.'

'Scout's honour.' Younis watched the warden go, then laughed. 'Honestly, Nelly. You were a shit cop and you make a much worse private eye. Didn't even spot me.'

'Get out.'

Younis folded the paper and set it down beside him. 'I'm not giving you any choice here, you fucking muppet.'

'How did you get in?'

'You didn't lock the bloody door.'

Stupid. 'You're following me?'

'Nelly, I've had people following you for years and you didn't notice. Got to know your enemy, my friend.' Younis leaned forward, his acid breath rasping on Nelson's cheeks. 'Don't think you can turn the tables on me here. Drive. Now.'

Nelson tried to act calm. Looking around. The traffic warden attaching the ticket to Deacon's car. Nobody else around.

How the hell did Younis know he was here?

Nelson had spotted three cars over the last week, all tailing him at various points, standard shifts. They were good. Younis must have ex-cops on his payroll. Younis made so much money, he did what he wanted. Paid them in cash using his dirty money.

But there was nobody here and he hadn't seen them today.

That sick feeling sat like an off steak in his gut, bubbling away. Knowing that his guys were better than him.

'Nelly, are you deaf? I told you to drive. Now fucking drive!'

'Where are we going?'

'You'll just have to find out.'

Nelson set off along the road, taking it extra slow so the pedestrians had a good view of what was going on inside the car.

'First, you're going to stop following my associates or I will fucking kill you and they'll never find the body.'

'Deacon.'

'Deacon. And you should be grateful I'm warning you and not just killing you, Nelly. Keep away from him.'

'Of course.' Nelson knew that he'd be the first person he'd investigate as soon as he was free. His brain started fizzing, thinking he could concoct any number of schemes. Get to know him. Find Younis's weak point.

'Left here.'

Nelson took the turning, heading away from London Bridge and the Shard. 'Where are we going?'

'That's a secret. Next, that client of yours, I need you to stop working for her.'

'Can't do that.'

'Come on, Nelly. I'm doing my best here, but you don't make this easy. She's the wife of Edwin Deacon. Good friend of mine. Stop it. Or else.'

'Why?'

'Nelly. All I'm saying is let their divorce happen naturally. I don't care if you sit there playing *Tetris* on an old Gameboy, just don't give her anything on my client. Yeah?'

What was their connection?

Nelson didn't quite see what, but Deacon was up to something with Younis. Meeting him in Peckham. Why? Why Peckham? He looked around at Younis. 'What's the "or else" here?'

'You don't want to test me, Nelly. If I don't fucking kill you, I will fuck you up. Not physically, but I'll completely ruin your life. And they'll never pin it on me.'

Nelson didn't say anything, just stuck to following the traffic, merciful that it was still flowing, no matter how slowly. Heading towards Tower Bridge.

'Mrs Deacon is a nasty piece of work, Nelly. Her husband's a good friend of mine, sorted out an injury I sustained when I was inside. And that whole thing's on you, so you owe me.'

'Can't do the time...'

Younis laughed. Fenchurch's trick of humouring him... it worked... 'Nelly, you think I'm some kind of animal. Don't you?'

'You are. The number of lives you've ruined.'

'The number I've saved, you mean. I give gainful employment to thousands of people.'

'Dealing drugs isn't gainful.'

'Nelly. Shut up. Your client's antics got her husband into a lot of trouble. Trouble that has a risk of blowing back on me. If it blows back on me, all that stuff about ruining your life?' Younis clicked his teeth. 'Well.'

'What antics?'

'She's your client, Nelly. You should know. But she's got you following her husband around. I've got people following her, meaning they're following you too.'

Nelson looked in the mirrors and tried to spot anyone. He'd been tailed before, had spotted them. But assuming it was true, his people were good.

Wait.

No.

Younis wouldn't have that shift of ex-cops watching him. He was probably deep in his IT equipment. Much cheaper to get into his phone. He'd know where he was at all times.

Nelson needed to bin the current ones. Get brand-new ones. Get a new wi-fi router at home. But that was soon, this was now. He was in danger here. He needed to play this really carefully.

'Course, it's the cops you should be worried about, Nelly. They've got that gun you tried to shoot me with.'

'Not mine.'

'Come on. We both know that's bollocks. Have to say, I thought more of you. You don't have the bollocks to shoot me? I'm a cunt, Nelly. A fucking cunt. I deserve to die. But that's the only chance you'll get.'

'I've got another—'

'No, you don't. I've been through this whole motor, Jon. Pull in here.'

'Here?'

'What I said.'

Nelson did. Left the engine running. He waited for the bullet through the seat. The knife in his neck.

Younis passed a bit of paper through the gap. 'Have a little look at this address in about an hour.'

'What is this?'

The door clicked and Younis was gone, walking down the street in his long jacket, despite the weather.

Nelson unfolded the paper, but didn't read it.

If he went there, what was he going to find?

Part of him knew he was being set up, but the rest of him knew he had to go.

CHAPTER TWENTY-EIGHT

Reed shot out of the car. 'I'll see you inside.' She ran across the car park towards the station.

What the hell was up with her?

Fenchurch sat in the driver's seat, struggling to bear his pain. His knee was throbbing almost as badly as his head. He needed to get inside, take one of those pills. Just one. That'd tide him over. Numb the pain.

Christ, the getting inside part felt like climbing Everest.

He managed to stand up on one leg, then rested the other foot down on the ground. Felt stable enough. Right. Now to walk. He set off, slower than his old man with a skinful inside him. Left, right, left, right.

There. Not too hard.

'You okay there, chief?' Tom Carling was standing in the smoking shelter, sucking on an untipped cigarette.

'Tom.' Fenchurch walked over and rested against the frame, trying to look subtle but completely failing. 'I'm fine.'

'Cool. Cool, cool, cool.' Carling exhaled deeply. 'Had Steve

THE LAST THING TO DIE

Clarke's DS on the blower, like you asked. Went over what they have on BRO.'

'And?'

'Well, if someone's pimping out NFTs to kids, BRO aren't involved. Certainly not directly.'

'Steve agree with that?'

'Backs them up totally.'

Well, that would've been too neat. 'Was there a sign that Curtis was involved?'

'We know he was. Seventeen separate videos on YouTube. A hundred or so tweets. Similar on Instagram. Did a School-book Movies thing too.'

'Who's been going over his social media?'

'Susan. Over a million followers on Twitter and Instagram. Not all of them were bots.'

'And he was using that to advertise these NFTs?'

'Not technically advertising. But if you ask me, the kid probably thought his career's going to be over so needs whatever he can get. If it involved pimping out dodgy investments to his fans, then damn right he's going to, right?'

'Does Steve's guy have any idea who was directly involved?'

Carling took another long drag. 'Jolly Roger's World of Pirates. They reckon it's run by a business in Seattle. Neoxis Industries, Inc.'

'Why do they only reckon?'

'This is what's dodgy about crypto. The ledgers are open, but there's so much grifting goes on around the sides.'

'So they're not legit?'

'Oh no, they are. Or seem to be. American sports are much more innovative. And exploitative. But this Neoxis Industries are running a scheme, that's for sure. They've recruited a lot of British footballers to sell pirate cartoons. A few ex-pros have been getting stuck in too. Images of each player drawn as a pirate. Curtis Archer was Redbeard, for instance. Only thirty images, each one unique. The players don't understand the tech or the risk, but they all love the money.' Carling scratched at his stubble. The guy needed another full shave at half past five. 'And their fans definitely don't.' Another drag on his cigarette. 'But Curtis's old man is possibly involved.'

'He told us he's not.'

Carling rolled his eyes as he exhaled. 'You believe him?'

'Fair point.' Fenchurch felt a deep ache in his knee. 'Okay, can you dig into this whole thing with Clarke's lot? See if you can connect Oliver Archer to this Jolly Roger thing?'

'DS Bridge has been taking the lead on that.'

Fenchurch held his gaze. 'Can you get someone else?'

'Why?'

Because you're a handsy pervert who I can't trust. 'Just find someone else, Tom.'

'But she's got a perfect skill fit. Degree in computer science. Four years working the City police before joining the Met as a DS.' Carling smirked. 'Don't you trust her?'

'Oh, I trust her.'

'That mean you don't trust me?'

'That's right. I don't.'

'Charming.' Carling laughed. 'Well. I was a bit upset you didn't take me to BRO Capital.'

'You know them?'

'One of the managers turned up dead in Borough Market a few months ago.'

'You catch who did it?'

'Oh, of course. But the thing is, we had to figure out precisely why he'd been killed. That was the tough bit.'

'Some crypto scheme?'

'I wish. But we had to explore that to find out why he'd

been killed.' Carling sucked down a fresh drag. 'He was shagging his cleaner. Hungarian girl. Her boyfriend found out.'

'Was he Hungarian?'

'Nah, he was from Watford. Didn't take it well.'

'Well, if you can—'

'Sir?' Bridge was scuttling across the car park. 'There you are.'

'Lisa, I need you to work with Tom here.'

She smiled politely at Carling. 'Sir, I've tried calling you.'

Fenchurch checked his phone. Sure enough, three missed calls from her and the sodding ringer was off. 'Sorry. What's up?'

'I've set up a video call with Curtis's girlfriend. Wondered if you wanted to sit in on it?'

CHAPTER TWENTY-NINE

The video conference suite was on the station's top floor and had a great view of a brick wall six feet away.

Fenchurch swallowed down a pill with a drink of ice-cold water. Glorious. The jolt of cold cleared his head a bit. He smoothed out his notebook but couldn't really focus on anything he'd written. The timeline seemed to curve back on itself.

'You okay, sir?' Bridge was at the door, carrying two clear cups of water.

'I'm fine. Just struggling to make sense of this case, that's all.'

She rested one in front of him, then sat next to him. 'It's a strange one.' She fiddled with the remote and the TV lit up. Just a waiting screen, the service's logo in the middle of the screen. 'Some of the team think Curtis was murdered.'

'Do you?'

'Not sure.' She took a sip of water. 'You?'

'I'm beginning to see that it's more and more possible he

was. And we're finding more and more suspects, Lisa. Someone at the club. His mother. His father. Anyone he pimped a dodgy NFT investment to. Anyone he potentially encouraged to pimp out dodgy NFTs. And Terry Monaghan was the last person to see him, and he ran away from me and DI Reed. Weird stuff going on here, Lisa. And none of it makes sense.'

Bridge nodded. Didn't say anything.

'You okay there?'

She smiled, but it was thin. 'I'm fine.'

'Is this about me asking you to work with Carling?'

'No.'

'Come on, is it?'

She sighed. 'Look, I've heard that he's handsy.'

'I've heard that too, but I've not seen. That's the trouble. Nobody has any evidence.'

'He's very clever like that, sir. Waits until his victims are alone.'

Fenchurch felt that stinging pain in his gut. He didn't know what to do. He didn't want a dodgy cop on his team, but he wanted him to get a fair crack of the whip. Maybe someone who had an axe to grind started spreading rumours. But this was all under his watch now and he needed to know, conclusively. 'Look, what do you want me to do about this?'

'What?'

'Well, it's a rotten situation for everyone involved. You've got the particular skills and experience I need to get Steve Clarke's lot working for me, rather than against me. I could get someone else—'

'No. It's my task. I've got the experience, like you say. I worked there for a bit. I'll work with Tom.'

'I could get someone else instead of him?'

'But he's tight with DI Clarke, sir. It'll hamper any investigation.'

She was right.

Fenchurch let out a sigh. 'Are you okay?'

'Well, it's hard not to feel... em.... slighted that you're not sticking up for me.'

'Lisa, I know what to do officially, of course I do, but allegations like that cut a huge wake in an officer's career.' Fenchurch raised a finger. 'But if Tom's dodgy, I want him gone. For good. I want him to pay the price for what he's done. If he's not, then I want these whispers to stop.'

'And if he's dodgy but careful?'

Which seemed to be the case. Fenchurch scratched at his neck, thinking it through. 'Look, how about I get that Manc lad from Uzma's team to work with him?'

'No, I said I'll do it, so I'll do it. It's only a rumour and if people listened to rumours, you wouldn't have a team.'

'What do you mean?'

'I'm winding you up, sir. I'll work with him.'

'Okay, but make sure there's another cop with you at all times.'

'Jesus, that's...' She seemed to shiver. Goosebumps rode up her bare arms. 'That's not cool. Is it?'

'No, it's not. I'd rather you didn't have to put up with it, but if he's not to be trusted, I don't want him overstepping any mark. Engagement ring or not.'

Hers was glittering under the spotlight. 'Some men don't even notice the ring. Others see it as a challenge.'

'How's Jon—'

The screen erupted with a notification:

Incoming call...

Bridge hit a button on the remote and the screen filled with a video, shaking and wobbling like it was taken with a hand-held phone. Someone's living room, maybe.

Even in green makeup, Casey Bosch had one of those faces – Fenchurch knew her from somewhere, but couldn't place it. Probably some shit Chloe had been watching on Netflix when she still stayed with them. 'Hey guys. Sorry about my skin. I'm in Australia filming a Marvel movie. Can't say which one, but this green stuff takes hours to apply. I've been up for hours already.'

Bridge was grinning at her. 'I'm guessing it's something Hulk-related.'

'Oh God, no. I auditioned for She-Hulk but they turned me down. This came from that so I'm hella grateful. And it's a good role. Five-movie deal rather than just one show.'

'Wow, that's cool.'

'Super cool.' Casey leaned forward onto her elbows. It looked like she was in a kitchen, but it must be a trailer on set. All wooden surfaces. An exercise bike sat behind her. 'So, uh, I heard about Curtis.' She swallowed hard.

'I'm sorry to have to do this so soon.'

'Well. It's tough. I loved him. Like, *really* loved him, but things were tough between us. They were *always* tough between us.'

Bridge gave a sympathetic smile. 'How did you guys meet?'

Casey frowned. 'When I was filming *Shot*. A lot of it was on location in the Highlands, in the castles and glens and lochs.' Her Midwest accent slipped into a very passable Scottish one. 'Most of it was shot at Pinewood Studios near London, though. We met at a party, one weekend, and just hit it off. Our relationship's been over for six months now. Haven't heard from Curtis in that time. It's so sad. My heart was broken into tiny pieces.'

'If you don't mind me asking, was it you who broke things off?'

'Um. Yeah, but... It's a long story.'

'It's okay, we've got time.'

'Not sure I do... I'm due on set soon.' She sighed. 'Look. He was going through a real tough time. Constantly worried about money.'

'In what way?'

'About running out of it. Obsessed about it. Kept going to the bank to get a statement. Every night at midnight.'

'How did that make you feel?'

'It was weird. He always had tons of cash in there. He earned tons. And I mean, *tons*. Even by movie-star standards. He made way more bank than me. And his money was all invested.'

'He ever talk about the investments?'

'Not to me.'

'Never mention any specific worries about them?'

'No. But his injury was making him angry and depressed, I think. He hadn't played for over a year. He couldn't run because he was in constant pain.'

'He take anything for that?'

'He was taking something. Don't know what.'

'Was it oxycodone?'

'I don't know. Why?'

Bridge glanced at Fenchurch. 'We found a lot of it in his blood.'

'Shit. You're kidding me?'

'No.'

'I lost an uncle to that shit. Back home. He... Uh... He overdosed. Nobody found him for two weeks.'

'I'm sorry to hear that.' Bridge left a pause. 'Did you ever see him taking anything?'

'No. But we weren't joined at the hip. I mean, I was up in Tain and Ullapool for, like, two months, then on a soundstage down here for eighteen-hour shoots. We didn't get a lot of time together.'

'So you didn't see him with any pills?'

'Well. He was taking *something*. Could've been whatever you guys call Tylenol or Advil over here. Could've been oxy. I just don't know.'

'Casey, why did you break up?'

She gave her movie-star smile, intimate and real-looking. Designed to dazzle and deflect. 'It's a long story.'

'Was it because of the drugs?'

'No. God, no. I didn't know he was on that shit.'

Bridge snorted. 'Okay. Casey, Curtis died of a heart attack.'

Casey clasped a hand over her mouth. Eyes wide. 'Oh my God.'

'We think it was partly exacerbated by his drug addiction. But it could also be from covid.'

'Right, he had that when I was seeing him. He told me to keep away.' She shook her head. 'Turns out *I'd* given *him* it. So he got super angry. Bringing that into his home.'

'How angry?'

'Like, *super* angry. Shouting. Screaming. I've never seen anything like it.'

'This was in person?'

'We both had it, so it wasn't like either of us would catch it. A lot of soccer players hadn't had a vaccine. He was one of them, so he got it super bad. I was, like, bad, but he was *bad*. Almost called an ambulance. He could barely breathe. His oxygen was like seventy-eight percent? But he got over it.'

'Was that why he ended it?'

'No. We made up after that.'

'So what was it?'

Casey stared at something to the side. 'I've got to get on set.'

'Casey, this is important. It's possible he was killed.'

'Shit.' She shut her eyes, clamping them tight. 'If you must know... Curtis found out I was having an affair with someone.'

'Who?'

'It's none of your business.'

'It's potentially material to our—'

'I'm not going to say.'

'Casey, he's dead.' Bridge's words rattled around the empty room. 'He was chased by someone. His lungs were compromised. Put a strain on his heart. I'm worried it could be this guy who did it. Maybe Curtis went after him in a rage. Maybe he got more than he bargained for.'

'I can't say.'

'Casey, was it a woman?'

'What?'

'It's okay if it was. I won't judge. I understand that the media might—'

'No. God no. It wasn't a woman. It was a man.'

'Okay, so who was it?'

Casey stared at the space in front of her, thousands of miles away. 'Okay...'

CHAPTER THIRTY

The training ground car park was much quieter now. A vintage Daimler parked right by the entrance to the sprawling complex, and a couple of sports cars further over. A stack of boxes teetered by the door, flanked by two giant pot plants and the security guard from before, hands on his hips, shaking his head.

'Wait here, Kay.' Fenchurch got out of the car. His knee managed to handle it. Thank God for oxycodone, eh?

Even at this time, someone was kicking a football. Then another. Must be two of them at it, practising free kicks and long passes from any angle on the pitch until they were pure instinct. That cliché – last to leave training – explained two of the sports cars.

The other was a white Toyota, flash but not on the scale of the other two, and branded with 'Guthrie's Cars' and 'Jack Walsh'.

So he was still around.

Sure enough, Walsh was struggling across the tarmac,

carrying two cardboard boxes in front of him. Looked like he'd drop them at any second.

'Here.' Fenchurch took the top one.

Walsh frowned at him, then nodded. 'Alright.' He stormed over towards his car, moving more freely now. He dumped the box into the boot, then grabbed Fenchurch's one back and shoved it in on top. Walsh tried to shut the boot but the parcel shelf blocked it. He tore it out and tossed it on the back seat. He tried to get past, back towards the building.

Fenchurch blocked him. 'What's up?'

'Need to get on.'

'Well, I need a word.'

'It'll have to wait.' Walsh waved a hand over to the training building. 'That prick sacked me.'

'Sacked you?'

'Yeah. Absolute joke. I've been here *years* and I'll make him so much money, but was he prepared to invest in the future? Was he fuck.'

'What did you do?'

'Fuck all.' Walsh shook his head. 'Absolutely fuck all.' He stared back at the training complex. 'Honestly, this geezer... He bought out Gold and Sullivan last May, but he doesn't appreciate what he's got here, what I bring to the table. I've been bringing through lots of young kids from around East London, Essex, Kent, you name it. Local lads. Raising them in the West Ham way.'

'Jack, you played for Charlton.'

'Yeah, but I was a West Ham boy, through and through. Cut my veins and they bleed claret and blue.' Walsh smirked. 'And that's the Irons' colours, not bloody Villa. Or Burnley. Lesser clubs, you know? Without an identity.'

'Did he say why—'

'They want to bring in the lad who used to be at Chelsea.

It's a totally different approach to what I was doing. This new shower talk about doing things the West Ham way, but this place is going to be full of bloody Africans and South Americans.'

Fenchurch heard the dog whistle – Walsh was a racist. Or a bigot. 'Football's a global game, Jack.'

'Yeah, I get it. Thing is, only two of the first team squad are lads who came up from the youth setup. They aren't exactly sparrow-eating Cockneys born a mile from the ground. A Geordie and a half-Irish lad from bloody Bristol.'

'What difference does it make to the club if your lads come from Buenos Aires or Bridge of Allan, so long as they're top-drawer talent?'

'A huge one. Where's the cultural fit in that? Where's the continuity? Where's the community? This is just going to be a disaster.'

Fenchurch kept his silence for now, but his ears were pricked for more dog whistling. The fact that Curtis Archer was a local lad from a mile or two down the road was one thing – the colour of his skin was another entirely. 'I'm very sorry, Jack. Must be heartbreaking to lose your job like that.'

'Absolutely crushing.'

'You know a lot about heartbreak, don't you?'

'Eh?'

'Breaking hearts, more than having yours broken.'

'What are you talking about?'

Fenchurch held his gaze, eyebrows raised. 'Casey Bosch.'

'Who?'

'Come on, Jack. You must remember her. The actress.' Fenchurch knew how to play a guy like Jack Walsh. He added a leery grin. 'Punching above your weight there, mate.'

'Oh. Yeah.' Walsh ran his hand through his hair. 'Bit more than sleeping with her. She was in love with me.'

'Sure.'

'I'm serious.' Walsh gave a coy grin. 'She said she wanted a real man, not her kid of a boyfriend.'

'Even though you're old enough to be her father.'

'Mate, I've exploited daddy issues my whole life.'

Fenchurch laughed, but his stomach clenched. 'Soon it'll be grandaddy issues.'

'Harsh.' Walsh laughing. 'But fair.'

'So you were seeing her for a while?'

'Yeah, but it was just a bit of fun for me. You know?'

'I know, yeah.'

'Met her at this club do. She was doing a bit of acting for the end-of-season DVD. Can't believe they still make them, but the fans lap 'em up. Back in February, so we had no idea whether we'd make Europe or finish eleventh, twelfth. Anyway, the bubbly was flowing afterwards. We got chatting.' He was staring into space. 'Had a lot of fun with her. That show she's in on Netflix, *Shot Through the Heart*, she's even worse behaved in real life than Margaret in that.'

'Oh?'

'Oh God, yeah. Like, I'm a man of the world, or at least I thought I was, but she's shown me things. Unbelievable.'

'Actually, I believe it. And I know how these things draw unintended consequences.'

'What's that supposed to mean?'

'People get hurt. People like Curtis Archer.'

Walsh looked down at his trainers. 'Right.'

'You broke up her relationship with Curtis Archer.'

'If you say so.'

'I know so. Didn't think to mention it when I spoke to you earlier?'

'Had put it out of my mind.'

Yeah, that was how he coped. Everything was compartmentalised. Boxed away. And those boxes were taped shut and shoved in a locked room, never to be opened again.

'Casey ever talk about Curtis?'

'I'm a man of action, mate. No time to talk. I just do.' Walsh stood up tall with another sigh. 'Now, I need to get on.' He made to get past Fenchurch again.

'No, you don't.'

'Mate, I really do. Got to clear out of the grace-and-favour pad by Monday and find myself a new gaff.' Walsh booted the car's tyres. 'Got to take this back to the dealer too.'

'Jack, did you have anything to do with Curtis's death?'

'Me?' Walsh laughed. 'Mate, I haven't spoken to the kid in ages. And that's the truth.'

'Seems a bit funny how you were sleeping with his ex. Kid blames you for the love of his life leaving you. Comes at you. You're a tough guy; things go too far. He runs off, you follow. He dies.'

'Mate, that's bollocks. He pegged it this morning, right? If you want to know where I was, I was dropping a bird off back at hers.'

'And she can vouch for you?'

'Can. Whether she will is another matter. But you're barking up the wrong tree here, sunshine. Me and Curtis made amends after that.'

'Just got to take your word for it, yeah?'

'You cops...' Walsh stepped closer, fists clenched. 'You want to know what really happened to Curtis? A little bird told me he was here yesterday, speaking to the new owner. About getting his contract paid up early.'

CHAPTER THIRTY-ONE

Football training complexes should smell of grass and sweat, maybe that stuff they used to polish the boots or the stuff that made them waterproof. Instead, it was like duty-free at the airport, a fug of perfumes all mixed together. All the lads on TV carried their giant wash bags into the stadiums, stuffed full of hair gel and aftershaves. Changed days from a splash of Old Spice after the session, followed by eighteen pints of lager and two portions of fish and chips, all run off the next day.

Stairs used to be so easy. Used to be able to run up them, two at a time, sometimes three. Now, Fenchurch could only do it one step at a time. Left foot, right foot, then up, same again. And he needed to grip the handrail. Still, he was a stubborn bastard and taking the lift for less than four flights was admitting defeat.

He stopped at the landing halfway up to catch his breath.

Through the window, Jack Walsh was carrying two pot plants across the car park. Kept having to stop to get a breather. Those things were heavier than they looked, not to mention the pots filled with soil. He was too proud to leave one and go back for it.

Nice to see that Fenchurch wasn't the only one struggling.

'Guv...'

'I'm fine, Kay.'

'I wish you'd take the lift.'

'I'm injured, not decrepit.' Fenchurch stared at Reed, concern riven on her face. 'Look, this meeting sounds fishy to me. Can you speak to his agent? See what he knows?'

'Guv, I think I should be here with you.'

'Kay, this is going to be easy. I'll be back down those stairs before you've finished your call.'

'I wouldn't bet on it.' She sighed. 'Fine.' Then scurried off at a speed Fenchurch could only dream of.

After his operation, he'd be doing that again.

He grabbed the handle and started hauling himself up once more. He even managed to take adjacent steps a couple of times.

Most people would expect the stadium to be where the owners' offices were, but the players were only there every second Saturday, give or take. Now West Ham were in Europe they played there more frequently, but the players were here every day. So the chairman had an office overlooking the main training pitch.

Glass bricks ran along the corridor, down the length of the office, obscuring what was inside, but not hiding the music playing. Early Prodigy, from their novelty rave days before they got all edgy and spiky.

Fenchurch knocked on the door.

Chairman

RyOB

Wasn't that a range of power tools?

The music turned down. Then off.

'Come in.'

Fenchurch opened the door. Place was like a posh hotel lobby. Sofas filled with too many cushions. Meeting area. Desk over the far side with a baby-blue iMac.

'Hey.' A lean guy stood on a gym mat, wearing short shorts and a vest, exposing a torso so hairy he might have been confused with a giant ape. Sculpted body, curling some free weights to boost both biceps. Trimmed beard, American teeth that shone like floodlights. Hard to guess his age, could be anything from thirty to fifty. 'Ryan O'Brien. Friends call me RyOB.' His accent was halfway between East London and Miami. 'How can I help?'

'Mr O'Brien, I'm DCI Simon Fenchurch.' He held out his warrant card but O'Brien didn't look at it.

'Proud of you, man.' More curls. O'Brien was grimacing, but it was hard to tell if it was from the exercise or what he was looking at – not the panoramic view of the almost-empty training pitch, but the giant TV that showed the car park.

Jack Walsh was carrying another box full of stuff over to his car.

O'Brien glanced over at Fenchurch. 'Heard you were at my old firm today?'

'Huh?'

O'Brien smiled. 'I'm the R in BRO.' He frowned. 'Well, I was. Guess I still am – nobody wants to work for BO Capital, do they.'

'BRO is a bit on the nose.'

'That's true.' O'Brien laughed, then dropped the dumb bells onto the mat. Sweat was glistening all over his body. He grabbed a rope and started skipping. 'Sold my stake to an anti-Putin Russian.' Fwip, fwip. 'Good guy, but it's probably why the others are toiling.' Fwip, fwip, fwip. 'Nobody looks at the anti-Putin bit, or the fact his son was poisoned and his daughter's in a gulag.' Fwip, fwip. 'They'll get hit with sanctions. And the crypto market is crashing. Poor guys.'

'But you got out while the going was good?'

'Damn right. I hated that business. Couldn't sleep, just kept worrying all the time. Made my money from YouTube. Got in at the right time. Doing videos of just shit. Pranks, wind-ups. Then pivoted to game streaming and the kids lapped it up. I made like a hundred million quid just from that and... some ancillary activities. Enough to invest and boy, did it pay off. Big time. Seems like I sold at the peak, or as near as damn it, and I'm a multi-billionaire. And not on paper either.'

'Congratulations.'

'My former business partners aren't anymore.' O'Brien wasn't losing any breath as he skipped. 'Focus right now is on investing that capital in real-world assets. Property and, well, buying West Ham. Doesn't give me the sweats like owning a vast number of cryptocurrencies does. Got a plan to make this lot worth over two billion in five years. Get into the Champions League and stay there.'

Fenchurch smirked. 'Well, I'm a Hammer myself, so I'd love to see that.'

'Hey, good to meet a fan.' O'Brien looked over without losing stride. Fwip, fwip. 'You a season ticket holder?'

'Have been for... Too long.'

'We're not that bad, are we?'

'No, I was a young man when I first signed up and now I'm an old git with a buggered knee. And my old man's thinking of not renewing his season ticket, even though we're doing well on the pitch, all because we're not at the Boleyn Ground anymore.'

'We'll do a lot better at the new ground, you mark my

words.' Fwip, fwip, fwip. 'And if he gives it up, he might not get it back. Got big plans for this club. Lot of people will be wanting to see us from all over the world.'

'Hope you can fulfil on those plans.'

O'Brien dropped the rope. Then dropped himself down onto his hands and feet, pushing through some very slow press-ups where his nose touched the mat and he held the position before rising back up slowly. 'What brings you into my office, DCI Fenchurch?'

'Understand you had Curtis Archer in here yesterday?'

'Sure. That punk was here.'

'Care to tell me why?'

'What have you heard?'

'That he wanted his contract paid in full early.'

'And I wonder who told you that.' O'Brien vaulted up to standing, then started squatting, watching Jack Walsh dump another box onto the back seat of his car on the screen. The pot plants were wedged along the middle. 'Why would a confidential club matter be an issue for the police?'

'We've got wind of Mr Archer being in financial difficulty.'

'Bloody police state.' O'Brien twisted and raised his left hand up, then twisted and did the mirror image. 'Listen, I invited him in. This was my meeting.'

That didn't tally with Walsh's story. Then again, Walsh was a man with an axe to grind, rightly or wrongly, and causing mischief was a good way to do that.

'Offered to give him half the value remaining on his contract to end the deal now. Fairly standard in, uh, situations like that, where a dude's been injured a long time. Meant he could get a move to America, Turkey, or wherever. It'd be less money, sure, but he'd effectively be earning double, or twice at the same time. If you follow my drift.'

'I do. He'd get half the cash up front and have an income from his new club.'

'Exactamundo. And that would be worth more than half his current deal, so he'd be up on the whole thing.'

'What was his agent saying about it?'

'Wasn't here.'

'Seriously?'

'Curtis Archer is a shark. Or he can be. He took the meeting without his agent. Came in here, sat down on that couch, said he wanted his contract paid up in full. Wouldn't listen. I told him to speak to his agent, he said no way. So I said I'd see him in court.'

'Why's that?'

'Because he wouldn't see sense. Wouldn't listen. Started threatening me, saying he's got a contract. We should honour it by paying it up.'

'And he wouldn't accept half?'

'Nope. No compromise. Kid wanted it all.'

That seemed a bit strange to Fenchurch. Surely if he was in the shit, he'd need whatever cash he could get. Unless he was so deeply in the hole that he needed the full amount. Millions of pounds.

'And you don't want to pay the contract in full?'

'Correct.'

'Why's that?'

'You'll know about his injuries. He's never going to be the same player he was. Not even half that.'

'Gather you don't have him insured?'

'Where did you hear that?'

'Around.'

'Well, it's bullshit. Trouble is, the insurer wouldn't touch all of his contract. Only paid about forty percent of the amount, while he wasn't playing.'

'So why did you say you'd see him in court?'

'Thing is, I've got a deal with him. I hold his registration until 2028. While he's not playing, I'm on the hook for his salary. I was trying to offer him an out that'd be mutually beneficial.'

'But?'

'What forced my hand was I've heard his agent's been cooking up a transfer to a couple of Turkish sides. So they're trying to get the money now and get another big signing-on fee.'

'But?'

'I won't see a dime of that. I told the kid if he wants that deal to happen, it's half of the remaining term now, plus a transfer fee for any deal. Ten million, say, would repay a lot of the lost wages and, more importantly, he'd be off my books.'

'But he refused that?'

'Outright. Just demanded the full amount now.' O'Brien bounced up from his deep squat, then sat down and started crunching his abs, hands clasped together in front of him. 'What of it, anyway?'

'Curtis was found dead this morning.'

O'Brien collapsed back, arms flopping by his sides and smacking off the mat. 'Shit, really?'

'Really. You hadn't heard?'

'It's... It's been a day.'

Fenchurch updated his suspects list. Maybe O'Brien wasn't the chief suspect, but certainly his motive was becoming much more concrete. 'How much was he on here? Two hundred grand a week?'

'At West Ham? Hardly.' O'Brien laughed. 'A hundred. It was the old mob who arranged it, so I'd need to check the exact amount and terms, but I know a lot of it was performance-based. Him sitting at home means he's not earning half of that.'

'I thought a finance guy like you would be all over this?'

'Sorry. Not at my best today, hence me only training now. Always need to do a full workout when I get het up about shit.'

'Like Curtis?'

'God, no. That's the stuff I live for. Staring someone down over a deal.' He was twisting to the side in a way Fenchurch hadn't been able to move in a long time. 'No, I had to let someone go today.'

'Jack Walsh, right?'

'Right.'

'I get why you did it.'

'Thank you. I hope you'll be speaking to him in a formal capacity.'

Fenchurch frowned. 'Excuse me?'

'Well. After what he did.'

'You fired him so you could replace him with someone from Chelsea.'

'That's what he said?' O'Brien laughed, bitter and sharp. 'That bloody nonce.'

'What do you mean by that?'

'Well, my daughter's sixteen, so he's technically not a nonce, but—'

'He was—'

'I was about to approve a spend of a hundred million on a serious upgrade to this place at his behest. Came in with a plan that looked good. He'd become the director of football here, we'd develop young talent we could bring into the team or sell on. And he's fucking my *daughter*?'

That wasn't what Fenchurch had expected.

'Someone caught him with her in his office. Can you imagine?'

Fenchurch could. 'It must be difficult.'

'Damn right it was. Talk about a cliché...' O'Brien pushed himself up to standing. 'When I came in, I spoke to all the staff. I'd heard about what Jack was up to in a hotel a few years back. I asked him and he said categorically no. He didn't fuck around. That wasn't him. Now I saw with my own eyes what a lying arsehole he is.'

Fenchurch had stepped into another pile of dog shit here. Murky Jack Walsh shit that was tied up with this case. 'I understand you firing him for—'

'Listen, if you could report this to the nonce squad, I'd appreciate it.'

'Sir, I think you should be with your daughter just now.'

'Yeah, pull the other one. Jadzia's not going to speak to me again, not after that. She fucking ran off.'

'Is she okay?'

'Mother's taking her round Harrod's.' O'Brien shook his head. 'See what a prick like Jack Walsh does? He fucks girls and women, then drops them. Makes them feel like shit. Just for a little bit of how's your father. She's only just turned six-fuck-ing-teen!

'I can help, but the report needs to come from your daughter.'

'Thank you.' O'Brien leaned in close, spraying Fenchurch with sweat. 'Thing with that prick is, after I spoke to Curtis in here, that punk was speaking to Jack bloody Walsh about something.'

'Do you know what?'

'Stitching me up, no doubt. The guy's a monster.'

Fenchurch had a better idea. Contact with the man who'd ended his relationship. Yeah, there was something there. 'Thank you, I'll be in touch.' He stormed over to the door, his knee twanging like a bass guitar string, and got out his phone in the corridor. 'Kay, is Walsh still there?'

'Eh, hang on. Let me see.'

'Stop him leaving!'

CHAPTER THIRTY-TWO

'Simon, Simon, Simon.' Bell slammed the door behind him. 'When I said you were good at handling high-profile cases, arresting the West Ham academy director wasn't what I had in mind in terms of keeping this all on the down low.'

Fenchurch hid behind his coffee mug. Tempted to toss the hot liquid over his face or smash it and stab the prick with the shards. 'Walsh hasn't been arrested. He came willingly. Just waiting on his lawyer to show up.'

'All the same, he's a figure with some profile.'

Fenchurch set his mug down and hobbled over to the door, slamming it with a loud thwack. 'Sir, I'm managing this case, so please keep your beak out of it until I come to you asking for help.'

Bell stood there, wide-eyed.

'Once I've got him in a room, I'll tear his story apart. Find out why he was talking to Curtis Archer. Find out the truth about O'Brien's daughter.'

'Do you believe it?'

'Don't know what to believe, sir. Everyone's lying to us. Everyone. And if Walsh has been sleeping with the owner's daughter, it's such a cliché – but then Jack Walsh is a walking cliché.'

Bell was frowning. Just stood there, saying nothing.

Fenchurch sat behind his desk and took a long slug of tea.

'Are you okay, Simon?'

'I'm fine.'

'After our earlier chat, I have to admit to being a tad concerned about you.'

'I'm okay.'

'You're sweating.'

And so are you. 'Just the heat, sir. It's August in London.'

'Well.' Bell collapsed into the chair opposite and looked around the office with a sour expression on his face, like he was sucking lemons. And hated lemons. 'The Acting Commissioner is pleased with how it's going so far. My work in establishing a coherent media strategy, for instance, is bearing real fruit.'

'In what way?'

'We're on all of the main news sites. Alerts on Facebook, Twitter, Instagram, TikTok, Schoolbook, you name it. BBC and Sky are leading with it on the hour. Getting traction in America.'

'And how much of that has yielded any leads?'

Bell didn't have an answer for that. He sat there, hands on his lap, palms facing upwards. 'I need to ask you why were you out at the club.'

'Investigating his death, sir.'

'But Sky have you and DI Reed in the background as they reported on the first day of training.'

'That was earlier, sir.'

'Wait, you've been there twice?'

'Right. We spoke to Ryan O'Brien... The club owner. He'd been seen chatting to Curtis at the training ground. There's a lot of money to be made or lost from Curtis's contract. DI Reed is with his agent just now, trying to figure out why the hell the player was there on his own.'

'Why not you?'

'Because I trust Kay.'

'Okay. Simon. Do you think Walsh killed him?'

'I certainly think it's possible, sir.'

'So you believe this is a murder?'

'I am keeping an open mind on that front. I've got the feeling deep in my gut that this is a murder. Too many people have benefited financially from his career. His parents, the club, Jack bloody Walsh. Everyone except for Curtis Archer himself. Kid was almost out of cash thanks to his stupid investments.'

'Eh?'

Fenchurch sighed. 'Curtis lost a lot of his money from speculating on cryptocurrencies.'

Bell nodded along with that. 'I myself have dabbled in crypto, but I got out before it collapsed. Luckily. Enough to buy a holiday home in Wales.'

'Alright for some.'

'Got to get out while the going's good. But you can't be serious. This isn't a murder.'

'I am, serious. Curtis might've been plied with oxycodone and he didn't even know he was on it.'

'You think he was poisoned?'

'That's the long and short of it, yes. Someone went into his property and cleared out any sign of the drugs Curtis was clearly on. That's suspicious in and of itself. But it raises the possibility that might mean he didn't know he was on anything.'

'Wasn't that his mother who cleaned the place?'

'It is, and she made all his meals. His father... Maybe someone at the club. They all have motives.'

Bell let out a deep breath. 'I still think you're expending a lot of man hours on a long shot.'

'We still don't know who took Curtis's key fob.'

'What about this light-fingered paramedic?'

'Good question. I don't think he could've killed him.'

'No, but could he have stolen the key fob?'

'He could've done, but he was on duty from before Curtis's death until pretty much the time we arrested him, which was after Mick Clooney's team had been around. So he didn't have any opportunity to go there and clean up.'

'Okay. With you now. Could be he handed it to someone?'

'Could be, but that's an even longer shot, sir.'

'True.'

Bell smirked. 'This is a bit beyond Jack Walsh, don't you think?'

'What do you mean?'

'Well. I'm a season ticket holder at the Valley so I saw him play for Charlton many times. Walsh was stupid. Incredibly stupid. And I mean thick. One time, I heard the ref speak to him after a bad tackle. Gave him a long warning and said "off you go". Jack took that to mean he'd been sent off. The manager had to run into the dressing room to fetch him back onto the pitch.'

'What's your point, sir?'

'I just don't believe, if this is a murder case, that Jack Walsh is behind it.'

'I get that. I'm trying not to exclude the possibility, sir. If Curtis's heart had exploded when he was out for a run, I'd buy that. Possible covid damage, depleted respiratory system, and so on. But he was being chased, sir. We've got witnesses.'

'But chased by Jack Walsh?'

'Lots of connections to Walsh, sir. Walsh had an affair with his ex-girlfriend.'

'On top of all that stuff he was up to at that hotel? Where does he get the energy from?'

'I suspect it's a deep-rooted need for love, sir. He talked to me about exploiting daddy issues. I think he's got mummy issues at the heart of it. Or something similar. A need to feel loved by a woman. But he's the one who breaks it off, so he feels in control.'

'My, that's impressive psychological work.'

Fenchurch ignored it. 'I could buy it.'

'What about the street kids who reported it?'

'That's a good point. Let's just see.' Fenchurch hauled himself up to standing, then walked over to the door.

'Simon, where are you going?'

'Come on, sir. Let's see what's what with those kids.' Fenchurch limped along the corridor, each step feeling like it took a day off his life. Maybe a week. The one thing he needed, other than another pill, was Bell off his back.

'Your knee doesn't look good.'

'It's fine, sir. Just a bit stiff.' Fenchurch pushed through the incident room door.

The place smelled of stale armpits and staler coffee. The pot in the corner was spitting. Thing was a fire hazard – no matter how many times he binned one of those machines and told people to get coffee from the canteen, one magically reappeared. Probably the same bloody one, belching out thick tar.

Bridge and Carling were by the machine, drinking coffee.

'Si.' Carling was all smiles. 'Heard about Jack Walsh. Dirty bugger.'

Bridge was scowling at Carling.

Fenchurch made eye contact with her, mouthing, 'OK?'

She nodded, short and curt so nobody else would see.

But Fenchurch wasn't too relaxed or reassured.

Carling lifted the coffee pot. 'Can I get you one?'

'We're both fine.' Bell stepped towards them, smiling and nodding. 'Tom.'

'Sir.' Carling topped up his own mug. 'So, Si, what brings you into the lion's den?'

'These kids who found him. You're pulling together the timeline, right?'

'Correct. Trouble is, we're drawing a blank on some of the concrete details for the timeline.'

'In what way?'

'Well. Their stories are all over the place.'

'In the sense that one of them could've taken Curtis's key fob?'

'Possibly. But...' Carling frowned. 'No, the two uniforms who were first attending saw the big guy, Jamie I think it is, helping Curtis. We've got their body-worn video. At no point did he appear to take anything, let alone a key fob.'

'There was a gap from his call, wasn't there?'

'Not very long. They were responding to an incident on Queen Vic Street up at the top. Was only about a minute between the call and them arriving. And they got there before him.'

Bridge was nodding. 'Besides, Jamie was with my officers all morning and didn't pass anything to anyone. So if you're looking for who cleared out the flat? It wasn't him.'

'Okay.' Bell smiled. 'And the paramedic?'

Carling went through his notebook. 'Full confession from him, sir. There were cops with him at the crime scene at all times and their body-worn video checks out.'

Bridge was frowning. 'Besides, they didn't find a key fob. So unless it was spilled by accident... Anyway. And Jon Wardle doesn't have it.'

Bell sniffed. 'You honestly believe a junkie?'

She shrugged. 'Thing is, he was full and frank about taking a two grand ring off his finger. And the phone. He would've mentioned the key, don't you think?'

Bell nodded. 'But, Tom, please make sure your guys are leaning on the paramedic.'

'Sir, they're DI Reed's—'

'I'm asking you to make sure.'

'Sir.'

'So there's probably someone else who did it – find them.' Bell swept across the room. 'I'll be in touch, Simon.'

'On it, sir.' At least Bridge waited until Bell had turned his back to roll her eyes.

The door clicked shut.

Fenchurch let out a held breath. 'Well. That's us told.' And his ploy had worked – the illusion of activity had got Bell off his back.

Carling raised his eyebrows. 'That guy is such a—'

'Prick?'

'No! Force of nature. He gets shit done. You can see why he's got where he has.'

Only because you could see Bell's feet sticking out of any senior officer's rear end...

'You really can.' Fenchurch clamped his shoulder. 'Can one of you get someone to ritually destroy that coffee machine before it burns down the building? Swear that thing is cursed.'

Bridge walked over to it. 'On it, sir.'

The door clattered open.

Fenchurch looked over, expecting Bell again.

It was Reed. 'Walsh's lawyer's here.'

CHAPTER THIRTY-THREE

'Simon...' Dalton Unwin shook a hand like a car door would. 'Pleased to see you again.'

Fenchurch took his paw back, resisting the urge to check for bruising. That would come later. Talk about dominating tactics and mind games. 'Thank you for coming in to represent your client.' He smiled like he meant it.

Behind it, he was sweating in a cold room. His watch showed his heart rate over a hundred. From doing nothing. He was in withdrawal. Shit. He couldn't handle this.

'Not a problem. All part of the job.'

'Been a while, Dalton. How are you doing?'

'I'm well, thank you.' Unwin splayed his jacket and sat down. 'I must say, it's unusual for a client to be interviewed by someone of your rank.'

'Very unusual case, sir.' Fenchurch was still smiling. 'High-profile death. Lots of money at stake. Means we are forced to put a lot onto it. Not that we don't for people with nothing, but a lot more attention from the media makes it much harder to run a case.'

'I totally understand that.' Unwin finally returned the smile. 'Now, Mr Walsh and I have had a discussion and it's in his best interests to be as open as possible. No question is off-limits. We both want him walking out of here a free man in an hour's time.'

'Sure. We all do. If he's innocent.' Fenchurch nodded at Reed. 'Please start the recording.'

She started talking and Fenchurch tuned her out – words he'd heard a thousand times a year – and instead focused on Walsh's body language.

A man who was used to being king of his manor, ruling whatever roost he was in, be it a football pitch or a dressing room. Pulling whatever alpha male bollocks he needed to push himself up the pecking order.

But this was Fenchurch's domain and Walsh seemed to shrink in on himself. Head bowed, staring at the desk. Lips constantly twisting into a pout. Whatever he was thinking, it was giving him a lot of turmoil.

Reed splayed her hands on the table and focused on Walsh. 'Jack, how about we start with you lying about why you were sacked by West Ham.'

Walsh looked up and to the side. 'Lying?'

She nodded. 'You told my colleague you had your contract terminated because of a disagreement in the vision for the club's youth development.'

'I mean, that's right.'

'Is it? Because Mr O'Brien said he was going to spend many millions of pounds on redeveloping the training complex to your design? Going to make you director of football?'

Walsh shrugged.

'For the purposes of the recording, is that a denial?'

'That fucking prick sacked me.'

Reed was nodding. 'That's the bit everyone agrees on. It's why that seems to be the sticking point.'

Walsh sat back and folded his arms. Gnawed at his bottom lip. Then shook his head, eyes shut.

Arrogance.

Denial.

'Mr Walsh, why was your employment terminated?'

Another shrug.

'You do know that you're a suspect in a potential murder case, right?'

Walsh snorted. 'I ain't killed anyone.'

'But you've been lying about things. You have a plausible motive for murdering Curtis Archer. You have unexplained movements.'

'A second.' Unwin smiled at Reed, then leaned in to whisper, 'Jack. You're doing yourself no favours here. Remember what we talked about?'

Walsh frowned.

'Transparent honesty, Jack.'

'Transparent honesty.' Walsh sat back and stared up at the ceiling. His Adam's apple bobbed up and down. He swallowed. 'Okay...' He looked at Reed, eyelids flickering like candles in a strong draught. 'It's been incredibly hard to admit to myself, but I've got a problem. I'm addicted to having sex. To the pursuit of sex. It's something I've had therapy for, but it's a continual affliction.' He looked Fenchurch right in the eyes. 'The reason I was fired from West Ham was because I was caught having sex with the owner's daughter.' He leaned forward, resting on his elbows, legs jigging. 'I'm a cliché. The number of times you hear of lads who've done the same thing... None of them hit the press, do they? Injunctions and superinjunctions. This will, though, being a bloody murder investigation.'

'We can make sure this stays locked up tight.' Reed held his gaze until he looked away. 'Nobody has to know, Jack. But we need the full truth here.'

'The full truth... Right.' Walsh dragged his hand down his face. He was sweating, giant beads dripping like rain on a drainpipe. 'Thing is, Jadzia was hanging around the place a lot. Even when her old man wasn't there.'

'Jadzia?'

'Jadzia O'Brien.' Walsh nodded. 'She'd be speaking to the lads and she was a real flirt. Because of my condition, I kept well away from her. But one day, she tried it on with me. I pushed back. Couldn't help myself. I'm like an alcoholic drinking zero percent beer. It's still the same taste, the same habit. Soon I'll be on half a percent. Then a half-pint shandy. Then someone will buy me a lager top by mistake and away we go. And that's what happened. I just slipped back into it.'

Reed was nodding along. 'Thank you for your candour.'

'Do you think I deserved to get fired for this?'

Reed shrugged. 'It's nothing to do with me. It's a matter between you and your employer. It's a private business, so what he says goes.'

Walsh was shaking his head.

'Do you believe you should've been fired?'

'No!'

She frowned. 'But you've got to admit that having sexual relations with a girl that age means you shouldn't be in charge of—'

'Eh? Those are *boys*! I'm not gay!'

'It doesn't matter. You're entrusted with their—'

'Of course it does!' Walsh barked out a laugh. 'Jesus Christ, you think I'm some kind of nonce, don't you?'

'Well, how old was she when you met her?'

Walsh looked away. 'She started it. Not me.'

'I'm assuming she was over the age of—'

'Jadzia's sixteen. I've not committed a crime. You brought me in here to ask me questions about having consensual sex with a woman?' Walsh laughed. 'No wonder people want to defund the police.'

'Those people are genuine victims, Mr Walsh. You're someone who's—' Fenchurch stopped. This bloody brain fog was stopping him seeing the wood for the trees. 'Actually, Jack, with you being a coach, and someone senior in the organisation, you could be deemed a "person in a position of trust or authority" over her, which then raises the age of consent to eighteen.'

'What?'

'Say Jadzia meets a guy in a bar. He could legally have sex with her. But a doctor, a teacher, a pastor, a cop or a person with whom she has a relationship of dependency could not.'

Walsh was sweating hard now. 'Listen to me. There's no dirt here. I'm an addict who's had a moment of weakness. For what little I did, I've lost my job. Unfairly in my view. I'll pay that price for the rest of my life, because all these mugs talk, don't they? I'll be blackballed. But I'll work with my therapist to become stronger for it.'

'Okay.'

'Listen, are you going to let me go or are you going to charge me here?' Walsh scraped back his chair and stood up. 'Because I've got to find myself a bleeding house by Monday and take my motor back to the garage.'

Reed gave a curt smile, then turned the page in her notebook. 'You were seen speaking to Curtis Archer yesterday.'

Walsh frowned. 'Was I?'

'You omitted this from our discussion earlier.'

'Not yesterday, darling.'

'You were seen talking to him. What did you discuss?'

Walsh sat down again and looked at his lawyer. Unwin was a wall, unreadable. He looked back at Reed. 'Now you mention it, I think I might've nodded at him, asked how he was. Made a joke about him not scoring anymore.'

'Nothing to do with you having sex with his ex-girlfriend?'

Walsh laughed. 'You're *obsessed*, darling.' He rubbed at his nose. 'And I discussed that matter with your boss here. Casey's what made me seek help for my condition. Casey told me, about how she'd seen... it in acting. That made me seek help.. Football and acting, same sort of industry. All about image. They pay big bucks for youth. Lots of exploitation. Lots of fame people struggle to handle. I didn't handle it well. That tendency to show off, made me bugger my back as a kid.'

'Jack. You ruined Curtis's relationship.'

'I feel really bad about that. But Casey... She did what she did.'

'Sure that didn't make Curtis come after you?'

Walsh shut his eyes. 'He'd be fucking entitled to. I'm a scumbag. I'm a sex addict. I shag all these birds. Over and over again.' He brushed away tears. 'Even that word is loaded. Birds. Women. They are women, but I treat them as objects. And it's robbed me of love. Of happiness. I couldn't find a woman who loved me, I just exploited weaknesses in ones I met.'

The door flew open. 'Simon.'

Fenchurch swung around.

Bell was standing there, eyes wide, thumbing behind him into the corridor.

Fenchurch got up. 'Pause it, Kay.' He left the room and took one last look at Walsh, sitting there, fingers on his nose, tears streaming down his cheeks. 'I appreciate how hard this must be to open up about, Mr Walsh. I'm glad you're getting the help you need.'

Walsh was staring into space.

Fenchurch left the room.

'Simon, you need to let him go.'

'Sir, we've not—'

'Jack Walsh is a broken man who's lost everything. You're chasing down this lost cause here, and I don't like it. This long shot of yours is getting longer and longer. If the best you've got is Jack Walsh did it, you've got nothing. Correct?'

Walsh was a pathetic man. Curtis's love for Casey Bosch was collateral damage in his race to the bottom. To numbing his own pain. At least he was now getting help for it.

'Fine.'

'Good man.' Bell smiled at Fenchurch then opened the interview room door. 'Kay, can you show Mr Walsh out?'

Fenchurch stepped away. His watch rumbled with a reminder – he needed to take another pill. He was losing track of how long he was going to space the drugs out for.

Walsh walked out into the corridor, bawling his eyes out. He looked at Fenchurch, clenched his jaw, then let Reed walk him on, head bowed.

'Dalton.' Bell grinned at Unwin. 'Been a while.'

'Well, of course.' Unwin clamped his brutal handshake on him. 'You're too important to deal with actual crimes. Statistics and spreadsheets now, yes?'

'You cheeky so and so.' Bell pinched his cheek. 'I'll see you around, Dalton.'

'We should get lunch soon.'

'Definitely.' Bell watched Unwin jog down the corridor after his client, then focused on Fenchurch. 'Do you still think Walsh could've killed him?'

'No, but...' Fenchurch blew air up his face. He didn't know what to think. What was up or down. Just juggled the pill bottle in his pocket. He rubbed at his nose. He got out his hanky and blew. Didn't clear anything and the thickness in his head was getting worse. Right at the front, like his nose was being pushed into his brain.

Bell stepped back. 'Simon, have you got Covid?'

'No, sir.' Fenchurch put his hanky away but his nose was like a knackered tap. 'I tested negative this morning.'

'Are you still testing negative, though?' Bell grabbed his arm and pointed down the corridor. 'Get yourself home, Simon. You don't look at all well.'

'I'm fine.' Fenchurch tried to shake him off, but the whole corridor swayed around. He stumbled over, bounced off the wall and went down. Felt like his knee had been sawn off. He swallowed down a scream.

Bell grabbed his wrist and hauled him up to his feet with astonishing power. 'Simon, get yourself home!'

CHAPTER THIRTY-FOUR

Windows down, Nelson sat there like a guy waiting to pick up his girlfriend. Borough Market bustling around, the smells of Lebanese, Mexican, Thai and American cuisines mixing with the pie and mash stall nearby. Tunes playing. Bit of SUGARMAN on the radio, the new single with Kanyif Iqbal, both of them keeping it old school. Trying to calm himself down.

Nelson was so over this. Since he'd left the police, waiting in a car had been how he'd spent most days.

All day.

Every day.

Younis.

He should've killed him when he had the chance this morning.

He'd frozen.

If they traced that zip gun back to Nelson...

Or back to Jenny...

He did another scan of the vicinity. Nobody around, nobody watching him.

Such a bad idea.

He looked at Younis's piece of paper.

He was in the right place.

Almost the right time.

This was a trap.

Had to be.

Nelson had tried to kill Younis.

This was Younis's way of getting back at Nelly.

Jesus, he hated that name.

Younis had to be framing him for something. Some drugs shit that would fuck Nelson up. Hit him where he'd tried to do the most good.

Maybe taking a rap for something one of Younis's guys had done.

A murder.

Anything.

He should leave. Get out of there. Protect himself. Ignore Younis.

Lisa was right – they were starting a family, his second one. He had to focus on that.

Nelson twisted the key in the ignition and the engine growled.

A car pulled up next to him. A Travis, covered in the new signage.

Marie Deacon got out and smiled at the driver. She looked around the street like she was being watched. Tall and elegant, dressed in a stripy blue and white dress, clutching a leather bag. She knocked on the door and waited, checking her phone. She didn't notice Nelson. A sharp sigh, then she got back into the Travis and it shot off.

Nelson followed it at a distance, passing around the maze of South London at the foothills of the Shard. Onto Borough Street, just as it became London Bridge.

Marie walked into the pub, while the car stayed there.

The Barrowboy and Banker.

Nelson knew it from the dim and distant, a previous life before he joined the police. Old-school pub with glass windows so you could see inside.

Nelson's angle made it hard to see much in there. Not the bar, just the corniced ceiling.

There she was.

Marie Deacon.

She sat in a seat by the window opposite a man, someone Nelson recognised but couldn't place. Not the guy who'd knocked on her door that morning. They were frosty. Not lovers. Not friends. Maybe colleagues. Or ex-lovers.

He was doing all of the talking. Quick, like he was hurrying to convey a message.

She was just listening. Not looking at him.

Then a woman came over and said something. Younger, much longer hair, much heavier makeup.

Marie got up and pecked the man on the cheek. Gave the other woman a smile and pat on the arm, then walked off.

Nelson lost sight of her until she emerged from the far entrance, passing through a few lads lurking by the door, smoking and vaping, all laughing and not looking at their phones.

She got back in the Travis and it drove off.

This had to be it.

Younis had warned him off her, but now this?

Was he testing him?

How the hell did he know she'd be there?

Did he want him to follow her?

Sod it.

Nelson drove off. If nothing else, this would prove to Waheed that he was actually doing his job.

He had to do a wild U-turn to follow, but a bus blocked most of the view, so he figured he'd got away with it.

The flow was good for this time of night so he followed them along the road, windows down, SUGARMAN and Kanyif Iqbal still his companions. Just a dude out for a drive, listening to hip-hop.

Left at Borough Tube, down Great Dover Street. A road with post-war brick flats on either side. No character. Trees, mature and covering the road. Not even trimmed back by passing buses.

The Travis stopped at the lights outside the Roebuck, a pub Nelson had always fancied the look of but had never visited. Two cars between them.

Then they were off again, past some shops on the right and student accommodation for Southwark Uni, and they pulled up at the lights guarding the Bricklayers Arms roundabout.

Left would be back to Marie's home, to that part of Shoreditch that had recovered its Victorian grandeur.

The car set off and they headed on towards Elephant and Castle.

Back to the address...

Weird. Where was she going?

The car pulled up outside a Domino's Pizza and Marie got out. Not the worst area in South London, but far from the best. And not the sort of place where Marie Deacon belonged.

Nelson pulled up across the road, half a street back.

She pressed a flat buzzer. A nice building, but rundown. She waited, fussing with her hair. Then she tried again.

No reply.

She opened her bag and pulled out a key, then let herself inside.

This was weird.

THE LAST THING TO DIE

She'd met a guy. Got spooked by a woman. Come here and had a key to get inside.

And had come here, to the address Younis had given him. In advance.

A light flicked on upstairs. The window was open to a crack, curtains drawn behind it.

Nelson felt like someone was tickling his shoulders. Shivers ran up his arms.

A scream burst out of the open window.

Shit.

Did someone have her?

Nelson got out of the car and darted across the road. The street door was wedged open – did she do that? – and he got inside.

Up two flights of stairs at full pelt, then into the flat on the right.

Quiet.

If she'd been attacked, someone could be in there.

Fuck.

If only he had that zip gun on him.

Sod it.

He stepped in, everything tensed. 'Hello?'

'Oh my God.' A murmur from the left, the room facing the street. Dark in there.

Nelson walked in. 'Hello? Are you okay?'

Marie was hovering over a man.

He lay on his back, mouth hanging open, white foam dribbling out. Skin slack and thin.

'Shit.' Nelson got out his phone and hit 999.

CHAPTER THIRTY-FIVE

Fenchurch tossed his keys in the bowl. 'Honey, I'm
home.'

No response.

Abi was probably out.

He limped through the flat, itching for another pill, but
knowing he needed to push it back. He stepped into the
kitchen, set his phone on to charge and washed his hands.

The stack of covid tests was wedged between the
microwave and the fridge. He set about tearing at the package,
then started assembling the test. Ready. Here goes. He
swabbed at his throat, feeling like he was going to gag. No
matter how many times he did this – every morning and every
night – it never felt anything less than an invasion. He popped
the swab into the tube then mixed it. Two drops onto the test.

More waiting.

Great.

He felt okay. Just... Thick-headed. Heavy. Like he needed
more painkillers. Not covid-y but with all these variants and
sub-variants, who knew?

Lights on in the living room, though.

He popped his head in.

Abi was curled up on the sofa, legs under her, Kindle in her hand. Didn't look up.

Al lay on the rug in the middle of the floor, his iPad propped up in front of him, watching some football videos at full blast – the crowd noise was like waves at the seaside.

'There you are.'

Now she looked over. 'You going to come and have a seat?'

'Doing my test.'

'Well, you don't have to stand over there while you wait.'

'I'm okay standing here.'

'You're not symptomatic, are you?'

'Well, kind of.'

'Simon, if you've got symptoms, we've all got it now. Come over here.'

'Sure?'

'Sure.'

Fenchurch walked over and sat next to Abi on the sofa.

'Hey you.' She reached over to kiss him on the cheek. 'Do you honestly think you've got it?'

'Always worry I've got it.' Fenchurch smiled at her. 'But I think it's... for other reasons. Anyway. How was your day, love?'

She looked over her reading specs with *that* look. 'Challenging.'

'Oh? School?'

She shook her head then nodded at the floor. 'Had to explain to someone about their hero.'

Fenchurch could now see he was watching Curtis Archer videos on his iPad. 'Oh, right.'

'Yeah. Right.' She locked the Kindle and set it down. 'Doesn't understand that he's unalive, as the kids say. Can't process it.'

'That why he's up so late?'

'Tried putting him to bed, but he won't go.'

'Meltdown?'

'More a major tantrum.'

The joys of having a six-year-old when you were getting on a bit. His sister had been much easier, but they were both in their twenties. He got up with a crunch, then leaned over and tapped Al on the back.

The boy swung around, frowning. Then laughed. 'Daddy!' He ran over and smothered himself all over Fenchurch.

'Hey there, tiger. You okay?'

'I'm sad, Daddy.'

'Oh, why?'

'Mum said Curtis died.'

'That's right, son.'

The boy didn't seem to understand and hugged into his old man.

Fenchurch sat there for a while.

The iPad blared away. Onscreen, Curtis Archer hit a scissors kick against Man City in slow motion – that jump off the ground, that swivel to catch the ball at the top of its arc – then it cut off to a dummy he did against Liverpool. Didn't show the fact his scissors kick blazed into row Z or that West Ham lost 6-0.

In Fenchurch's day, landfill indie soundtracked the goal of the month. Now, there were countless highlight videos all set to the worst possible dance music.

He tapped Al's side. 'Bedtime, sonny.'

'Daaaad!'

'Come on. You know the rules.'

'Just a little bit more.' Al squeezed his fingers until they were almost touching. 'Just a teensy bit?'

'You've already had it.'

'Pleeeeeease.'

Fenchurch's head was thumping so he was in no mood for this. 'Come on, scamp.' He picked him up and put him over his shoulder.

'Daaaaaaaadddddeeeeeeeeeeeee!'

Fenchurch just about made it through to his bedroom without falling over. Had to brace himself against the door frame, then set his son down. 'Come on, Al. Off to bed, son.'

'Don't want to.'

'You'll feel bad at school in the morning, okay?'

'But Dad...' He looked like he was going to punch something. Then he stared up at his father. 'Did Curtis really die?'

Fenchurch would love to crouch down to his level, but that wasn't happening. 'I'm afraid so.'

'But he's my hero, Dad.'

'I know. It's sad, but you've got all those memories of him. That time me and your sister and your granddad took you to see him.'

Al stuck out his lip. 'Will I really never see him again?'

'There's all those videos you can watch.' Fenchurch winked at him. 'And a little birdie tells me we'll be signing a replacement pretty soon.'

'Who?

'Georgiev.'

Al's mouth hung open. 'Wow!'

'Now, you go and brush your teeth.'

'Done.' He beamed wide. 'Mummy let me stay up another five minutes if I did it all myself.'

Probably half an hour ago...

'Okay, well you get yourself to bed and Mummy will come and read you a story.'

'But I want Daddy!'

'I'll be through soon, okay?' Fenchurch kissed his head and nudged him on his way. He stayed in the doorway, making sure he did get changed for bed. Kid was a handful at times, but he was getting on with things. Growing up a month for every day. Or at least it felt like it.

Abi joined him, wrapping her arm around his back. 'I miss Chloe living with us.'

Fenchurch couldn't look at her. This used to be Chloe's bedroom. Then... it happened. And it was just Abi here, and this was a spare room, a room she'd filled with broken typewriters, spending her empty evenings refurbishing them for people, while Fenchurch hunted for their missing daughter. Both driven apart by their unprocessed grief.

Now it was their son's room. A second chance for them both.

'Weird how much time we missed with her. Now she's living with her flatmates and we don't see her.' Abi leaned back against the door, hiding from their son. 'I haven't heard from her in a while.'

Fenchurch watched Al slip on his West Ham pyjama top backwards. He'd figure it. 'I saw her for lunch on Friday.'

'Oh. Do you do that often?'

'Couple of times a week.'

'Hard not to take that personally.'

'Well, we work in the same station, whereas you're up in Walthamstow.'

Abi nibbled at her fingernails. 'Are things okay between you?'

'Good, yeah.'

'I'm pleased. For you both.' She brushed her hair back. 'I did what I did and she won't forgive me. After all we've been through...'

'Ab, she'll come around. In time. I've been trying to—URGH.' Pain screamed up his thigh. His knee was throbbing.

'Are you okay?'

He couldn't catch his breath. What was it Pratt said about lung damage? 'I'm fine.' Jesus, he wasn't. He tried to shake it off, but the pain just got worse.

'Kay's worried about you.'

'*I'm* worried about me.'

'Simon, what's going on?'

'Well, you know how I've been taking oxy for this knee?'

'And?'

Fenchurch nodded into the room. 'His hero, Curtis Archer... I'm investigating his death. Looks like it might be a result of him being on oxy. Same dose as me.'

'Jesus Christ.'

'I'm coming off it.'

'You're not going cold turkey, are you?'

He looked away.

'Jesus, Simon!'

'I'm not, but I'm reducing it. I spoke to a doctor. It's all fine. Called tapering. I've been okay. I'll *be* okay. Just got to get through this until my op, Ab. I'll be fine. We'll be fine.'

She pursed her lips, thinking it all through, then walked away through to the kitchen. He hated it when she didn't voice the thoughts. Just left him fearing the worst.

Fenchurch's watch stabbed at his wrist.

Was the time up for his test?

No, his heart rate was spiking.

Time for another pill.

He pushed through into the bathroom and locked the door. Alone. Going an extra half an hour had been tough, but then he'd pushed it to an hour. Stupid. Bloody stupid.

This is what hell would feel like.

And it was all he could think about. He was sweating. Even fell over in the station in front of Bell.

He felt like he was underwater.

Fuck, he *was* an addict.

Any excuse to take a pill.

Only one way to beat this.

He opened the bottle and held them over the toilet. Ready to tip them in, flush the rest of them down the pan. The whole bottle. The whole prescription.

He couldn't.

Abi was right. Cold turkey would destroy him.

He needed to be on his A-game.

'Simon!'

Fenchurch opened the door. 'What's up?'

'You left Al on his own!'

The boy was standing with his pyjamas on back to front.

'I'm sorry, love. I—'

Fenchurch's phone blasted out from the kitchen.

Abi had her hands on her hips. 'You go and get that, I'll sort him out.'

Fenchurch wanted to stay, but the sound of the phone itself was scratching at his brain. He walked through to the kitchen, grabbed it and answered without looking. 'Fenchurch.'

'Simon, it's Jason.' Bell. Great. 'How are you?'

He checked his Covid test. Just the single control line. Not even a faint smudge.

He let out a breath, but the deeper realisation hit – he was feeling like shit because he was reducing the oxy.

'I'm okay, sir. It's not covid.'

'Okay. Are you fit for duty?'

'Depends, sir. What do you need me to do?'

'Well, I need you to attend a crime scene.'

'Text me the address. I'll see you soon.' He hung up and walked back through. 'Sorry, love. I've got a call out. Can you read Al his story?'

'I want Daddy to!'

CHAPTER THIRTY-SIX

Fenchurch looked around the flat, his Tyvek suit crinkling. The open window was letting in a breeze. A welcome one. His goggles were all misted up from the sweat. He was a furnace someone had just shoved more logs into. Dark outside, but still nowhere near cool enough for him. 'Well, we're going to get our arses kicked for this.'

Terry Monaghan lay on his back, facing up. His mouth open, showing those missing teeth. White foam had dried on his cheeks. Eyes wide, full of surprise.

Bell was next to him. Somehow he was able to crouch low. 'We didn't have anyone posted here?'

Fenchurch shook his head now. He was sweating, despite swallowing a pill. 'We just wanted to speak to him, sir. He saw us and ran. No reason to stick guards on his door.'

'Why did he do that?'

'I presume it'll be connected to why he's dead, sir.'

'Less of that, please.' Bell stood up tall, a good few inches shorter than Fenchurch. 'Why did you want to speak to him?'

'Because he'd been arranging for young footballers to

promote an NFT scheme. Pay them money, they tweet or post on Instagram to their followers, get sales of these cartoon pirates they're selling.'

'I see. Well, it's not a crime, I suppose.' Bell didn't seem impressed. 'I need you to speak to whoever is involved in this.'

Oliver Archer. Ryan O'Brien.

'On it, sir.' Fenchurch scanned around the room, taking his time. Clooney's team were working away. Analysing and cataloguing. Typical bachelor pad. Living room and kitchen in one place. Mess everywhere. No sign the cooker or the crockery in the cupboards had ever been used. Takeaway cartons filled the sink. Might find a new form of life in there, but unlikely to get anything pinning down what happened to him.

A figure crouched by the body, the suit swelling around the neck. 'Om pom tiddly om pom.' Dr Pratt was working away, oblivious to them. 'Tiddly-oh, tiddly-om, pom pom pom.'

'William, what's your take on this?'

Pratt looked up, bloodshot eyes peering through his goggles. 'Why are you looking at me?' He was shouting. 'Sorry.' He reached up and tapped at his ear. 'I just received these in-ear headphones, which are marvellous inventions. Listening to Brahms while I work is how I handle things. Being able to listen to the same music at a crime scene? It's *invigorating*.'

'I'm pleased for you.' Bell tilted his head towards the body. 'So? How's it looking?'

'It appears the victim died as a result of—'

'Hang on.' Fenchurch felt himself frown. 'Victim?'

'Well, yes. He was clearly murdered.'

Fenchurch shared a look with Bell. News to both of them. 'It's not an OD?'

'Yes. It is.'

'So how can it be murder *and* an OD?'

'Because he overdosed as a result of someone stuffing twenty-four transdermal patches of fentanyl down his throat.'

Fenchurch felt all the air escape, like he'd been punched.

Fentanyl?

Christ.

The step up from the oxy, if things got too much for him. Hundred times more potent than morphine.

'If he didn't suffocate from his airway being full of patches, that much fentanyl would be fatal almost instantly.' Pratt scratched at his beard. 'Excellent way to kill someone. No messing about.'

'How do you know he didn't take them himself?'

'Because his wrists are bound together.'

Fenchurch spotted the black cable ties digging into dead flesh. 'Couldn't he have—'

'I suppose he could've done that to himself *after* he took them to prevent getting help.' Pratt was frowning through his goggles, wisps of beard hair trapped up by his eyes. 'But no. The scratch marks around his lips, the bruising on his throat... It all suggests someone coerced him into this. Forced him to swallow it all down.'

'It's not—'

'It's possible the suffocation killed him, of course, but I think it bears all the hallmarks of an overdose. They held his mouth shut while they waited for the patches to do their business. I need to get him onto the slab and excavate deep inside to figure it all out, naturally, but either way, it's clear that someone's killed him. And done a dreadfully bad job of it.'

Fenchurch tried playing it all through and nothing made sense. Monaghan had a connection to Curtis Archer. Both played for the same club at the same time, though Monaghan moved on. They were involved in the scam to promote NFTs.

Did any of the suspects for Curtis's death fit Monaghan? Hard to see any.

'How long ago did this happen?'

'Oh... The sheer volume of drugs... Plus there are fresh track marks on his arms, so he could've been injected too...' Pratt pressed a glove against his skin, then tilted his head back and forth. 'I'd say this looks like at least two hours.'

Not long after he'd run from them. Must've returned and been attacked.

'Thanks, William.' Bell walked over to the flat door and crossed into the hallway, then tore off his mask and goggles. 'Well, we've got another dead footballer. I'm going back to the Yard to report this up to the top. Simon, I need you to find out who killed him. I'm counting on you, okay? We're all counting on you.'

CHAPTER THIRTY-SEVEN

Fenchurch stepped out into the street and felt like a horrible sweaty mess. His head was throbbing, his gut was churning, his heart was racing and he should be at home. Should be reading his son a bedtime story.

And he had another dead body. One with a profile that would keep him up for the whole night.

Just perfect.

People milled around the street. The Domino's next door was doing a decent trade to bystanders, all standing around watching and eating pizza like this was street theatre.

Inside the cordon, various cops paired off with witnesses.

Two of his better officers were speaking to a woman in a stripy blue dress. Uzma Ashkani and DS Dan Baxindale, a male officer over six five tall but stooping so he was barely Fenchurch's height.

Two of Carling's lot were speaking to Jon Nelson. Inglis was the female sergeant's name. Wasn't it?

It'd been a long time. Too long.

Fenchurch walked over to Uzma. 'Can I have a word?'

'Sure thing, sir.' Uzma stayed there, fists on her hips. 'Sir, this is Marie. She found the body.'

'This is DCI Simon Fenchurch. He's the Senior Investigating Officer on this case.'

'Okay.' She wasn't making eye contact with anyone.

Fenchurch waited until she looked at him then held her gaze. 'It must've been a shock when you found his body.'

Poor woman looked like she'd been turned inside out and not put back together in the same way. Her eyes were black smudges. 'Thank you.'

'Do you know the deceased?'

She nodded.

'How did you get inside?'

'I have a key to the property.' She ran her fingers along the bottom of her eyes, trying to restore some stability to her makeup. 'I've been feeding his cat when he's away.'

Fenchurch frowned. 'I don't believe there were any animals in the property.'

'No, Nippy passed away a few months ago.'

'I'm sorry about that.'

'He was a lovely old thing.'

'Do you know if Mr Monaghan had been taking any prescription medication?'

'We're barely friends. Acquaintances, really. Listen, a mutual friend asked me to pop around and see him. He hadn't heard from Terry in a while and he knew I had a key.'

'Who's that friend?'

Marie was crying. Tears streaming down her cheeks.

Fenchurch exchanged a look with Uzma. They both gave her space. 'Marie, is there something you'd like to tell us?'

She wheeled around, facing away from them now. Head bowed. 'Jesus Christ.' She swung back around, sniffing. 'It... It was more than that. We were... We were in love. I've been seeing Terry since I left my husband. Edwin. He's a doctor.'

Shit. This wasn't a good thing. 'Edwin Deacon?'

'You know him?'

'In passing.' Fenchurch tried to keep calm. 'You've divorced him?'

'I... I found out my husband was using prostitutes. It was over long before then, but that was when I knew. You know? When I knew I couldn't keep living that lie. Pretending I was happy. He didn't want me to leave. So I've hired a private investigator to find what I can on him.'

Nelson.

This was getting stranger and stranger.

'I met Terry through a friend. It was... He was what I needed at the time. Someone younger. Full of fun. Not boring. He didn't want to go to the *opera*. We went to the pub instead. To the football. For walks. To the gym. We had fun. We laughed.'

'But?'

'I found out he was on fentanyl and it broke me.' She shook her head. 'My husband was involved in prescribing drugs, but Terry was taking it illegally. Buying it off the street.' She sighed. 'This evening, I met that friend, the man we met each other through. He had a message for me. Said he'd given Terry some fentanyl.'

'He sold him it?'

She shook her head. 'Coerced him to supply it. And he regretted it. Said Terry was in a bad way. Terry had been clean for so long. And I...'

'Who was this?'

'I had to find out. Had to see him. And I... I discovered him like that.' She stared at Fenchurch. 'Suicide. Who does that to someone else? Sending a message like that? Luring them to see that? It's cowardice!'

Fenchurch held her gaze. 'No, that's not on you. If it was suicide, it's not your fault. He's angry at you. He's angry at the world. It sounds like you did what you could for him, but you left when it became too much. Addicts are only interested in their next hit. It's not your fault what happened.'

Or that it was likely a murder...

She seemed to take some solace from that.

'Who was it gave him the fentanyl?'

'I'm not... I can't... I made a promise.'

Fenchurch nodded at Uzma. 'Look after her, okay?'

'Sure thing, sir.'

Fenchurch leaned in close. 'And get her to identify this dealer.' He walked over and nodded at the other lead, DS Inglis. 'Mind if I step in here?'

'Sure thing, sir.' Inglis smiled and led her big lump partner away. 'Come on, Josh.'

'Evening, Jon.'

Nelson couldn't look at him. 'Simon.'

Fenchurch waited for eye contact. It didn't happen. 'Gather you called this in?'

'That's correct.' Nelson let out a deep breath. 'I...' He finally looked over, but it was hidden behind a wall of rage. Anger. Undeserved anger. 'You look like shit.'

'I feel like shit.'

A frown flickered and died on his forehead. 'You okay?'

'I'm just fine and dandy, Jon. Now. Why were you here?'

Nelson raised his eyebrows. 'If you think I'm going to answer that...'

So that was how he was going to play it. 'Why not?'

'After what you put me through?'

'Me? Jon, I tried to stop it, I tried to—'

'No, you didn't. Barely lifted your finger. After all we'd been through.'

'I tried to get you reinstated, Jon. I appealed it all.'

'Oh, well done.' Nelson clapped his hands. 'You're the best.'

'I've let you stay in my flat for the amount I pay to the bank. Not a penny more.'

'Out of guilt.'

'After what *Younis* did to you? No, Jon. I don't feel guilty. You did what you did and you paid the price. Other people cut corners and get away with it. You were just unlucky. I'm helping because you're a friend and something really shit happened to you. I've no guilt or shame for it, Jon. You did it to yourself and I tried to protect you.'

'Well. I blame you.'

'Blame me all you like, Sergeant. This isn't—'

'I'm not a cop. And I haven't been a sergeant for years either.'

Fenchurch laughed. Couldn't help himself. 'Jon. Why were you here?'

Nelson swallowed something down. Maybe his pride. 'I'm working a case. Followed a client over here.'

'Your client around?'

Nelson nodded.

'Where?'

Nelson gestured over to Uzma. 'With her.'

'Okay. So, you were following this client?'

'Just logging what she did. Making sure she was on the level.' Nelson looked away.

'Who are you working for these days?'

'Waheed Lad.'

It felt like a punch in the stomach. 'Christ.' Fenchurch pictured the incident, years ago, where Waheed was hit by a train. His police career over after he lost an arm. 'How is he doing?'

'Well, he's almost able to use a can opener with his prosthetic arm.'

Another gut punch. One that caused internal bleeding. 'Tell him I was asking for him.'

'I don't think he'd appreciate that.'

'No.' Fenchurch tried to shake it off, but the guilt was a tight cloak. 'Still don't get how you could be here to call it in, Jon.'

'Like I told you, I was following my client.' Nelson pointed at an old VW Passat with 56 plates. 'That's my car. I was waiting there and she screamed.'

'She screamed?'

'Right.'

'So she was inside the house?'

'Right.'

'How did she get in?'

Nelson shrugged. 'Had a key.'

So that checked out. 'She said she hired you to get evidence into her husband. Why were you following her?'

'Like I told you, just to make sure it was all on the level. To see if she was being followed by someone else.'

'Sounds like bullshit to me.'

Nelson shrugged.

'Jon, I know when you're lying.'

'Do you.'

'Okay, Jon. If that's how you're going to play it, I need you to give a statement. Okay? Everything you've got.'

'I can't do that.'

'Why?'

'It's protected work, Simon.'

'I get that.' Bloody PIs, cosplay cops. 'Give us as much as you can. Okay?'

'Sure.'

'I mean it. A man's died here, Jon. I know you're a good guy. I know you want to help.'

'Fine.'

'And we need to clear the air.' Fenchurch got eye contact. 'I'm sorry about what happened to you. I'm sorry I've been distant. I've tried, Jon, but you've got to meet me halfway. And if we aren't friends or you don't want to know me anymore, you'd best get your arse out of my flat.'

'Okay.' Nelson snorted. 'I'm not sure a coffee's going to fix this.'

'No, but it'll be a start. And I want to try, Jon. You're a good mate. You *were* a good mate. I want to be your friend again. And I hate seeing you like this.'

Nelson frowned. 'Like what?'

'Not working as a cop.' Fenchurch beckoned the DS back over. 'Take a full statement, please.'

'Sure thing, sir.'

'Guv.' Reed was bouncing across the pavement, still in most of her crime scene suit, clutching an evidence bag. 'Found Monaghan's phone in the bedroom. There are a ton of messages and missed calls from Jack Walsh.'

Weirder and weirder.

'When did we let him go?'

'Two hours ago.'

Walsh could've killed Monaghan. Just bloody perfect.

Marie was looking at Reed. 'Did you say Jack Walsh?'

CHAPTER THIRTY-EIGHT

Reed parked the car down the road from Jack Walsh's grace-and-favour pad. More than the flat he'd alluded to – a big house, four or five bedrooms, and a big garden out the back. Decent views across Hampstead. 'How the other half live, eh?'

'Mm,' Fenchurch was kneading his knee. The pill was kicking in but the ache was still hovering around.

Reed scowled at him. 'Are you sure you're okay?'

'I'm fine, why?'

'It's just...' Reed bunched up her hair and let it fall back. 'Abi said you've stopped taking your meds?'

'I'm fine, Kay. It's under control. I'm here, right?'

'Yeah, but you look like you're the one who's overdosed.'

'That's a bit harsh.'

'Well...'

'I'm fine.' Fenchurch twisted around and locked eyes with her long enough that she got the message. 'Now, let's just see what Jack has to say about this, okay?'

Their uniform back-up arrived, parking down the street, so

they could converge on him. Catch him if he ran. What happened earlier with Monaghan made Fenchurch determined to not get burnt twice.

He got out first into the cooling night.

A black cab pulled in between the cars. Jack Walsh got out, accompanied by a woman. Younger than him. Both swaying. Laughing. Keys tinkled on the ground.

Fenchurch tugged Reed's sleeve back.

The cab's yellow light came back on then it drove off at speed.

Walsh managed to navigate the front path. Dropped the keys again. Then took several goes getting them into the lock.

'Now!' Fenchurch walked after Reed, who was running. The uniform pair were younger and fitter and got there first.

Walsh was kissing the woman in the doorway.

She swung around. Frowned at them. Then ran off, rounding the uniforms and sprinting away.

Fenchurch couldn't give chase, but he managed to grab Walsh and pin him to the door, holding his right arm in place, locking his wrist against the wood.

Reed shot off with the uniforms, back out onto the street. Screaming and shouting.

Fenchurch felt like he was going to fall over. Took everything he had to stay upright.

'You.' Walsh was swaying.

What a pair they made, one absolutely shit-faced, the other suffering from opioid withdrawal.

'You.' Walsh tried to turn around. 'Fucking cocksucker.'

Fenchurch let him go a touch, but kept his wrist in a tight grip. 'Okay, Jack. You and me are going to have another talk.'

'You prick. You got me fired! You. It was you! It was all you!' His face was twisted into a snarl.

'No, Jack, that was your own fault.'

'You and fucking Terry.'

'Monaghan?'

'Yeah, he caught me with her then grassed me up to the boss today. Told him to keep it to himself, but he couldn't. He just couldn't. I love her. Man. I love her.'

'Who?'

'I know she's young but I love her. I fucking love her. Jadzia's the one.'

Reed was dragging a hissing ball of hair and swearing along behind her. Dressed in a slutty school uniform, everything way too short and revealing.

Jadzia O'Brien. Bloody hell.

'Let's take you both back for an interview.'

'You pricks. Let her go!' Walsh lashed out, missing with his punch but catching Fenchurch in the face with his fingernails.

Fenchurch grabbed his arm.

Walsh lurched forward, powering his neck muscles like he was back on the pitch and Fenchurch's head was a Mitre Delta.

Fenchurch caught the flash and jerked to the side.

Walsh fell face forward, landing on the flagstones. 'You fucking pricks. She's done nothing.'

Fenchurch stood over him. 'Jack, did you give Terry the fentanyl?'

'Terry?' Walsh's eyes bulged. 'Fentanyl?'

'The stuff you used to kill Terry Monaghan.'

Walsh frowned. 'He's dead?'

'I'm afraid so.'

'Ah, shit.'

Fenchurch sighed. 'Jack Walsh, I'm arresting you for the supply of a controlled substance.'

CHAPTER THIRTY-NINE

Leman Street was in that lull between shifts, where the night shift were keying themselves up and the back shift were still working, but keeping quiet and trying to avoid staying back. Finding those odd little bits of paperwork that just needed doing. Not running a last check down the Minories or along Mile End Road that might end up in processing an arrest into the "wee sma' hours", as Fenchurch's old boss would've called it.

Down the corridor, Uzma Ashkani was on the phone. 'Okay, Mick.' She winced at Fenchurch and covered the screen. 'Clooney's team are going to be all night at Monaghan's flat, so they *could* call in a lot from way out west to do it. Overtime job, guv.'

'Meaning Bell will be spitting teeth.'

'Yeah, but at least he's got himself a potential murder to hang it to.'

'True.' Fenchurch rasped at the stubble on his chin. 'Tell Mick to do it.'

She turned away, speaking in a low voice. Then back. 'Mick

says Bell is going to nail your balls to the wall with cocktail sticks. His words.'

Fenchurch gave a hard stare. 'Tell him I've had words with him before about his kinkshaming.'

She frowned, then got the joke. 'It's approved, Mick. Sure you're sure? Thanks.' She ended the call. 'Like dealing with my uncles...'

'Oh?'

Uzma put her phone away. 'How do you want to play this?'

'She's definitely sober enough to be interviewed?'

'Cleared by the duty doctor.'

'What about Walsh?'

'Dalton Unwin is insisting his client is too drunk to submit to interview.'

'But she's not?'

'Nope. Looks like she had two vodkas whereas he's drowned himself in a keg of beer.'

Fenchurch smiled. 'Okay. You lead.'

'Sure.' Uzma entered the interview room and started the recorder.

Jadzia sat opposite, arms folded, looking pissed off at the world. Skin darker than Uzma's – amazing what a bottle of tan did. Her stick-on nails seemed even longer than the rest of her fingers. Tiger patterns on one hand, zebra on the other. She looked up at Fenchurch standing in the doorway, batting her long lashes, then looked away.

Fenchurch took the seat next to Uzma. His knee was okay, giving him some movement. Maybe this dosage was enough. He stretched out his leg, away from their feet.

Uzma drummed her fingers on the table. 'Must be tough, Jadzia.'

'What?'

'Being the daughter of someone famous?'

'My dad. Right.'

'RyOB... I used to watch his stuff on YouTube. He was really funny. Then he stopped doing it.'

'Right. Wouldn't know.'

'I bet he still gets stopped in the street.'

Jadzia shrugged. 'Hardly.'

Uzma gave Fenchurch a flick of her eyebrow. 'Okay, you're sixteen and you've been drinking.'

'So?'

'I don't make the rules, Jadzia. We've got people collecting the CCTV from the pub you were in. The Barrowboy and Banker. The landlord will get into a lot of bother because of that.'

'Seriously. You're interviewing me because I had two drinks?' Jadzia sighed. 'What's this really about?'

Wise beyond her years.

'The man I was with. Right?'

Uzma nodded.

'Why have you got such a hard-on for Jack?'

Uzma smiled. 'Because he's involved in a complex case. Someone died earlier today. And we found the body of another man this evening.'

'You want to shag him. Is that it?'

Uzma laughed. 'No. I'm not the one sleeping with him. We need to talk to you about—'

'He got sacked because of us. Can you believe that? My dad told me to quit him.' Jadzia shrugged. 'I can't. And I won't. And we'll be fine. All three of us.'

Uzma's mouth hung open. 'You're pregnant?'

'Two months gone.'

Uzma shut her eyes. 'When was your birthday, Jadzia?'

'Three weeks ago.'

'And it's Mr Walsh's child?'

THE LAST THING TO DIE

'Saying I'm a slag?'

'No, Jadzia, but Mr Walsh is in a position where he safe-guards the welfare of young people. If you were *under*—'

'I'm winding you up.' Jadzia rolled her eyes. 'God. Just messing with you.'

Uzma was blushing. Caught out by a schoolgirl. 'This is a formal interview. This is being recorded. We can get a warrant for a pregnancy test and then get an additional warrant for a paternity test.'

The girl's face fell. Maybe she wasn't playing them. Maybe she was pregnant.

'If you had a lawyer in here, they'd be—'

'I told you, I don't want a lawyer. And this is *such* bullshit. I'm in love with Jack. I want to marry him. I want to have his baby.'

'Jadzia, he's three times your age.'

'So? It's love.'

Fenchurch sat back. 'Jack has got previous.'

'Eh?'

'Having sex with lots of women, often at the same time, but not in the same bed. It's a compulsion. An addiction for which he's seeking counselling. You're just the latest in a—'

'I know all of that. And I know I can change him.'

Fenchurch laughed. 'Nobody can change Jack Walsh. Only Jack can. Believe me.'

'I will.'

She was deluded in the way teenagers often were. Quite a few adults too.

'Jadzia, I want to let you go, but I need you to answer some questions about Jack, okay?'

'I'm not going to drop him in it.'

'No, I just want the truth. It'll help us out a lot. It'll help Jack too, because he's in a lot of trouble.'

The girl let her hair out and it spilled around her giant eyes. 'What do you want to know?'

'Did Jack ever talk about Terry Monaghan?'

'Yeah. Good mate of his.' Jadzia was frowning. 'When we were in the pub, I went to the toilet and came back and he was talking to this old woman about him. Saying how Terry loved her and missed her. See, that's the Jack I know. He cares about people.'

'That woman, she found Terry's body about ten minutes later.'

'Shit.'

'Someone had given him a controlled substance and he overdosed on it.'

'What?'

'Did Jack know anything about it?'

'No!'

'When did you see him this evening?'

'He called me about half past four. Asked to see me. His car was full of stuff like pot plants and boxes. Told me he'd been sacked by my dad. Asked me to speak to him.'

'And did you?'

'I said, no way.'

'And that was it?'

'No, he called me later. Said he wanted a drink and we went to that pub. Told me you'd interviewed him.'

Fenchurch played the timeline through in his head, which was like shoving a rock through a pasta maker. The state of Walsh meant he must've gone straight to the pub after being let go, probably dropped off by his lawyer. Met her there. No time to kill Monaghan. 'Okay, Jadzia. That's been helpful.' He stood up and felt dizzy, like he was going to fall over. 'DI Ashkani, can you take her to her father's?'

Uzma's turn to roll her eyes. Not only teenagers who used that level of sass.

'Uh uh.' Jadzia had folded her arms again. 'No fucking way.'

Uzma leaned forward. 'Why not?'

'Because he's a dick. Take me to Jack's.'

'That's not going to happen.'

'Why not?'

'Because he tried to assault a police officer. He'll be in all night.'

'You forced him to do that.'

'He supplied the fentanyl to Terry Monaghan.'

'Shut up.'

'Jadzia, do you know anything about it?'

'No! Take me to Mum's, then. God.'

Fenchurch had to get out of there. Way too hot. Walls closing in. He pushed out into the corridor. Empty and cool. But he still felt like he was going to be sick.

'Fenchurch, isn't it?'

He swung around.

Ryan O'Brien was standing in the corridor.

Reed was on the phone behind him, facing away.

O'Brien was frowning at him. 'You okay there?'

'I'm fine. Just came to see you.'

'About my little lady, right?'

'Not quite. Did you hear about Terry Monaghan?'

'Right. Heard a whisper. Poor guy.'

'Well, your daughter's ready to go home, but she doesn't want to go with you.'

'Little bitch.' O'Brien pushed past Fenchurch and entered the room.

Fenchurch stumbled. He tried to grab at anything to keep him upright, but his fingers just clawed at the wallpaper. His arse cracked off the floor.

Shit.

He sat there, like his son just after he'd learnt to walk.

Nobody noticed. Nobody around to notice. Hopefully the CCTV camera was off.

He took two goes to get up.

Shouting came from inside the room, muffled by the door.

Fenchurch dusted himself off then followed O'Brien in.

'Jadzia Kira O'Brien, you're coming with me.' He was jabbing a finger at her. 'No questions.'

'Fuck. Off. You don't own me!'

'Do you hear the level of cheek I have to put up with?'

Fenchurch wanted to get between them, but everything hurt. He was burning up and his heart was pounding in his chest.

'You're shacking up with a fat old drunk, missy. That guy's riddled with more STDs than I have millions. And I'm a billionaire!'

'I might as well just sit here and tell them how you made all that money.'

'I'm clean, you ungrateful slut.'

'Fuck off.' She was shaking her head. 'You just had to tell them about me and Jack, didn't you?'

'Only because Jack had been committing a crime. Turns out he's giving people drugs! Did he give anything to Curtis Archer? You know he died, Jadzia. I'm thinking your boyfriend knows why.'

She looked away. 'Jack needs to take these pills. His back hurts.'

Uzma held up a hand. 'What pills?'

'I don't know.'

'Are you talking about fentanyl?'

'No, you stupid bitch. Fentanyl is like in patches? He was getting oxy pills off a guy.'

'Who was he getting—?'

'I don't know.'

'Was it Terry?' O'Brien was leaning across the desk. 'Was he bringing them in when... When he caught you and Jack?'

'No! I don't know who it was! Curtis put him on to some guy.'

'Curtis Archer?'

'Right.'

'Who?'

'I keep telling you! I don't know.' Jadzia folded her arms. She realised she'd said too much.

'Right, come on.' Fenchurch grabbed O'Brien and dragged him out of the room.

Reed had a pair of burly security officers with her now.

'Kay, can you escort him back downstairs please?'

O'Brien knew he was defeated. He nodded and let them go.

Fenchurch could barely take it in.

Jack Walsh was on oxy. Probably explained the state of him. Don't mix those pills with booze – Fenchurch had made that mistake once and half a glass of red felt like four bottles. Never again.

But if Curtis Archer had been the link in the chain between Walsh and Monaghan.

If...

Fenchurch went back in the room and whispered. 'Uzma, process her. Get a statement. Rock solid. No holes. Then she can go home with her mother.'

'Will do. Are you okay?'

'Sorry about this, but I've got to go home.' Because I'm an addict and I feel like I'm going to die. 'I'll see you tomorrow morning.'

CHAPTER FORTY

Nelson got back to the flat but didn't want to go back inside. In there, it'd all feel real. Out here, he could fool himself that it wasn't. That he wasn't a fucking idiot.

But he was.

So he sat there, car door half open, cabin light on, trying to deny reality. That he hadn't spent hours giving a police statement to former colleagues. That his life was now that of an ex-cop, kicked off the force for going over the line, for lying.

All of that he could live with, except for the fact that nobody defended him.

No matter what Fenchurch said, or told himself, he hadn't tried hard enough.

He looked up at the block of flats, a turn-of-the-millennium six-storey building, its stark-white grandeur faded over the years to dull grey. The number of times he'd sat up there on the balcony with Fenchurch, drinking cheap supermarket wine, listening to all of the pain he was going through because he'd lost his daughter.

Being a friend.

Being his best friend.

His only friend.

Helping.

Giving up time he could've spent with his own kids to search for what happened to her.

Not that he'd done it transactionally, expecting a return on all the hours he'd devoted to it.

But Fenchurch just turned his back on him.

Let him go.

No longer a Met officer.

He tried to cast it out of his mind.

And Younis popped back in.

What the hell was he going to do about that?

The man who'd got Nelson to follow Marie Deacon to Terry Monaghan's flat.

He must've known.

Had he killed Monaghan?

From what Nelson heard from old cop mates, someone had crammed fentanyl patches down his throat and forced him to overdose. A brutal death, one that had all the hallmarks of Younis and his craven empire. Punishments that fit the perceived crimes.

But it felt like Younis wasn't just happy with ruining Nelson's career. He wanted his life too.

Another car pulled up opposite and Lisa got out, face like she'd murdered someone. He knew that expression, that prickly fire in her. Something had happened. He needed to know what. He needed to help her.

Nelson got out of the car. 'Hey, are you okay?'

Lisa jumped and yelled. 'Jesus, Jon!' She was scowling at him. 'What the hell are you doing creeping up on me like that?'

'Sorry, I was just processing stuff.'

'What's up?'

'Nothing.' He shrugged. 'You don't seem okay.'

'I'm fine.'

'Come on, Lisa. I know that face. You're pissed off.'

'Just the time of the month.'

'But I thought you were at your—'

'Leave it, Jon.' She charged off, then got inside and was just a pair of shoes racing up the stairs.

Nelson got out and locked his car, then followed her up.

She was talking to someone. Raised voices.

Nelson stopped at the landing.

Waheed Lad stood there, his only hand in his pocket. The prosthetic arm dangled by his side like a fake ventriloquist as he worked his crazy bird puppet.

The boss.

Weird how things had been inverted.

'I'll see you around, Lisa.' Waheed stood up tall but he didn't have any height on Nelson. 'Just need a word with your man here.'

Lisa looked over, frowning.

Nelson nodded – this was okay. He'd handle it.

A flash of eyebrows and she went inside the flat.

Leaving the two of them in the staircase.

'What's up, Waheed?'

'Knew you'd be here, Jon, because I track your phone. Happened to be in the area, so thought I'd come and say this face-to-face.'

'Say what?'

'This case you're on, Jon. I've been through your billing time and... Well.'

'Well what?'

'You've been billing some personal time to a client, haven't you?'

'Excuse me?'

'Don't.' Waheed raised a finger. 'Okay? Don't. I've caught you, you pillock. There's no reason for you to be at Southwark court on her dime.'

'I was following her husband!'

'So why haven't I got a report, eh?'

Nelson looked away. That flickering light needed fixing. 'I've been busy.'

'With some kind of vendetta, right? Heard you got picked up by the cops. Twice. What's going on, Jon?'

'Nothing I can't handle.'

'Come on, Jon. That's bollocks. We're both ex-cops, so we know the lay of—'

'I'm *fine*.'

'Well.'

'Are you here to fire me?'

'No.' Waheed laughed. 'God no. You're my number one guy, Jon.' He clicked his fingers and pointed finger pistols at Nelson. 'Thing is, though...' He scratched at his neck. 'I've got a curious proposition. The husband of our client is... This is weird. He came to my office, Jon, and he's offered to buy us out of the contract on him.'

'Are you going to?'

'It's not that simple. He wants copies of the reports on his wife. Wants her followed.'

'You're double dipping on both sides?'

'No reason not to.'

'It's unethical.'

'We're private eyes, Jon. Ethics shouldn't concern us.' Waheed grinned. 'I dug into his background. He's got lots of cash. Made a ton from cryptocurrencies and all that Web3 shit. He can afford it.'

'It's not about affording it, Waheed. I don't think it's a great idea.'

'Jon, he's got a lot to lose. A lot of money at stake in this divorce. He wants to find out what she's been up to and take her down before she grabs him.'

'Still think it's—'

'I hear you, but it's what we're doing.' Waheed held up his hand. 'Two things.' He extended his thumb. 'First, how did he know?'

'No idea, Waheed.' Nelson rolled his eyes. 'Having me following him around all day might alert people.'

'True.' He extended his forefinger. 'Second, I don't care how this happened. This is a big gig for us. It's why I had you following her earlier.' He clapped Nelson's arm. 'This is all great work, Jon. I'll cancel the time from the system, so she won't get billed, but he will. And don't do any of this cowboy shit again, okay? You fleecing me makes me think I shouldn't keep you on.' He walked off, skipping down the stairs.

Leaving Nelson feeling like utter shit.

Waheed used to be a good cop and now he was all twisted and bitter, ready to take bent money.

This wasn't supposed to happen. It wasn't supposed to be like this. He hated doing this work and it was gnawing away at his soul.

Nelson got out his keys and went inside the flat.

Water hissed from deep inside.

Nelson walked through to the bedroom.

Lisa was in the shower. She wasn't singing. Not a good sign.

He stepped into the en-suite. 'Hey, are—?'

She squealed. 'Stop sneaking up on me!'

The stall was all misted up.

She wiped it away.

'Hey, I'm just seeing how you are.' Nelson held up his hands. 'Are you okay?'

'I'm fine.'

'Are you sure?'

'Of course I'm sure.'

'Because you can talk—'

'I don't want to talk about it. Going to bed, Jon. Got an early start tomorrow – sure you understand what goes on during a case like this.'

'Right, I do.' Nelson wanted to stay with her, force out of her what was really going on. But that could backfire, drive a wedge between them. 'Well, I'm a bit keyed up, so I'll go and watch some telly.'

'You do that. Night.' She turned away and squirted more shower gel into the puff ball.

Nelson wanted to stay, to ask her what the hell had happened, how he could help... but he left the room. Took his time, crossing the bedroom.

She started singing and it made him feel a bit better.

He went into the living room and sat on the sofa. He flicked on the telly and a baseball match was just starting. Not his favourite sport, but it'd occupy his brain.

Waheed...

What the hell was he doing?

Was there something he just didn't see?

The marriage was over... and paying for both sides was expensive. And exploitative.

And there wasn't a lot Nelson had unearthed.

Marie was just a woman who did her own stuff. Marched to her own drumbeat.

And Waheed was screwing her over because her rich husband wanted to hoard his wealth like a dragon with its gold.

Great.

He was still thinking about work.

Marie found the body. Terry Monaghan, a lower-league footballer.

There was no obvious connection there, which meant they were probably sleeping together.

That could be the smoking gun her husband needed to cut a lot of her value from their settlement.

Jesus, this work made his skin crawl. Having to do this... It wasn't right. It wasn't real work.

His laptop was charging, so he grabbed it and rested it on his lap.

Her husband was Dr Edwin Deacon. Rich enough to pay twice. Rich enough to seriously care about losing half of his fortune.

But there was a link to Younis. He'd been meeting him in the arse end of Peckham.

Why?

Waheed had said Deacon made money from crypto. A lot of it. There might be something in that.

A lot of criminals used it to hide their assets or bury the transactions.

Nelson knew he was still a good investigator. Forget about killing Younis. There might be a better way to take him down.

CHAPTER FORTY-ONE

Fenchurch woke up with a start.

He felt like he'd been run over by a car. His heart was at the kind of tempo it took twelve ecstasy pills to appreciate. A pneumatic drill, rattling at his ribs, reverberating into his skull, his jaw, his whole body.

The bedsheets were soaked through. His hair was as though he'd just been swimming.

Abi was up, her side of the bed empty.

He moved his leg and his knee throbbed. The pain felt worse everywhere else, his head feeling smashed in.

The drug was killing him. He was sick because it wasn't in his system at the level it was before.

Dope sick.

Christ.

And all he could think about was taking another pill. This craving would not stop. He'd gone hours without one.

And he needed another.

Could he do that to himself?

He had no choice.

He sat up and felt like his head was going to topple off. He managed to reach over to the chair still covered in his clothes from yesterday.

The drugs weren't in his trouser pockets.

Where the hell were they?

He staggered into the en-suite and used the sink to keep himself upright. It shifted the plinth underneath or whatever it was called.

He caught his reflection in the medicine cabinet's mirror. He looked like death warmed up in the microwave. Still rock hard in the middle and boiling hot on the surface.

Caught a smell from the toilet.

His gag reflex kicked in.

He collapsed onto the floor, gripping the pan.

Bile burnt his throat, but nothing came up.

Right then, he'd welcome death – cool, cool death – with open arms.

He wasn't going to be sick. He knew that now.

Took him a fortnight to lever himself up, one hand on the cold toilet pan, the other on the sink.

He reached into the medicine cabinet. Just bottles of shower gel and over-the-counter painkillers.

Had Abi taken his drugs?

Where would she have put them?

He padded back into the bedroom and his knee was throbbing like a bastard. 'Abi!'

Nothing.

Into the hallway. 'Ab?'

No reply.

He managed to make it into the master bathroom and tore open the drugs cabinet.

Empty.

Shit.

'Abi!?'

He collapsed onto the toilet. His leg was numb now. The pain was digging into his side, all the way up to his ribs.

He needed to get more drugs from somewhere.

Go to Deacon. Say he'd lost them. It was the truth, after all.

But what if he refused?

There were people on the street. He could get hold of them that way.

He had to face the truth – he was a junkie. Might've been an accident, might be a real reason behind it, but he was as much a junkie as the guy sleeping in a phone box.

After all, he knew more than anyone else that those people had reasons they took the stuff. Deep traumas they tried to hide. The ex-squaddie who couldn't face what he'd seen or done. The woman who left home a teenager to escape an abusive stepfather.

Maybe Fenchurch should just kill himself.

No more pain.

No more suffering.

All through what he'd experienced with Chloe's disappearance, he had a goal – to find his daughter. His thoughts got dark, sure, darker than this. But he had hope. That hope almost killed him, but she came back.

Now, hope was dead. The last thing to die.

He had no hope.

The operation wouldn't fix him. He was just another useless junkie. He'd still crave those demonic pills.

Nobody would miss him. Nobody would care about him being gone.

His dad would laugh it off like he did everything.

The team at work would get a new boss, forget all about him. Kay Reed, Lisa Bridge, Uzma Ashkani, Mick Clooney, Jason Bell. They'd all forget him.

Abi would move on. Like she'd tried to before.

Al was so young he would forget him in time. Fenchurch would just be this memory as he became an adult. Maybe he'd have a stepdad and wouldn't remember him.

Chloe...

Christ. Chloe.

She would remember him.

She would care.

She knew how hard he fought to find her.

No.

He needed to get better – he owed it to himself and to her.

He stood up tall, swaying, but stepped into the shower. He had to brace himself against the wall to stay upright, but he was determined to kick this shit.

CHAPTER FORTY-TWO

Fenchurch had faced down guns and knives. His daughter and wife had both been taken as hostages. He'd stopped a bomb designed to kill tens of thousands of people, including his son and father.

Getting across the car park in this state was going to be at least as tough as any of that.

Fenchurch had managed to drive here on autopilot, taking it slowly. In this condition, soaked with sweat and as many paracetamol and ibuprofen as he could manage. Felt like he was rattling. The rest of them were stuffed into his pockets.

He took a drink from his ice-cold water bottle, though it was a struggle to reduce his temperature.

He hit dial on his phone and put it to his ear.

Voicemail.

Again.

'Abi, it's Simon. Just wondering where you are? I'm at work, but call me anytime. Okay? Love you. Bye.'

She had been there when he got back last night.

Hadn't she?

He couldn't remember.

These drugs were tearing him apart.

Focus.

Focus on the task at hand.

He got out into the cool morning.

'Sir?'

Fenchurch swung around, frowning. The sun was at that irritating low level that blinded him – the height it'd be most of the short day in midwinter. Sparkles of light around the edges.

Uzma was frowning. She had a halo glowing around her head. 'You okay there, sir?'

'I'm fine.' Fenchurch set off towards the station, feeling like he might topple over with each step. 'You're in early.'

'I was in late too.' She was quicker than him, already swiping through the security system. 'You don't look well, if you don't mind me saying.'

'And if I do mind?'

'Sir, are you okay?'

'Just don't feel well.' Fenchurch stepped inside. His knee was a dull throb. His head was a screaming klaxon. 'Did a covid test this morning, so it's not that.'

'Well, since you asked... The reason I was in so late last night was I managed to speak to the surgeon in the US who redid Archer's knee.'

'Oh?'

'He says it should've been fixed by now, and he should've at least been back training, if not playing.'

'So why wasn't he?'

'He said he didn't have the case history to hand, so couldn't give a concrete answer. He did give me a few options to investigate. Said he's seen this with a few NFL players. They're out so long with a recovery like this, particularly when the first op is a bust – his exact words, not mine – that they get out of the habit of being athletes. Doing the fitness stuff day in, day out. Instead, they focus on the pain they're enduring way more than the joy they get from training and playing.'

'Sounds like a roundabout way of saying he suspects Curtis has got himself hooked on those painkillers.'

'That's right, sir.' Uzma winced. 'The amount in his blood is way stronger than the dose he should've been taking, even just after the procedure. So he reckons Curtis was taking it recreationally.'

'That stacks up. Kay hasn't found a prescription after the one from Dr Deacon, which means he was getting it either from another doctor, which would leave a paper trail we've so far been unable to unearth, or—'

'Or from a street dealer.' Uzma nodded as she led him down the corridor with the interview rooms. 'Ties in with the obsession too. Everything becomes about taking those drugs.'

'That makes sense.' Fenchurch knew the temptation. 'Jack Walsh's girlfriend told us he'd sourced some oxy from a dealer Curtis had recommended to him. Can you find who was—'

'Come on, guv. There must be hundreds of street dealers around here. That's impossible.'

'I don't think it is. Uzma, I asked you to speak to the drugs teams yesterday. They should know enough street dealers to give us a ton of leads to chase down. Curtis Archer was a superstar, it can't be that difficult to find a street dealer who was dining out on stories of selling oxy to West Ham's number nine. And I'll ask Jack Walsh directly, see if there's any way of narrowing it down.'

'Fine.' Uzma took a deep breath and let it out slowly.

'I hope you're not pissed off with me.'

'I'm not. I just... people shouldn't be prescribed oxy for recovery like that.' She stormed off down the corridor.

Hard to disagree with that.

Fenchurch only had himself to blame for getting sucked into it. He'd thought he was smarter than the average cat.

But he'd trusted his doctor that he was on a safe track. He was in pain and someone took it away.

He took another oxy pill – sod it – and swallowed it down. He needed to be on his A-game. Hell, his Z-game would be better than how he'd felt first thing.

Monaghan...

Was he the one sourcing the street oxy for Curtis?

There was a connection there, so someone needed to explore it.

And who benefited from *his* death?

All roads led to Jack bloody Walsh. He was still here.

CHAPTER FORTY-THREE

Christ, Fenchurch felt almost normal. The drug kicked in hard when it needed to.

He walked down the corridor to the room Walsh had been in last night. Voices in there. He had to brace himself against the wooden door surround. Finish his water. Calm himself down. Cool himself.

He opened the door and popped his head in.

Not Jack Walsh.

Oliver Archer was sitting with Bridge.

She looked over, frowning, then beckoned him in.

Fenchurch took his time walking over and sitting – last thing he needed was to fall over in front of a member of the public, especially someone whose son had just died.

Bridge got up and left the room.

Leaving Fenchurch alone.

'I'm stunned by it.'

Fenchurch frowned. 'By what?'

'By Terry Monaghan's death.'

Took Fenchurch a few seconds to recalibrate his thinking.

Why Archer would be in here. 'You told us yesterday he was working with your son on these NFTs.'

'That's right. Neoxis Industries. Jolly Roger's World of Pirates.

'A Seattle firm, correct?'

Archer shrugged. 'Ish.'

'Ish?'

'Well, they've got local footing, but it's hard to pin them down. Trouble with a business like Neoxis is they can easily shift where they're based at the drop of a hat. It's not like Apple or Google or Microsoft, where they've got these massive headquarters buildings or data centres everywhere and thousands of members of staff. Neoxis can leave their Seattle office and pick up in Mexico City like nothing's happened.' Archer was bouncing his fists off the table rhythmically. 'Still, I wasn't happy my boy was doing that.'

'Rather do that yourself?'

He raised his hands. 'Not my game.'

'Do you think his death could have anything to do with that scheme?'

'Hard to say. I heard Neoxis were in trouble. Need more people to keep buying in. Almost like a pyramid scheme, but there are underlying assets being bought. But that's all I know.' Archer waved at the door. 'And I told your colleague that.'

Why was Bridge leaving this to Fenchurch? Felt like there wasn't anything concrete to explore, no smoking gun. Nothing. Then again, he was pig ignorant when it came to this stuff. What was blindingly obvious to a computer science graduate like Bridge was triple Dutch to someone like Fenchurch.

'Okay.' Fenchurch sighed. 'Give me a minute, sir.' He took his time getting up and hobbled over to the door.

'You okay there?'

Fenchurch turned back to Archer. 'Just slept on it, I think. Dead leg.'

'Well, I know a good sports masseur if you need a recommendation.'

'I'll maybe take you up on that.' Though it was going to take a hell of a lot more than that. Fenchurch smiled at him and pushed out into the corridor.

Bridge was standing in the middle, clutching her phone. Looking like she was going to smash it against the wall.

'Lisa, are you okay?'

She looked over at him, tears filling her eyes. 'No.'

Now Fenchurch had an idea what was going on.

He opened another door and checked the room was empty. 'Come in here.' He held it for her.

She shuffled past but didn't sit, instead standing by the whiteboard, facing away from him.

Fenchurch nudged the door shut behind him. 'Hey, what's going on?'

She just stood there, shaking her head.

'Carling?'

Her head dipped.

'What did he do?'

'He grabbed me in the office last night.'

'Grabbed?'

'Ran his hand over my arse. I told him to stop. Then he grabbed my... my breasts.'

Fenchurch felt that fire burning in his chest. In his stomach. 'Lisa, I'm so sorry this has happened to you.'

'Sorry? She turned back around and glared at him, hatred spilling out of every pore. At least it had found direction – Fenchurch – and wasn't aimed at herself. 'I knew the rumours and I chose to work with him solo. *You* knew this would happen.'

'Lisa, I'm going to put a stop to it all. Okay?'

She shot him a glare. 'Oh, so you're going to save me? My saviour.'

'No, Lisa. It's not like that. I'm going to take him down. You don't deserve this. Nobody does. It has to bloody stop. I'm sorry it hasn't before now and that you're facing this.'

She looked at him with damp eyes. Didn't say anything.

'Have you told Jon?'

She shook her head. 'I couldn't. He'd lose his shit. And he already blames you for everything, so...'

Fenchurch had seen flashes of his anger over the years. 'Okay. My priority right now is making sure you're okay.'

'I'm fine, sir. I can work.'

'Okay.' But Fenchurch would keep a close eye on her. 'Can you escort Mr Archer outside, please?' He opened the door. 'I'm going to put a stop to this.' He fixed her with a stare. 'File the complaint and I will back you from here.'

She looked away. 'Thank you, sir.' Then walked off.

Leaving Fenchurch alone in that room. Everything ached. Felt like he'd been poisoned.

But he had a target now. Someone he could direct all that fizzing rage at.

CHAPTER FORTY-FOUR

The incident room was throbbing with enough noise to make Fenchurch's head even worse. Like he was trapped inside a giant marshmallow. He scanned the room, forty or so officers waiting for his appearance in ten minutes time.

No sign of Carling.

His phone was thrumming in his pocket.

He left the room.

By the time he'd caught his breath and taken out his mobile, Abi had rung off.

He waited a few seconds to see if she'd left a voicemail.

Nothing.

He tried calling but it just kept ringing.

What the hell was going on?

So much for being supported. For being loved.

After what she'd put him through. After he'd insisted on counselling, then agreeing to move back in for the sake of Al.

Who was the idiot now?

Right. No time for this.

'Morning, guv.' Reed barged past him and walked over to the photocopier, staring into space as it flashed below her.

Fenchurch made his way over, his knee like a lump of brittle toffee. 'Kay. I need a word.'

She swung around, smiling. It turned to a frown, then a scowl as she looked him up and down. 'Guv, are you okay?'

'I'm fine.' Fenchurch gave the room another thorough search but no sign of him. 'Have you seen Carling?'

'Are you sure you—'

'Right. Okay.' Fenchurch set off over to the door.

'Guv.' Reed followed him out into the corridor. 'Listen, I heard from Abi.'

Fenchurch tried to keep calm as he walked. 'Where is she?'

Reed frowned. 'You don't know?'

'Her and Al were gone this morning when I got up.' Fenchurch felt his whole body shaking. 'What's really freaking me out is there should've been a blow up. That's Abi's style. But she's just... gone.'

'She called me when she was driving.'

'Driving? Where's she gone?'

Reed shot in front of him. 'Guv, she told me about your addiction.'

Fenchurch stopped. He couldn't look at her.

'Don't expect sympathy from me.'

'I don't expect any, Kay.'

'You look like shit. Are you going cold turkey?'

Fenchurch gave a tight shake of the head. 'I was. But I can't hack it. Reducing it down, big time.'

'Jesus, guv.'

'I'm sick, Kay. I'm in more pain than you can imagine.'

'I've had two kids.'

'Well, imagine them both coming out at the same time,

then make it happen all the time. Everywhere hurts. My knee, my thigh, my hips, my back. Everything. I need help.'

'That's why Abi's gone, Simon. She can't help you. She doesn't want Al to see his old man like this.'

'Right.' Fenchurch looked at the door to the stairs. 'Do you know where?'

'Guv. Give her time and space to process it, okay? You'll come to a new understanding. I know things have been tough for you for a while, but just give her that space.'

Fenchurch tried to see through it all, see any way in which—

He nodded. 'Fine. Where's Tom Carling?'

'Tom? Why are you looking for him?'

Fenchurch stared right at her. 'Carling assaulted Lisa last night.'

Her eyes bulged. 'What?'

'Don't make a big thing of it. I'm going to put a stop to any more of it. Where is he?'

'Saw him first thing. Said he was going to the gym downstairs. Reckons it's better than his station's one.'

'Run the briefing for me, would you?'

CHAPTER FORTY-FIVE

Fenchurch had to stop at the bottom of the stairs. The basement was dank and cold. Just the drip of a tap and the slow clanking of weights. He set off along the dark corridor as fast as he could. The gym was even darker, just the daylight glow of a phone next to the bench press in the corner. 'Come on, Carling! You've got this!' Timed with his exhales. Tinny music bled from headphones, like he was listening to 'Now That's What I Call Hi-Hat!'.

Fenchurch walked over and stood just in his field of vision. 'Morning, Tom.'

Carling rested the bar down. Weights so heavy the bar was curving in the middle. Over-compensating. He eased out his left earbud. 'Oh, hey. Morning.'

'Should you be doing that without someone to spot you?'

'Been doing this a long time, Si. Can spot myself.' He was pumping away again. Even in the cold, he was sweating.

Fenchurch knew that feeling. 'You're going to be late for the briefing.'

'What briefing?'

'Seven every morning.'

'Shit. I didn't know.' And he wasn't stopping his workout. Had no intention of making it.

'Okay. So how's it going with the NFT stuff?'

'Hard work. But we're getting there. I like working with Steve Clarke on the City stuff. Bridge less so.'

'Oh. Why's that?'

'Women.' Carling was smirking.

'Sorry, I don't get what you mean?'

Carling laughed. 'No, you wouldn't. Half your team's female. No wonder.'

'No wonder what?'

'Well, you know. Your results aren't exactly stellar, are they?'

Carling was an expert interviewer, always capable of finding the needle-thin chink in anyone's armour, then widening out until he could shove a sword through the gap.

Fenchurch took a deep breath. The cold down here was helping. 'Tom, I need to talk to you about an allegation.'

Carling stopped pressing and carefully returned the weight to the rack. He sat up, grabbed a towel and dabbed at his face. 'What *allegation*?'

'About you being up to your old tricks again.'

'My old tricks?' Carling tossed the towel back onto the chair. 'This to do with Lisa Bridge.'

'So you know?'

'Mate, I'm not interested in her.'

'Really? Single guy like you, with your reputation?'

'Fuck off, Si.'

'Tom. This isn't a joke. You groped her, didn't you?'

'I did nothing!' Carling let out a deep moan. 'That makes me sick, Simon. That you could even *think* I would do that.'

'Sure. So why is she complaining to me?'

'Because she can't handle the pressure. She's out of her depth. Surprised Clarke hasn't said anything to you.'

'Really.'

'I'm more surprised you can't see that she's useless. Clarke's running rings around her.' Carling was shaking his head, beads of sweat flying everywhere. 'This is the problem. Women get away with this shit because it used to be all about doing the job, now it's about how woke you are. Kissing the right ring. It's bullshit, Si. Fucking bullshit.'

'Sounds a bit misogynistic to me.'

'Misogynistic?' Carling laughed. 'Good one. Come on, Si, don't try and deny it. You've got a team full of birds. Eye candy over skill, am I right?'

Fenchurch was blushing. 'That's bollocks.'

'Yeah? Don't give me this bullshit, Si, because we all know you're a pervert. I've seen you looking at DI Reed's arse. Down Uzma's blouse. Makes me wonder what *you've* done with DC Bridge.'

'Don't try and tar me with the same brush as you.' Fenchurch wanted to smash his face against the wall. 'I'm going to report you for this, Tom.'

The words rattled around the room.

Carling broke the silence by grabbing the weight and lifting again. 'You know what, Si, you can fuck off. I'm heading back to Sutton after this. And I'll be reporting *you*.'

'What for?'

'Bullying. Intimidation. Sexual misconduct. All of it.'

Fuck this.

Fenchurch grabbed the bar and pressed it down, using his superior weight to pin the bar against Carling's chest. 'I know what you did to Lisa, Tom Thumb. You've got a reputation for being handsy. That's not a good thing. You'd think it'd make you stop. But no, you doubled down. You wait until you're alone, then you just can't help yourself. How many others are there? How many haven't spoken up? How many have you intimidated into silence?'

Carling was struggling to breathe.

'You'll pay for this, you little worm.'

'Simon.'

Someone was in the doorway. The faint light caught on his bald head. DCS Julian Loftus stepped into the gym. Full uniform, cap under his arm.

Fenchurch let go of the bar and stood up tall. 'Sir.'

The rack rattled as Carling returned the weight, sucking in deep breaths. 'Did you see what he just did to me?'

Loftus sighed. 'Tom, Tom, Tom, you'll never learn.'

'What? He tried to kill me!'

'I saw nothing of the sort.' Loftus was between them now. 'But I have just been upstairs speaking with DI Reed and DS Bridge. DI Carling, fetch your clothes and kindly Foxtrot Oscar.'

'Eh?'

'Go home, Tom. No shower, just get out of here. You're suspended, pending an investigation into your antics.'

'My *antics*?'

'DS Bridge isn't the first, Tom, and, unless someone does something about it, she won't be the last.'

'I thought you were a friend, Julian.'

'And like a lot of people, I thought you were a good cop and an honest man.' Loftus leaned forward. 'Now get out of my sight.'

Carling stood up, sweat dripping off him. He shot a glare between them, then grabbed his towel and scuttled off, shaking his head.

Leaving Fenchurch in there with Loftus.

'I'm sorry to intrude like this, but I was upstairs when DI Reed called me.' Loftus snorted. 'I saw what you did, Simon.'

'I'd do it again.'

'Quite right.'

'I should've called you, sir.'

'That's true.' Loftus smoothed a hand over his head. 'I've heard that story from him before. We almost got him last year, but somehow he persuaded his last victim to not comply with the investigation. DS Bridge came to you, am I right?'

Fenchurch nodded.

'And she will stand up, won't she?'

'I believe so.'

'Excellent.' Loftus clapped him on the arm like he would a trusty dog. 'Sorry I've been absent from this case. The new broom upstairs needs to be kept on a tight leash, I'm afraid. I've got Jason Bell's updates coming thick and fast, but I wanted to speak to you and see your take on it. But that can wait. Simon, please write up your statement on this matter.' He leaned in close. 'We have another to discuss, though.'

'What's that, sir?'

'Your addiction.'

'My *addiction*?'

'Don't do me the disservice of pretending you're not suffering from oxycodone addiction, Simon. Upon hearing through sources about your issues, I came to speak with you directly...'

'That source will be Kay Reed?'

'I'm not going to comment on that. But upon learning that you went to the gym to confront DI Carling, I followed you. And I overheard the whole exchange. Nothing to see here and I'll make sure of it.' Loftus fixed him with a hard stare. 'You know how I like to operate. I need good cops who owe me one. And you're now both.'

Bloody hell.

Fenchurch had been the one in charge of that dynamic, but now it had flipped on its head – he was the one who owed.

Loftus walked over to the door. 'Now, I'm off to see that buffoon, Bell. I'll be in touch.'

Fenchurch stood there, fizzing with adrenaline, but also feeling the drugs waving over him. He had to sit on the bench, soaked with sweat. With Carling's sweat.

He'd lost it.

This junk sickness. This withdrawal. It made him lose control.

If Loftus hadn't been there...

How far would he have taken it?

'Simon?' Loftus was back, peering around the door. 'Forgot to say. DI Reed said the duty doctor has cleared Jack Walsh for interview.'

CHAPTER FORTY-SIX

F enchurch walked along the corridor, his shirt soaked through. His suit jacket hid the worst of it, but it was only a matter of time before that was sodden too.

The painkillers were doing their job, at least. His knee was less like a hammer had struck it and more a subtle throb. But the rest of him...

The dope sickness had cleared.

He could try to deny it all, but he *was* a junkie.

He checked his phone. Still nothing from Abi.

A message from Chloe:

Just got off shift so apols for delay. No, not heard from her, but haven't in weeks. You on for lunch tomo?

Tomorrow felt like a lifetime away.

He tapped out his reply:

Lunch sounds great. You choose where.

Chloe Fenchurch is typing...

> Is Mum okay?

Fenchurch had no idea.

No, he did. He knew she was strong, just like their daughter. But...

> Must be her phone.

A stupid lie and a blatant one.

He needed to fix it, send her the truth. He called her.

'Dad? What's up?' She was yawning.

'Listen, your mum's gone somewhere and I don't know where.'

She paused. 'Right.' Another pause. 'Are you still here?'

'I am, why?'

'First floor meeting room.'

'I'll be there.' Fenchurch hobbled off around the corner.

Chloe was standing in the doorway, frowning. 'God, your leg looks bad.'

'I'll live.' Fenchurch got past her and took a seat. A pleasure to take the weight off it. 'Just... Your mother's gone. Haven't seen her this morning.'

'Oh.'

'I know things aren't great between you, but have you—'

'No, not for ages. What's happened?'

'She got upset about the painkillers I'm on.'

'The oxy? She got upset by that?'

'It's not like I've been hiding it, but...'

'Weird.'

'Let me know when she gets in touch.'

'Of course, but don't hold your breath.' She paused. 'Dad, I saw Jon Nelson yesterday.'

'He mentioned it to me.'

'Did he say he had a zip gun?'

'He *what*?'

'He was going to kill Younis.'

'Wait. Back up.'

'I arrested them both. Jon was following some doctor.'

'Deacon?'

'Right. He's working for his wife.'

'Bloody hell. And he tried to kill Younis?'

'Well, that's the thing, Dad. I *think* it was Jon's gun, even though it's more likely the criminal would have the gun. If I had reasonable grounds, rather than just a gut instinct, someone would be in handcuffs. But it's fifty-fifty in my mind. Professionally.'

'And personally?'

'Personally...' She blew air up her face. 'Personally, I worry it was Jon's gun. He tried and failed. Couldn't do it.'

'Thanks. And if you hear from your mum?'

'Will do.'

Fenchurch heaved himself back up and left the room.

'Whatever dose you're on, Dad, you clearly need a stronger one.'

Fenchurch didn't have the heart to tell her he was going cold turkey. One secret he'd keep until he was clean again. 'See you tomorrow, love.' He kissed her cheek and walked off down the corridor.

What the hell was Nelson doing with a zip gun?

Assuming it was his...

This was getting uncomfortable.

A door opened and Bridge shot out. She stopped dead, eyes

THE LAST THING TO DIE

wide. 'Sir?' She clocked Fenchurch and blinked hard a few times, then brushed at her cheeks.

'Are you okay?'

She shrugged. 'I submitted the complaint.'

Fenchurch nodded. 'I spoke with DCS Loftus after you.' He stared hard at her, the intensity to underline the magnitude. 'DI Carling has been suspended.'

'Good.' She let out a deep breath. 'That's... Thank you.'

'None of it was my doing, really. DI Reed deserves some of the credit, but you deserve most of it. You've experienced a terrible thing and you—'

'Okay... Listen, I need to clear my head, so can I take five?'

'Sure thing, Lisa. Take as long as you need.'

She smiled at him, then dashed off down the corridor, stomping away.

Fenchurch stood there, wiping sweat from his brow. He wanted to go after her, to reassure her, to make her realise it wasn't her doing.

But he didn't.

Instead, he opened the door she'd come out of.

Reed was sitting there, staring at two evidence bags. 'Guv?'

'Just saw Lisa. I told her Carling isn't a problem anymore.'

'What's that supposed to mean?'

'Suspended.'

'Shit, really?'

'Really. Thank you. You filed the paperwork very quickly.'

'Lisa was in such a bad way that I needed to do it.'

'Loftus said you called him?'

'He called me.'

Lying sod. 'Well, thank you for doing that, anyway.' Not least because Loftus stopped Fenchurch from taking things way too far.

The door opened and Dalton Unwin led his client in.

Jack Walsh looked like he'd got drunk, lost his house keys, slept in a hedge and woke up to find a badger defecating on his face. And then his day only got worse from there. Deep bags under his eyes, thick stubble. Hair like a toilet brush that should've been chucked out months ago.

They sat opposite and didn't say anything.

Unwin smiled.

'Okay.' Reed leaned forward and started the recorder. 'Continuing the interview dated Monday eighteenth July, 2022. Present still are DI Kay Reed, DCI Simon Fenchurch, Jack Walsh and Dalton Unwin, representing Mr Walsh.'

Fenchurch sat back and shifted his gaze between them. 'I gather congratulations are in order?'

Walsh was scratching at his ear. 'Eh?'

'Jadzia told us she's pregnant.'

Walsh gasped. Eyes bulging, looking everywhere. 'What?'

'Two months, she reckons. Which is very naughty of her.'

Walsh let out a deep breath. 'Well, it ain't mine!'

'Sure about that?'

'I told you I'm not a nonce. I didn't touch her until she was sixteen.'

'I bet you wanted to, though.'

Walsh shook his head. 'Saying nothing to that.'

'She was in the training ground all that time. Seeing her dad, but speaking to the lads. Speaking to you, no doubt.'

'Nope.'

'Sure about that?'

'Of course! Soon as I clocked her, I knew she was trouble. Plus the fact she's the owner's daughter?'

'But you couldn't help yourself, could you?'

'I'm a weak man. I couldn't resist.' Walsh was starting to twitch a bit. Little jerks here and there. 'I'm trying to be strong, but... Admitting you've got a weakness is the hardest part, you know?'

Fenchurch clocked the tremors, so he reached into his jacket pocket for a prop he'd gone back to the car for. Had to root around in his pigsty of a glove box for it. 'Don't mind me.' He rested the empty bottle of oxycodone on the table.

It was all Walsh could focus on. He'd gone twelve hours without a pill now. Must've been closer to eighteen since he'd had a dose.

Fenchurch wasn't the only one in that room suffering from opioid withdrawal.

Reed tossed the larger bag onto the table. 'This is from your flat. Our forensics team found it first thing this morning. How do you explain this?'

Walsh looked at it and jerked his head away. 'No idea what that is.'

'It appears to be stuff that went missing from Curtis Archer's home. Empty bottles of oxycodone prescription. Plus we found a load of crime scene cleaning gear.'

'Woah, woah.' Walsh raised his hands. 'This is bullshit!'

'Deny it all you want, Jack, this is stacking up against you.'

'Listen, I haven't been home since yesterday morning at five. You stopped me going in at night!'

'When you tried to assault DCI Fenchurch.'

'That's bullshit. Total bullshit.'

Reed held up a hand. 'Jack, level with me here. Did you kill Curtis Archer?'

'No!' But he seemed too hungover to put up an effective defence.

'Inspector.' Unwin rested forward on his wrists, his fingers playing with the opposing cufflinks. 'Throwing baseless accusations at my client is not going to get you results. We all sat in here yesterday and I, in good faith, promised to work with you to establish the truth of the matter. We have held up our part of that bargain, but you're accusing him of cleaning up a murder victim's home?'

Reed nodded. 'That's exactly it. Except Curtis Archer isn't officially a murder victim.'

'But he will become one, I suspect.' Unwin shook his head. 'And you've got forensic evidence to back up these claims?'

Reed held his gaze then held up the evidence bag. 'We'll be processing these in due course for prints and DNA.'

'So why have you brought them in here?'

'Because I'm giving you and your client a chance to get ahead of this. Admit what you did. It'll save us all a lot of heartache.'

'Love, when the lad was killed, I was in the training ground with the boys eating bacon sarnies, discussing the day's schedule and a bit of bother with a foreign lad.'

'You could've been in to his home before that.'

'This is preposterous.' Unwin sat back, arm draped on the back of his chair, motioning at his client with the other hand. 'Guys, it's time to just let Mr Walsh go. This is a circus and you know it.'

'Last chance, Jack.'

'Ain't got nothing to do with me, love.'

'Okay, Jack. We want to ask you about all the calls you made to Terry Monaghan last night.'

'No idea what you're talking about.'

'Really? Because they're on his phone screen.' She held up an evidence bag containing a phone. 'Jack Walsh. Plain as day.'

'You'll no doubt have read them, yeah?'

'Terry's phone's encrypted. We can't get into it without his passcode.'

'That's your problem, not mine.'

'Well, it's yours too, Jack, because Terry Monaghan was murdered.'

Walsh looked up at Fenchurch, his forehead creased. 'Terry was one of the good ones.'

'Someone killed him. Was that you, Jack?'

'No! I was with my bird!'

'By bird, I take it you mean Jadzia O'Brien?'

'Right. It wasn't me! I was with Jadzia all night!'

Reed was standing her ground. 'When did you last see Terry Monaghan?'

'Ages ago. Why?'

'Okay, and what about talking on the phone? Texts?'

'Well, last night.'

'This is why you were calling him?'

Walsh looked at his lawyer, got a curt nod, then gave a stern one. 'Got a worrying call from him. Asking about this woman he was seeing. Marie. She wouldn't speak to him, but she still messaged me occasionally. Knew her through a mate. Terry wanted me to act as a go-between, fix things up. So I met her last night, told her Terry wanted to see her. Urgently. She hot-footed it out of there.'

'This is Marie Deacon?'

'That's her. Absolute ball ache, I tell you. Jadzia came back from the ladies', thought I was seeing her on the sly! Bloody hell, that's a lesson I've learnt about five times over.'

'What about all the calls you made to Terry Monaghan, Jack? The texts?'

'When?'

'Last night. What were you talking to him about?'

'He didn't answer. And I just tried calling him to let him know I'd dropped the bomb on Marie. That's it.'

'And that took five messages?'

'Love. In my game, you don't leave anything unsaid. You

say it. If they're not listening, you still say it. If they're not picking up, you call back. Understand?'

'Same as in our game, Mr Walsh.' Reed ran a hand over the evidence bag. 'But Terry called you back, didn't he?'

'I've no idea.'

Reed held up another phone in an evidence bag. 'This is your mobile, Jack, which we confiscated after your arrest last night. It appears that Mr Monaghan called you and left a message. What did he say?'

'None of your business.'

'Jack, we have a statement to the effect that you were supplying people with a controlled substance.'

'What?'

'Oxycodone.'

'That's bullshit!'

'Gave it to Curtis Archer. Fentanyl to Terry Monaghan.'

'No way.'

'Listen, if you want to clear your—'

'Fine.' Walsh sighed. 'Give me my phone.'

Reed frowned at Fenchurch.

He nodded.

She rested it on the table.

Walsh reached for it.

'No, sir. This is evidence.' Reed snapped on a pair of gloves. 'What's the passcode?'

'I ain't giving you that!'

'Come on.'

Unwin raised an eyebrow. 'I suggest you let my client go should this prove fruitful.'

'We'll consider it.'

Unwin motioned at his client. 'Over to you, Jack.'

Walsh dropped his head onto the desk. 'Passcode is 696969.'

Fenchurch watched Reed tap it in.

Bingo.

His home screen was filled with dating and messaging apps, each with numbers in the hundreds and thousands. Tinder, Hinge, Sugardaddio. WhatsApp, Facebook Messenger, Snapchat, Schoolbook Live.

'You like chatting to people, Jack?'

'It's good to talk.'

'How do you have any time to coach kids?'

'What can I say, I'm a grade-A shagger.' Walsh snorted. 'Sorry. I'm an addict and this is my bottle of vodka hidden at the back of the cupboard. Under the sink. In the wardrobe.' He sighed. 'Not even my main phone, that. This is my one for all those apps. I gave it to Dalton here for safekeeping. Gave Terry the number for emergencies.'

'You and he ever—'

'He's a shagger too. We chatted a lot about tactics. He was my wingman sometimes. Others, I was his.'

'Still. Two phones, Jack. Why?'

'I don't want my kid finding those messages when she's playing with me phone.'

'Your *kid*?'

'Yeah... Got three girls. All between three and ten.'

'Same mother?'

'Two mothers. Me trying to fix my life. And failing. And another was... Well, when I was on loan in Holland.'

What a way to make a mess of your life and three others. Plus the mothers'.

Christ.

'Here we go.' Reed was in the text message app.

Money Shot Monaghan:
Call me.

Money Shot Monaghan:
Dude! Call me!

Money Shot Monaghan:
Mate!

She went into the phone app and there was a missed call:

Money Shot Monaghan:
Missed call, 19:36

'That wasn't long before he died, guv.' Reed looked at Walsh. 'Do you mind if we call your voicemail?'

Walsh shrugged.

Reed hit dial.

A sparkly female voice answered. 'Welcome to the GoMobile voicemail service. You have... one... unplayed message. Press one to—'

Reed stabbed the one button.

'Jack. Jack, it's me. Tez. Money Shot. Listen, thanks for the ... little help earlier. Much appreciated. Cops were here, no idea what they wanted. Thing is, he's going to kill us. Both of us. Get out of London now. You hear me? Get the fuck out of London!'

'Shit!' Walsh leaned forward, resting his head onto the desktop. 'What the hell?'

'Who is he talking about, Jack?'

'I've no idea!'

Reed played it again.

Fenchurch focused on the background noise this time. It sounded like Monaghan was packing, which checked out with Clooney's initial assessment.

If he'd just heeded his own advice and run, he'd still be alive.

Maybe.

Fenchurch stared at Walsh, but he was still resting his head on the table. 'You've no idea who that would be about?'

'Absolutely none.'

'Come on, Jack. You were doing so well there.'

Walsh looked up at them. 'What?'

'Not lying. Telling us the truth. Helping. Why ruin it all now?'

Walsh just shook his head.

'We heard you got a recommendation from Curtis Archer.'

It was like a light went on inside his head. 'Look, I've got an idea. Terry spoke to me last week. Came to the training ground. Bit out of the blue, but I thought, okay. Told me his dealer had gone to ground.'

'His dealer?'

'He was on fentanyl for his knee. A patch on there. Only thing that kept him playing. I mean, daft prick... As soon as he did a random drugs test, game over. But he said he had no other option. Needed the money until he had his coaching badges, then he'd be sorted.'

'And?'

'Well, I told him about a guy I go to about my back.'

'I take it this isn't a doctor.'

'Let's leave it at a guy.'

'I need his name, Jack.'

'I don't know it.'

'But you know where he is, right?'

CHAPTER FORTY-SEVEN

Fenchurch found Uzma not in the incident room but in their office space.

Staring at her laptop like she wanted to smash it down into its component atoms. Phone to her ear, teeth bared. She clocked Fenchurch and killed the call. 'Sir, I'm looking for Pinkie. I mean, Tom.'

'DI Carling's no longer part of the investigation.' Fenchurch lowered himself into the seat next to her. 'Why?'

'I needed to check something with him, but hey ho.'

'Can anyone else help with it?'

'I'll find Lisa Bridge.' She looked up at him. 'Take it you're looking for me?'

'Just wondering how your contact with drugs is going?'

'I've linked up with both the Central Task Force and Middle Market Drugs. I'll spare you the details, but they're both helping so you don't need to grass to teacher for me.'

A tall, chunky man was sitting opposite her. He looked over at Fenchurch and grinned. One of his front teeth had a sliver of gold running down it. He stood and held out his hand. 'DI Richard Hay. Middle Market Drugs.'

Fenchurch shook it. 'You took over from thingy O'Keefe, right?' Jon Nelson's old boss. He couldn't remember his name and he'd found his body.

'Thingy.' Hay laughed. 'Sure, I did. Want to thank you.'

'What for?'

'I spoke to Uzma here. The stuff your lot found in Walsh's flat has hallmarks of street oxy. A particular dealer too.'

'Which one?'

'Sounds like you know?'

'Well, I've got word there's someone selling oxy from a cafe on Mile End Road. Mark and Dean's. Heard of it?'

'Strangely enough, I have. There are six dealers selling oxy on the street around there. That guy's one of them.'

'Mark or Dean?'

'Not sure. Think it's both and an accomplice.'

'It's true?'

'It's just intel.'

'Right. Is this the guy who's selling the stuff you found?'

'Yep.'

'Well. We need to speak to them. So, I'm wondering if Dean and Mark are a discrete unit—'

'—or if they're connected?' Hay shut his laptop and stood up. 'Thing is, sir... We think that's part of a highly layered operation possibly leading to our old chum Younis.'

'Possibly?'

'There are others it could be.'

'Younis...' Fenchurch sighed. 'Figures that he'd still be at it.'

'We don't have any direct evidence. His time inside has made him too wise. He got very smart.' Hay stuffed his hands in his pockets. 'When he was released two years ago, he stuck lots of people

---

and shell companies between him and anything illegal. And the word on the street is the first thing he did when he got out was to slit someone's throat for running a side hustle. Put the fear of death into the rest of them. Not had a single actionable item of intel since. Tightened his operation like a camel's arse in a sandstorm.'

'But?'

Hay smiled. 'But the bottom line is we think he's still selling drugs, still laundering money.'

'He's using this Mark and Dean's café?'

'We believe he might be. Well, someone is.'

Fenchurch nodded along with it. 'Okay, let's go and pick up this guy.'

'Not so fast, sir.'

'Excuse me?'

'These are critical investigations of strategic value.'

'Yeah, you guys are so bloody funny.' Fenchurch wasn't laughing. 'Why aren't they in custody?'

'Because we're looking to build an operation against them.'

'Meanwhile, they're ruining lives?'

'It's the age-old tightrope we have to run across in drugs.'

'Well. This place has come up in a murder case, so we've got a chance to leverage them for our benefit and yours. How's about we run across together?'

Hay shifted his gaze between Fenchurch and Uzma. 'We do it all together or not at all. Okay?'

CHAPTER FORTY-EIGHT

Mark and Dean's was a café on Mile End Road, set back from the street and wedged between a Tesco Express and a Boots chemist. That bit of Stepney that used to be dodgy at half four, let alone after dark.

Fenchurch's first beat as a uniformed cop.

Place used to be the Last Knight of Avalon, a pub that couldn't look less heroic and probably hadn't been refurbished since Arthur sat on the throne of Albion.

Now it was all stripped back to its bare brickwork.

Fenchurch pushed inside for the first time since he'd separated two grandmothers from smashing each other's heads off the bar top. They'd been mid-forties at best and seemed impossibly old back then. Now he was beyond that age, he didn't know how to feel about it.

Doing a brisk trade, though. The dark smells of Ethiopian coffee mixed with the caramel of Colombian beans.

The two baristas – Mark and Dean presumably – looked identical. Hair in topknots, bushy beards covering most of their hooped shirts so it was hard to see the granddad collars.

Three tables filled with workmen, though they were enjoying small coffees and paninis rather than vats of instant and bacon rolls.

Sonic Youth blasted out of the café's speakers, their mid-Nineties commercial peak, but still way too abrasive and experimental for this time of morning.

Fenchurch clocked the suspect already.

A hipster, sitting at the end of the bar – the same scarred wood that Shelly and Emma-Jane had been fighting at all those years ago – working away on a MacBook. No headphones on, though. He scratched his jet-black beard.

Fenchurch sat next to him, leaving a space between them, and picked up a menu. A wooden clipboard with typewritten text on brown paper. Half of it was devoted to coffee and its various forms – at least seven types that Fenchurch had never heard of, and a few countries too. A quarter was savoury food, a load of paninis but also hearty stuff like meat pies, fish and chips, even a side order of jellied eels. Irony wasn't dead with these guys. Or rather, snark at the East End's heritage.

The target was looking at him. Smile and a nod, then back to his computer.

The good side of being in partial withdrawal from oxy was Fenchurch looked like he was in withdrawal from oxy. Pale, sweaty, desperate. Not a detective, just some junk-sick loser looking for a fix.

He frowned at his menu again, even though he knew he'd just order a cup of filter coffee. Though there were four different ways it was served.

He let out a sigh.

'Tough choice, huh?'

Fenchurch looked over at the target. 'Too much choice.'

He was grinning. 'First time I came in here, I thought I knew coffee but these guys *know* coffee.'

'What's the difference between the filters?'

'Well. I'd go with the V60 drip, personally, but then I don't like a bitter coffee.'

'Me neither.' Fenchurch picked up his menu and limped over to the counter. Typically, neither Mark nor Dean were free now. One was through in the kitchen, while the other was working at an espresso machine, making a big order. 'Be with you in a sec.'

It was going to be hours, by the looks of it.

Fenchurch waddled back over, wincing as he sat. 'I'll give them a minute.'

The target was frowning at his leg. 'You okay?'

'Waiting on an op. You know how it is.'

'Right, right.'

Fenchurch picked up the morning's *London Post*. 'Shame about what happened to Curtis Archer, eh?'

'God, yeah. Kid was some player. To just die like that. Heart attack, they're saying.'

'Heart attack?' Fenchurch was shaking his head. 'At his age?'

'Happens.'

'Yeah, I guess it does.' Fenchurch stretched out his knee until it popped. 'You bugger.'

'Mate, that doesn't sound good.'

'It ain't good.' Fenchurch exhaled slowly. 'Not good at all.'

They sat in silence and the hipster sipped at his coffee.

Sonic Youth became that Pavement song about mulleted hair.

The target looked over at Fenchurch. 'Take it you've been to the doctor about it, yeah?'

'Keep trying to get a date for my op, but they knock me back. NHS waiting times are brutal just now.'

'That's covid for you. Total joke.'

'You believe that shit?'

'Oh God, no. It's all a way to control us. Turn us from subjects into peasants. The new feudalism.'

'So true.' Fenchurch grimaced. 'I can't keep on like this.'

He sniffed and looked back to his laptop. 'What you need is something for your knee.'

'Asked, refused.'

'Mate of mine is on these pills that take all the pain away.'

'Yeah? Sounds like nonsense to me.'

'Oh, it's true. Says the only thing that's ever touched his pain was oxycodone.'

'I was on that. Doc said I was getting addicted.'

The guy looked him up and down. 'Name's Ben.'

'Simon.'

Ben leaned in closer. 'Listen. I can get you some oxy.'

'Doc said I shouldn't be on that anymore.'

'What does he know?'

'Mate, I'm fine.'

'You ain't fine. Look at you.' Ben laughed. 'How much do you need?'

'Oxy? Well, anything really.'

'What were you on?'

'Eight eighties.'

Ben's eyes almost popped out. 'A day?'

'A day.'

'Mate... Well. I can do you forty.'

'That's five days' worth, right?'

'Right. You come back here on Friday or Saturday, I'd be able to do the same again?'

'Mate, I've only just got off them.'

Ben nodded. 'But you look like you should still be on them. Could double it with some notice too.'

'Just not sure.'

'Well. That's your lookout. I'll be here. Every day. Rain or shine.' Ben tapped at his notebook. 'Writing a novel here.'

'What's it about?'

'Ain't telling you. Don't want you nicking my idea!'

'Trust me, last thing I'm doing is writing a novel.'

Ben closed his laptop lid. 'How about it, then?'

Fenchurch got out his wallet. 'Sounds ideal.'

'Woah, woah. Don't pay me.' Ben shuffled closer. 'Go up to the till. Order a long black with a cronut. And a bag of beans to takeaway.'

'Right.'

'You'll get charged fifty quid. Pay it. Come see me.'

'Fifty quid?'

'I mean, you'll actually get the coffee and the cronut as well.'

'I meant, that's it? Seems cheap.'

'I'm providing a service to people. The government are too fixated on vaccines and controlling people. I'm just helping out the man on the street.'

'I appreciate it.' Fenchurch reached over for a serviette and dried his forehead. 'Thank you.' He got up and staggered over to the till.

One of the hipster baristas was looking over the top of his glasses. 'What can I get you, pal?' As Scottish as a fight in a chip shop.

'Can I get a long black with a cronut?'

Eyes glanced over at Ben. 'Sure thing. Milk in the coffee?'

'Please. And a bag of beans.'

'Colombian or Ethiopian?'

Fenchurch leaned forward. 'What do you recommend?'

'Ethiopian this month is pretty special.'

'Then Ethiopian it is.'

'Coming right up.' The hipster looked away. 'That's it ready for your card.'

Fifty quid flashed up on the display.

Interesting how Mark or Dean didn't read it aloud.

Fenchurch pressed his card into the reader and typed in the PIN. 'There you go.'

The hipster passed him a big bag of coffee beans. A kilo, maybe, but nothing like forty quid's worth, unless they were *special* beans. 'I'll bring the rest over.'

'Thanks.' Fenchurch lugged his package over and sat down.

Sure enough, sitting on top of the *Post* was a tub of oxy. Same generic manufacturer his own pills were. He inspected the tub – a little corner of a sticky label was still attached, then he put them away in his pocket.

So bloody tempting to just pop one.

Fenchurch stood up and held out his warrant card. 'Benjamin Morris, I'm arresting you for the supply of a controlled substance.'

The front door clattered open and Hay burst in with a squad of drugs cops. They swarmed the bar area.

The workmen were all on their feet, fists clenched, ready for a scrap.

Uzma joined Fenchurch by the bar.

Ben looked like he was going to bolt.

Fenchurch grabbed his wrist and squeezed, pushing him down to his knees. 'You don't have to say anything but anything you do say—'

CHAPTER FORTY-NINE

Nelson charged along Bishopsgate, not quite back to the pre-pandemic level but not far off. A lot of lunchtime takeaways had shut and half of the Prets were gone – still left what felt like a hundred just on that stretch. The noise of commuters walking, talking, eating, smoking, drinking...

It all drilled into Nelson's skull.

The fancy coffee wasn't yet touching the sides of his fatigue – he'd been chaining them all night, so it was maybe no wonder.

Stupid.

Well. He'd get his mischief out of the way, then head home for as much shuteye as his wired mind would allow.

He stopped outside the station and yawned. Everything seemed haloed, the buses passing each other on the street, the man smiling at him.

'Jon.' DI Steve Clarke waved as he passed him. Suited and booted, *FT* folded under his arm, swinging his briefcase. 'Come on in.' He held the station's front door.

Nelson hadn't been inside Bishopsgate station in years. Place hadn't changed in that time, probably hadn't in over a century.

This lot were like a private army, the British equivalent of the Swiss Guard protecting the Vatican. Ancient capitals like London and Rome had their deep secrets. Nelson had heard the City was the only part of Britain not under the direct governance of Parliament. A square mile cleaved off in pursuit of money and power, beholden only to itself. Forget your conspiracy theories, this was a real-world conspiracy, the British establishment conspiring not so much to own the world as take a big cut from those that did.

'In here.' Clarke opened a heavy door and led into a wood-lined room. Paintings on the wall of many unnamed moustachioed Victorian policemen. The window to the street was leaded and obscured by misting. Made the place glow.

Clarke waited for Nelson to enter, then had a peek out into the atrium before he shut the door. As though he didn't want anyone to see him smuggling a normal person in. He dumped his briefcase and paper on the table. 'You look like shit.'

'Feel like it.' Nelson rested his coffee and laptop, then sat opposite. 'Been up all night working. Didn't get much sleep.'

'Now, Jon, you can get away with that in your twenties, but at our age it's not to be advised.'

'I'll never learn. I'm like a dog with a bone.'

'And you've got something for me?'

Nelson took his laptop out of the bag and rested it on the table. 'I've found something.'

'Before you open that monster, why me?'

'Why you?'

'Yeah. Why have you come to me? Why are you, ex-DI Jon Nelson of the Met, coming to me, DI Steve Clarke of the City of London Police, with this?'

'Because you're the only one I can trust.'

Clarke laughed. 'Things must be pretty shit for you if that's the case.'

'I can't trust any of them in the Met. Least of all Fenchurch. And I don't want him to win.'

'Win? Jon, this isn't a game. It's not about—'

'Can I trust you, Steve?'

'Of course you can. We've worked together so many times over the years.' Clarke held up a finger. 'But I'll warn you. If you're trying to get into the City police, don't think it'll happen. Not with your recent record.'

'My recent record?'

'Jon, you screwed up. Big time. This isn't your chance to recover lost ground, okay? This is just you helping a mate.'

The truth stung.

Nelson grinned. 'Fine.'

Clarke reached into his briefcase for a chilled bottle of water and set it down on the table. 'Okay. What's this about?'

'Younis.'

'You don't pick the easy targets, do you?' Clarke tore off the cap and took a sip. 'If you want to take him down, you should speak to your old mob's drug squad. This is the City. I'm not going to deny that there's coke being snorted in most buildings here, but we've got different fish to fry.'

'This isn't about drugs.'

Clarke held the water bottle over his lips. 'Go on?'

'Not directly. It's what I believe he's doing with all that money he's been creaming off the streets.'

'Okay, I'm interested.' Clarke took a glug of water and put the cap back on. 'Spill.'

Nelson took a drink of coffee, trying to assemble his thoughts. It was like building a brick wall in the dark. Drunk. With less than half the cement you needed. And it was raining.

And your bricks were all Lego. 'Okay. I'm offering you this help for free. I don't want anything other than one promise.'

'What's that?'

'That you'll at least *try* to take Younis down.'

'Half of my time is spent on that prick, so please. Fire away.'

'Okay. Have you heard of a DAO?'

'You pronounce it Dow, Jon.'

'Right.'

'And of course I have.' Clarke shrugged off his suit jacket and rested it on the back of his chair. 'Web3 and crypto is a big focus of my life. DAO stands for Decentralised Autonomous Organisation. It's a Web3 object that sells tokens in exchange for a vote on what they do with their pooled cash. It's all programmed in on the blockchain and gives the owners collective power and decision-making. You can buy and sell your tokens of ownership.'

'Okay, so what would one buy?'

'Like being back at high school, this.' Clarke rolled his eyes. 'There was one in America that bought an original copy of their Constitution, so they could preserve it, independently of any museum or government body. And another bought the original unmade screenplay to Jodorowsky's *Dune*, written way back in the Sixties. That wasn't filmed, but different adaptations were made in the Eighties and again last year. But that original screenplay was different. It had a big influence on *Star Wars* and *Alien*.'

Nelson laughed. 'Quite the film buff.'

'Damn right. It's how I cope with life. That and a bottle of red every night.'

'I read about that DAO. That lot thought they could buy a copy of the screenplay at auction and it gave them rights to make the film.'

Clarke laughed. 'Yeah. It's like buying a Lee Child novel in a charity shop and thinking you can make a Reacher TV show. Spending a few million just because they didn't understand copyright law.' He narrowed his eyes. 'What's your point here?'

'I've been thinking about it all night. Reading about it too. Some people have theories that it's a scam. I'm not sure if it is or if it's just stupidity, but I saw a few ideas on how you *could* execute a scam like that. For instance, instead of buying a screenplay or a copy of the US Constitution, why not use a DAO to buy NFTs.'

Clarke leaned forward, resting on his elbows. 'Go on.'

'It's all digital. Nothing in the real world. NFTs can be a few hundred quid a pop or a few million. Totally unregulated market. Lots of data security issues.'

'Have you got a specific one?'

'Well, yes.'

'Now I'm intrigued. Go on?'

'I'm a PI now. Working for a divorce client. Her husband's big into crypto. And I know he's in league with Younis.'

'Huh.'

'Saw them on the street. I thought it was some scam relating to his day job. He's a doctor. I found out last night that he's deep into crypto investments. Or was. Turns out he's lost a *lot* of money.'

'How much?'

'Tens of millions.'

'Shit.'

'Right. My firm has access to some data we maybe shouldn't, but it let me see what he was invested in. And he'd invested it all in one set of NFTs. Who doesn't want a picture of a pirate?'

Clarke frowned. 'A pirate?'

'Jolly Roger's World of Pirates.'

'Run by Neoxis. Seattle-based firm.' Clarke took a glug of water. 'Fenchurch was asking about that earlier.'

'Interesting. I did a lot of digging into Neoxis. They're just a front. The technology that underpins it all is someone else. Someone local. BRO Capital.'

'Jon, I know them. It ain't them.'

'I've spent all night scouring the blockchain ledger they use for these Jolly Rodger NFTs. It's the blockchain BRO run for their coins.'

Clarke slumped back in his chair and huffed out a sigh. 'Lying bastards.'

'Come on, Steve. You just left it at believing them?'

'No. Just hadn't got around to checking.'

'Well.' Nelson cracked his knuckles and got a satisfying ping of pain. 'Just as well I did. Ran a lot of queries against his transactions and started spotting patterns.'

'In this doctor's transactions?'

'No. In the whole thing. Sure enough, most of the investors bought them as long-term investments. But the values for the NFTs have all plunged and are worth fractions of what they paid for them. Like about two grand each.'

'It's the crypto winter, Jon. Huge losses everywhere. The bubble's burst.'

'I found ten accounts that look funny. These accounts bought tons of NFTs *before* the initial offering. One hundred quid each.'

'*Each?*'

'Right. And they sold them all to the same DAO for between one and three million quid each.'

'Seen that a lot, Jon. The founders are allowed to buy them before trading. Sell their private ones after the initial offering, pocket the difference. I don't think it's morally great, but it happens.'

'Great way to clean dirty money.'

Clarke twisted up his lips, then shut his eyes. Rubbed at his forehead. 'Explain?'

'You're Younis. You've got a big pot of filthy money. You use it to buy NFTs for bugger all. Then you sell them to a DAO you control for millions. You get one hundred percent of the initial amount, but the DAO's now saddled with the assets, which are now worthless.'

'Right.' Clarke rocked back. 'Holy shit. That's... That's genius. Most money laundering, twenty percent would be good. This is close to a hundred percent, plus you've got the value of the NFTs still there for a long-term investment. So when the next bubble expands, you can rinse and repeat.'

'So that all checks out?'

'So far. Who owns these accounts who bought before the start?'

'I can't tell. The cleaned cash received from selling the NFTs to the DAO has been taken out as cash. I can't track it, but you could.'

Clarke nodded at Nelson's computer. 'This is all on there?'

'Down to the account, yes.'

'Christ, Jon. This is good.' Clarke rubbed at his smooth chin and seemed to find a patch he'd missed in his morning shave. 'Okay, so I'm with you. This doctor, how does he fit in?'

'Well, he doesn't. He's just a mug. Bought five NFTs for over a million each. Sitting at a value of about ten grand.'

'Jesus.'

'Yeah. My problem, Steve, is how a money laundering scheme like this cleans actual dirty cash.'

'You mean, *cash* cash?'

'Right. Real money. Banknotes. Taken from addicts on the streets.'

Clarke tilted his head. 'I don't get it.'

'Okay. Say you're in charge of an illegal East End street business, hoovering in cash from drugs or enforced prostitution. How do you get it into the system?'

'Oh, I've got an idea.' Clarke cracked his knuckles. 'Most schemes fake the income from vape shops, tanning salons or sweet shops, any cash business. But if you could get a bunch of the guys dealing for you to buy a share in the DAO with the dirty cash, then each transaction is so small that us lot in the City police or the NCA won't be looking at it. Ten grand's the minimum for one transaction to go into their scope. And Younis has hundreds of guys. Stick in, say, five grand each a day over the six months, it soon adds up to a lot of half-cleaned cash in this DAO. Execute those ten transactions and the account that bought those NFTs for hundreds now has millions of cleaned money.'

'That's how you'd do it.'

'Nobody would know.' Clarke got to his feet and walked over to the window.

Had Nelson persuaded him?

Was it enough?

Had he made a mistake and now looked like an idiot?

His last chance to take Younis down – or at least completely derail his empire...

Had he squandered it?

Clarke turned back to him. 'So, let me get this straight. Younis buys these NFTs for a hundred quid each. He sells them to himself for at least a million quid each in half-dirty cash, then withdraws the money, now cleaned. His DAO owns the worthless NFTs but he's cleaned all that cash?'

'That's pretty much the size of it.' Nelson smiled. 'And I've got an idea where Younis runs this scheme from.'

CHAPTER FIFTY

Fenchurch and Richard Hay sat opposite Ben Morris in an interview room in Leman Street. The clock above the door was ticking.

Fenchurch had to focus all of his efforts on Ben. Anything else and he'd have to think about—

Ignore it.

Focus. Here and now. Here and now.

Ben looked absolutely terrified. Hands shaking so much he tucked them under his armpits. In the café, he'd seemed older, wiser. But in this interview room, Fenchurch could see how much the beard aged him. He was barely twenty-one. Acting older. Looking older. But just a kid.

'Ben, you're a drug dealer. You will do time.'

The kid looked up at Fenchurch. 'There a but here?'

'If you give us a full confession, the choice is yours as to how long the time you serve is going to be.'

'You think you're going to flip me or something?'

'That's not *my* focus.' Fenchurch sat back and thumbed at

Hay. 'Richard here, sure. But me? I'm a murder squad detective.'

Ben frowned. 'Murder?'

'I'm a Senior Investigating Officer, too. I wouldn't normally be sitting in an interview like this. But it's a high-profile victim. Two, in fact.'

'Who?'

'Curtis Archer's one of them.'

'Shit.' Ben looked away. Yeah, he knew him. 'Who's the other?'

'Terry Monaghan.'

A bob of his Adam's apple.

'You supply drugs to people, Ben.'

'I don't.'

'You sold oxy to me.' Fenchurch put the evidence bag on the table. 'You've sold oxy to Curtis Archer, haven't you?'

Ben shook his head.

'What about Jack Walsh?'

Ben swallowed hard. 'Don't know what you mean.'

'Who else did you deal that stuff to? Terry Monaghan?'

'No.'

'Sorry. Terry died of a fentanyl overdose this evening. Was that stuff you sold him?'

'No!' Kid was getting rattled now.

'Did you kill him, Ben?'

'Why would I?'

'Easier if you answer the questions and I ask them.'

'I can't.' His voice was tiny. The microphone wouldn't pick it up.

'Ben. You're in deep, deep trouble here. The best case for you is you're going to do serious time. That's the best. At least ten years.'

Hay coughed. 'At *least* twelve, I reckon. Time served.'

Ben was focusing on Hay. 'What's the worst?'

'Depends on how many drug counts we're looking at here.' Hay fixed a heavy stare on Ben. 'We've only just begun with you. There'll be tons and tons of people crawl out of the woodwork. For each one we can definitively tie back to you, that'll be twelve each. Plus two murders...' Hay tilted his head from side to side. 'You're, what, twenty-one? You'll be lucky to be out in time to collect your old-age pension.'

Ben swallowed something down. Something heavy and thick, like his guilt or his conscience. 'And if I help you?'

'Well, I'm not going to mess you about with lies and false hope. You're going to do time, Ben, like DCI Fenchurch here said.' Hay folded his arms and looked up at the clock. Let the tick reverberate around the room. Five seconds. Ten. Fifteen. Then he watched Ben twitch. 'But I've seen cases where a year is deemed perfectly fine. A year's sentence and you're out. A year in a soft prison where you can study for qualifications. Come out and get a good job. But those cases are only for people who help.'

'How do I help?'

Fenchurch left him a long pause that made it look like he was thinking it all through. Fifteen. Sixteen. Seventeen. Eighteen. Nineteen. Twenty. 'First, Ben, you need to prove to me that you didn't kill them. Second, if you didn't kill them and you help us find out who did, then me and my pal here will have words and I'll push for you to only get the minimum sentence.' Three. Four. Five. Six. 'One year against at least forty.'

Ben rubbed at his beard. Every time he took his hand away from his face, it was shaking. 'Curtis put Jack Walsh onto me. Then Terry Monaghan.'

'How long had you been supplying him.'

'About six months.' Scratch, scratch, scratch. 'Curtis came

in once. Said his prescriptions ran out a long time ago, but he'd been getting street stuff. All too often it turned out to be paracetamol or ibuprofen. Or just chalk. He needed an opioid. Oxy, fentanyl. Anything. And he heard that my stuff's good. No idea who told him about me, but there he was. Desperate. Hungry. In dire need. Me and the boys in the café... We... have a source. Legit stuff. Prescription labels steamed off. Don't charge through the nose. Fair price. Build a good rep.'

Hay was frowning. 'You going to name your source?'

'I thought this was about the murder?'

'Right. But every little helps, Ben.'

'Thing is, I don't know. Dean and Mark don't either. Just have this guy come in. Wears a hoodie. Tall. He gives us the pills every Friday morning at ten.'

'And he takes the money?'

Ben shook his head. 'No.'

'So this guy who gives you the pills—'

'—he doesn't take anything from us, no.'

Hay was scowling. 'This sounds like absolute nonsense to me. The guy who gives you your pills doesn't take the money back?'

'That's correct.'

'So what happens?'

Ben sighed. 'We've got to put the cash into this bank account at a place nearby. I put in three quarters and keep the rest for myself. I live a good life with that cash. Pay for my rent, my shopping, whatever else, with cash. Even put a little bit into my bank account. But just a little.'

'So, the money's not really dirty if you're just spending it on yourself in cash. And not a lot.'

'Something like that.'

Decentralised money laundering.

Fenchurch had never heard of a scheme like that. 'Who owns that bank account?'

Ben shrugged. 'No idea.'

'But?'

Ben leaned forward, elbows cracking off the table. 'The way I heard it, the guy who runs the operation banked tens of millions of clean money.'

'You know his name?'

Ben nodded. 'And the rumour is he's leaving the country for good. You won't be able to prosecute him for anything if you don't catch him before his flight to Bangkok.'

'Ben. What's his name?'

CHAPTER FIFTY-ONE

The door clunked. 'Hate doing this, Jon.'

Nelson jerked awake. Blinking against the harsh light. He looked around the street, heart thudding. Where the hell was he?

Looked like the East End. Hard to name the street. Used to be his beat, but as a detective so he didn't have that same intimacy as a uniform would. He hadn't grown up around here. And he knew the back streets – people's homes, not their businesses.

The smell of hash filled the car. No wonder he'd been sleeping.

He wound the window up and stretched out. 'Hate doing what?'

'Sitting in a car with someone snoring like my mum.'

'Funny.'

'Seriously, you need to get one of those rings.'

'Rings?'

'She swears it works, but my old man still moans about it.'

Clarke looked around the street. 'No, what I hate is staking out a place that's outside of my jurisdiction. Especially as we haven't formally told your lot.'

'Not my lot anymore, Steve.'

'You know what I mean. They get very touchy when we don't go through protocol.'

'Your lot are the same.' Nelson recognised where they were. Mile End Road, looking at Amir's Wine and Beer. Probably the only building not to be gentrified in the immediate vicinity. A corner shop advertising local newspapers for as many ethnicities had even visited London, let alone lived around here. The *Midwest Telegraph* logo took up more space than the shop's own one. Cash transfers, the friend of the money launderer the world over.

Clarke passed him a cup of Captain Ribeye's Coffee. 'Sorry, but the usual one I go to is shut.' He nodded over the road. The hipster coffee joint – Mark and Dean's – was hidden by a few uniformed cops standing out the front. 'Any idea what that's all about?'

'Not my beat anymore, Steve. Keep telling you.'

'Right.' Clarke slurped coffee through the lid. 'Not bad at all. Anyway. Did you see anything while I was gone? Other than sheep jumping fences.'

'Very funny.' Nelson tore the lid off. The coffee was a shade lighter than his own skin. Perfect. 'No, I didn't see anyone.'

'Well, have a look at that.'

Two shifty guys strolled along the street, heavy-duty rucksacks hanging from their shoulders, and both entered the building.

'Not exactly the types to go off yomping through the Yorkshire Dales.'

An old man toddled out with his newspaper. Something shiny slid out onto the pavement. He knelt to pick it up, stuffed it back inside, then hurried away, looking around.

Both men followed him out, minus their rucksacks.

'No prizes for guessing what was in them.' Clarke yawned into his fist. 'Still. This is all checking out. Is the DAO still going?'

'I mean, it's still live.'

'And it's registered here?'

'The many bank accounts are.'

'How do you know that?'

Nelson tapped his nose. 'But if they're still paying money into a bank account, it can be used for other schemes. You could vary that model, so you could buy hundreds of ten grand NFTs or one fifty million quid one. All adds up to the same amount cleaned.'

Clarke slurped coffee and gasped. 'I'm impressed by your work, Jon. Didn't know you had it in you.'

'I was a management consultant before I joined the police. I've got some pretty solid analytical skills and I know a thing or two about the world you lot focus on.'

'Have you got anything else to back this up?'

'This is a lot, isn't it? Soon as your guys finish trawling through their records, you'll be able to get a warrant.'

'But you don't have anything else, do you?'

'No.'

'I'm not having a go, Jon. Just want to move fast on this.' Clarke finished his coffee and dumped the empty in the back footwell. 'Well, I think there's someone who might be able to help us.'

'Who?'

Nelson's phone blasted out:

Lisa calling...

He answered it. 'Hey, you okay?'

'Not really. Can you meet up?'

'Sure. Where are you?'

'At the station.'

'Hang on.' Nelson stuck it on mute. 'Mind if we head over to Leman Street?'

'Sure thing.'

'You don't mind?'

'Need to see a man about a dog myself.'

Nelson unmuted the call. 'Hey, I'll see you outside. Two minutes. Love you.' He hung up. 'Do you really not mind—'

Clarke was already doing a U-turn back towards Leman Street. 'Lisa's a good cop.'

'You know her?'

Clarke nodded. 'Done some work with her recently.' He grinned. 'You're punching above your weight there.'

'On so many scores.'

Clarke shot through the red light, almost back onto his territory.

Nelson finished his coffee. He had no idea what Lisa wanted. But something was up. Her shower last night, refusing to talk.

Clarke pulled up outside the station and got out into the thin summer rain. 'See you in a minute.'

Nelson followed him out onto the street.

Lisa was leaning against a lamppost, checking her phone. She looked up and didn't smile. Barely reacted to his presence.

Nelson walked over and she lost herself in a deep cuddle, her arms wrapping tight around him.

He squeezed his around her. 'Hey.'

'Hey.'

'You okay?'

She looked up at him, then away. 'No.'

'What happened?'

'Last night, I was working with Steve Clarke. And he left, went back to Bishopsgate. The incident room was empty.' She swallowed hard. 'And Tom... Tom Carling tried it on with me.'

'What?'

'I told him to fuck off. He didn't listen. Grabbed my arse. Grabbed my tits. Tried to kiss me.'

'Jesus, Lisa.'

'I pushed him away and ran.'

Nelson pulled her even tighter. 'This is what you didn't tell me, right?'

'Sorry. I...'

'It's okay, Lisa. It's okay.'

'I... I'm just trying to process it, Jon.'

'I'm not judging you, okay?' Nelson grabbed her in a big hug. 'I love you, Lisa. I want you to know that. I'm here for you.'

'I've raised a formal complaint with DCI Fenchurch.'

Nelson let her go. 'You told *him* before me?'

'Jesus, Jon. It's not like that.'

Nelson stood there, fire burning in his veins. Of all the bloody people. 'Sorry. I... That's good. I'm glad you did that.'

'It was Kay... She...' Lisa shut her eyes. 'Jon, he's been suspended.'

'Right. Good.' Nelson tried to see the good that could come from it. 'Carling has a reputation.'

'You knew?'

'Right. Uzma calls him "Pinkie" because they used to go out and he flashed her once in the office. She laughed it off, but it's... It's not cool.'

'Kay said there are lots of others. I'm standing up for them all, Jon.'

'Jesus Christ. I should've stopped it years ago.'

'Look, whatever. Just don't do anything. Okay?'

'Okay. I won't. I'm trusting the process. After all, it kicked me off the force for my stupidity. Hopefully it'll do the same for Carling.'

'I mean it, Jon. Don't do anything.'

'I won't.'

'Good.' She wrapped her arms around him. 'I need to go back to work.'

'Are you sure—'

'I'm sure.' She pecked him on the cheek. 'Thank you.' She broke free and walked towards the entrance.

Carling.

Nelson had worked with him. Never got a good read from him. Slimy, oily. But he thought that time he flashed Uzma was a one-off and in a consenting relationship. She'd given him that nickname to wind him up.

But no.

Carling kept doing it. Without consent. Treating everything as a joke.

'What are you doing here, stranger?'

Nelson looked over – Kay Reed was standing there, frowning at him. 'Hey there. Wow. It's been a while.'

'Hasn't it just...' She was looking distracted but he couldn't tell what by. 'What brings you here?'

'Lisa wanted a word.'

Kay stared right at him. 'Did she say what it was about?'

Nelson nodded. 'She told you first, didn't she?'

Kay nodded back.

'Thank you.'

'I thought you'd be mad.'

'I'm just glad she could tell someone.'

'Don't do anything, Jon.'

'I won't.'

'I mean it. It's important he goes down this time.'

'This time?'

'Lisa's not the first. He's been getting away with it for years.' Kay stared at him with burning intensity. 'He tried it on with me once. In the evidence room. He pinned me against a cabinet. Ran his hand down my back. Over my arse. Grabbed it. He's short, but he's strong, Jon. Bigger than you or Simon. He tried to kiss me, but I pushed him away.'

'I... I don't know what to say.'

'I reported him but it went nowhere. Just my word against his. Typical.' She was brushing tears out of her eyes.

Jesus Christ.

Not only his girlfriend, but other women too.

'I mean it, Jon. Don't do anything about this. Lara Bishop in Professional Standards is leading it.'

'Lara's good. She kicked me off the force.'

Kay narrowed her eyes at him. 'Promise me.'

'I promise, Kay.'

She came over and gave him a big hug. 'Don't be a stranger, okay?'

He smiled. 'Okay.'

She walked off, hands in pockets, head dipped.

Nelson got out his phone and searched Waheed's special service for Tom Carling's home address.

Bermondsey.

He didn't know what he was going to do, but having it was good.

Clarke jogged over. 'Get back in, Jon. Good news – I've got a friend who's been investigating Amir's.'

CHAPTER FIFTY-TWO

The lift pinged and Fenchurch stepped out into an atrium. Three separate offices, each with its own door. He took the one for Vivant Entertainment, leading into a reception room, overlooking a square in the City that was all bushes and trees and benches now, rather than heroin addicts and alcoholics.

The receptionist was immaculately dressed. Black suit, purple shirt open three buttons to the chest. Cropped hair. Designer stubble. 'Can I help you, sir?'

'Looking for your firm's owner. He in?'

'In his office, but he's not taking meetings.'

'Oh, he'll take a meeting with me. Simon Fenchurch.'

The PA touched a control on the desk. 'Sir, it's a Simon Fenchurch to—' He grimaced. 'Of course.' He gestured towards one of the two other doors. 'He's through there, sir.'

'Thanks.' Fenchurch walked into the office.

Empty.

A spartan room. A desk with a sleeping laptop. A chair. A

safe. Nothing else, no windows, no paintings. Just another door.

And it was absolutely roasting in there.

Maybe it was just Fenchurch's withdrawal, but he was dripping with sweat.

'Coo-ee! I'm in here!'

Came from the door.

Fenchurch walked over and opened it.

A blast of dry heat hit his face.

Younis was sitting in the middle of a sauna, stark bollock naked. 'Hello, Fenchy. Get your kit off and join me.'

Fenchurch slipped off his jacket and kicked off his shoes. Left his phone inside one. Then went in.

'Oh, come on, Fenchy. Don't I get to see your old fella again?'

'I've had enough sexual humiliation from you to last a lifetime.'

'Suit yourself.' Younis adjusted his groin area, but all Fenchurch saw was movement from the corner of his eye.

He sat on the edge of the bench. Burning. His heart was already going like the clappers and now...

'What?'

Fenchurch frowned at him. 'What?'

'What are you here for, Fenchy? Sorry, is this because I haven't done our daily catch up yet? Do you miss me?'

'No, it's not about that. Wanted to ask you why you'd risk going back inside.'

'I ain't doing anything that'd get me inside.'

'Sure about that?'

'Sure, I'm sure.'

'Well, if that's the case then all I can do is wish you well in Thailand.'

'Oh, you've done your homework. Very sexy!' Younis cackled. 'You always did know how to charm a fella. Thailand of all places. Whatever would I do there?' He winked. 'Of course, I'm not really heading there. I spread a rumour around a few people, but I watermarked each one. Thailand, Guam, Morocco, Guatemala, Costa Rica. Each one's as much of a fabled destination for an enthusiastic gentleman like myself. But now I know who's blabbing to the cops.'

Shit. Ben was in danger.

'Enthusiasm isn't the same as exploitative degeneracy.'

'Don't judge me, Fenchy. It might turn me off.' Younis splayed himself out on the bench. 'Why are you here?'

Fenchurch still couldn't look at him. 'I know you're still in the drugs trade.'

'I'm not. And I wouldn't tell you if I was. Too much money to be made legitimately these days. Vivant Entertainment is doing a roaring bloody trade, I tell you. See the price of beer in pubs? Coke dealers dream of that price, my sweetheart. I've got bars, clubs, you name it. Security firms. Ticket companies. Gig venues. All legit. All lucrative.'

'It's the other stuff I want to know about.'

'Ain't no other stuff.'

'You promised to tell me the absolute truth. I'd hate to think you were lying to me.'

'Go on.' Younis rolled his eyes. 'Spell it out. How am I lying?'

'There's a dealer on Mile End Road, selling prescription drugs to people.'

'What kind?'

'Oxy, fentanyl. That I know about.'

'Well, colour me impressed, Fenchy. Sounds like a wrong 'un and no mistaking. Thing is, I'm just not involved. Sorry. Now.' Younis stood up, his pencil-thin penis dangling. 'I've got to go and see some people about some stuff. Catch you later, my love.'

Fenchurch stood up and grabbed his wrist. 'You knew Monaghan was going to die, didn't you?'

'Who?'

'Terry Monaghan. You told someone to be at a certain address and she led him to the body.'

'Oh my, that's shocking.'

'Admit it.'

'No way. I was winding Nelly up, you stupid clown.'

'I'm going to prove your involvement in this murder. How this is all still you. All of it. All of that misery you inflict on people.'

'You'd have to be very good to do that. I'm not the least bit worried about you having the wherewithal to manufacture something against an innocent businessman like myself. Let's face it, Fenchy, with your drug problem and your wife leaving you, you ain't up to much.'

What the hell?

Fenchurch tightened his grip. 'What do you know?'

'About the good lady Fenchurch?' Younis winked. 'A lot more than you do, clearly.'

'What the fuck do you know?' Fenchurch squeezed. 'Where is she?'

'Cornwall.'

'What?'

'She called in to school sick this morning. Took your boy down to see his grandparents at the crack of sparrowfart.'

Fenchurch stared into his venomous eyes. 'If you're lying, I swear—'

'I'm not. Like I told you, I only tell you the God's honest truth. And I've got someone on her twenty-four-seven.'

'Why are you—'

'It's not a bad thing, Fenchy. There's no malice. I heard about what happened to her a few years back, before my time. What you did to those geezers who took her. I'm just looking out for you and yours.'

Fenchurch tightened his wrist. 'I'm going to fucking kill you. Right here, right now.'

Younis squealed. 'It's her phone!'

'What?'

'I've hacked her phone. That's it. I'm not stupid enough to man mark your missus. I've got people listening in on her, though. Just looking out for my guy.'

Fenchurch tried to ignore the feeling he was burning in his skin. The mallets hammering at his skull.

Everyone's lives were on those things, either overtly like a post on Schoolbook, or covertly on a WhatsApp message. You didn't need a squad of round-the-clock PIs like Nelson to monitor someone. They did it all for you.

The data the phone captured.

The information people put out there.

The secrets they shared by texts.

Fenchurch let go of his wrist. 'If anything happens to her, I swear—'

'Nothing will.' Younis was rubbing at his wrist. 'You've got that on my son's life.'

'You haven't got a son.'

'Three of them. Not telling you which one's life belongs to you, though.'

Fenchurch stared him down, but Younis wasn't looking away. He opened the door and left the creep standing there in his own private sauna. He stepped into his shoes. His phone was still in one of them. He pocketed it and walked as fast as he could manage through the office, laces flailing, through reception and over to the lift. He hammered the button and wished he was in a fit-enough state to take the stairs.

He should go back in there. Confront him again. Hurt him, chuck him out of a window and screw the consequences.

No.

Younis had someone on Abi. Insurance. If Fenchurch acted, she'd pay the price. Her or Al.

Shit.

He hit dial.

Abi answered. 'Hello?'

'Love.' Hearing her voice made him melt inside.

'Simon?'

'Abi. Are you okay?'

'Not really.'

'Has someone—'

'No, Simon. I'm just trying to process things, okay? It's a lot to discover your husband's... Well. I'm sure you understand.'

'I don't. I want to. But I thought you understood. That you knew. That you accepted this.'

'Simon, I knew. Of course I knew. But I just didn't know the extent. It's... It's a lot to take in.'

'I get it. I don't want to force your hand. I just want to know that you're okay.'

'I'm fine.'

'Abi, I think someone's hacked your phone. Buy a new one. New number. Clean install of all your apps. Change the passwords. Okay?'

'What?'

'I'm serious.'

'I need to go. Lunch is ready.'

Click.

Fenchurch stepped into the lift and hit the button for ground. He held onto his phone, hoping she'd listened to him.

The Thailand thing had to be a ruse.

Watermarking stories so you knew who was leaking when you heard it back.

Then again, someone like Younis knew how to work people. Because Ben had blabbed to them, Younis now knew who his weakest link was.

Fenchurch needed to take him down.

Yesterday, Younis called him when he was at the pharmacy next to Dr Deacon's surgery. He knew where Fenchurch was because he'd hacked into his phone. His and Abi's.

Younis had called him at that precise moment because he could wind Fenchurch up. Let him know that he knew where he was. What he was doing.

But phones could only tell you what you put into them. Locations, messages, voicemails.

Fenchurch had never told anyone about his addiction over the phone. Just in person.

The only people who knew about Fenchurch's drugs were Abi and three police officers: Reed, Bell, Loftus.

Sure, Bell had probably told a couple of others, but Reed and Loftus wouldn't.

And Bell might be many things, but corrupt wasn't one of them. He wasn't the leak.

For Younis to know he was on oxycodone, it had to come from one source.

Dr Edwin Deacon.

A shiver ran up Fenchurch's spine. He was melting, but that thought chilled him.

Nelson had told Fenchurch he saw Deacon speaking to Younis down in Peckham.

That had to be it – Younis knew Fenchurch was on oxy because Deacon had told him.

Meaning Younis could influence Deacon, make sure Fenchurch was doped.

Jesus Christ.

Younis had kept him high when in all likelihood he didn't need those drugs or nothing like that dose.

Deacon betrayed that trust.

Why didn't he see it before?

How was Deacon able to fool him?

He shouldn't have been on the dose he was on, but he'd told himself his pain had been so bad he just had to escalate the dose, instead of managing it himself.

And Younis would soon be in Thailand or wherever, off the board. Given how well he'd run things from prison, he'd manage it just as well from overseas.

The lift chimed and the doors opened.

Fenchurch walked out into the atrium. He needed to take Younis down before he flew off.

CHAPTER FIFTY-THREE

Fenchurch stormed across the white reception area, his knee crunching with each step. Ignoring the pain, pushing on through.

'He's with a patient, sir!' The receptionist raced around much faster than Fenchurch could manage.

Still, he made it to the door he'd been through just the previous morning. Tore it open and it cracked off the wall.

And that was a complete lie.

Deacon was sitting at his computer, typing, sipping from a bottle of water. He turned and stared at Fenchurch. 'Ah, Inspector. How can I help?'

The receptionist got between them. 'Edwin, I tried to—'

'It's okay, Minty.' Deacon rose to his feet. 'DCI Fenchurch is a patient of mine.'

'All the same, he can't just barge in here like—'

'Ms Silk, need I remind you that this is my surgery?' Deacon stared her down until she turned and left them to it. 'Honestly. You can't get the staff these days.'

Fenchurch was momentarily shaken. 'Her name's Minty Silk?'

'Not her birth name. More a stage name.'

Fenchurch scowled at him. 'Listen. I need to have a word with you.'

'How's the knee?'

'It's absolutely shocking.'

'Oh, we can up your dose, if you—'

'That's why I'm here. Did Dimitri ask you to—'

'Dimitri?'

'Younis.'

'Sorry, I don't know him.'

That glance away, though. Subtle. You could almost miss it. A tell.

'You're lying, Edwin.'

'What?'

'You know him, you lying bastard. You met him yesterday lunchtime down in Peckham.'

'What?'

'Don't. Lie. To. Me.' Fenchurch towered over him. 'You prescribed opioids for my condition. I should never have had them at the strength I've been taking. Did he give you instructions to overmedicate me?'

'No!'

'I'm in so much more pain from the drug withdrawal than from my fucking knee. I feel like I'm dying and all because of you.'

'This is nothing to do with me!'

'I told you to stop lying!'

Deacon stared at him, then looked away. He walked over to his chair and just crumbled. 'I'm so sorry.'

'I don't care. What happened?'

Deacon swallowed a pill down with some water from

another bottle. 'The waiting time is... You can get an op in two weeks, if you want.'

'Two weeks? You said it'd be months.'

'I know.'

'You're a doctor. You sign up to the Hippocratic oath. Do no harm. You've been milking me for the consultation and prescription fees, haven't you?'

'Simon, I'm absolutely skint. I lost all of my savings.'

'Crypto investments?'

'How... You should've seen the returns I was getting. Forget about twelve percent, this was doubling every year. And... It lost ninety-six percent of its value overnight. I've lost everything.'

'So you're taking it out on me?'

'But what about *me*? Or my kids? This is fucked up. I've worked hard all my life to... to... to look after them.' Deacon took another drink. 'All I've done is the right thing. And it's all crumbling down around me. I've lost so much money, all because of my investments tanking. I've done things I didn't want to, just so I could protect my kids' futures.'

'That's your decision to go with the riskiest bets you could. Might as well have stuck that all on a random horse in the three thirty at Chepstow.'

Deacon looked at Fenchurch with piercing eyes. No emotion. Sweating, pale skin. 'You want to know what's really going on?'

'No, I'm here for you to gaslight me some more. Maybe hand over some of my hard-earned cash in exchange for drugs that are slowly killing me.'

Deacon took another drink. 'I'll tell you it all, but you have to let me get out of here with some dignity.'

'I'll let you get out with functioning legs. Spill it all. Now.'

'Okay, you're right. Younis is behind it all.'

'How did you meet him?'

'He came in here. Had some injuries from his time in prison. Not even someone like him escapes scot-free, I guess. And we got talking. I just supplied the drugs to him. I started out by getting partly used bottles of oxy from people I knew and trusted. Doctors. Orderlies who worked in care homes. Could even get them from house clearances. They were supposed to destroy it, but when the dead left their medication anywhere in East London, I took it. I forged the paperwork and sold them on.'

Fenchurch was frowning. 'This has been going on a while, right?'

'Almost two years. Started out as small potatoes. I was getting hundreds a week, but Younis saw the potential in it. Saw the untapped demand. So he started sending mules into pharmacies with copious fake IDs, and that turned to thousands, then tens of thousands a week. There are a lot of doctors out there who are willing to prescribe to order. We write the scripts in different names, they fulfil them at various pharmacies all over the south east. Risky if they just keep them, but those that buy from Younis have a habit of overdosing. So we had people taking their drugs and putting them back into the system. And the street dealers sell them for five times the markup.'

'Curtis Archer was your patient. You kept selling to him off the books, didn't you?'

Deacon nodded. 'The club didn't want it showing up. He paid me cash. Cash I sorely needed after... the crash.'

'Did you kill Curtis?'

'What? No, he died... of a heart attack.'

'Okay, but someone was chasing him. Took his drugs from his flat. Was that you?'

'No... but... Well. I know who it might be.'

'Who?'

'You found his drugs all in Jack Walsh's flat, didn't you?'

'How do you know that?'

'It's Younis's business to find out.'

'He did it?'

'Not personally. But Jack was a good customer. Always paid on time. Not all of the drugs were Curtis's.'

Fenchurch played the whole thing through. It all slotted in so neatly. His supposition had paid off. Dr Edwin Deacon had supplied drugs that killed a lot of people. And there was only one small problem. 'All this cash you were coining in, you needed a way to launder that.'

Deacon nodded. 'Through my investments. It wasn't all dirty money. My savings, I remortgaged my house, got business loans, sunk it all in. Made it look legit. Another two years and I could retire.'

'And this was with Younis?'

Deacon nodded again. He took another slug and finished the bottle. 'He's behind it all, but you'll never trace it to him. He's layered it so well, you'll never get at him.'

'I'm a patient man. I'll do it all. If it means getting him.'

'He's leaving the country.'

'I know.' Fenchurch grabbed his arm. 'Right, sunshine, you're coming with me. This is all going down in a statement. You're going down for your part in it.'

'Not with the amount of fentanyl I've just ingested.'

'What?'

'I've swallowed ten patches' worth. Not enough naloxone in the world to bring me back from this. Good luck.' Deacon collapsed onto the floor. 'If you want to know who chased him... Speak to his father.'

CHAPTER FIFTY-FOUR

The trouble with knowing Carling's address was the closer they got to his house, the more Nelson wanted to visit and have a stern word.

A stern word.

Sure. That was it.

He wanted to kick the shit out of him. Make him really pay for what he'd done.

Lisa didn't deserve that – no woman did – but the fact he was still doing it after all these years. Someone needed to put a stop to it.

Clarke pulled up outside an Eighties terrace of two-up two-down houses. Curtains drawn. Only one car parked outside the whole row, a silver Vauxhall Astra. The only one with a porch. 'Here we go.'

The porch door opened and Tom Carling walked out, his face all chewed up and tight.

Nelson glared at Clarke. 'He's your contact?'

'Right. And?'

Nelson felt the veins in his neck tighten like power cables.

'Fuck this.' He opened the door and got out. Stormed across the road. 'You!'

Carling spotted his intensity, his ferocity. He grabbed Nelson's shirt collar and jerked him forward. Not often Nelson came up against someone as strong as him.

Nelson caught him with his foot and Carling tripped up. 'You are going to pay for—'

'Jesus, Jon!' Clarke was tugging at his arm. 'Stop it!'

'What the fuck?!' Carling was wriggling, scrabbling back against the porch, pushing his head back against his door. 'What the fuck is this about, Steve?'

'This piece of shit doesn't—'

'Jon!' Clarke got him free. Separated them. Between them, stopping Nelson getting at Carling.

'Fuck did I do to you?' Carling was like a spider, crawling away from him.

'You know!'

Carling scrabbled to his feet. Circling, keeping Clarke's body between them. 'What are you talking about?'

Nelson stood still, fists clenched. 'I know, Tom. I fucking know. What you did. What you've been doing. What you're still doing!'

'Guys, guys, guys.' Clarke got between them. 'What the *hell* is going on?'

Carling was cornered, trapped between the car, the porch and Clarke. 'Nothing!'

Nelson kept his distance, but jabbed a finger at him. 'He... He's... I'm going to—'

'Jon!' Carling held up his hands. 'Jon, mate, we go way back—'

'Don't!'

'Come on, Jon. We're mates. I did nothing and they've suspended me for it. I'm the victim here!'

'You?' Nelson laughed. 'You ruin lives, Tom.'

'I don't ruin anything! I haven't *done* anything!'

'Admit it, Pinkie.'

'Pinkie?'

'Don't you remember? Thought it was all fun and games, didn't you? A laugh.'

'That was a joke!'

'But you couldn't help yourself, could you? I'm surprised you've lasted this long.'

'I've lasted this long because it's bullshit, Jon. All of it.' Carling blinked hard a few times. 'Jon, I swear—'

'Jon!' Clarke was pointing at his car. 'Get in the motor. Now. Or I'm arresting you.'

Nelson stared at him, then at Carling. 'Fine.' He turned around and walked over to the car.

He didn't doubt Lisa. Not for a second.

Carling was the worst kind of offender. Someone who committed crimes and got away with it.

He wished he still had that zip gun on him now. Fuck prison, fuck ruining his life – Carling deserved it.

Deserved it all.

The driver door opened and Clarke got in.

Carling was over by the door, staring into space.

'Okay, Jon. He told me all about it. How he's been suspended. Fenchurch has reported him to Professional Standards. You directing your rage at Carling isn't solving anything. Sure, he deserves it, deserves it all, but how far will you take it? There's a process in place here, Jon. Trust it.'

Nelson tried to play it all through. Every possibility. He'd been reported. He knew Lisa was telling the truth. He'd seen what Carling did to Uzma, which was 'just a bit of banter' between lovers. And he'd heard the stories. Seen the look on Kay Reed's face. 'I shouldn't have gone after him like that.'

'Damn right. There's a process here. He'll get what's coming to him. But you and I, Jon, we think we've got half of the puzzle. But the reality is we're short. If we want to take out Younis, we need Tom's help.'

'I've got to work with that scumbag?'

'That's right, Jon.'

Jesus Christ. What a decision.

Nelson sighed. 'Fine. I'll let him face the music in due course. If he helps take down Younis, then I'll take that. But this is not cool.'

'Believe me, I know.' Clarke opened his door. 'Give me a minute.'

Nelson watched him get out and walk over to the house.

Carling was twitching, jerking his head around. Staring at Nelson, listening to Clarke. One thing Nelson had achieved was scaring the living daylights out of him. Carling nodded.

Nelson got out of the car and held up his hands. 'Let's do this later.'

Carling was rubbing at his throat. 'There's nothing in it.'

'Drop it.' Nelson stood over him. 'You're going to tell us what you've got on Amir's Wine and Beer.'

'Well, nothing.'

Nelson glared at Clarke. 'So why are we here?'

'Tom, tell him about the Last Knight of Avalon.'

'Pub on Mile End Road. I investigated it as part of a really shit case last year. Body found in Lambeth. Traced him to working in that boozer. I was undercover. Turns out they were up to all sorts. Drugs, hookers, you name it. Had to get Steve's lot in.'

'Why?'

'If you ordered a pint and a pie in the pub, along with a packet of French cigarettes, you got charged six hundred quid for it. Hand over a passport photo and your old passport, come back the next day and you've got a new passport under a new name. Steve and I investigated how they were laundering all that cash. As a result, we shut it down.'

Nelson looked at Clarke. 'It's a scam, that's for sure. But would that extend to crypto?'

'Heard it's reopened as a hipster café now. But the same woman owns both places. Janice Royle. The shop and the pub.'

'And we've got an active operation on her.' Carling shrugged. 'If you want her address, you're taking me with you.'

'No way!'

'I'm serious. I need a big tick on my side, so I want in on whatever you two are cooking up here.'

CHAPTER FIFTY-FIVE

Reed and Bridge were waiting in the building's entrance doorway.

Bridge waved at him, then headed inside without speaking.

Fenchurch watched her go – she seemed distant, like she'd lost something. He really needed to say something to her, to show his support. And he needed to pressure Professional Standards into throwing the book at Carling. But the whole thing needed to be handled fairly and objectively.

Christ, what a bloody mess.

'Is Lisa okay?'

Reed seemed distracted too. 'She's a fighter, guv.' She entered the atrium and led over to the lifts.

Bridge was holding it open for them. 'I'll take the stairs.' She scurried off towards the door, even though there was space for all three of them.

Fenchurch got in and hammered the button for the BRO Capital floor. 'I hate this, Kay. I hate that people like Carling can do this. Have been doing this.'

'It's not people, guv. It's men.'

'That's true.'

Reed leaned back against the wall. Her lips twitched like she was going to add something, but the moment passed. 'Do you really believe Curtis's dad was chasing him?'

'Don't know, Kay.' Fenchurch shrugged. 'I've only got Deacon's word for it.'

'Will he survive?'

'He was dead by the time the paramedics arrived.'

'Shit.'

'And he played me, Kay.'

'Deacon?'

'No. Younis. He played me. Got a desperate or greedy doctor to overprescribe fucking opioids. I can't believe I fell for it. I—'

The lift pinged and the doors opened.

'It's okay, guv. You'll be okay.' Reed stormed out. 'You're a fighter too.'

Fenchurch followed, wishing he had her conviction. Maybe it was adrenalin from the impending collapse of Younis's house of cards, but he barely noticed his knee.

The office was pretty much empty now, just a boffin in the corner sitting in front of three monitors. Headphones on, not even looking in their direction. Completely oblivious.

Reed was ahead, by Oliver Archer's office. She looked around, eyes bulging. 'Guv!'

Fenchurch jogged through, his knee wobbling every time he put weight on it.

The corner office was empty, but the door to the balcony was open. Oliver Archer was resting against the barrier, staring down at the ground several storeys below.

Fenchurch stepped out into the bracing wind. 'Oliver. Stay right where you are.'

'I'll jump.'

'Don't. Please. I'm begging you.'

'You don't understand. It's all over. All of it. I've got nothing left to live for. I'm losing my business. I've lost my son.'

'We know you were chasing him.'

Oliver looked around at Fenchurch. Then dipped his head. 'I was.'

'Why did you want to kill him?'

'Kill him? I was trying to *save* him. Curtis was too deep in his addiction. I was going to take him to the Priory. The last of my fucking money, too. I wanted to clean him up. Start to fix his career. Or... I just wanted him to be well. Sod his career. Sod any of that. I just wanted him to be alive and happy.' He wiped tears from his face. 'Then his heart exploded. I've lived longer than Curtis. He did nothing to help me during his life, but I helped him in ways he couldn't have known. Curtis gave money to his mother, whereas I had to earn it all myself, didn't I?'

'You told us half of his income went on crypto investments. He bailed out your business, pimped out your NFTs for you.'

'They weren't *my* NFTs. He didn't invest with us.'

'Whose were they?'

'That whole scheme's taken down my business. I've lost everything because of it.' Oliver was back to looking down at the ground again. 'And Curtis was the mastermind, not me.'

'What?'

'He came in with the idea. He had the contacts, the connections. He just needed me to make it happen on a technical level. He had lots of money to invest. Him and his mates.'

'You told us it was Neoxis?'

'That's just a brand. We own it through a number of shell companies. I told him it wasn't wise to throw all of his money into a scheme like that. But he was insistent. Had this fervour in his eyes. I never wanted a son, not at that age. But I had one and I tried to do everything I could to protect my boy. To help him. I wanted to be part of his life, but she poisoned him against me.'

'Candace?'

'Right. That boy was nothing but a cash cow to her. I knew about these investments his mother had made in his name. It was all bollocks. She never does anything for anyone else, not even her own son. I should've protected him from her, but she had him hooked on those drugs. I tried to stop it! Tried to get him off them! But he wouldn't listen to me. Heard he even went to the club, asking to get his contract paid out, just so he could give all that money to fucking Younis!'

'Younis?'

'Younis had his hooks into my boy. Into his mother too. He was using them both to launder his money. Younis told my son he had to pay more because the money laundering scheme wasn't pulling in as much cash as he needed anymore. And Curtis didn't stand up to him, did he? And I... I just let it happen to my boy. To save my own neck, I stepped back... just a businessman who milked his son like a cow.' He leaned forward, eyes closed.

Fenchurch might've been severely injured, but he was still fast enough to catch him. He grabbed Oliver by the neck and pulled him away from the barrier.

'Let me go!'

'No!' Fenchurch got him up against the wall, pressing him against the stone. 'No, you don't. Not again. The way to pay your son back, the way to put all of this right, is to talk to me. I can put Younis away, but I need your cooperation.'

'What do you want?'

'Everything. The whole story. On the record. And how I can charge Younis.'

CHAPTER FIFTY-SIX

Nelson had been here the day before, when he watched Dr Edwin Deacon climb the stairs to the flat at the top. He spoke to a woman, then came back out, where he spoke to Younis. He still didn't know why, but he had more of a clue now – this was central to Younis's scheme. Illicit sources of legal drugs, sold on the street to the desperate, then turned into dirty money, all cleaned by this machine. Elaborate as hell. But it was over.

He cracked his door open and planted a foot onto the pavement. 'What's the plan?'

'Nothing for you, Jon.' Clarke stepped out of the driver's side. 'You're staying here.'

'But I've handed you this on a platter.'

'And you ain't a serving cop.' Clarke reached in to pat his arm. 'Come on, mate. You've done really well, so thank you but—'

'He's on suspension!' Nelson was pointing at Carling. 'You're going in there with a cop on suspension?'

'Jon. Let it go. Stay here. Call me if anything happens out here. Okay?'

Nelson sat back in the car and let out a sigh. He watched Clarke and Carling head inside, just like Deacon had the previous morning. Up those stairs to the top flat.

This close to the heart of what Younis was up to, this was a job that needed support. Two cars of detectives. Uniforms too. Not just two idiots – a City spreadsheet monkey and a rapist.

Jesus.

The traffic was thick, a passing bus obscuring the view of the flats as they knocked on the door and waited.

By the time the bus had passed, a black Range Rover had pulled up in front of the entrance.

Younis got out of the back.

Shit.

Clarke and Carling were nowhere. Must've gone inside.

Shit, shit.

Nelson could be the good boy here and stay put. Do what he was told.

But he needed to do something.

Didn't he?

Younis looked around – didn't seem to spot Nelson – then set off up the path.

No choice here.

Nelson slipped out and ran across the road through a gap that seemed a lot bigger when he started running. He stopped, waiting until Younis was inside, keeping an eye on the driver. Act naturally. He strolled up the path like he lived there and caught the door just before it shut, then slipped inside and pulled it behind him, so it sounded natural and to stop anyone else getting in. Well, anyone without a key.

Younis's footsteps padded up the stairs. Humming that old Cliff Richard tune, *Summer Holiday*.

Nelson kicked off his shoes and carried them up, his socks cushioning his climb.

Up to the top floor and Younis was rapping on the door. The same one as Deacon.

Nelson hid behind the banister. Not much of a barrier, but Younis seemed preoccupied by the door.

'Bugger this.' Younis got out a key and opened the door. 'Mum, you okay?'

Mum?

Younis had a mother?

Nelson had never really considered it. A guy like Younis seemed like he'd been carved from stone a million years ago, or dropped from orbit. Or hatched.

Stupid to have spent so long going through Younis's life history and trusting that his immediate family was all dead. Like everyone, Dimitri Younis had a history, but whether it matched the person Nelson saw here and now was a completely different matter.

Nelson wedged his foot in the door as it slammed shut, and eased himself into the flat, leaving his shoes on the mat outside.

'Mum?' Younis was walking down a long hallway, cream walls and engineered wooden flooring. Paintings on the wall. The place was way bigger than a council flat should be, like two or three units had been knocked together. 'Where are you?'

Voices came from a room at the end.

Younis was standing in the doorway, arms out at his side. 'Who the hell are these pair?'

'They're cops, Dimitri.'

'Mum. How many times... Never let the filth in!'

'Dimitri, my name's Steve Clarke. I work for the City of

London police. We're just asking Mrs Royle here a few
questions.'

Younis stepped into the room. 'Well, you can fuck right off!'

'No, Dimitri. We're doing this here. Now.'

'Fuck off, I told you.'

'Dimitri, how many times do I have to tell you not to swear
in my house!'

'Sorry, Mum.'

Nelson made his way over to the doorway. He leaned out to
inspect it.

A massive galley kitchen with an island. Expensive units.
Silver coffee maker. American fridge.

Younis wasn't far from Nelson. He could just grab him and
take him down.

A silver-haired woman stood by the sink. Immaculately
dressed. Smooth skin.

Clarke was next to her, acting all casual as he leaned back
against the counter, but his eyes were swivelling around the
place. Nervous at Younis's presence. 'Mrs Royle, we just want
to know about the Last Knight of Avalon and Amir's Wine and
Beer.'

'How do you—'

'Mum. Shut up. I love you, but shut up. Let me—'

'How dare you talk to me like that?'

Younis had his phone out and tapped out a message, then
put it away again. 'You've got five minutes to clear out. My
squad is on its way here.'

Mrs Royle was scowling at her son. 'What on earth is
going on?'

Clarke couldn't even look at her. 'Is this man your son?'

'Yeah, and what of it?'

'Do you know what he does for a living?'

'No, because I don't understand it. He's tried explaining but it's beyond me.'

'He runs a criminal empire, Mrs Royle.'

'What?' She laughed. 'That's nonsense. Dimitri, tell them!'

'Mum, of course it's bollocks. The filth hate it when a geezer from round here does well for himself. Can't handle it!'

Clarke was staring at her now. 'Mrs Royle, there are at least three properties and businesses directly involved in criminal activities which are registered in your name. Now, you can come with us willingly to answer our questions, or I can arrest you.'

'Arrest me?' She scowled at Younis. 'Dimitri, what the hell's going on?'

'Mum, I've no idea. I'm innocent here. I'm heading off on my holiday and this lot are thinking I'm something I'm not!'

'Your son's a criminal.'

'No! No, he's not!'

Nelson entered the room. 'Why do you think he was in prison?'

Everyone turned around to face him.

Younis gave him the up and down. He winced, like he realised he wasn't just outnumbered anymore, but massively outgunned. 'How are you here?'

'Thought you'd set me up, right? Send me to the address where you'd killed Terry Monaghan.'

'Fuck off!'

'Dimitri!' Mrs Royle was scowling at him. 'Prison?'

'He got out just over two years ago.'

'He was in Goa! Dimitri, tell them where you were!'

'*Goa?*' Nelson laughed. 'He was in Belmarsh. I've got the visitor logs to prove it. Hours and hours of CCTV. Prison guards.'

'This is... What?' She was glaring at her son. 'Dimitri, what the hell have you been doing?'

'Mum, it's not—'

'All that money, you said it was from your business.' She smacked the side of his head. 'What the hell have you been doing?'

'Mum, I can explain!'

'You've been lying to me, haven't you?'

'They're all lying!'

'You lying little shit!' She stepped forward and slapped him, the contact like a drum skin. 'All that money you paid me, where did it come from?'

'Mum! It's legit!'

'Dimitri, are you into drugs?'

'No!'

Clarke started counting on his fingers. 'Drugs, enforced street prostitution, online sex work, gambling...'

'Jesus Christ.' She collapsed onto a chair. 'Dimitri, I thought I raised you better than this.'

Younis looked around at them. 'You lot happy, eh? Broke her heart now, haven't you?'

She looked like she was going to be sick. Furious eyes glared at him. 'Well, you can have it all back, you ungrateful little shit.'

'It's your money, Mum.'

'I don't want it!'

'Mum... I want to look after you. I gave you it so you'd be secure.'

'You're getting it all back. I'll call them up and transfer it back to you.'

'Mum. It's yours.'

'You filthy little bastard.' She stormed across the room and reached into a drawer, then flung a load of paperwork at him.

'Take it! I invested it all in your name, anyway. Take it. It's yours. I want nothing to do with it!'

'Mum...' Younis caught a page and read it. 'Oh fuck... Why did you invest with *them*?'

'Why not?'

'Because this a scam!' Younis rubbed his temples. 'Mum, BRO Capital are so bent they're almost straight again.'

Clarke nodded. 'That's why we're investigating you, Dimitri. You've been using them to launder millions.' He smiled. 'Good news for us is all that money's worth diddly squat. BRO's coins have gone to zero.'

Younis stood there, mouth hanging open.

'Believe it, mate.' Clarke bent over to pick up some pages. 'All that cash on these statements is gone.'

Mrs Royle stood next to her son, her mouth hanging open as well. A family trait. 'Fuck.'

'Live by the sword, Dimitri.' Carling winked at him. 'You knew it'd come to this, didn't you?'

'Fuck you.'

'Come on, Dimitri. You can't do the time—'

Younis lashed out with an elbow and cracked Nelson square in the nose.

He went down, clutching his face.

Saw Younis stick the head on Clarke, who stumbled back against the counter. Clarke tripped and knocked Janice over.

'You pricks!' Younis grabbed a knife out of a block and lashed at Carling. He sliced at the air, caught Carling's ear, his arm and slashed his shirt wide open. A slit of blood appeared.

Carling screamed. Then his shirt soaked red. He grabbed Younis's wrist, screaming even louder. The knife dropped onto the floor. They both tumbled back against the worktop. A marble mortar and pestle set fell off, landing on Clarke, prone on the floor. Janice was sitting up now.

Nelson pushed up to standing. Everything was swaying. His face was a ball of fire.

Carling had the knife now. He wrapped his arm around Younis's neck, then moved to slit his throat, but Younis thrust his head backwards.

Carling went down on his knees. Wheezing.

Younis picked up the knife. 'You think you can come into my mum's—'

Carling punched him in the balls.

Younis squealed. Dropped the knife, the point digging into the floorboard.

Carling grabbed Younis's balls and squeezed.

Younis was roaring with pain now. He slapped at Carling's arm. Carling caught his wrist with his free hand and twisted Younis's arm. Twisted until it cracked. Twisted it until Younis wasn't screaming anymore.

Clarke was on his feet again, clutching his head. He grabbed Carling by the arm. 'Come on, Tom. That's enough.' He hauled him back, away from Younis.

Curled up into a ball, crying.

Carling turned around. 'What the fuck do you think you're doing?' He stepped around him and did a judo throw.

Clarke flew through the air, landing on his back.

Carling grabbed the mortar in his hand like a drunk wielding an ashtray and clattered the bowl off Younis's skull. He pulled his legs apart and crashed it into his balls. Over and over again.

Nelson grabbed him by the throat and pushed him over. 'That's enough!'

CHAPTER FIFTY-SEVEN

Fenchurch charged through the hospital as fast as he could manage, sweating. Soaked in it. Stinking of it, like off cheese.

'Well, well.' DCI Thompson swanned over, fingers clasped in front of him, all bloated like a pack of sausages. 'Simon Fenchurch. How the devil are you?'

'We saw each other yesterday.'

'Ah, of course, but we didn't have much of a chance to talk. Word comes from on high that you've solved the poor lad's death?'

Fenchurch nodded. All he could do. The noise of the hospital was like a jackhammer in his ears.

Screaming came from the room behind Thompson.

Fenchurch angled his head to look past. He caught a flash of black hair, streaked with blonde. 'Is that—?'

Thompson nodded. 'Younis.'

'What happened to him?'

'Tom Carling.'

'What did he do?'

Clarke joined them, handing a coffee to Thompson. 'Sorry, Si, didn't know you were here. Would've got you one.'

'Cheers, Steve.' Thompson raised his cup. 'Listen, I need to report back, so I'll return. Thanks.' He walked off, shoulders back, chest thrust forward.

Fenchurch focused on Clarke. 'What did he mean, Tom Carling happened?'

Clarke blew on his coffee. 'He was working with me on this case and—'

'You know he's on suspension.'

'I do, but I needed his help.'

'You should've come to me first, Steve.'

'I can't so much as sneeze outside the Square Mile without having to fill out a form, can I?'

'Same rules apply inside. You know that – you've come down on me and my guys like a ton of bricks many times.'

'It's more like a ton of feathers, Si.'

Fenchurch grimaced. 'Anyway. Tom attacked Younis?'

Clarke nodded. 'Don't worry, he's sitting in an interview room in your station waiting on Professional Standards.'

'I'm not impressed.'

'He had information that he'd share with us at a later date. He's a good one for keeping things back, isn't he?'

'Secrets are what he's all about.' Fenchurch fixed a hard stare on him. 'You know he's—'

'A sexual predator? So I gather.' Clarke sighed. 'He swore to me his suspension was because he's a gambler. But Jon Nelson's given me the full story and backed it up. Well.' He took a sip. 'Almost all of it.'

'What do you mean?'

'This case Tom worked on was the reason I went to him in the first place. Man was murdered by one of Younis's people. That's what Carling told me. But he'd been raped, by Younis.

And Carling knew the guy. An informant on other cases. He lost a lot of man-hours to that. But the guy had become a friend. Tom was his sponsor in AA.'

'Jesus Christ.'

'Yeah. So that's why he went mental at him.' Clarke took a bracing sip of coffee then laughed. 'Don't think Younis will be having kids any time soon.'

Fenchurch tried to tune out the screams coming from the room. 'I need to speak to him, but I guess that's not going to happen for a while.'

'What about?'

'Well, this scheme he's been running.'

'Money laundering using NFTs from BRO Capital?'

Fenchurch frowned. 'How do you know?'

'Jon Nelson figured it all out.'

'Jon Nelson did?'

'Right. He's a good guy.'

'He's among the best cops I've ever worked with.'

'I can see why. Thing is, we pretty much proved it. The pipeline from street drugs to cleaned, laundered cash in accounts Younis controlled. But we needed Tom's help to track down who ran it. Just so happens it was being run by Younis's mother.'

'His *mother*?'

Clarke snapped the lid back on his coffee. 'Janet Royle. And she's not an innocent party in all of this.' He thumped Fenchurch on the arm, a playful smile on his face. 'We've got him. I know what's going on inside that head of yours, beating yourself up for not knowing, but we've got him. And once Younis is out of here, he'll be going away for assaulting Carling and myself. As a minimum. On top of that, whatever we can pull together on this NFT scheme, that'll keep him in prison for a very long time. Data is king now – no witness statements that can be overturned. A solid, locked-in conviction.'

'Believe it when I see it.'

'He's not getting off with it this time, Si. And the best thing – all of his money's gone.'

'What?'

'All of it. He gave it all to his mother and she invested it in his own scheme. It's lost all of its value.'

'Shit.'

Clarke looked Fenchurch up and down, his lip curling. 'Take care of yourself, Si. See you around.'

Fenchurch stood there, close to losing it. Rattled. He wanted to shout, to scream, to punch, to kick.

Instead, he walked away. His feet squeaked as he limped along the corridor towards the lifts, one stride longer and louder than the other.

He desperately needed that operation. Now.

The lift opened and Jon Nelson stepped out.

CHAPTER FIFTY-EIGHT

'Afternoon, Jon.' Fenchurch stood in front of Nelson, face as pale as a vanilla milkshake. Off-white, yellowed. Eyes like scrunched-up paper. Sweat soaked his silver hair. A couple of days' worth of stubble, which was totally unlike him. His shirt was too loose, like he'd lost weight.

Nelson stepped out of the lift. 'Guv, are you okay?'

'I'm fine.' Fenchurch tried to barge past into the lift.

'Not so fast.' Nelson got in his way, blocking him.

Fenchurch huffed out a sigh. 'Jon, I need to get home.'

'Okay, but I can't keep going on like this. I've been an arsehole to you. I'm sorry.'

Fenchurch looked at him, forehead twitching, eyelids flickering. 'Apology accepted.'

'That's it?'

'What, do you want us to have it out here? No chance.' Fenchurch shut his eyes and took a deep breath. 'Look, Jon. Sorry. I'm... In a bad place.' He swallowed hard, eyes opening again but staring at the floor. 'I'm trying to kick oxycodone.'

'Oh shit.'

'That's how I feel. Shit.' Fenchurch smiled at him. 'But I appreciate your apology.' He scratched at his neck. 'And I'm sorry for not sticking up for you over Younis.'

'It's okay, guv. You're processing Lisa's complaint. Supporting it. I'll take that.'

'Can't promise anything, Jon. But I'll do what I can.'

'I've realised a lot about that. It's Lisa's to deal with. Not yours. Not mine. Hers. All we can do is support her and all the others. I recognise that now. Just do it right.'

'I will. You or me acting all caveman here isn't going to help that. And I get it, if someone did that to my wife, I'd be exactly the same. In this day and age, we shouldn't have to protect women. We stand with them, support them. And that's what we'll do. Stand with Lisa.'

Nelson could see the logic, even if it butted up against his instincts. 'Right. But Carling... He's wriggled out of this so many times now, Jon. Who's to say he won't do it again?'

'Speak to Uzma.'

Fenchurch frowned. 'Why?'

'Something happened when she split up with him all those years ago. The "Pinkie" stuff is crueller than banter.'

Fenchurch nodded slowly, getting that distant look in his eyes when he was thinking things through too much. 'Maybe I'll catch up with her.' He patted Nelson on the arm. 'I'll see you around, Jon. Maybe grab a beer and a burrito one day?'

'Sounds great.' Nelson grinned and felt a sting in his heart, in the pit of his stomach. It felt good. He stepped out of the way. 'I'll see you later.'

'See you, Jon. And I mean that.' Fenchurch entered the lift and pressed the button. The doors closed and he tipped his head.

Nelson let out a deep breath, then charged off down the corridor.

Clarke was sipping a coffee by the door to the ward. Bedlam reigned inside, screaming and shouting. He spotted Nelson and raised his head. 'Jon.'

'How's it going?'

'We'll get there, I think.' Clarke put the lid back on his coffee cup. 'Fenchurch reckons he might have some stuff that'll back up what we've got on Younis's little scheme.'

Nelson glanced back at the shut lift doors. 'We should've worked together.'

'That's true. We should've done. And I shouldn't have brought Carling in. Should've put him in an interview room, got his intel out of him. He's a loose cannon. And... He told me it was gambling.'

'Well, he'll be taken down soon. Don't you worry.'

'Who will?' A big guy appeared, more farmyard animal than human being. Suited and booted, fingers like bananas wrapped around a coffee cup, same branding as Clarke's.

'Carling, sir.'

'Right. Him.' He held out a hand to Nelson. 'DCI Thompson. Pleasure to meet you.'

'And you, sir.' Though Nelson had a feeling they'd met before. Still, he didn't want to upset the big ogre.

'Listen.' Thompson wrapped an arm around Nelson's shoulder. 'Steve's had a word with me. I've looked at your work and your record. If you're up for it, I think you'll be an excellent addition to my financial crime team.'

Nelson let himself be walked by him. 'I... I don't know what to say, sir.'

'"Thank you" would be a start.'

'Of course. Thank you.'

'Assuming you want it?'

'I do.'

'Good. Obviously have to go through the rigmarole of interviews and what have you. But you'll be DI Jon Nelson again.'

CHAPTER FIFTY-NINE

Fenchurch rested the phone on the cradle and sat back in his chair, arms folded. Eyes shut. Hard to process that.

But he would. In time.

He reached into his drawer and found a bottle of oxycodone. Two tablets left in there, enough to rattle. He needed to last longer for the next one. To hold out that little bit.

Sod it.

He needed the drug. The pain – in his arms, his chest, his head – was a hundred times worse than in his knee. He tipped one out onto his palm and stared at it. The little bastard, so much pain and temptation in a tiny object.

The door opened and Loftus stepped in. 'Evening.'

Fenchurch dropped the pill back into the bottle. Unlike with everyone else, he didn't hide it. Just left it there. He took a drink of water. 'Sir.'

Loftus didn't sit, instead planting himself in front of the desk. 'How are you feeling?'

'Well. I'm not sure we'll get Younis for what he's done.'

'Oh. I'm confident we will.' Loftus walked over to the corner. 'Other than that, how do you feel?'

'Honestly?'

'Always.'

'Like I've died, sir. I feel like I'm a zombie, dug up from the grave. And... And all I can think about is these.' Fenchurch tossed the bottle at him.

Loftus caught it with a rattle. 'I'm sorry this has happened to you.'

Fenchurch shrugged. 'I let it happen to me, sir.'

'Maybe you did, or maybe he got the better of you. Hard to say for certain.' Loftus tossed the bottle in the air and caught it. 'Listen, I wanted to give you some good news and some bad. I'll do the good first. Your fear over failing to convict Younis is unfounded. Initial reports from the searches show that Dr Deacon was up to his eyeballs in crime. Over-prescribing to celebrities, issuing prescriptions to non-patients who filled them and turned them in for resale. Supplying Younis's street trade. We can pin it all on Younis. DS Bridge has unearthed six patients using ten different names at ten different pharmacies. Each. And each one has offered a statement. I mean, it's a good living for them and it's far cleaner than selling crack or heroin. Besides, house-wives and accountants don't buy off the street. Nor do police officers.'

'I'm sorry, sir. I shouldn't have let it happen.'

'Drug addiction in this sense isn't fireable. You were taking those pills to manage a condition, a serious injury you incurred in the line of duty, which has only been exacerbated. I get that. But here comes the bad news – if you are that deep into oxycodone, then you need to detox. I've approved a residential treatment programme. Methadone, addiction therapy, compulsive behaviour therapy. And you can go voluntarily on medical leave throughout it.'

'And if I refuse?'

'Then you're suspended. You've always got a lot on your plate, Simon. Take the course, get clean, get your marriage back on track, be a father to your kids and maybe you won't even want to be a police officer when you're done.'

'Is this your way of trying to get rid of me?'

'No. You've just been through a lot more than most people. If the perspective you gain makes you want to leave, that's a good thing.'

Fenchurch sat there. Maybe he was right and he'd been a cop too long. Endured too much. Put up with too much. His injury was on duty, a useless junkie getting lucky.

A change would do him good, let him figure out what he wanted to do next with his life. Be it as a cop or otherwise.

The door swung open and Bell stormed in, face like a lightning storm. Fizzing with rage. 'What the hell is going on?'

'About what?'

'Your drugs, Simon.' Bell laughed. 'I've got a direct report on heroin, someone running a major investigation for me is a junkie. Simon, I've been your friend for years. Why couldn't you tell me?'

Fenchurch bit his tongue. Actually rested his molars against it. He was so contemptuous of Bell and he felt so shit... he couldn't trust what came out.

'Okay, Simon. I get it. You've been pushed back and pushed back for your knee operation so many times. You must be in crippling pain.'

'I am. I went to a private specialist to get fast-tracked, but they gave me painkillers. Oxy is an opioid, sure, but I thought I'd kick it. And nothing else could touch the pain. Do you know what that feels like? To walk around limping all the time?

Unable to do your job? Used to be I could chase and catch the best of them. Now I'm confined to a desk.'

'And that's what you're supposed to do! You're a DCI, Simon! It's a desk job. You're the only one in the Met who still does things like that.'

If Fenchurch was standing, he would've attacked Bell.

'Jason.' Loftus walked forward from the corner, fiddling with the oxy bottle. 'Can you leave us alone?'

'Boss... I, uh, didn't know you were there.'

'You don't talk to people like that.' Loftus whistled and pointed out into the corridor. 'Scram.'

Bell took a final look at Fenchurch, then buggered off.

Loftus kept the door open and watched him go, then turned to Fenchurch. 'I don't know what I was thinking in promoting that clown, but we are where we are, I suppose.' He tossed the bottle back.

Fenchurch caught it and played with it, letting the pills rattle with each rotation. And he was throwing an idea around too. 'Sir, I know a way of getting rid of him.'

'Oh?'

'Here's something to think about. How do you think Carling got away with his behaviour for so long?'

'Bell?'

Fenchurch nodded. 'Bell's protected him for years. Before you arrived, I spoke to Uzma Ashkani. She's got the whole story, sir.'

'Oh my.'

Fenchurch grabbed his coat off the rack. 'Now, if I'm officially on medical leave, I'll see you in a few months.'

CHAPTER SIXTY

Fenchurch was gripping the handle above his door. The air conditioning wasn't doing anything to stop him sweating and the evening sun was in about three different places at once. Every time he blinked, it moved again. 'Steady there, Lewis Hamilton.'

Chloe was behind the wheel, powering down the narrow road, great thick hedges on both sides. 'Are you criticising my driving? I passed my advanced driving two months ago.'

'Chloe, if something comes, you'll—'

'—pull in. Let them past. I'm courteous.'

'These are Cornish hedges, love. That's about six foot of stone in the middle of all that bushy tree stuff.'

'Oh, shit.' She slowed right down.

'Next left, anyway.'

'I mean, I have been here before.'

'Yeah, but me or your mum always drives.'

Chloe took the left, onto an even smaller lane and trundled along it. 'Mum's not Cornish, so why do Nana and Papa live here?'

'They used to live not far from your grandad. Over the river in Greenwich. Sold their three-bedroom house and bought half of Cornwall.'

The old farmhouse appeared over the low hedge, restored and improved. Not a lot of love in it, and not much class. And it was colossal. Eight bedrooms, enough for the whole clan to descend on at Christmas. Not that they had.

Chloe pulled into the drive and crunched across the pebbles. Just Abi's car in the drive.

She was sitting in the swing seat under the hulking great oak, scowling at them. It shifted to a frown, then a smile. 'Simon?'

He was first out. 'Evening, love.' He tried walking over the patch of lawn, but his leg was still half-asleep. Just a lump of numbness hanging off him. 'You on your own?'

'Mum and Dad are out. Ballroom dancing tonight.'

Chloe got out of the car and walked over to her mother. Gave her a hug. 'Where's Al?'

'He's inside on his iPad.'

Music came from the house, that annoying-as-hell shit Al listened to about a fish. On one-track repeat, all day.

Fenchurch tried so hard to claw it out of his mind.

'If only you could use those things outside, eh?' Chloe smiled. Her gaze shifted between them. 'I'll go and see if he's okay.'

'Nice to see you, love.' Abi watched her daughter cross the grass towards the house's ornate front porch. Took her a few seconds to look over at Fenchurch. 'Hey.'

'Hey.' Fenchurch held her gaze for a few seconds. 'Mind if I sit next to you? Leg's bloody killing me.'

'By all means.' She sat back down and locked her Kindle. 'You came.'

'I almost didn't. I was going to give you some space, let you think it all through. But Chloe persuaded me to come.'

'Well, I'll have to thank her.' A smile flickered across her lips. 'What's going on, Simon? Why are you here?'

'I've got a date for my op.'

'When?'

'Two weeks.'

'Blimey.'

'I know. I'll be a while on the painkillers afterwards, but once it's done... I'm already tapering off. I don't need to be on anything like this dose. But...' Fenchurch settled back in the seat and it swung backwards. 'Love, I've got a problem. I've been given an addiction and I'm going to need help getting rid of it. I can't do it on my own. I'm accepting that fact. I could go on and on about how it's not my fault, but... I let it happen.' He leaned forward, planting both feet on the grass. 'After the op, I'm going into rehab. I've been dosed long-term, so I'm going to need help quitting. I thought I could handle it. But you left and I didn't know what to do and... This has got me beaten. I'll be in there for a fortnight, give or take. When I come out, I'll be clean again. The old me. If I'm that bad, I may need to attend Narcotics Anonymous afterwards. But I will get clean.'

'Well, that's a lot to take in.'

'I know. When you took Al, it...'

'Simon, I came here because... I panicked. I ran. I woke up in the middle of the night and you were rolling around and moaning. Talking in your sleep. The realisation hit and it hit hard. I'm not going to have a junkie in my son's life.'

'Abi, I'm not a junkie. My doctor... He was being paid to keep me on those drugs. I was weak, I was in pain and I was fooled, but I'm going to get help and get off the stuff for good. We've been through so much together, you and I. And the times we've been apart.'

She swivelled around to stare at him. 'After what you've put me through?'

'After what *you* put me through, Abi?'

She closed her eyes. 'I was hurt.'

'We both were. And you're hurt now. I see that. I'm not demanding anything, but one thing I've learnt about us is that when we stick together, nothing can stop us. Nothing.'

'I'll think about it.'

Fenchurch took out the bottle of pills from his coat pocket. 'I could be overly dramatic and say this lot is hopefully the last one I'll ever take. Flush them down the toilet. But I have to come off them gradually and get my knee surgery. Once I've removed the source of the pain, then I can transition off of the painkillers. There's no magic bullet here.'

She took the bottle off him. 'I'll keep a hold of them. Give you some when it's your dose.'

'So you're not thinking about it anymore?'

'Nope.' She leaned over and kissed him. 'We will get through this together.'

AFTERWORD

Thank you for reading this book.

After my own health worries over the last two years, it's been interesting to write about Fenchurch and that infernal knee of his causing so much pain for him. I hope it wasn't too traumatic to read about, but he had to go there to come back, I guess.

If you or someone you know is having difficulties with opioid addiction, then you can seek help with the NHS (in the UK):

https://www.nhs.uk/live-well/addiction-support/drug-addiction-getting-help/

I wrote the books in trilogies and this is the third. The first three were about Chloe's fate, then about reconnecting with her. This last trilogy has been a "business as usual" series for Fenchurch, where he's out of his comfort zone as a DCI with a knackered knee. The next three will be NEW YORK MINUTE, GLASGOW KISS and LONDON EYE/CALLING/SOMETHING ELSE THAT I'VE GOT YEARS TO DECIDE ON, so let's see where it takes him. New York, Glasgow and London, probably.

As ever, massive thanks to James Mackay for the editing work at outline stage and after the first draft, it fixed a lot of howlers, especially around the opioids. And for the insight into a cop going through the addiction to opioids.

As usual, huge thanks to John Rickards for his copy editing, one day I'll remember some of the things you point out in comments. And last but not least to Mare Bate for proofing it. If you notice any errors, which are all my fault, then please email ed@edjames.co.uk and I'll fix them.

Finally, the tenth Fenchurch book, NEW YORK MINUTE, will be out in October, two months earlier than the recent schedule. No prizes for guessing where it's set, but it'll be a chance for him to restart with his bionic knee and new-found sobriety.

And if you could leave a review on Amazon? That'd be a huge help, cheers.

Cheers,

Ed James

Scottish Borders, October 2022

ABOUT THE AUTHOR

Ed James writes crime-fiction novels, primarily the DI Simon Fenchurch series, set on the gritty streets of East London featuring a detective with little to lose. His Scott Cullen series features a young Edinburgh detective constable investigating crimes from the bottom rung of the career ladder he's desperate to climb.

Formerly an IT project manager, Ed began writing on planes, trains and automobiles to fill his weekly commute to London. He now writes full-time and lives in the Scottish Borders, with his girlfriend and a menagerie of rescued animals.

If you would like to be kept up to date with new releases from Ed James, please join the Ed James Readers Club.

Connect with Ed online:

Amazon Author page

Website

OTHER BOOKS BY ED JAMES

SCOTT CULLEN MYSTERIES SERIES

Eight novels featuring a detective eager to climb the career ladder, covering Edinburgh and its surrounding counties, and further across Scotland.

1.GHOST IN THE MACHINE

2.DEVIL IN THE DETAIL

3.FIRE IN THE BLOOD

4.STAB IN THE DARK

5.COPS & ROBBERS

6.LIARS & THIEVES

7.COWBOYS & INDIANS

8.HEROES & VILLAINS

CULLEN & BAIN SERIES

Six novellas spinning off from the main Cullen series covering the events of the global pandemic in 2020.

1.CITY OF THE DEAD

2.WORLD'S END

3.HELL'S KITCHEN

4.GORE GLEN

5.DEAD IN THE WATER

6.THE LAST DROP

CRAIG HUNTER SERIES

A spin-off series from the Cullen series, with Hunter first featuring in the fifth book, starring an ex-squaddie cop struggling with PTSD, investigating crimes in Scotland and further afield.

1.MISSING

2.HUNTED

3.THE BLACK ISLE

DS VICKY DODDS SERIES

Gritty crime novels set in Dundee and Tayside, featuring a DS juggling being a cop and a single mother.

1.BLOOD & GUTS

2.TOOTH & CLAW

3.FLESH & BLOOD

4.SKIN & BONE

5.GUILT TRIP

DI SIMON FENCHURCH SERIES

Set in East London, will Fenchurch ever find what happened to his daughter, missing for the last ten years?

1.THE HOPE THAT KILLS

2.WORTH KILLING FOR

3.WHAT DOESN'T KILL YOU

4.IN FOR THE KILL

5.KILL WITH KINDNESS

6.KILL THE MESSENGER

7.DEAD MAN'S SHOES

8.A HILL TO DIE ON

9.THE LAST THING TO DIE

Other Books

Other crime novels, with Lost Cause set in Scotland and Senseless set in southern England, and the other three set in Seattle, Washington.

- LOST CAUSE

- SENSELESS

- TELL ME LIES

- GONE IN SECONDS

- BEFORE SHE WAKES

FENCHURCH WILL RETURN IN

New York Minute
1st December 2023
Preorder now:
https://geni.us/EJF10

AFTERWORD

Thank you for reading this book.

After my own health worries over the last two years, it's been interesting to write about Fenchurch and that infernal knee of his causing so much pain for him. I hope it wasn't too traumatic to read about, but he had to go there to come back, I guess.

If you or someone you know is having difficulties with opioid addiction, then you can seek help with the NHS (in the UK):

https://www.nhs.uk/live-well/addiction-support/drug-addiction-getting-help/

I wrote the books in trilogies and this is the third. The first three were about Chloe's fate, then about reconnecting with her. This last trilogy has been a "business as usual" series for Fenchurch, where he's out of his comfort zone as a DCI with a knackered knee. The next three will be NEW YORK MINUTE, GLASGOW KISS and LONDON EYE/CALLING/SOMETHING ELSE THAT I'VE GOT YEARS TO DECIDE ON, and I'll try and do them at a faster cadence, so every eight months rather than year. If it keeps selling, then let's see where it takes him.

As ever, massive thanks to James Mackay for the editing work at outline stage and after the first draft, it fixed a lot of howlers, especially around the opioids. And for the insight into a cop going through the addiction to opioids.

As usual, huge thanks to John Rickards for his copy editing, one day I'll remember some of the things you point out in comments. And last but not least to Mare Bate for proofing it. If you notice any errors, which are all my fault, then please email ed@edjames.co.uk and I'll fix them.

Finally, the tenth Fenchurch book, NEW YORK MINUTE, will be out in October, two months earlier than the recent schedule. No prizes for guessing where it's set, but it'll be a chance for him to restart with his bionic knee and new-found sobriety.

And if you could leave a review on Amazon? That'd be a huge help, cheers.

Cheers,

Ed James

Scottish Borders, October 2022

ABOUT THE AUTHOR

Ed James writes crime-fiction novels, primarily the DI Simon Fenchurch series, set on the gritty streets of East London featuring a detective with little to lose. His Scott Cullen series features a young Edinburgh detective constable investigating crimes from the bottom rung of the career ladder he's desperate to climb.

Formerly an IT project manager, Ed began writing on planes, trains and automobiles to fill his weekly commute to London. He now writes full-time and lives in the Scottish Borders, with his girlfriend and a menagerie of rescued animals.

If you would like to be kept up to date with new releases from Ed James, please join the Ed James Readers Club.

Connect with Ed online:

Amazon Author page

Website

ED JAMES READERS CLUB

Available now for members of my Readers Club is FALSE START, a prequel to my first new series in six years.

Sign up for FREE and get access to exclusive content and keep up-to-speed with all of my releases on a monthly basis.
https://geni.us/EJF9FS

MEET DI ROB MARSHALL

The first new Ed James series in six years starts here.

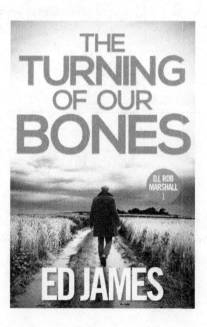

The Serial Killer he couldn't catch is dead...

Can DI Rob Marshall save his final victim before she dies too?

Met cop DI Rob Marshall is hot on the trail of the serial killer known as the Chameleon, who has abducted, tortured and killed a series of young women in north-west London. As they close in, the Chameleon - who switches identity to get close to his victims - shoots Marshall's partner and escapes.

But when the Chameleon's body is found two years later, Marshall must return to his home town of Melrose in the Scottish Borders and face the tragedy that's haunted him for twenty years, which made him leave in the first place.

The Chameleon's final victim is still missing – can Marshall unpick the Chameleon's latest identity in time to save her from a lonely death?

THE TURNING OF OUR BONES
1 February 2023

Preorder now for a bargain price!

Made in the USA
Coppell, TX
07 December 2022